GONE DRAGON

BOOK I

T.P. SHEEHAN

QUERENCIA
BOOKS

Published by Querencia Books

ISBN: 978-0-6480928-0-3 (paperback)

Querencia Books
info@querenciabooks.com
Querenciabooks.com

Follow the Gone Dragon series: GoneDragon.com

For Nic. You are my sunshine.

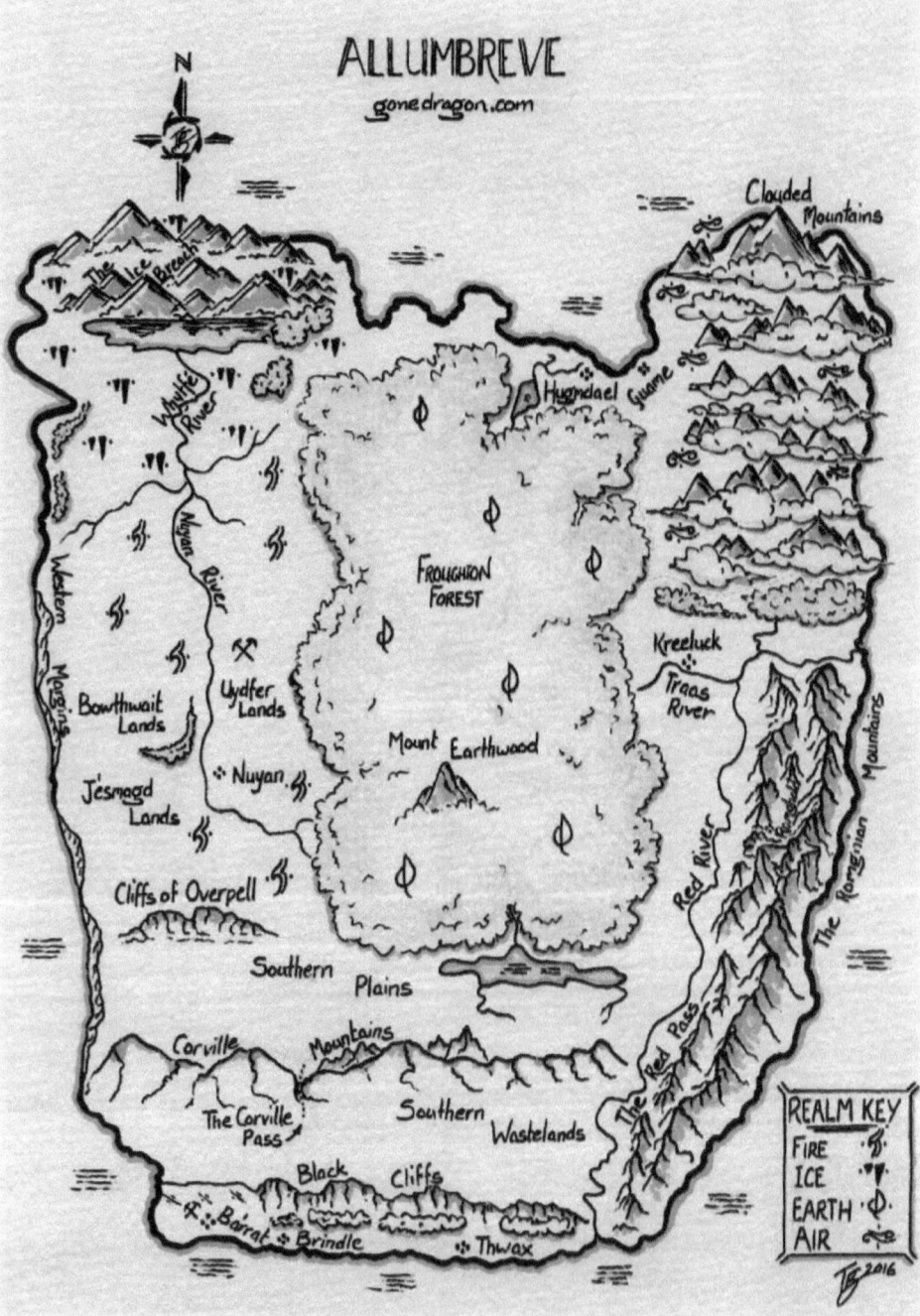

PROLOGUE

"Will the chosen one turn the tide on the war with the Quag?"

"Yes, Semsarian, I believe they will."

"Then who, Semsdi, is worthy to receive the blood of the fire dragon?"

"In time we will know. The *Electus* will present themselves to us when the time is right."

"How will we recognise them? How will we know for sure they are the chosen one?"

"We will know Semsarian. They will not be able to hide from who they are…"

MAGNUS

"Magnus. You're up."

Magnus took the sword from Ganister.

"No holding back," Ganister instructed. Magnus gave a small nod and blew through pursed lips. He looked back to the other students—five pairs of eyes on him. They had already sparred for rank. None had beaten Lucas. Magnus twirled the sword in his left hand.

"You ready?" Lucas snarled.

"We've been through this before, Lucas," Magnus smiled.

"Only this time you're going to lose."

"Is that so?" Magnus appraised the training sword. It was a little heavier than he preferred. Ganister had been trying to improve his strength with heavier, larger swords for the past few months leading up to the trials. He need not have bothered—Magnus never lost a bout, no matter which sword he used.

"Begin!" Ganister shouted.

Lucas lunged toward Magnus, bringing his sword down hard. Magnus caught the blow and pushed back, their swords locking at the cross-guards. Magnus grimaced, pushing harder to keep from losing his footing.

"Break!" Ganister demanded.

Magnus pulled back. Lucas came again, shouting and swinging furiously. He used every move he knew—every move Ganister had taught him. Magnus dodged each and every one of them, expelling no energy at all to avoid Lucas's attack. Lucas soon tired and lowered his blade. He took a moment to catch his breath, pointing his sword at Magnus. "Quit playing with me."

Magnus skipped about and stumbled into Ganister. He felt the large man's powerful hands grasp his lean shoulders, steadying him. He pulled Magnus closer and whispered to him, "I said, no holding back."

"He's your son," Magnus whispered.

"And he can take care of himself. No holding back. Show us what you've learned."

Magnus circled his shoulders and cracked his neck to one side. He raised his sword and let the leather grip slip beneath his fingers until the cross-guard touched his hand. With a firm grasp, he whispered a spell in Fireisgh tongue—*"Fara gin parshin-ar."* A delicate shaft of flame danced up the blade of his sword and vanished. A cheer came from the small audience of students. Magnus was pleased—his father had taught him the spell just days before and it was only the second time it had worked. He was certain, however, his father would not approve of its use at this time.

Magnus pointed the blade at Lucas, who crouched into a battle stance. They both charged at once and their swords clashed. Blow after blow, Magnus drove Lucas back, never allowing him the chance to counter. Lucas soon shifted his weight onto his back foot. This is what Magnus was waiting for. He swept Lucas's leg away with his own and Lucas fell onto his back. Magnus's blade was at his friend's throat as his head hit the ground.

"Do you yield?" Magnus demanded.

Lucas grimaced. "Aye... I yield."

Another cheer rose as Magnus helped Lucas to his feet. They bowed to one another and Lucas rubbed the back of his head.

"Are you alright?" Magnus placed a hand on his friend's back. He hated injuring people in a sparring contest.

"I'll live," Lucas grimaced. "I almost bested you." He feigned a smile.

"Yes, and I almost bested his father once too." Ganister shook his head, joining them. "Magnus has proven to us that showmanship and skill can be mutually beneficial." The students laughed. Magnus looked to Lucas and shrugged.

When the students were silent Ganister spoke again. "You've done well. All of you have. As far as I'm concerned, you are all worthy of selection into the knighthood of the Authoritarium." Magnus gave a wry smile. Ganister was always so diplomatic. The truth was, only he and Lucas netted the results needed to gain favour with the selection panel.

"But as you know, in all the lands of Allumbreve, only forty candidates are chosen each year," Ganister clarified. "Ten from the Air Realm of the Northeast, ten from the Ice Realm of the North, another ten from the Earth Realm in the forest region and of course ten for us of the Fire Realm. Each realm has its own means of selection. A fortnight ago, we of the Fire Realm completed our trials." The students cheered. "Ten will have their fates chosen and every second year one more will have the honour of selection into the order of the Irucantî."

It had been two weeks since the trials and the students waited eagerly for the selection results. Magnus knew the results were predictable. He and Lucas performed better than anyone else.

"We at the western margins usually gain two candidates at best, but we have an advantage. Not in selection, but in alternatives." There was a collective moan from the students. Magnus caught Ganister's eye, who flashed him a sympathetic glance. Ganister continued, "Those of you not fortunate enough to be accepted into knighthood or who, for other reasons, are not able to join the knighthood, can rest easy because all of you come from good families, good farmland or good trades."

The alternatives gave Magnus no inspiration. *I need to become a knight,* Magnus thought to himself. *How can I be with Catanya and remain a farm hand? At my father's property no less.* He shook his head. He thought it no life to offer the woman he wanted to marry. The other students voiced concerns of their own among themselves.

"I know all your fathers. They are each noble men. Each of you should feel worthy to follow them."

"Yeah sure," a voice mumbled. Magnus looked and saw it was Ruben. He was a heavy-set lad from the coast who lost most of his bouts at the trials. Magnus felt almost as sorry for him as he did for himself. It was one thing to fail selection, quite another to win a candidacy and turn your position down. That was unheard of, but Magnus knew... *My father will never let me become a knight.*

"If I should not be a knight, why then should I train?" Magnus asked of his father long ago.

"There is no harm in mastering the sword, nor to prove yourself as capable as any other," his father had replied. His words sounded wise enough at the time but did little to appease Magnus now. His father was not forthcoming with the reason he despised the Authoritarium.

A messenger entered the tall, wooden building in which they were training. He walked across the cobbled floor toward Ganister. "Sire, I have delivery from the Authoritarium. I bring documents of importance and..."

"Yes, yes, yes," Ganister interrupted. "Importance and urgency for my attention. I've heard it all before. Does old Trager send his greetings?" Ganister took a large scroll and a selection of envelopes from the messenger.

"Sire?" the young messenger cleared his throat.

"Never mind. Send the old bugger my regards. He is still alive isn't he?" The students stifled their laughs.

"Yes sir. The honourable elder of the Authoritarium is alive… just…" His eyes trailed away. Ganister gave him a firm slap on the back.

"Good lad. Head over to the house and my wife will fix you a hot meal. But eat sparingly—I'm famished after a long day of training this lot. To that effect, be sure to tell old Trager that his new recruits from the West are the best he's ever had."

"I will sire, thank you sire." The messenger bowed, turned and hurried off toward Ganister's home across the field.

Lucas nudged Magnus. "Who do you think has been chosen?"

"Most certainly you two," observed one student—eavesdropping to Magnus's left. "And with any luck a couple more of us."

Magnus chewed the inside of his cheek. He had both dreamed of and dreaded this moment for as long as he could remember. He wanted more than anything to become a knight. He and Lucas had grown together, trained together and imagined the moment when they, together, would be chosen.

"So here we are then." Ganister broke the seal on the scroll and pulled it swiftly open. The students stood to attention with their hands behind their backs. Ganister read in silence, his face set in a concentrated frown. "Ahah…"

"Well, come on Father, the suspense is killing us!" Lucas complained.

Ganister's eyebrows rose and he looked up from the scroll. "Hmm? Sorry, yes. The results are in… This year two of you have been selected. The primary candidate is Magnus of J'esmagd."

The students approached Magnus and congratulated him. Magnus thanked them, feeling shallow and dishonest at the achievement. He smiled, but found it painful to make eye contact with any but Lucas. *At least he'll be chosen with me.* Lucas had lost only a single bout in the trials. He was the only other candidate from the western margins to lose so few. He was the logical choice for secondary candidate.

"The secondary candidate is Alfret of Benstart." Ganister brought the scroll slowly down. The room fell to silence.

Alfret? Magnus was dumbfounded. Alfret had lost three bouts at the games and had never beaten Lucas in years of training. A good chance at third perhaps but… *Alfret?* Magnus's heart sank. Lucas was as still as a statue and almost as grey as one too. He looked to his father, as did Magnus. Ganister appeared to fare no better. He had never seen shock like that carved on this great warrior's face.

Ganister cleared his throat. "There is more." The large room fell to silence again. "A tertiary candidate has been chosen in reserve. That candidate is Lucas of Bowthwait."

Things were going from bad to worse. *Reserve? What in all the realms does that mean?* Magnus had never heard of such a thing. Candidates were chosen and that was it.

"Reserve?" Lucas exclaimed. "Reserve for what?"

"If one of the chosen candidates from our region declines their offer of knightship, you may take their place."

Lucas threw his sword to the ground, sending a sharp sound ricocheting off the hardwood beams overhead. He strode out of the building toward the house. Magnus turned to follow but Ganister called to him.

"Magnus, wait." Ganister approached and together they saw Lucas crouching in the field. "Leave him be. I will talk to him directly. Take this." Ganister handed Magnus a sealed envelope. "Congratulations, Magnus. You more than any deserve it."

"No more than Lucas. It is not fair, Ganister. He wants this more than anyone."

Ganister looked at Lucas before he spoke. "There is more than just swordsmanship that makes a good knight. I'm sure Xavier and his affiliates have fit reason for their choice."

Magnus gave a nod but did not agree with Ganister's words any more than he believed Ganister did. Ganister tapped the envelope in his hand. "I know the conflict you face with this Magnus. Would you like me to speak to your father about it?"

"Thank you, but I think I can handle it." Magnus appreciated the offer. Ganister and his father were the best of friends, yet their views on knighthood differed greatly.

"I can clear things up here and accompany you home, speak to your father, see if a few mugs of ale might make him more malleable."

Magnus smiled and then winced as Lucas disappeared into the house. "I think Lucas needs you more than I, and besides, my father made his decision long ago."

Ganister looked sympathetically at Magnus, making him feel even more uncomfortable. "I fear you're right. Be off home then, Magnus. But know this—there was never a more accomplished knight than your father under the old regime, before the days of the Authoritarium. Had things been different, he would be an elder of this realm, seated in the Great Hall of Guame among his peers."

"Aye, but he is not. He is a farmer of the western margins. And I am the farmer's son," Magnus mumbled.

"Your father sees things my naive eyes do not, so heed his words." Magnus sighed and Ganister continued. "Give my regards to your mother. I must go now and wish Alfret all the best." He winked and Magnus felt the heaviness of Ganister's slap on his back.

BONSTAPH

A mile south, Magnus entered the Crescent Woods that marked the end of the lands of Bowthwait. The woods got their name for their semicircular shape that curved from east to west with the central, thickest portion of pine and oak a mile deep. Magnus rode his chestnut stallion, Esmder, through the woods and beyond the gate at the low stone wall that marked the northern boundary of his own lands—the J'esmagdlands.

Magnus's stomach twisted thinking of the conversation he was about to have with his father. He looked at the envelope clutched in the palm of his hand. He had no wish to open it for he knew he would give it to Lucas. It made perfect sense. Lucas would be happy and get what he wanted and Ganister would be proud of his son—a knight of the Authoritarium. *There was no such pride to be got from my father. He despises the Authoritarium. Regardless of what I say, Father will not give me his blessing.*

Magnus's father, Bonstaph, spoke little of his time as a knight. What Magnus knew was gleaned from stories told by Ganister, or others who remembered Bonstaph's time as Knight Commander. His father led the knights of the realms to the last great battle against the Quag—the Battle of Fire. They fought alongside the dragons and the elite Irucantî, or *Ferustirs*, as the priests were called when they went into battle. The Quag were driven back to the wastelands, but not before Delvion, their leader, slew the greatest dragon of all—Balgur. *And with a priest's own fire-sword no less…* Magnus sighed. He always believed the stories to be fanciful.

Magnus's thoughts strayed for a moment to the one thing this whole debacle would seriously affect. It was the one reason he would consider disobeying his father and accepting the offer of knighthood for himself—*Catanya.*

Catanya's father was due home on leave from the Authoritarium in a month and Magnus planned to ask his blessing to marry his daughter. He was sure that being a primary candidate would sway him to bless their engagement. After all, he was the one who had chosen Magnus for the candidature, for her father, Xavier, was Knight Commander.

Magnus rode over the rise and looked down at his family home. Smoke rose from the stone chimney that poked through the thatched roof. In the fields, two draft horses pulled a plough steered by Bonstaph. Magnus took a deep breath and rode down the embankment to the right of the house and over to the stables, where he took the saddle and bridle from Esmder and led him to feed and water. Magnus stood at the door of the stables and examined his envelope, running his thumb over the Authoritarium's purple seal before stuffing it in a pocket beneath his tunic.

Walking toward his father, Magnus shouted across the half ploughed field. "Good evening!"

His father turned and looked across at him. Bonstaph was tall and powerful. He had a less bulky frame than Ganister but was not lean like Magnus, who was more his mother's build. He was a strong man who carried himself with pride.

Bonstaph turned back to the horses as he replied, "Good evening to you."

Magnus rolled his eyes. His father knew what this day meant to him. It was the most important and talked about day for all young men of Allumbreve. It had been for generations. Now Magnus had in his possession the one thing each seventeen year old craved. None had worked so hard as he to receive it.

"Do you intend to finish the field by nightfall?" Magnus decided he would not raise the topic if his father did not.

Bonstaph pulled on the reins, driving the horses to a stop and setting the plough down. He removed his leather gloves and looked over at Magnus. "I assume congratulations are in order?" Bonstaph finally asked.

"Why would you say that?" Magnus could taste the bitterness in his own words.

"You've proved yourself better than all other contenders, no doubt."

"It does not matter what I've proved. As you said, my place is here, on the farm."

"I said there is no place for you in the knighthood. Not under the regime of the Authoritarium. There will be other options. What is important is you proved to yourself…"

"I've proven nothing," Magnus interrupted. "Nothing more than disloyalty when I decline their offer."

"They are not worthy of you, Magnus!"

"You are the only one who believes that," Magnus replied.

Bonstaph sighed and shook his head. "Someday you will understand."

Magnus walked over to his father, unhitching the first of the horses from the harness, then the second. "What options are there for me father, if you forbid me to follow in your footsteps as a knight? What other post can a farm boy of the outer margins fill?"

Bonstaph pointed a finger at him. "Being a farmer is nothing to be ashamed about."

Magnus led the draft horses to the stable. "I can finish here."

Bonstaph opened his mouth to speak but thought differently and gave a nod. "I'll see you inside for supper then."

Magnus felt his father's eyes watching him for a moment before he moved off to the homestead. He mucked out the stables and dragged in two fresh hay bales for the horses to eat. Leaving the stables, he walked over to the stone well in the gravel-strewn courtyard south of the homestead where his father had left a pail of water. Magnus washed his hands and face of the day's grime and began to rub the back of his neck when he felt the soft touch of another's thoughts brush over his mind. He turned about and saw Breona—his mother's white Astermeer horse—by the nearby watering trough. She was looking at Magnus. Magnus stood as still as a statue. Breona was very reserved and only ever spoke with his mother—Alavia.

"Hello Breona," Magnus said softly. Immediately, the beautiful white horse withdrew her thoughts from Magnus and turned back to the trough. Magnus smiled. He was rarely able to feel her thoughts. That was the way with Astermeers—they would only speak with their foresworn, and being the only Astermeer in this entire realm, Alavia alone knew how they thought. Magnus had often tried, especially as a child. *She's curious about you Magnus, but it's not in her nature*, Alavia would tell him.

Magnus gave Breona a quick pat then headed to the homestead.

The front door was ajar and Magnus could hear his parents conversing inside. He kicked off his boots and walked in. His father was seated at the small table near the kitchen, drinking a pitcher of ale. His mother stood beside him, unbuttoning and removing her long black robe. She spotted Magnus and came over to him, embracing him. Magnus was as tall as her but had only grown so in recent months.

"Look at you two," Bonstaph mused. "Blonde hair... blue eyes. Who is your father again?"

Alavia smiled at her husband's jest then turned back to Magnus, who tried his best to hide his disdain at the day's dramas. Nevertheless, Alavia frowned and her eyes flashed brilliant like sapphires—she knew something was wrong.

"We'll talk about it later, Magnus," Alavia whispered. Magnus smiled weakly. Alavia turned back to Bonstaph, her face serious. "Breona and I rode our usual route today, from the Cliffs of Overpell as far as the Uydferlands. Then further, to the fringes of Froughton Forest."

"That's quite a ride," Bonstaph remarked.

"None of the knights were at their posts."

"None?" Bonstaph put his pitcher down with a clatter.

"I returned the same route. Not one. All six posts were unmanned."

Magnus looked to his father, waiting for his reaction. The southern borders of the Fire Realm were supposed to be patrolled at all times. It was the frontline of defence. The posts gave vantage over the southern plains all the way to the Corville Mountains. The post closest to them was at Overpell. From there, they could see as far as the Corville Pass—the only passage through the Corville Mountains. It was through here the Quag warmongers would come to attack and had done before. *Surely there must be an explanation for the knights' absence,* Magnus thought.

"Twenty leagues and not a single guard. This is what comes of a dictatorship." Bonstaph brought a fist down hard on the table, sending his pitcher spinning, spilling half its contents. "In my day, patrols were not left to the fickle ways of men. That's what dragons were for."

Bonstaph stood. He threw his heavy cloak over his shoulders and walked to the large wooden chest in the living room where a fire burned brightly in the fireplace. He opened the chest and removed his longsword, strapping his scabbard about his waist. He turned back to his wife and son. Magnus took a seat at the table. He knew there was more of his father's speech to come.

"Well it's true, is it not? The dragons have been guardians of the realms for an age. The Authoritarium, in all their piety, stepped in and made it the role of men. What good are the beasts and their warrior-priests hiding away in the Romgnian Mountains? The Gods certainly did not intend for this." Bonstaph turned and pointed to a large brown book upon the fireplace mantel. "It is written—four breeds of dragons bestowed upon the realms, one for each, sworn in guardianship. In the Great Hall of Guame I'm sure the heathen rulers burn such books to keep themselves warm at night. Place me before them with an Icerealmish sword and I'll chill their night."

Magnus had heard it all before. He was not in the mood for his father's resentments. Bonstaph made for the front door and Alavia stepped forward.

"Wait till morning, Bonstaph," Alavia said. "There is an ice-wind rising from the north. It carries with it memory and warning of things past and will do you no favour."

It was not like his mother to voice such trepidation. In her support, Magnus tried to reason with his father.

"Stay, Father. We can ride out together in the morning."

Bonstaph turned to Magnus. "This matter is urgent. I will not let day turn to night with the borders unguarded." He pointed once more at his son. "Stay here Magnus. Look after your mother."

"Bonstaph!" Alavia spoke in a forceful voice. It was too late. Bonstaph slammed the door behind him. Alavia flashed a glance back at Magnus. "He will learn to respect your wishes in time, Magnus."

"It's fine, Mother." He did not want her upset on his account.

"Always remember. You are as much a man of the North as you are your father's son." Alavia re-buttoned her robe. "There is a Rhyderman in you. Be proud of it. Always stand up for what it right. It is in your blood. It is your birth right." Alavia made for the door.

"Mother wait, I'll ready Esmder and ride with you."

"There is no need. Wait here. Keep the fire warm until we return. The night will be cold." She smiled lovingly at Magnus and closed the door behind her.

CATANYA

Magnus walked through the kitchen and out the side door. The sun had shifted to the west and the air grew bitterly cold in the late autumn afternoon. *Mother is right. It will be a cold night.* To his right under a lean-to was a stockpile of pine logs. He had stacked them in his arms up to his chin when he heard movement across the eastern field. Magnus put down the wood and stood back.

A great warhorse was thundering toward him. He recognised the horse at once for it was a silver Wardemeer horse. Only one of such a coat lived within riding distance to the western margins.

That's Xavier's horse.

The horse was coming fast. Magnus squinted. At a hundred paces he could see the rider. It was a familiar face, but not Xavier's. His heart leapt with joy.

Catanya!

Even before she had drawn the horse to a halt, the young woman jumped from its back and ran to Magnus. Her black hair and white summer dress flowed behind her. Magnus ran to meet her, all troubles of the day forgotten. At the edge of the field they flung their arms around one another. Magnus could feel Catanya squeezing him as tight as ever she had. After a good moment they stood apart. Magnus took her hands and held them gently. Catanya was short of breath from the ride. Her brown eyes fixed on Magnus and a beaming smile came to her face.

"Catanya, what is it?"

"My father. He's returned home early from his posting. Many knights have come home on leave this day. The whole town of Nuyan is celebrating."

Magnus was happy for her. He knew how hard it had been on her family with her father away. A knight's calling was that of a nomad, constantly patrolling the length and breadth of Allumbreve, and even more so for a Knight Commander.

"That's wonderful news. I'm guessing that's why you ride his horse?"

"Aye. I'm sure he doesn't mind me riding Trillium, although I didn't ask. It was the only way to come to you so fast." Catanya jumped with excitement. "Magnus, I spoke to him. He said he will see you today."

Magnus's heart leapt. "Catanya…"

"What is it, Magnus?"

Magnus wondered if perhaps Xavier had told Catanya of his candidacy already. "It can wait. Let me get Esmder and I will explain on the way."

Pulling his boots on as he went, Magnus hurried to the stable and prepared his horse. He returned to Catanya, who was standing high in Trillium's stirrups, eager to go. The great warhorse reared up, but Catanya sat back in the saddle, smiling. Magnus marvelled at her confidence. She looked like a child seated on the great silver beast.

The horses galloped across the fields toward the town of Nuyan and Catanya's home. After a spell, they both slowed to a trot. Magnus leant over and handed Catanya the sealed envelope he had been guarding.

"Is this what I think it is?" Catanya studied the envelope.

"Aye." Magnus wanted to tell her to open it. He desperately wanted to know what the letter said. Did the Authoritarium elders congratulate him for doing so well in the trial? He wanted to see his name in their neatly scribed purple ink printed on the same parchment as the words—*to be trained as knight of the Authoritarium.*

Catanya looked back over her shoulder at Magnus's homestead, then to him. "I take it this did not go down well with your father."

"Not the slightest bit." He spurred Esmder onward, trying to keep up with Trillium, who had picked his pace up once again.

"You always knew it would be this way." Catanya reached to Magnus and handed back the letter as the two horses drew neck and neck.

"I know, but somehow I hoped…" Magnus sighed. *I was silly to hope.* Magnus sat up straight and rolled his shoulders back. *Enough of feeling sorry for myself.* "I will go before your father and tell him what is what," Magnus announced in a comical, formal voice.

"That's the spirit." Catanya beamed again. Magnus found it intoxicating. After all the years of knowing Catanya, he was still mesmerised by her. They both slowed their horses. Catanya reached out and took Magnus's hand, squeezing it tight. "I love you, Magnus of J'esmagd. We are to be married and live the happiest of lives together here at the margins. We will have many children and they will run among the lambs and chickens and collect the irises

13

that grow along the banks of the Nuyan River. Nothing could make me happier."

Catanya turned on her saddle and stood, crouched. With the horses still moving, she leapt onto the front of Magnus's saddle and landed facing him. Catanya took a breath and sighed. Magnus placed a hand on her waist, their bodies pushed tightly together in the saddle. Catanya lent forward and gave Magnus the gentlest of kisses. He felt the soft warmth of her breath and let go of the reins to cradle her face in the palms of his hands, caressing her cheekbones with his thumbs. Too soon they broke away. Catanya stood and leapt back onto Trillium.

Magnus felt as if he were glowing from the inside out. He smiled then laughed at Catanya.

"What? Spit it out!" Catanya teased, a playful smile on her face.

"I hope your father is ready!"

"It's not every day a father gives his daughter away." Catanya smiled out one side of her mouth. "Go easy on him."

Magnus's stomach twisted. *Who am I kidding?* He was more anxious about speaking with Xavier than he was with his own father. *Still,* Magnus reasoned, *it couldn't be any worse...*

XAVIER

Magnus had not given any thought to his appearance. He wished he'd bathed, changed and seen to the state of his hair before leaving home. The common room of Xavier's family home felt strange. In all the years he had known Catanya he had never set foot inside it, though Magnus knew her family well enough. As he and Catanya entered, before them stood Catanya's mother Alessandra and her six-year-old sister Hannah, who insisted on holding Magnus's hand.

"I learned my first spell today," Hannah said. Her big brown eyes stared unblinking at Magnus. He was fond of Hannah. She was so much like her older sister—strong willed, inquisitive, and a dreamer. These were all the qualities he loved about Catanya—the same he knew drove her father to frustration.

Magnus knelt down beside Hannah, still holding her hand. "Is it a good spell?"

Hannah grinned, nodding her head. "Do you want to see it?"

"I'd love to see it," Magnus said enthusiastically.

Hannah led Magnus over to the fireplace where a small fire burned. He glanced at Alessandra and Catanya who were both smiling. Hannah let go of Magnus's hand and stared hard at the fire. Her lips moved as she rehearsed the words quietly. Then she raised a hand to the fire and said, "*Fara mi parina.*" The flames flared angrily in a burst of light and the glowing coals beneath hissed back at Hannah in response. It was as if she had thrown a cup of oil over the coals. The fire settled back into a weary, orange glow as quickly as it had responded to the spell.

"That's fantastic!" Magnus said. "Do you know I didn't do my first spell until I was seven?"

"Really?" Hannah's eyes widened and a look of pride came over her. She held Magnus's hand again.

"Really," he replied.

"Magnus..." Hannah said, "Are you going to marry my sister?"

15

"Hannah—be silent!" Catanya lifted her sister up and carried her to a wooden chair in the kitchen.

"But I want to wait with Magnus," Hannah protested. Catanya crouched and spoke quietly to her. Magnus took the moment to brush his hair with the palms of his hands before realising Alessandra was looking at him. He stopped and stood with his hands behind his back, clearing his throat. Alessandra smiled politely, but it seemed to mask sadness. Magnus thought hard for something to say to break the ice between them. It was ridiculous. He had known Catanya's parents almost as long as he had Catanya and never struggled before now.

"How is you mother, Magnus?" Alessandra eventually asked.

"Very well, Ma'am."

"Don't be so formal. Call me Alessandra."

Magnus nodded. "She is very well, thank you, Alessandra."

"And your father, is he well?"

"He is well, yes." The conversation seemed strained to Magnus but he appreciated Alessandra making the effort.

"Tell me, does Alavia travel back north at all—to the Ice Realm?"

Magnus thought for a moment. He had never known his mother to travel back north to her people. She was proud of them, always reminding Magnus of his maternal origins, but never spoke of her family. She certainly had not in the years he could remember.

"Not in some time, Ma... Alessandra," Magnus struggled. "I don't believe she has much to do at all with her people. The Rhyder folk I mean."

Alessandra gave a nod. "Xavier shan't be too much longer."

Hannah giggled, drawing Magnus's attention. Catanya was tickling her.

"Magnus," Alessandra continued. He looked back to her and saw the sadness return to her face. "I want you to know that if there was ever a suitor Catanya was meant to marry it would be you... if things were not as they were..."

Alessandra was interrupted when the front door swung inward. In walked Xavier. He was dressed befitting a knight of the Authoritarium. His uniform was impressive—a well-tailored dark blue tunic emblazoned with the Authoritarium coat of arms across his chest in white. It carried the symbol of each of the four realms with an oak tree in the middle representing Froughton Forest. Hannah broke from her play with Catanya and flew to her father's arms.

Before a word was spoken, another figure entered the house. Taller than Xavier and wearing a black robe, a hood hid the stranger's identity.

"Xavier. Not now!" Alessandra forced through a whisper.

"Father?" Catanya questioned.

"Good evening to you all," Xavier said, seemingly oblivious to his family's remarks. "Catanya, Hannah, you remember your uncle—Austagia?"

The figure drew back his hood revealing tattooed markings over the left side of his bald head. The man bowed slightly but said nothing. Magnus knew the markings. He had never seen them before but knew what they meant. *He is a priest—an Irucantî.* Magnus drank in the sight of the man. *This is what becomes of those who are drafted into the priesthood.* There was an air about him that Magnus found intriguing. He seemed reserved, yet certain of himself, and so he should—the priests were the ultimate warriors who trained alongside dragons. It was said that in battle a single Irucantî was worth ten knights and a hundred untrained men. Magnus wondered if this Irucantî had come to Nuyan with a fire dragon, for the Irucantî were known to travel with them.

"Right. Magnus. At my daughter's request I am to give you counsel," Xavier said, giving no further explanation as to the presence of the numinous uncle. Xavier pulled the gloves from his hands and walked toward a door at the back of room.

"Father!" Catanya exclaimed, walking up to Xavier, who looked at her intently. "Why is your brother here?"

Xavier looked to the priest then back to Catanya. "We will discuss that soon enough." A bleak expression washed over his face.

Catanya looked to Magnus then her father, scowling. "Be nice. Please."

"I see you took the liberty of procuring Trillium for the afternoon?" Xavier countered.

"He's a fast horse. If not for him, Magnus and I would have kept you waiting rather than the other way around." Catanya took a step toward her father, placing her hands defiantly on her hips. She looked then to Austagia and frowned.

"Hmm. I'm sure when the Rhydermere honoured me with a purebred Wardemeer they did not account for meddling daughters." Xavier turned to Magnus. "Come then Magnus. Let us talk in private." He opened the door and waited for Magnus to enter.

Magnus smiled at Catanya and gave a polite nod to Alessandra. Both returned in kind. He wished he could have heard all of what Alessandra had to say, for she seemed to be telling him something of importance. *"It would be you if things were not as they were."* *What did she mean?* He walked to the door and followed Xavier in.

"Congratulations." Xavier extended a hand to Magnus. Magnus shook it. He was unsure whether he was talking about his selection into knighthood or taking his daughter's hand in marriage. "Primary candidate no less. And deservedly so." Xavier held Magnus's hand firmly in both of his.

"It was you who made the decision?" Magnus asked. He wondered if Xavier had also made the decision not to select Lucas.

"Honestly, there was little decision to be made." Xavier opened a tall cabinet on the wall next to him, removed a flask and poured two glasses of wine. "Tell me, have you ever lost a bout with the sword?"

Magnus tried to relax. "In competition, no. In training I have only ever lost to Lucas," he lied and looked to Xavier to see his reaction. Xavier stared at him closely as he handed him a glass.

"That I highly doubt." Xavier raised his glass. "To you, on your selection with the knighthood."

Magnus raised his glass. "Why do you doubt Lucas would best me?" He was curious.

Xavier took a large draft of his wine. "What you really want to ask me is why your friend was not selected as a candidate." Magnus said nothing, but took a sip of his drink. Xavier carried himself with such confidence that Magnus dared not give the impression he was challenging his decision. "His father was a great warrior, as was yours. As for Lucas—he strives for the approval of others—a corruptible quality where loyalties can shift. You on the other hand have your own cause, your own motivations. You try to be the best regardless of the price or prize. Such a quality is not so malleable."

"Would the Authoritarium not seek those who do as they want?"

"That may suit the Authoritarium. Right now our people need warriors who fight for what is right."

"And his selection as a reserve candidate?" Magnus dared to push the issue a little further, not half because it delayed the issue of Catanya.

"That may become apparent in a moment." Xavier gave Magnus a moment to weigh on his words. Magnus however, was not sure what to make of Xavier's intimations.

"To you," Xavier charged his glass, "On your selection to the knighthood." Magnus and Xavier both took a sip of wine. "Of course, when you're on duty as a knight you won't be drinking any of this stuff." He flashed a smile revealing teeth equally as white as his daughter's. "It makes it all the better when you're not!" With that, Xavier downed the rest of his wine and returned to the cabinet to refill his glass. Magnus took a long draw of his own drink.

"Now, to business." Xavier pointed to one of two leather-bound chairs in the room. "Please." Magnus took a seat as Xavier did. Clearly Magnus was getting no further about the subject of Lucas and so he decided to get to the point of his visit.

"As you know, Catanya and I have known each other for a very long time…"

"You wish to marry my daughter," Xavier interjected. Magnus was surprised at his frankness.

"More than anything. Yes. We both do." Magnus sat straight in his chair. Xavier sniffed at his glass of wine, apparently deep in thought.

"What are your intentions, Magnus? I ask you this because I know your father. I know him very well." Magnus frowned, waiting for Xavier to get to the point. "Do not get me wrong, I have the utmost respect for the man. I trained under him for several years and his accomplishments are second to none. However…" Xavier raised his glass and took a big sip. "His disdain for the Authoritarium is well known. You are aware of this?"

Magnus sighed, hoping it was not too obvious. "Sire, I do not see what this has to do with Catanya and I."

"What I'm getting at, Magnus, is will your father approve of you joining the knighthood under the current regime? Under the rule of the Authoritarium?"

Magnus felt trapped and even worse—it was a trap he had not considered himself. *Damned if I do and damned if I don't.* He decided there was nothing he could do but speak the truth. "No, he will not approve. And I have no intention of joining the knighthood. I will stay with my father on our lands and become a farmer as my father is. Catanya knows this and supports my decision."

"Tell me, why did you train to be the best all these years only to decline such an offer?"

"I wished to prove I was as capable as any other."

"And for how long will that give you peace?" Xavier leaned toward Magnus. "Watching, knowing you could be a better knight than your peers and bowing before each succession of knights for all the years to come?"

Magnus had no counter argument. Xavier had spoken the exact thoughts he often dwelled on.

Xavier sat back into his chair and sighed—a far more obvious sigh than Magnus's. "I am sorry Magnus, I will not let you marry Catanya." Magnus sank back into his own chair. His heart seemed to sink even lower. "Catanya deserves someone who will pursue the best for himself and for her. Someone true to himself and true to her. If you compromise on your choices now, where will you stop?"

Magnus stared blankly at Xavier. Was the man seriously telling him to go against his own father's will? Magnus could not help but point out the irony in Xavier's words. "You are telling me to stand against my father's judgement. By the same measure is Catanya not able to decide for herself what is right for her?"

"If you were one of my men, such words would see you disciplined for insubordination. But you aren't and have no intention of being. I think therefore our conversation is at its end." Xavier stood and walked to the cabinet once again. "You can see yourself out."

Magnus knew any further argument would be fruitless, particularly after the *insubordination* remark. However, he could not leave without voicing one last truth.

"If I am going to make a stand it will be for a more worthy reason than the Authoritarium's knighthood. It will be for Catanya." Xavier turned with a hard look on his face. Before he could retort, Magnus concluded. "You do not give us your blessing and I respect that—for now." He was unsure why he said what he did other than refusing to accept Xavier's decision as final.

Magnus left the room as instructed and immediately made eye contact with Catanya. He could see she was evaluating his facial expression. He opened his mouth to speak but Xavier's voice shouted from the room behind him. "Catanya. Here. Now." Catanya moved toward the door, not taking her eyes off Magnus. He grabbed her arm as she passed. He had to say something. He had to speak to her. There had to be a way...

"Wait for me by the river," Catanya whispered as she hurried into the room Magnus had just left. She looked at Magnus once again then closed the door behind her.

PRIESTHOOD

"Father?" Catanya looked to Xavier who seemed reluctant to turn from the cabinet, where he poured himself another glass of wine. "Father, look at me." Xavier finally turned to Catanya but did not say a word. "You said *no* didn't you. You told Magnus you would not approve."

Catanya had feared the worst. Her mother had been too quiet. *Mother knew.* "Father, all my life Magnus has been the one. We are meant to be together."

"Catanya, it is not to be." Xavier spoke gently. Catanya could see he believed his words no more than she did.

"It *is* to be. I *will* marry Magnus."

Xavier's voice sharpened. "Your place is elsewhere." He walked to the door and opened it. "Austagia," he called.

Catanya watched as the robed priest entered the room. Something was not right.

"Father, what's going on?" She looked at her estranged uncle. All she knew of him came from stories her father had told of their childhood together. His face broadened when he spoke of him. But the tales he told always finished with silence—his thoughts drifting. It was as though he was harbouring some regret.

A priest came to her father's family years ago. His name was Steyne, and Austagia was to be his understudy. It was considered an honour to have one's child drafted into the order, but it was an unspoken truth that it broke the hearts of loved ones. The priesthood was for life. It was a life of celibacy and commitment. This held no appeal to Catanya, or Magnus, or most of their friends in the realm. All the Irucantî were born of fire—of the Fire Realm. At the end of the harvest, on the even counted years, a single candidate would receive the call.

Austagia had come to visit once, when Catanya was five years old. Her grandmother had passed and Austagia came for the funeral. He seemed so tall and so serious to her then. He never smiled and paid her little heed short of staring at her occasionally. Catanya had put it down to his grieving. Looking at him now though, she saw not much had changed.

"Catanya." Xavier walked over to her and gently cupped his hand over her left shoulder. "The order of the Irucantî has kindly requested that you be inducted into their order."

Catanya smiled at her father's jest. "There is to be no induction into the priesthood this year. Not until next year."

"There is to be this one concession." It was Austagia speaking for the first time.

Xavier looked to his brother then to the ground. "You have been chosen over all others, Catanya."

"What? What are you saying? I am to become a *priest?*" Catanya pushed her father's hand away and stepped back.

"It is an honour to join our order," Austagia said.

"I'll decide if it's an honour!" Catanya looked to her father. "Is this to stop me marrying Magnus? What if he was to become a knight? Would you allow me to marry him then?" Xavier kept his silence. "That would make no difference, would it?" Catanya deduced. "You were going to send me to the priesthood regardless. You lied to Magnus."

Xavier kindly asked Austagia to leave the room. The priest gave a nod and there was a brief, quiet exchange between them. Catanya watched them closely. Anger boiled in her at her father's betrayal. She knew he had a part in this. It was most certainly not a regular induction into the order. Austagia left, closing the door behind him and Catanya was quick to speak.

"You had Magnus leave here believing he was not good enough for you. Not good enough for *me*. It didn't matter what he did, he was always going to be rejected. Am I right?"

"There is a lot more at stake here, Catanya. In time you will understand."

"I understand perfectly well." Tears brimmed Catanya's eyes and she turned to leave the room, not wanting her father to see her so upset.

"Catanya," her father snapped. She hesitated then looked back at him. Her tears spilled down her cheeks. She could see her father hesitate, sympathy in his eyes. It angered her ever the more. But then he stood tall, pulling himself to attention and addressed her formally. "You will have your chance to say your farewells, then leave for the Romghold in the morning."

"I have nothing more to say. Not to you. Not ever again. But then, that is the will of the order anyway, is it not?" Catanya turned and stormed out of the room.

NUYAN RIVER

Magnus sat on the western bank of the Nuyan River among the irises and tall grasses that lined the bank for many miles. He peered into the river's crystal waters then across to the eastern bank and up the knoll toward the township of Nuyan and Catanya's home. He picked a selection of the purple flowers and tied their long stems together with a thick reed of grass before setting them aside. Magnus gazed once again into the depths of the river where a trout swam against the current toward the small waterfall a hundred yards up stream. "What then, when you reach the waterfall?" he lamented.

Magnus threw a pebble across the surface of the river, attempting to skim it, only he threw too hard and the stone dove deep into the water before settling on the gravel at its bed. His ponderings were interrupted when he heard faint footsteps across the river.

"Magnus?" It was Catanya. She shielded her eyes from the late afternoon sun. Magnus stood and walked to the edge of the water as Catanya stepped across stones placed evenly across the river and landed beside Magnus on the other side. They embraced. Catanya buried her head against Magnus's chest and clasped her arms around his back. Magnus picked her up, pulling her even tighter against him. Catanya shifted her arms around his neck, kissing him firmly on the lips. Magnus could feel the warmth of her tears on his cheeks.

A long while passed before they slowly pulled away from one another. Magnus handed Catanya the bouquet of irises, feeling the softness of her hands as she took them. She smiled weakly.

"The flowers of J'esmagd," Catanya said. "I still remember the first time you gave me some. I took them home and placed them in the pitcher on the kitchen table. My mother accused me of trespassing over to J'esmagdlands— your lands—and stealing them." Catanya looked to the ground and Magnus saw a tear fall. He placed his hand gently under her chin and tilted her head up, looking into her watery eyes.

"But I dared not tell her they were from you," Catanya continued. "I looked at them each day until time made them wither. I had taken a part of you home and I have dreamt thereafter of the rest of you coming someday."

Magnus traced her long hair with his fingers, over the olive skin of her shoulders and across the straps of her dress. He was at a loss for words.

"My father is giving me away," Catanya said, looking down again.

"What do you mean? To whom?" Magnus asked, puzzled.

"To the order of the Irucantî. Apparently, I am to become a priest." Catanya looked at him again.

Magnus feigned a smile. He tried to see the humour in Catanya's words, but her face told a different story—she was serious. "Your uncle... That is why he came to Nuyan," Magnus realised.

"Aye."

Magnus froze. "The priesthood? Why?"

"I do not know. Magnus, something is going on. I know it. I have not seen my father this way before."

"I think your mother knew too." Magnus recalled his brief conversation with Alessandra. "She said we would marry if things were not as they were. What did she mean by that?"

Catanya seemed lost in her own world. She walked a little way down the riverbank before turning and heading back again. Magnus watched her, trying to form a vision of Catanya as a priest. She had such a lean build and was barely up to his shoulders in height. *Hardly a fighting warrior.* To become a dragon priest was not a sedentary calling. Catanya would become one of the most formidable warriors in all of Allumbreve. She would be a fighting Irucantî—*a Ferustir!* He found it hard to imagine her in the priesthood with her hair shaved to the scalp, her head tattooed in the markings of the Fire Realm. A smile came to his face.

"What is it, Magnus?" Catanya wiped her cheeks, an inquisitive smile on her face.

"Catanya the dragon warrior... Does this mean the next time we meet, you'll be able to give me a hiding?"

Catanya's eyes lit up and her jaw dropped. Her expression quickly morphed into a scowl. "No more than I could now." They both laughed.

'You could never..." Magnus teased.

"Says he, who didn't do his first spell until he was seven!" Catanya teased.

"How old were you?"

"Six—like Hannah."

"If only I could have been so gifted," Magnus mocked. Catanya shook her head.

A fleeting idea suddenly came to Magnus. He bit a thumbnail and looked about, trying to find the sanity in his ludicrous idea. There was nothing for it—it was the only option.

"Catanya, we could run."

Catanya thought it over, but not for long. "Let's. Now! We could make for the Crescent Woods."

"No, they would surely find us there. The woods are too small. Unlike Froughton Forest—we could hide there for an age." Magnus grew excited. This surely had to be the way.

"Froughton is far too dangerous. I have nightmares about what lurks there. But then again, no one would suspect we'd go there."

"We could go north to the Ice Realm… to my mother's people. That is, if we do not freeze along the way, what with winter coming. I'm sure they would welcome us." Ideas and possibilities poured into Magnus's mind. Yes—running was the only way.

Catanya could not stand still. "Or we could go south, through the Corville Mountains. No one will ever suspect we'd gone that way."

Magnus chuckled, certain she was joking. Only mad men and gypsies travelled south of the realms. No normal man who ever travelled that way returned. The mountains were home to the black wyverns. These vile creatures were thrice the size of a Wardemeer—more like that of a young dragon. They had long fangs and poisonous barbed tails. Magnus had only ever seen them from afar, taking to the skies like giant bats above their mountainous turf. The caves beneath the mountains hosted creatures far worse. South of that was stuff of nightmares surely worse than Froughton Forest—the Southern Wastelands and the black city of Ba'rrat—home to the Quag clan.

"It is true Catanya, no one would suspect. True as much we would be killed or put into slavery."

Catanya seemed unperturbed. "We'd disguise ourselves as gypsies and travel with a gypsy train to the coast, procure a ship and sail away through the Southern Gap to discover new lands."

"I've never seen a ship before," Magnus said. "Perhaps there is one waiting for us to sail beyond the Neverseas."

"So which will it be then, Magnus? The Ice Realm or south beyond the seas?"

"If it's all the same to you, I'd have us take our chances with the Ice Realm." Magnus held Catanya close again.

"So be it. Northward to the Ice Realm it is," Catanya said. "But I've never known a Northern winter. You'll need to keep me close to you at night." She raised her eyebrows and bit her lip.

Magnus poked Catanya in her side, making her squirm. He summoned Esmder and helped Catanya into his saddle. "Best we don't return to our homes, Catanya." Magnus did not like their chances of getting away again if either of them risked returning home.

"Aye. I've told my father I want nothing more of him anyhow." Sadness washed over her face, but she was quick to shake it off.

"And your mother and Hannah?" Magnus felt it rude not to ask.

"I will see them again and they will understand. As will your parents." Catanya flashed Magnus the quickest of smiles. "Shall we go?"

"Aye." Magnus sat in front of Catanya and she wrapped her arms firmly around his waist, her head against his back. "We can travel through the Crescent Woods. I'll give my letter to Lucas and have him give us provisions to see us through to the North."

"That's a good plan," Catanya said. Magnus sensed the reality of what they were about to do had suddenly dawned on her. He would not have it any other way. Esmder carried them up the western embankment and emerged from the thickets of grass to the field beyond. But they were not alone.

"There will be no travelling north this evening."

It was Xavier, sitting upon Trillium with a blank expression on his face. Two other knights on black Wardemeers flanked him. They were swift to move either side of Esmder, forcing him toward Xavier. There was no escape. Esmder grew skittish. Magnus patted his side to settle him, not taking his eyes off Catanya's father.

A sudden darkness fell over the afternoon sky and Magnus heard a deep beating sound overhead. The darkness shifted slowly to the north and descended into the shape of a great beast, casting aside its shadow revealing its bronze markings and huge wings that held the large creature in its descent until its hind legs struck the ground hard.

A fire dragon...

Austagia was seated at the base of the creature's neck. The dragon tucked its wings against its body and stood tall. It opened its large jaw to the sky and yawned. Its body shook for a moment before its jaw snapped shut and its head lowered to survey the group of men and horses before it.

"No. No, Father. I won't go." Catanya leapt from Esmder's back and walked past the knights to her father. Magnus went to do the same but the knight to his left rested a gloved hand on his leg.

"Best you stay seated, boy."

Magnus stared at him, noticing how his other hand gripped the pommel of his sheathed sword. He turned to the other guard, who winked at him.

"You're going to the one place I know you'll be safe," Xavier said to Catanya. He turned to his fellow knights, addressing them. "Travel southward to Realms End. Place two men at each of the posts from Overpell to Froughton Forest. Stay fast until you hear otherwise." The riders pulled their horses away from Magnus and charged southward at speed.

With the two knights gone, Magnus alighted and stood beside Catanya.

"Father, what is going on?" Catanya asked. She grabbed Magnus's hand, squeezing it tight. Magnus tried to think of a way out. Should they run and hide, or reason with Xavier? He knew, though, that it was too late for such things. He looked at the dragon. Its large pupils reflected the amber of the setting sun. It looked from him to Catanya. Magnus felt its abrasive presence in his mind like a dream pushing to be heard. Magnus tried to resist, keeping his thoughts to himself. Catanya let go of Magnus's hand and rubbed her temples with the tips of her fingers, staring at the dragon. *She feels it too...*

"Leave her be, please," Magnus said, looking at the dragon. The priest spoke to the creature softly and the beast's presence withdrew from his mind. Catanya lowered her hands.

"Father?" Catanya questioned again, "Why do this? What good am I to the priesthood?"

"I know you do not understand, but it is for the best."

"I know what is best for me," Catanya retorted.

"Sire, please," Magnus said. "Give us your blessing and you will see I can give Catanya the life she deserves." He felt desperate and, worse still, powerless.

"We have been through this," Xavier said. "In another time and place I would see my daughter suitored to the right man, but fate sees otherwise. As for you, Magnus of J'esmagd, I should have you disciplined for attempting to defy my decision. This is the second time you have done as much. There will not be a third." The large silver warhorse shifted impatiently beneath Xavier who pulled hard on the reins to steady him.

"I am not one of your subordinates." The words escaped Magnus's mouth without proper thought. "You've no authority to make such a call over me."

"Magnus please, don't." Catanya placed a hand on his chest. She turned to Xavier. "Father, I will do as you ask, but let Magnus be."

Magnus looked at her. "No Catanya. He must let *you* be." A dreadful thought crossed his mind—a thought that could save Catanya but at great cost. Magnus stepped around Catanya and stood in front of Trillium.

"If you must, send me to the Romghold in Catanya's place. I will become an Irucantî." He looked at the priest and walked over to him, now standing directly in front of the fire dragon, "I am gifted with the sword. I have been chosen as primary candidacy for the knighthood." Magnus nervously pulled the envelope from his trouser pocket. He fumbled, tore it open and pulled the letter free. He tried to hand it to the priest who simply stared back at him. Austagia's expression was cold and void of emotion.

Desperate, Magnus turned back to Xavier. "It was *you* who selected me. Give my position in the knighthood to Lucas. Let Catanya be with her mother and sister here in the Realm." Magnus stared at the Knight Commander.

Xavier had the same cold expression as his brother. But then the slightest smile came to his face. "I see there is more substance to you than I first thought. True as I said, you have your own cause, but I see now there is more. You do what is best for those you love."

"Thank you, sire." Magnus glanced to Catanya. She looked more worried than ever.

"Just don't let that be the chink in your armour. Everyone has one. Nothing is changed." Xavier addressed his daughter. "Catanya. It is time to leave."

Magnus fell to one knee, shocked.

Catanya pleaded, "Give me a moment with Magnus, please."

Xavier turned Trillium away from Magnus and toward the dragon. He fell into conversation with his brother. Catanya knelt beside Magnus. His heart skipped a beat. He went to talk, to reason with Catanya, but she placed a finger on his lips to silence him.

"You've done all you can. You've done more than you can. Be silent now, Magnus."

Magnus shook his head. Moments ago they were both excited to be fleeing and now... *this cannot be happening...*

With her back to her father, Catanya removed a plaited leather bracelet from her wrist and tied it fast to Magnus's left wrist. She whispered a spell, "*Shalla boyowa muto evavar*—bound forever, forever mine. Nothing will

28

separate this from you without breaking the spell. I am meant to be yours, Magnus of J'esmagd. Some day, one way or another, I will be. I promise." Catanya kissed Magnus then turned about before he had a chance to object.

Magnus stood. His boots felt rooted to the spot. Xavier helped Catanya climb onto the back of the dragon where she sat behind the priest. Xavier strapped her legs into stirrups that laced up to her knees. The priest pulled his hood up and seemed to peer out from beneath it at Magnus. Magnus wished for a sword. He wished to plunge it into the darkness of the priest's hood. His breathing quickened, his heart raced and still his feet did not move. At Catanya's request, he remained silent.

With one leap the dragon launched itself, kicking up great clumps of soil. Its wings beat hard, sending a rush of wind over Magnus as it climbed into the evening sky. Three, four, five beats of its wings and the creature was so high not even a cross bow could reach it. It turned back across the Nuyan River and eastward, no doubt toward its home far away at the peaks of the Romgnian Mountains. Magnus watched as Catanya disappeared from sight.

"Go home now Magnus." Xavier's voice blew over him with the cold wind from the north. "See to it your family is safe, for the days to come will bring darkness." With that, Xavier pulled hard on his reins and charged his horse southward.

Darkness… Magnus remained where he stood. *I see no days without it from this day forth.*

RUN

Dusk turned to night and the stolen sun gave over to endless trails of stars. Magnus found sanctuary in them, freeing himself from his weary game of blame and anger.

He scanned the four constellations, each reflecting a realm of Allumbreve. They were Ertwe, Jaat, Spindlefax and Couldradt—*Ice, Air, Earth and Fire.* Each realm had its god who looked down upon his own realm, looking over his people. He wondered what the god of fire was thinking of him just now. Magnus had looked into the eyes of one of his dragons and seen the fire in them. Some folk said the dragons were Gods themselves. Magnus was unsure. He hoped the dragon Catanya rode would get her safely to where she had to go.

It was an hour from the Nuyan River to his homestead and with less than a mile to go Magnus saw what looked to be the glow of the setting sun rise strangely again in the west. The glow grew more intense as he drew closer, and the light flickered angrily. He thought of his parents. They had left hours ago for the Cliffs of Overpell to investigate its abandoned post. He thought of the knights been sent home early on leave—including Xavier—and of Xavier commanding his men to return to their posts. The pieces began to click together and as Magnus came to the rise before his home, the final piece lay burning before him.

The stable, haystacks and wood yard were engulfed in fire. Flames clawed at the sky and roared with anger, hungrily leaping from one surface to another. A horse cart beside the wood yard caught some burning embers and ignited instantly, and in the middle of it all, Magnus's homestead stood, so far untouched by fire.

Magnus stifled a shriek. He dug his heels into Esmder's sides, driving the stallion down the slope of the field as fast as he would go. Magnus looked about for any sign of his parents but there was none. He could hear the screams of horses coming from beyond from the burning stables. Magnus guessed they were the draft horses. There was no sign of Breona, or Staeda—his father's Wardemeer.

He arrived at the house where flames started to take hold in the roof's thatching and spread quickly. Magnus dismounted and flew toward the house, shielding his face as he rounded the burning horse cart and pushed his way through the kitchen entrance at the back.

"Mother! Father!" Magnus tore through the house, going from room to room. The house was empty. Great wafts of smoke bled through the straw ceiling, filling the rooms. Magnus coughed and looked into the fire place that held nothing more than the faintest remains of glowing embers. *Mother and Father did not return.*

"Thump… Thump… Thump…"

Magnus turned. The sound was coming from his bedroom at the end of the living room. He raced across, opened the door and stepped into his bedroom. To his alarm it was just as hot and just as smoky as the rest of the house. He looked to the small window. Standing outside was Ganister. Magnus went to shout but was interrupted by a loud roar from behind him. He turned to see the ceiling of the house collapse into the living room. The supporting beams of hardwood splintered and cracked. Burning clumps of thatching and plumes of smoke wafted through the house, choking him. Magnus cowered back toward the window where Ganister was. In his bedroom, the roof started to creak and groan as the fire took hold of the weakening beams overhead.

Magnus's heart pounded. He turned back to Ganister who punched through the glass window with the pommel of his sword. The window shattered inward and Magnus reeled away from the shards of glass that scattered through the room. Ganister cleared the window frame of glass in the same manner and reached an arm through the window.

"Come Magnus, quickly!"

Magnus reached to Ganister, gripping his forearm. He hoisted himself up and through the small window opening. Once out to his shoulders, Ganister pulled him clean in one big tug. Magnus fell to the hard ground outside. With a loud crash the remaining portion of the roof tumbled inward, sending fire, smoke and debris shooting out the window after him.

Ganister pulled Magnus to his feet. He looked in disbelief as the walls of his family home began to crumble, falling to the inferno within. Spitting soot and ash out of his mouth, Magnus turned to Ganister, keen to ask if he knew where his parents were, but his gaze was drawn to something else—a tall black figure running toward them from around the back of the house.

"Ganister!" Magnus shouted, pointing to the approaching man. The assailant was equally as tall as Ganister, his chest and arms layered in metal armour finished in a dull, black hue. The rest of his body was covered in black cloth and his face was partially covered by a kerchief that tied into the spikes of the black helm that extended to his collarbones. He would have been invisible in the dark of night if not for the light of the fire.

The man came at them fast, wielding a pair of black swords finished in the same dull, black steel as his armour.

Ganister pushed Magnus aside with his free hand and reeled around just as the warrior swung one of swords down on Ganister. Ganister shifted at the last moment, parrying the blow with his own sword before raising it above his head and bringing it down on the man with all his might. The warrior swiftly knelt on one knee and raised a blade to bear the force of Ganister's blow. Magnus was frightened by the man's strength. He had always thought of Ganister as the most powerful man in all of Allumbreve, but this black warrior was equally as large and twice as menacing.

A Quagman! Magnus guessed.

The black warrior leapt toward Magnus as Ganister recovered his position. It was an unexpected move. Magnus tried to run, slamming his shins into the low stone garden wall, falling clumsily. He flipped onto his back and tried to scamper backward, slipping over the damp grass beneath him. The Quagman was moving fast. His dark eyes were fixed on Magnus. He raised both swords and held them as daggers then thrust them down. At the last moment, Magnus twisted and rolled over to his right and the blades sank into the soft ground.

Ganister was upon the overextended man in a flash, kicking his legs out from under him. The menacing Quagman fell to the ground hard, and before he could recover Ganister drove his sword through the warrior's back. He held it fast until the Quagman stopped struggling. Satisfied he was dead, Ganister pulled his sword free and moved to Magnus.

"Listen to me Magnus, you must follow me as fast as you can and don't look back. You hear me?"

Magnus was still staring at the dead man lying beside him. Ganister shook Magnus who nodded feverishly. "Yes... follow you."

Together they ran northward from the house. Magnus leaped across the rise of the open field like a gazelle in stark contrast to Ganister's bull-like, lumbering motions. Equally as effective, they never left one another's side. Fuelled by fear, Magnus felt as if his legs were propelling themselves. Once over the rise, Magnus tried to look back but Ganister grabbed his arm, forcing him to go on.

"Keep moving, don't look back," he panted. But Magnus stopped.

"My father, my mother. Ganister—where are they? They left the house hours ago." Fear started to grip Magnus and he began to shake. The cold night air pierced through him, accentuating the shaking. He stood in the field wearing only his loose tunic, pants and boots.

"I will look for them Magnus. But you are not safe here. The Quagmen will be looking for you."

"Why are they looking for me?" Magnus asked.

Ganister took a deep breath and appeared to Magnus to be stifling frustration. "Because you are Bonstaph's son."

This meant nothing to Magnus. He had more questions and was about to voice them when he heard a ghastly sound from back over the rise toward the house. It was unlike anything Magnus had heard before—a kind of bellowing shriek that reverberated through the night sky and shook the ground beneath him. It chilled Magnus even more than the cold. Ganister grasped his arm again, pulled hard and forced him to run. They sprinted down the plain of the north meadow, away from his home. A quarter mile away was the low stone wall and beyond that the Crescent Woods.

"We must get to the Woods!" Ganister panted, almost completely out of breath. Magnus had none left to reply.

Magnus and Ganister threw themselves up and over the four-foot wall and sprinted to the first of the oak trees. The amity of darkness came as they moved deep into the woods and the cold chill of the night air was replaced with a warmth and stillness afforded by the green canopy above. Magnus was glad for the respite but was no more certain what they were running from. *What was that screaming creature?*

The comfort of the woods was short lived. From the northern field came the awful shriek again.

"Get down, Magnus!" Ganister pushed Magnus to the ground and lay close beside him, his hand still holding him fast. Peering out through the woods and beyond the boundary wall, Magnus could see a dark blur of movement in the night sky, circling around the empty field twice before moving back northward toward his home.

"Let's move," Ganister whispered, jumping to his feet. The two of them moved deeper into the woods.

"What was that?" Magnus asked.

"Keep moving," Ganister insisted, still not answering Magnus's question.

They traversed half a mile deep to the dark centre of the woodlands and came upon a broad oak tree. Ganister trudged towards it. "Come Magnus," he motioned. Magnus followed him, treading carefully through the dark to the tree that was easily twenty feet thick at its base.

Ganister called out in a loud whisper. "Sarah? Sarah, are you there?"

A shadow appeared from behind the back of the tree. Magnus recognised the short, stout woman immediately. It was Ganister's wife.

"Magnus!" Sarah called as loud as she dared, running over to him. Her long, curly blonde hair billowing as she moved. She gave Magnus a quick hug then stepped back, looking at him. She held a small lamp supported by a shoulder strap that rattled as she moved. Lifting it up to his face, she examined him, holding his chin with the other hand and frowning as she turned his head from side to side.

"Are you hurt?"

"No Ma'am, I am..."

"*Sarah* will do," she interrupted. "I am no *Ma'am*. I've told you a thousand times." Still frowning, Sarah inspected Magnus from head to toe, looking for any signs of damage.

"I am not hurt, Sarah."

"No?" Sarah continued her examinations.

A second figure appeared from behind the large tree. He held a bow in one hand, with an arrow drawn at the ready in the other. "Magnus?" he called with a whisper.

"Lucas!" Magnus recognised his voice. Lucas released the tension in his bow. He walked over to Magnus and the two boys shook hands.

"It is good to see you well," Lucas said.

"And you."

Sarah seemed content Magnus was unharmed and walked to Ganister. "Bonstaph? Alavia?"

Ganister shook his head. "I will go back for them, now that I know Magnus is safe."

Magnus looked to Lucas, hoping to get more answers from him. "Lucas, how did you know we were in trouble?"

Lucas led Magnus to the back of the large tree. "It was Breona. She came to us less than an hour ago, making a good racket at the front door. We found her foaming at the mouth like she had near-killed herself to get to us."

Sure enough, Breona was there behind the tree. She waited beside three other horses including Tameror—Ganister's own black Wardemeer. While the other three were content chewing on the sparse grass that grew between the thirsty surface roots of the oak trees, Breona was trotting around in a state of unrest.

"Breona!" Magnus called to her, glad to see her. She trotted over to him, her white hide shining even in the sparse light of the woods. She blew through her nostrils and nuzzled into the palms of Magnus's hands.

"Yes, Breona raised the alarm," Ganister continued Lucas's story. He was checking over his armour, neatly laid out over a large blanket to the side of where the horses grazed. "Thank you for arranging this, son." Ganister looked at Lucas, smiling. Lucas nodded in return. Ganister removed his grey cloak and place it around Magnus's shoulders—he was still shivering from the cold. Ganister began to change into his armour. Sarah helped him into his steel chain mail and leather tunic.

"Ganister fell out the door pulling his boots on," Sarah said.

"Thanks to Breona, pushing and shoving me as she was. I was barefoot and half-naked." He nodded toward Magnus with a grin on his face but Magnus was in no mood for humour. Seeing this, Ganister lost his smile. "I left Lucas and Sarah to prepare my armour and planned to meet them here. Tameror and I followed Breona back through the woods and came across your place ablaze. It could be no accident, that I was sure of," Ganister explained further. "I sent the horses back to the woods, then came about the house from the west to see what was what. Your mother and father were there, further to the south, surrounded by six or more of those Quagmen." He shook his head as Sarah pulled his leather tunic over him and tied straps around his back.

"You saw them! They are alive?" Magnus was relieved and worried all at once.

"Aye, they were alive. But those wretched Quagmen weren't alone. They had *wyverns* with them—black Corville Mountain wyverns. Six as I counted, prowling around like hunger-ravaged dogs. That was the ghastly sound we heard as we made for the woods. What they are doing this far from their desolate home I do not know. It has been a long time since I've seen the likes of them but apparently they are in the service of the Quag now... Or vice versa, perhaps. What I want to know is, how did the Quag infiltrate the Realm?"

Magnus knew how. "The knights were removed from their patrol. All along the southern borders."

"Are you certain?"

"Mother saw it herself. And at sunset Xavier ordered knights back into position." Magnus was far more concerned about his parents. "Could you not have killed the Quagmen and helped my parents?" he asked, frustrated.

"Hmph," Ganister exclaimed, checking his sword then sheathing it again in its scabbard before pulling leather gauntlets over his hands.

"He could have, had he allowed me to go with him," Lucas interjected. He stood tall and proud next to Magnus with a demeanour suggesting he was ready to take on anything. Lucas had his mother's curly blonde hair but a tall, leaner build—much like Magnus's. It was something that always made Magnus curious, considering how heavyset his parents were.

Ignoring his son, Ganister continued talking as he dressed. "It was my first desire, Magnus, but I could see your parents were distracted by something other than the wretched Quagmen. Your mother was gazing toward the burning homestead. Worry was written all over her face. I knew then *you* must have been in the house. Low and behold, as I moved back to the north I saw you running *into* the burning house! I had to get you out."

"I went in to be sure my parents weren't there," Magnus said.

"You're lucky I was the one who saw you." Ganister put his hands on his hips. "We nearly got away unnoticed, but for the Quagman we killed. I fear the screaming wyvern suggests discovery of the body. They'll be looking for us, that's for sure."

Magnus nodded. He appreciated Ganister's honesty, but it did nothing to appease his worries.

"I will find them Magnus—know that," Ganister said. Sarah fitted greaves over his shins then bound them tightly about his calves. When she was done, Ganister mounted Tameror and retied his scabbard around his waist. Sarah handed him his shield.

"Ganister." Magnus walked up to him. "You said they would be looking for me because I'm Bonstaph's son. Why?"

Tameror grew skittish, as all warhorses do at the sniff of battle, and neighed loudly. Ganister patted his great horse's side with his gloved hand to steady him. He returned his attention to Magnus. "There are a lot of questions unanswered for you, Magnus. In time you will learn what you must.

But for now, you are not safe here. Go now with Sarah. She will give you warm clothes and all the provisions you need."

Ganister leant over to kiss Sarah and held her arm for a moment. "Farewell my love. I will see you soon enough."

"That you will, my husband."

Ganister rode to Magnus and reached to him. Magnus held his gloved hand.

"The night is still young, Magnus. Ride with Breona, for an Astermeer can traverse these lands faster than any other. Head east toward Froughton Forest as fast as you can. Cloak yourself in its darkness and travel nor'eastward along the road of the Outer Rim. You will travel with the Valley of Shadows always to your right, but on no account enter the Valley. At the northern most point of Froughton, travel the Northern Road to the city of Guame. Speak before the Authoritarium. They will afford counsel to the son of Bonstaph—former Knight Commander of Allumbreve. They may disagree on political terms but that amounts to naught during war. If that does not sit well with them, tell them I sent you. Let them know the Quag have invaded our lands. They will mobilise their legions to Realms End."

Ganister then took Lucas's hand. "Be safe my son. Travel with Magnus as far as the Nuyan River but no further, then return home to your mother's side. Don't come looking for me, Lucas. I will return to you both soon." Lucas nodded, although Magnus could see disappointment in his face.

Ganister waved to his wife. Sarah waved back then covered her mouth, holding back her tears. Tameror charged back through the woods, throwing up clumps of turf with his massive hooves, before disappearing into the darkness, back toward Magnus's home.

Sarah and Lucas prepared their horses for the ride back to their homestead north of the woodlands. Magnus stroked Breona's head.

"Will she let you ride her?" Lucas asked.

"I never have before. Not so as I remember," replied Magnus. "She was sworn to Mother. I've not known another to ride her." He thought of his own horse—Esmder—hoping he was okay and hadn't suffered at the hands of the Quag or the black wyverns.

Sarah walked her horse over to Magnus. "You rode with Breona as an infant in your mother's arms and sat at the front of her saddle as a child. She will remember you upon her back, I am sure."

Sarah spoke to Breona. "You know Magnus as you know Alavia. He is as much of the Ice Realm as he is of Fire. He is your kin." She placed the palms of her hands upon Breona's forehead, closing her eyes. *"Fara un icen du ralxva forr Magnus. Alavia shi wuden ralma vua fetrama Breona."* Sarah opened her eyes then looked to Magnus who waited for an explanation for her Icerealmish chant. She smiled at him, "I learnt much from your mother. I spoke the truth of whom you are Magnus—fire and ice. Alavia chose the father of her child wisely. Breona should be at one with you as she is with your mother." Magnus was not sure how to respond. "Talk to her. She knows you. She'll hear you," Sarah urged.

"I don't speak much of her tongue." Magnus felt awkward and even a little embarrassed that he did not know Breona better. Although he never shared his mother's intimacy with Breona, he knew how special she was. Astermeers were the most coveted of horses, bred by the Rhydermere for their speed, intelligence and loyalty to their sworn riders. They were rare. Outside of the Ice Realm they were even more so, for they could not be bought and were gifted at the discretion of the Rhydermere themselves. The same was true of the Wardemeers—cousins to the Astermeer, they are   warhorses   bred for battle. Such breeds as these were gifted only to the finest warriors of the realms.

"Your dialect matters not. Speak with your mind. She will understand you—much as a dragon would."

Much as a dragon would... Magnus continued to pat Breona's forehead along the silver blaze that ran down to her snout upon her otherwise pure white coat. *The blood of the ice dragon...* People often said Astermeers were bred with dragon blood. *"That would imply ice dragons were not extinct..."* his mother would counter, invalidating the claim.

Magnus closed his eyes and tried to relax. He slowed his breathing and in a moment felt emotions that were not his own. Then a voice that was as gentle as his mother's came to mind as a whisper.

"Where is Alavia?"

Magnus responded with his thoughts. *"I don't know. I miss her and I want to help her."*

In the background Magnus overheard Lucas speaking with Sarah.

"We need to hurry back home, Mother, we have no time to spare."

"We cannot go anywhere until Magnus can ride that horse. He will need her if he is going to travel to Froughton Forest before sunrise."

Magnus's eavesdropping stopped as Breona's thoughts permeated through his mind again. *"Can we find her together?"*

"We need to travel far to find help. Warriors from the South are attacking our lands." *"I saw them come… I saw them with Alavia."*

"And you came to Ganister and Sarah for help. You are brave, Breona. Will you run with me to find help?"

"I will run with you Magnus, to do what we can to help her."

Magnus smiled and opened his eyes, hugging Breona around the neck. *"Thank you."*

SARAH

Magnus, Sarah and Lucas traversed northward out of the Crescent Woods and across the Bowthwait lands. As they rode their horses, the silence of the night gave Magnus leave to think about his parents. *Are they safe?* He thought of the viciousness of the Quagman's attack. It took even Ganister a moment to best the warrior. He shook himself free of his dark thoughts and looked over to Sarah. She was observing him, much as his own mother would.

"These things weigh heavily on your mind, don't they, Magnus?" Sarah said with a sympathetic smile. Magnus felt his chest tighten—he was sick with worry.

Sarah rode to his left and placed a soft hand on his arm. "There is good yet to come from this evening's wrongs, Magnus, I know it." Magnus looked to Sarah as if expecting an explanation. The moonlight caught her face as it rose above the woods and Sarah winked. "Call it gypsy's intuition." Her smile broadened and her fleshy cheeks lifted her eyes much like a yawning cat. She tucked her long blond hair back revealing the various shaped piercings she had around the rim of her ear, under which was a small tattoo in the shape of a four-sided star. Both these qualities revealed her gypsy past.

Magnus smiled at Sarah, feeling slightly relieved of his worry. She was good company and had been for as long as Magnus remembered. He considered for a moment what unlikely events may have led Ganister to marry a gypsy, much as his father had met his mother years ago—Marriage to a young woman of the Rhyder clan of the northern Ice Realm was also an unlikely pairing. He could only assume that as knights the two of them travelled far and wide and met many people from each of the four realms.

"Ganister fell for the charm of the Gypsy, much as your father did for a lady of the North!" Sarah said, interrupting his thoughts and apparently peering into his mind.

"Mother, leave Magnus's thoughts to himself," Lucas remarked.

"That's okay, I enjoy the company in my head," Magnus said. Lucas and Sarah laughed.

Lucas sidled up next to Magnus and gave Breona a nudge with his knee, and then another. Breona snorted in protest. Magnus looked at Lucas for an explanation.

"One thing is for sure, Magnus," Lucas said. "In all of Allumbreve, I would bet you are the only boy outside of the Rhyderlands to sit astride an Astermeer."

"You call me a boy, Lucas?" Magnus asked.

"Aye, I do."

"And what of you… all of six months older than me?"

"What a difference six months makes." Lucas grinned. "You see that lamp ahead?" He pointed to the north where Magnus could see a single yellow glow. It was a lantern at Lucas's homestead half a mile away. "In a thousand years a *boy* couldn't get to it before me." With that Lucas spurred his horse into a gallop, taking off as fast as he could and laughing as he went. Magnus smiled to himself. He knew what Lucas was doing—trying to take his mind off troubling thoughts.

"Not in the mood for a race, Magnus?" Sarah asked, grinning once again.

"I haven't decided yet. Either way, I only think it fair to give Lucas a head start." He was not in the mood at all, but watching Lucas disappear into the night was more that he could bear. He spoke with Breona. "*Shall we teach Lucas a lesson, Breona?*"

Breona needed no further encouragement. She reared up before charging forth with explosive speed. Magnus held tight to Breona's reins, pulling himself forward and down against the oncoming wind. He'd often seen his mother ride Breona at speed, but had never experienced something quite like this for himself. He could hear Sarah's laughter trailing behind him.

Two hundred feet out from the light, Lucas had a fifty-foot lead over Magnus, but Breona was gaining rapidly. Lucas steered his steed around the remains of an old horse-cart that sat weathered in the field. Breona did not deviate. She hurdled the cart and landed alongside Lucas, bolting ahead.

Breona and Magnus pulled up alongside the lamp with a fifty-foot lead of their own over Lucas, who finally arrived, his horse panting and heaving. "Look at her." Lucas pointed to Breona. "She's not so much as raised a sweat." He shook his head.

Breona had found a green patch of grass at the foot of the lamp pillar and was chewing on it. Magnus was glad she was no longer so anxious. It made him breathe a little easier too. The thought of Ganister going to help his parents gave him peace of mind—*surely there is no one more capable.*

41

Soon after, Sarah arrived and the three of them walked their horses around the back of the homestead. Lucas took the horses to feed and Magnus followed Sarah into the house.

The rear entry to the home led to the kitchen. As with his own home, the stone walls of the house were a mixture of locally sourced granite and sandstone from the quarry within the Uydferlands, north of the township of Nuyan. Magnus recalled the many times as a child he and Lucas had travelled there and helped their fathers load the stone onto Ganister's cart—the cart that now stood decaying in Ganister's field as a reminder of the hard labour they shared with their two young sons.

Magnus remembered the first time he arrived at the quarry and met Catanya, then a young girl. She would bring the travellers refreshments and always had a mug of lemon water for Magnus. They would sit together, talking for as long as they could while Magnus sipped his drink as slowly as possible, wishing to stay with her as long as he could before they were both called back to their duties. He looked forward to seeing her each time they ventured to the quarry where the Uydfermen worked the stone.

Magnus played with the bracelet Catanya placed on his right wrist. Comforted by its presence in her absence, he was glad she had placed enchantments to keep it with him. Even so, Magnus vowed to never take it off.

"Take a seat here, Magnus," Sarah said. Magnus woke from his reverie and sat at the square kitchen table. The house was decorated differently to his own home. Where his mother preferred elegance and cleanliness, Sarah was overtly expressive with ornaments, paintings and decorations that covered every surface possible. Most of the furniture she had made and engraved herself with symbols and glyphs of all the realms, each with its own story.

Sarah placed a bowl of food in front of him. "Pumpkin soup," she explained. "I know you love my pumpkin soup. Oh, some bread as well. I baked it today." She placed a large shred of grainy bread next the soup that Magnus had nearly finished. He ate keenly.

"Thank you, Sarah," Magnus muffled through a full mouth.

"Eat with your mouth full, speak with it empty."

Magnus gave a nod, watching her as he ate. She darted from one end of the house to another, gathering things into a woven basket. Once the basket was full, she placed it on a chair adjacent to him. "Here, I've put together some clothes for you, some food, coin and so forth. That should see you fed and warm on your trip to Guame."

"Thank you." Magnus smiled. Lucas came into the house through the rear door, closing it behind him.

"Keep the door open Lucas, so I can see the horses. They will warn us of unwelcome visitors." Sarah waved a hand at the door then returned to arranging the belongings for Magnus. Lucas did as told then seated himself at the table opposite Magnus.

"You need sturdy clothes for travelling. These fit Lucas until recently, so they should fit you well enough." Sarah handed the clothing to Magnus.

"Thank you Lucas. I appreciate it," Magnus said to his friend, who smiled and nodded in return. Lucas appeared a little distant to him.

Magnus removed his dirty, scorched tunic and put on a more fitted cream-coloured shirt of thicker fabric. Then he took a dark red leather jacket that Sarah helped him fit by tightening three buckles across his chest. It was firm around his body but comfortable. Its tall collars brushed his ear lobes. Together with the cloak Ganister had given him, he would be warm enough at night. Finally, Sarah had given him a pair of brown leather trousers with gold buckles running down the outer sides of the legs. Before changing into them, Magnus took the crumpled letter from the Authoritarium out of his back pocket. He folder it over and stashed it in the new trousers. *Now is not the time,* he decided.

Sarah looked Magnus up and down, nodding in approval. She made some alterations to his trouser buckles, pulled at the shirt beneath his jacket and peered closely at his face, before licking her thumb and rubbing a dirty mark off his cheek. Satisfied with his appearance, Sarah nodded once again.

"It suits you," Lucas said. Magnus looked at him. "Almost as much as it did me... when it fit." Magnus gave Lucas a shove.

Sarah lay out a green, tightly woven blanket across the table and started arranging the other items she had collected upon it. There was a spare shirt and food items including a full loaf of bread, a block of cheese, dried beef strips and dried fruit. Beside the food she placed a flask of water. "Just in case water is scarce, although you should do fine in Froughton Forest," Sarah explained. Finally, Sarah took out a small sack of gold coins that she put in the middle of the package. She folded the green blanket over itself until it presented as a tightly bound package, tying the corners off together.

"This can double as a blanket for you to wear if the nights grow cold." Sarah looked at Magnus. "The blanket has enchantments on it. If you sleep under it, it will hide you. Not visibly, mind you, but if you are hidden to the eye, prying minds won't pick up on any of your other senses, nor be able to read your thoughts. Handy—that is."

Sarah smiled deliberately and Magnus could see she was masking her concern. She scurried over to the living room and lifted the chairs away from the large stitched rug on the ground. She knelt down and began to roll the rug up over itself until the bare stone floor beneath was exposed. Lucas turned on his stool and looked at his mother with a curious expression on his face. She scampered back and started to feel the stones in the floor with the palms of her hands, her numerous brass bracelets clinking and clanging across the stone ground as she did.

"Four days," Sarah said, still feeling the ground beneath her.

"Sorry?" Magnus asked.

"It is four days journey to Guame. It will cost you a gold coin to enter the city gates. They will give it back when you leave. It's to keep the riff-raff out." Sarah thumbed a hand over her head. "And a sign of good will as you leave." She gave a thumbs-up in approval. "That were your father's idea, Magnus. A wise man he is and a brave knight he was." She mumbled as she continued across the ground, almost hidden under her long curly hair that fell to the floor. Soon, her hands settled on one of the stones and she paused.

"*Lif letta,*" Sarah chanted. She waited for something to happen. Nothing did. "Hmmm," she mumbled again, moving her hands across each of the stones set in the floor, pausing to push her bracelets up her forearms to stop the clanging. "Ahah!" She settled on one of the smaller stones in the floor and repeated her chant—"*Lif letta.*" Immediately the stone slid upward from the floor. It was only about an inch, but enough for her to get a grip on it and pull it out of the ground. Magnus and Lucas looked at one another. Lucas shrugged. It seemed he knew no more than Magnus did about Sarah's enchanted stone.

Sarah plunged one of her short arms shoulder-deep into the hole where the stone had been. She rummaged around for a few moments with her tongue out the side of her mouth, frowning as she concentrated. "Ahah!" Out of the hole she pulled a thin, three foot-long object wrapped in suede and tied off with a white ribbon. Placing the object beside her, Sarah reached back into the hole and pulled out a second object. It was the same as the first, only bound with a red ribbon. She stood, panting from the effort and brought the two objects over to the kitchen table and lay the one with the white ribbon in front of Magnus and the other with a red ribbon in front of Lucas.

"These are for you two. They were always meant for you. Your fathers were waiting for the right time to give them to you. Under the circumstances I think now is as good a time as any, don't you think?" Sarah loosened the ribbons on both objects and nodded in turn to Magnus and Lucas. "Go on then, open them." She rubbed her hands together anxiously.

Magnus could see Lucas was as curious and he was. They carefully unwrapped the cloths revealing a pair of swords. Magnus looked his over. Never had he seen a sword so beautiful. The pommel and cross guard were white-steel—the same steel as his father's sword—and finished with intricate engravings. The grip was wrapped in dark red leather. Lucas's sword was crafted the same, but for the pommel and cross-guard which were bronze rather than steel. The two swords were held in identical scabbards finished in engraved dark red leather.

Magnus and Lucas unsheathed their swords. The steel of each appeared as bright as diamond from guard to point. They looked to Sarah for an explanation.

"Your fathers were so proud of you both and so one evening, after they had toasted themselves silly with dewberry wine for the eleventieth time, Alavia and I suggested they celebrate in a more productive manner." Sarah took a seat beside Lucas. "Alavia's people gifted her some years earlier a measure of fleu-steel—or Icerealmish steel, as it is often known. It is the strongest steel in Allumbreve, mined by the Rhydermere of the North, beyond the Ice Breach. There was enough of it to make a large knight's longsword. She and Bonstaph insisted it was used to produce two lighter swords. One for each for you."

Tears formed in Sarah's eyes. "And so Ganister, son of a gifted swordsmith, used his learned skills to shape these two swords. They are different, yet the same. The differences between the two represent your maternal origins. The similarities show your link to the Fire Realm—the realm of your fathers. These swords tell of a brotherhood between you. A gift of the finest of steel from one family, and the finest of craftsmanship from another."

Magnus was at a loss for words. He felt honoured to be blessed with Lucas in such a way. Lucas was staring at Magnus but then he stood, sheathed his sword and placed it back on the table. "I shan't be needing this." Lucas folded his arms. "It's been shaped *by* a knight *for* a knight."

"Lucas… don't!" Sarah warned. "Whatever fate brings to the two of you this evening or for ever after, remember you are as brothers." Sarah wiped her eyes with the palms of her hands then lifted her chin up, sniffing. "Right then Magnus, we should pack your sword with the rest of your belongings and we shall have you on your way."

Magnus sheathed his sword, eyeballing Lucas. His friend was clearly having a hard time coming to terms with his 'reserve' candidacy news. Magnus just could not find the strength to talk to him about it—there seemed far more pressing issues at hand. He finished the last piece of bread. The nervousness in his stomach rose and he choked for a moment on his bread.

"Are you okay?" Lucas asked. Magnus nodded, swallowing hard and taking a deep breath.

"The horses!" Sarah whispered and quickly extinguished the numerous candles in the house. The three of them peered out into the dark of night. Breona and the other two horses were skittish and pacing about anxiously.

Magnus's heart pounded in his chest and he looked to Sarah who closed her eyes, joined her hands together and whispered a gypsy chant. After a moment's silence her eyes opened wide and she spoke in a low tone. "They approach from the Crescent Woods—Quagmen and mountain wyverns. There are many of them." Sarah blinked twice and shook her head as though waking from a trance and said in her normal voice, "Lucas… Magnus… you must go *now*."

Grabbing their swords, Magnus and Lucas followed Sarah out the rear door and over to the horses. With Magnus's belongings tied firmly to Breona's saddle, they all mounted. Sarah gave instructions.

"You both remember what Ganister said. You know what you are to do. I will provide a distraction until you reach the woods to the east. That is half a mile. Ride that half a mile faster than you have ever ridden."

Magnus looked at Lucas. "I will be by your side, Lucas." He had no intention of riding ahead of his friend even though he had the faster horse.

"I appreciate that," Lucas stammered.

Sarah approached Magnus, leant across and gave him a kiss on the cheek.

"Thank you for everything, Sarah," Magnus said, wishing he could show greater appreciation. Sarah smiled fondly. She rode over to her son, leaning toward him and embracing him before holding his face and kissing both cheeks. She spoke to him, but Magnus could not hear. Lucas nodded several times in response.

"I will. I love you too, Mother."

Sarah looked to both of them one last time. "Go now and don't look back for anything." She rummaged through the red velvet bag she held over her shoulder and pulled out a crystal ball that filled the palm of her hand. Raising it in front of her, she whispered a chant and a blue light began to swirl within the ball, building gradually in intensity. Sarah then rode off around the side of the house and out of Magnus's sight to face whatever was approaching from the south.

CHASE

Magnus and Lucas charged eastward. The moon was cloaked by an isolated clump of cloud and Magnus wondered if it was due to one of Sarah's gypsy spells. *Can she do that?* He shook the thought from his mind and focussed on remaining by Lucas's side. The meadow had a gradual rise making the ride even harder for Lucas's steed. The darkness of the looming woods seemed forever away. With barely a hundred feet remaining, Magnus dared to glance over his shoulder.

Sarah had stopped her horse midway between the Woodlands and the homestead and held the crystal ball high in front of her. An explosion of blue light pulsed out from the ball in a horizontal arc in all directions. The ghastly shriek of the wyverns pierced the night sky as the light reached them. Magnus gasped at the sight. "Go, go, go Lucas!" Magnus was terrified. It was just for a moment, but he saw the shadows of a great host of ironclad horsemen and lurking black beasts at the border of the woods.

The boys pushed their horses fast up the meadow into the first line of trees. Hidden in the shadows they dismounted their horses and doubled back, crouching behind the tall grasses of the woodland's verge. A long way from its source, they were still able to distinguish the brilliant blue disc of light pulsing from Sarah's crystal ball. All of a sudden it was gone and in its place was pure darkness.

"Do you see anything?" Lucas whispered, barely an inch from Magnus.

Magnus shook his head. "No." He strained his eyes and ears, looking for any sign of movement across the meadow, but in the light's absence, the darkness left him blind. A moment later the moon shifted out from behind the clouds and the grassy fields were illuminated by a dull, purplish glow. An advancing line of Quagmen divided the field. Twenty or more rode on great, black warhorses whose frightening eyes glowed red in the night.

"What are those beasts?" Magnus thought aloud.

"Delvion's sorcery."

"Delvion the dragon slayer? He's a sorcerer? Surely he'd be dead by now?"

"He'll not stop until he rules all of Allumbreve. He calls himself *King of Allumbreve*."

"Where'd you hear that?"

"People talk. Gypsies in Nuyan talk of it. They travel through there all the time."

Magnus sighed, "I don't trust a word those travelling gypsies say."

"Well, we can't all be bred of the Ice Realm, Magnus." Lucas's tone was condescending.

"Hey, I'm of the Fire Realm just as you are. There's no difference between you and me. There never has been." Magnus shook his head. *Well at least he's getting it off his chest.*

He looked again across the field. More Quagmen had appeared riding wyverns. Some took to the skies. One of the unaccompanied wyverns flew to the ground just before the house and landed on the old horse-cart. It kept its large, bat-like wings spread wide and arched its head up, screeching into the night sky. It made Magnus and Lucas jump. They both scuttled backward into the Crescent Woods.

"I can't see my mother, Magnus," Lucas said.

Magnus scanned the field one last time but couldn't see Sarah. *Was she captured? Was she killed?* "I cannot see her either. But she said to keep moving and not look back. She wouldn't want us caught, Lucas."

Lucas squinted, looking desperately for his mother. Magnus knew the Quagmen would advance across the field to the house and most likely burn it as they had his own. From here, he assumed the wyverns would track him, as they no doubt had to Lucas's house. They had to keep moving. Magnus stood up and grabbed Lucas by the shoulder.

"Come Lucas, we'd best be off."

Lucas looked at Magnus. Fear was in his eyes. "What if they have her? What if they have Father as well?"

Magnus was lost for words. He had the same concerns for his own parents. It appeared now the imminent danger of their situation had finally dawned on Lucas. "Then all we have is each other. And we need to get help!"

Magnus pulled Lucas to his feet and they scurried back to the horses. He could feel Breona breathing hard. Her emotions raced through his mind as though they were his own. He was surprised at the ease with which she communicated with him now. She was eager to get moving.

"Let's go." Lucas snapped out of his daze. He led the way through the woods. "We'll be clear of the trees in a few hundred feet."

They charged through the trees as fast as they dared in the darkness. Not a word was spoken as they reached the clearing at the eastern borders of the woodlands. Magnus peered out across the divide that would take them on to the Nuyan River. There was nothing ahead but the flat plains that formed the eastern part of Ganister's lands. They were several miles north of where Magnus crossed with Catanya earlier that day. It was an hour's journey at a casual trot, so he figured it would take half that at a sustainable gallop. *A long time to be exposed in the open,* Magnus considered. Once they had been seen, there would be no option but to run. If they could make it to the river they would have the cover of the hanging willows that ran along its banks this far north.

"The longer we hesitate, the greater the chance of them finding us," Lucas said. Magnus agreed. They charged out of the woods and across the moonlit field. The ground here was hard and uneven. They skittered across patches of flint that echoed the strikes of the horses' hooves across the field. Magnus cringed and begged for the anonymity of silence.

They progressed across the plain, their easterly direction becoming more northerly to distance them from trouble. They would cross the Nuyan River to the north, near the quarry. Magnus knew they could find refuge in the quarry's carved out tunnels and deep fissures. He hated to bring trouble to Catanya's people, the thought of which led to another dreadful thought— *What if the Uydfer folk are also under attack?* Magnus was consoled by the thought that Catanya would be half way to the Romghold by now. As for her family and the folk of Nuyan, they were strong in number and would soon band together to mount a defence more effectively than his or Lucas's family could, or any of the other sparsely populated areas at the margins.

Magnus was jolted out of his thoughts by the sound of a shrieking wyvern. He turned and saw its dark shadow circling overhead to the south. Magnus turned to Lucas, who reached for his sword, fastening its leather belt around his waist. Magnus turned back to watch the wyvern. It was no longer circling, but was motionless in mid air. He could hear the beating sound of its wings, keeping it suspended above the ground. Its head was focussed in one direction. There was no question—it had spotted them.

Magnus and Lucas picked up their pace, veering apart from one another to distract the wyvern. After a long pause, the black serpent-like creature's hover turned into a dive. It had chosen to follow Lucas. Magnus turned sharply back toward him, drawing his own sword out of the scabbard strapped to

Breona's saddle. The black beast came down on Lucas with an open jaw like a snake about to strike its prey. Magnus held his sword out in front of him. A white light shimmered its way from the blade collar to the tip of the sword without the need for a prompting spell. It distracted the creature for just a moment and Lucas, still charging his horse, swung his blade back, scoring the wyvern across the neck. It tucked its head in, letting out another shriek as it struck the ground and slammed into Lucas's horse, sending the two animals and Lucas tumbling across the ground.

Over and over they rolled, horse over wyvern with Lucas stuck in the middle. Breona pulled to a stop and Magnus leapt off her back just as the wyvern scrambled to its two feet. It was furious. Lucas stood with difficulty then doubled over, wincing in pain and guarding his chest with a bloodied arm. Magnus was close to the wyvern now. His head began to thump rhythmically, the pain making him wince. It was a little like the fire dragon that tried to scry his thoughts, only more brutal and obtrusive and without any objective but to tear his mind to pieces. It screeched at him then turned away, withdrawing from Magnus's mind.

Lucas's fallen horse distracted the wyvern, which sank the long claws of its feet into the horse's belly. The horse screamed but could not move. Lucas shouted at the wyvern as best he could, waving his good arm at it. Magnus seized the opportunity and swung his sword at the wyvern's left leg. The sword sliced deep and easily into its black, leathery flesh, almost severing its leg through the shin. It turned to Magnus, hissing with its jaw open, revealing its two-foot long fangs that hung like stalactites from the roof of its mouth. Greasy, brown saliva spat from its jaw.

Magnus swung his sword again, this time at its head, but the animal pulled back to avoid the blow. It swung back to Lucas and lunged clumsily off its good leg, knocking Lucas flat on his back. The wyvern thrust its head at Lucas like a striking snake, sinking its fangs into the flesh of his body. Lucas screamed. Magnus jumped over to the wyvern and swung down at its back, but the wyvern had smartened to Magnus's advances and swung its long, barbed tail, knocking his legs out from beneath him. Magnus fell to the ground, letting go of his sword.

The wyvern released Lucas and turned to Magnus again. Lucas's blood dripped from its fangs. The thumping in Magnus's head returned. He was astonished at its aggression and winced as he tried to keep the creature out of his mind. Once again the wyvern became distracted, this time struggling with its injured leg.

"Lucas!" Magnus called out. There was no response. The wyvern extended its long neck to Magnus, snapped its jaw shut and sniffed at him. Magnus pulled back from it, looking deep into its large yellow eyes with their thin-slitted irises that expanded and contracted as it focussed on him. He could smell the creature. It stunk like the decaying remains of a week old dead carcass. *"You've been eating a dragon's leftovers!"* Magnus forced the thought from his mind. The wyvern sneered angrily, revealing the edge of one of its fangs. It moved toward Magnus then yelped as it stumbled on its wounded leg.

With his attention on the wyvern, Magnus had not noticed Breona beside him. She reared up high and let out a high-pitched scream, then came down stomping toward the wyvern. The black creature, startled, stumbled back. Magnus rolled away from Breona's deadly hooves and grabbed his sword, jumping to his feet again. The wyvern hissed at Breona, then hobbled backward to Lucas's horse and sniffed it. It looked to Breona then again to Magnus, who held his sword at the ready. It seemed to consider its options for a moment, then pushed up off its good leg as best it could, flapped its gnarled wings and took flight back toward the Crescent Woods. *No doubt,* Magnus feared, *to tell his companions of our whereabouts.*

Magnus ran to Lucas, who was lying on his back. His eyes were closed but he was still breathing gently between coughs. Magnus took his hand and held it tight.

"Lucas, can you hear me?" Lucas groaned and opened his eyes slightly. Magnus looked closer at his bloodied arm, squeezing his forearm and then his upper arm. Lucas groaned again and Magnus could feel the broken bone moving beneath the torn flesh above his elbow. Lucas's beige shirt was covered in blood and there were two deep puncture marks in his torso from the wyvern's sharp fangs.

Breona walked over to Lucas and sniffed him, sharing her thoughts with Magnus. *"We must go Magnus, we must keep moving."*

Magnus stood and walked to Lucas's horse and tried to elicit a response but it was dead or close to being so. *"I need you to carry us both, Breona."* Breona shifted nervously. *"I will not leave him here to die."*

He returned to Lucas and knelt in front of him, wrapping his arms around his body and pulling him up to a sitting position. Holding Lucas's good arm over his shoulder he stood, dragging his friend up with him. Lucas cried out for a moment then began muttering under his breath.

"We're going to keep moving Lucas," Magnus insisted.

"Go…" Lucas mumbled.

"Not without you I don't." Magnus walked Lucas over to Breona who shuffled from side to side, unsure of what to do.

"Breona, please," Magnus spoke aloud. He sensed her disapproval but she relented, lowering herself down until her belly was on the ground. With a bit of difficulty and a huge amount of effort, Magnus lifted Lucas onto Breona's back. Breona then stood holding Lucas to the front of the saddle. Magnus leapt up behind him.

"My sword," Lucas mumbled, swaying in his seat. Magnus jumped off Breona and walked back to where Lucas had fallen and rolled. After a moment he found the unsheathed sword, and a little distance away, its scabbard. Returning to Breona, Magnus mounted again and slung the belts of both scabbards across his back, much as he would a quiver of arrows.

Breona needed no instruction to move on, and without the need to limit her pace to suit Lucas's horse, she ran at a much faster pace than before—even with the weight of two people. Magnus held tight to the reins with his arms wrapped around Lucas to keep him from falling. He could hear Lucas mumbling to himself incoherently as if in a dream state, then startling himself awake before drifting off once again.

Magnus feared the worst, both for Lucas and the wyvern that was surely moments away from raising the alarm as to their whereabouts. He expected a storm of wyverns to come screeching overhead from the woodlands to the west.

"We have to get past the Nuyan River," Magnus projected his thoughts to Breona. Breona galloped faster and faster. Under the light of the moon, Magnus felt as if they were travelling faster than time itself and very soon, he could see the willows by the distant banks of the Nuyan River.

Breona was closing the gap between her and the river swiftly. But even so, Magnus grew more anxious the closer they got. Then the terror he had been waiting for came from behind them—the ghastly scream and repetitive beat of wings. Breona released a pent up screech of her own and forced herself on, seemingly doubling her pace. Magnus could feel the fear she kept buried under a sea of determination. He dared turn, but the wyverns and Quagmen were not yet in sight, whereas the sanctuary of the river loomed large. Magnus's arms ached from holding Lucas and squeezing the reins but he tightened them even more as Breona jumped a verge then landed, bringing her rear legs skidding forward across the slippery grass at the edge of the Nuyan River. They were there. But they were not alone.

The tips of a half dozen arrows were aimed at Magnus the moment Breona slid down the embankment to a stop with her front hooves touching the waters of the flowing river. The archers shifted from the shadows of darkness, each of them dressed in flowing crimson cloth that draped across their faces and over their torsos with matching hoods. They looked nothing like the Quagman he had encountered earlier. Magnus calculated the distance to the other side of the river and up the western embankment, hoping to make a run for it, but he was too late—more archers moved out from beneath the trees in that direction, effectively surrounding Breona. They were trapped.

Magnus raised both hands in the air in surrender, but quickly brought them back down to support Lucas, who nearly fell from the saddle.

"I am Magnus of J'esmagd. This is Lucas of Bowthwait," he said. "We have been chased from our homes and seek safe passage to Froughton Forest."

Magnus's explanation was cut short by another cry from a vile black creature to the west. It seemed closer now, yet was still out of sight. One of the archers pulled the cloth from their face and nodded to the others. They lowered their bows.

"Come, hide yourselves amongst the foliage." It was a woman. She was of middle age and had olive skin like Catanya.

"You are of the Uydfer clan?" Magnus asked.

"Aye," she nodded. "The Quag attacked our lands this night also. We are here to ensure they do not breach our northern and western borders. Our people are positioned all along the river and north of the quarry." She took Breona's reins to lead her but Breona pulled against her in defiance.

'It's okay Breona, they are friends." He looked at the woman. "She will not be led, but she will follow."

The woman looked the horse over. "Very well then."

They moved into the shadows of a large willow and Breona lowered herself to her belly once again, allowing Magnus to alight and lift Lucas out of the saddle. He placed Lucas on his back on the soft grass beneath the tree. Lucas moaned with the movement and then coughed.

"And what of your friend?" the woman asked, watching them.

"We were attacked by a wyvern. They have overrun our lands."

The woman knelt beside Lucas. She placed a hand upon his forehead and another over his chest, causing him to wince. Unsure of her intentions, Magnus reached over his left shoulder and felt for the pommel of his sword, yanking it free from its scabbard. In quick response, one of the archers held a knife to Magnus's neck. The woman turned and looked at the archer, then to Magnus.

"Lower your weapons, both of you."

The archer did as he was told. Magnus tensed his grip on the sword and a bronze ring of light shimmered its way down the sword's blade. He took a closer look and realised he had unsheathed Lucas's sword, forgetting he held them both slung over the same shoulder. He was curious about the differences in the two swords—his glowing white and Lucas's bronze. *Ganister has forged these swords with an obvious difference in the metal work.* He replaced the sword into its scabbard. The woman watched him closely with a curious expression on her face. Magnus knelt beside her and took Lucas's good hand. Lucas gripped his hand tightly and smiled weakly at him. The woman watched them both for a moment.

"I mean your friend no harm," the woman explained, staring at Magnus. "But the next time you pull your sword on my lands it had better be to fight with us, not against us. Do you understand?"

"My apologies. I've had a troublesome night."

The woman stared for a moment longer then looked to Lucas. "He is not well," she mumbled to herself.

The thump, thump, thump of beating wings circled overhead, followed by the familiar scream that accompanied it. Through the dense foliage of the weeping willow, Magnus could see a wyvern circling around several times before moving away again. Another wyvern followed, then another, and a fourth wyvern landed at the top of the riverbank, not twenty feet from where Magnus and his companions hid.

A Quagman sat in a black leather saddle behind the wyvern's wings, holding onto a large horn protruding from the saddle's gullet with one hand, the other holding the reins. The wyvern wore a hard leather and iron chamfron upon its head to which the reins were fastened with iron rings. Pulling the reins, the Quagman directed the wyvern down the embankment to the river's edge. The wyvern moved slowly, sniffing at the ground. Magnus cautiously turned and placed a hand on Breona's head to ease her, lest she be startled and give away their position. He could feel that she was forcing herself to remain calm—her front hooves dug deep into the soft soil beneath her.

The wyvern continued its crawl down the embankment, crouching forward and moving with trepidation. The Quagman released the horn and reins to draw a pair of black swords from either side of the saddle, holding them as if expecting a confrontation. Magnus looked to the Uydfer woman, who held her fist in the air. She turned to Magnus and whispered, "Wait until he is alone. *Now* is the time to draw your sword." She turned back to look at the enemy, holding her fist to affirm the need to wait. Magnus looked to the sky as the last of the airborne wyverns moved on. He smoothly unsheathed one of the swords over his shoulder, unaware in the darkness if it were his or Lucas's blade.

Finally, the woman pointed in quick succession to several archers—each of them hidden within the willow trees out of sight. Instantly, they released several arrows that flew swiftly towards the wyvern, skilfully piercing its head beneath its armour. Several more pierced its chest. The wyvern fell to the river's edge with hardly a sound.

The Quagman leapt quickly from the dead wyvern and launched himself sideways in Magnus's direction. A volley of arrows pierced every part of his body, yet still the big man moved. Magnus stood quickly and scuffled to the river's edge, raising his sword. The Uydfer woman leapt down next to him wielding her own sword. The Quagman hesitated, raising his blades, but the Uydfer woman was too quick. She bounced off the bank of the river slicing at the Quagman's midsection. With his blades still raised he fell to his knees, his dark eyes staring at Magnus. Magnus took a tentative step forward, pulling his second sword free of its scabbard so he too held a blade in each hand—matching the Quagman. But he needn't have bothered, for the Quagman fell face forward into the river with six arrows protruding from his back.

The archers were quick to grab the man's dead body and carry it away, hiding it amongst the trees and undergrowth. Others brought branches and covered the remains of the wyvern, still resting on the western bank. In less than a minute no evidence of foul play could be seen from the skies.

The woman in command walked to where the fallen wyvern lay hidden. Magnus followed her. She examined the site for a moment before addressing her men. "They will return soon enough when they realise they are missing one of their own." She looked at Magnus, who still grasped the two swords. "You have done well to get this far. Having an Astermeer gives you a great advantage. Is she yours?"

"My mother's," replied Magnus. The woman had an inquisitive expression on her face.

"And yet you ride her?"

"It took some encouragement. But we share a common goal."

"Brilliant," said the woman, looking Breona over again. "I should introduce myself. I am Csilla. I lead this band of intrepid archers." Her fellow Uydfermen laughed at her description of them, then moved about, busying themselves with the task of fortifying a line along the eastern border of the river with long branches of felled trees. More swordsmen and archers arrived, placing their weapons behind the line and going to work with their kinsmen, lifting shovels and helping with the fortifications.

Magnus had several pressing concerns on his mind. First of all was Lucas. "May I ask of you, Ma'am, Lucas needs help. Do you have a healer among you?"

Csilla nodded. "Kriser!" she called out across the river. A man turned and she motioned for him to come to her. Csilla spoke to him in Fireisgh, telling him of Lucas. The man nodded. He spoke briefly to two other men who came to the willow tree and gently lifted Lucas, carrying him across the river. "Kriser is our finest healer, he will look after your friend as best he can."

"Thank you Ma'am," Magnus said.

"You can stop calling me Ma'am. We are hard working people, there is not a *Ma'am* among us," Csilla said. "Besides, should things have been different, you would marry Catanya and then you would call me 'Auntie'." She winked at him before moving on to attend to other duties.

HEALERS

The healers carried Lucas up the embankment on the eastern side of the river. Magnus stayed with them and Breona followed close behind. He looked back toward Csilla but could no longer see her. The news that she was Catanya's aunt thrilled him. It vexed him though, that she said the same thing Catanya's mother had—*"should things have been different..."* He was sure Csilla knew Catanya would be joining the priesthood.

They walked a narrow trail through the tall grasses that weaved between trees and reached a clearing where numerous tents were pitched. The tents were basic at best, made from canvas with basic wooden frames—clearly a temporary measure to be moved on with Csilla's company. Two of the tents already had injured men in them being attended to by other healers.

Lucas was taken into a third tent where he was placed on a narrow, knee-high bed. The three healers immediately set to work. They cut away his bloodied shirt and Kriser held a lamp over his body, looking him over briefly.

"A wyvern did this?" he spoke quickly.

Magnus moved in closer and the other two healers made room so he could sit beside his friend.

"Did a wyvern do this?" Kriser asked again, impatiently.

"Yes. After he fell and broke his arm." Magnus pointed to Lucas's left arm.

"The arm we will set and it will heal, that I am sure." He cupped a hand around each of the puncture wounds the wyvern had made in Lucas's body and looked closely at each of them. He examined his legs, feeling each bone and then looked at his face, prising his eyes open one at a time and shining his lamp in each, making Lucas wince. Kriser finally examined his broken arm.

"Your friend is lucky in a way, not so lucky in another," he concluded. Magnus sighed, frustrated.

Lucas forced himself up onto his good elbow then dropped again. "How am I lucky? How am I not?" he mumbled.

"You are lucky the wyvern did not puncture your lungs. The wyvern's fangs, however, give venom much like a snake's and they have poisoned you. As it takes hold, you will come to fever. We will draw out of you what we can of the poison. What you must do is stay awake, for the poison that remains will try to take you. You must resist."

Kriser felt Lucas's forehead in the same manner Csilla had earlier. "Tell me, did the wyvern speak to you?" Lucas did not answer.

"What do you mean?" Magnus asked.

"To his mind," Kriser said then addressed Lucas again. "Did you hear his thoughts? Did he speak to you?" Lucas shook his head. "That is good."

"He spoke to me," Magnus said. Kriser glanced at him. "He was thumping away in my head. Like he was trying to get in. But... I think there were too many distractions for the creature to persist."

"It seems the wyvern attacked one of you with its teeth, the other with its mind." Kriser pointed at Magnus. "You may have saved your friend today."

"What of it?" Magnus asked again. "What harm could come of it?"

"Wyverns are very near the nastiest of creatures." Kriser scratched his forehead.

"How so?" Magnus pushed for further information.

"There is malice in a wyvern's heart." Kriser's lip curled. "Their poison gives aid to a mental assault so they can manipulate and deceive the victim. Rhyme and reason is twisted into turmoil and madness. To be overcome in such a way is a cruel fate for the worst of men." He shook his head, looking from Magnus to Lucas. "I can extract poison from a wound, but a meddled-with mind is another matter. I am a healer, not a sorcerer."

The healer looked into Lucas's eyes again. "Yes, your friend will begin to fever soon." Kriser turned to one of the other healers, a young man who was grinding a powder within a stone mortar. The third healer, a slightly older man, was pouring small vials of fluid into the mixture. When the young man was satisfied, he handed the mortar to Kriser.

"Walt has prepared a potion that should help." Kriser sipped the fluid and savoured the flavour for a moment before handing the mortar to Magnus. "Here, feed this to your friend."

Magnus cradled Lucas's head forward, slowly feeding him the potion. Lucas drank quickly then laid his head back to rest. "That was disgusting," he murmured, looking at Magnus, smiling weakly. They both chuckled and Lucas coughed.

"Keep still and rest. You must stay awake as best you can, boy. Understand?" Kriser instructed. Lucas nodded. "Do you understand?" he questioned again.

"Yes!" grunted Lucas—clearly annoyed at being asked twice. "I'm not a boy. Neither is Magnus."

Magnus smiled at the compliment.

"Good. That's the spirit," Kriser said. "Keep fighting… you must always keep fighting. It may just save you."

Kriser shuffled around getting comfortable, and sat up on his knees. He closed his eyes and rubbed the palms of his hands together vigorously. He blew upon them then rubbed again, blew on them again and rubbed some more. After his fourth bout of blowing and rubbing Kriser brought his hands down over Lucas's abdomen and held them there, hovering an inch above his body. He started to mumble a long, wordy chant. A moment later, a faint red glow emanated from beneath his hands and spread over Lucas's bare flesh. Lucas grunted. Walt placed a tightly wrapped leather strap between Lucas's teeth then pushed down on his shoulders. The other healer held fast to his ankles. Magnus figured Lucas was about to endure a lot more pain.

The red glow beneath the healer's hands grew brighter and Lucas bit down hard on the strap in his mouth, cursing incoherently. Lucas held Magnus's hand in a vice-like grip. The red light twisted and twirled between Lucas's skin and Kriser's hands as though resisting whatever it was Kriser was trying to will it to do.

"What are you doing?" Magnus asked.

"Drawing out the poison," Walt said. The light soon started to lift away and through the two large wounds in Lucas's stomach, two thick trails of syrupy black matter spiralled out and mixed with the red glowing light. For a good long minute the black poison came. The smell of it was revolting, making Magnus gag. After a few moments, when the poison no longer had any contact with Lucas, but was entangled with the red light from the healer's hands, Kriser drew his hands away quickly, leaving the combined matter to spiral frantically through the air, making a hissing sound as it whipped across Magnus's face and around the tent. "Be off!" Kriser shouted and spoke a realmish chant that seemed to stop it in its tracks. The fragments of red light clung to the syrupy black poison and together, they floated silently out of the tent and dissipated into the night sky.

Kriser shifted back from Lucas, making room for Walt to give attention to Lucas's wounded arm. With long skinny fingers, Walt felt the length of the broken bone with a gentle touch, examining it carefully. He then took a hold of the arm directly over the break and held it firmly with both hands. Lucas grunted again. Walt then began mumbling chants of his own. Kriser placed the leather strap back into Lucas's mouth, who bit down on it once more. Magnus heard a nauseating crackling sound as the broken fragments of bone shifted and contorted beneath Walt's hands. Lucas writhed, trying to break free of the healers, but they had him well pinned to the bed. A minute passed and Walt stopped the chant. He examined Lucas's arm again, feeling the length of the bone. He smiled as though proud of his work.

"Good, Walt, good," Kriser commended him.

Lucas breathed easier. He spat the strap from his mouth. Magnus looked him in the eyes and felt his forehead. He was beginning to radiate a lot of heat.

"Are you okay?"

Lucas nodded. "Tired," he mumbled. "I feel cold."

Kriser stood and stepped past Magnus to leave the tent, tapping Magnus on the shoulder as he went and signalling him to follow.

"Rest," Magnus told his friend. "I'll be back soon."

Magnus stood and peered out of the tent. Kriser was washing his hands in a pail positioned on a small table a short distance away. Magnus left the tent, leaving Walt and the other healer to attend to Lucas.

Approaching Kriser, he pondered his next course of action. Ganister had told him to try to get to Froughton Forest by sunrise. Much had happened since then and he felt torn—he did not want to leave Lucas. He recalled that Ganister wanted Lucas to return to his mother's side. *Their home is surely burned to the ground and I doubt Sarah is there anyway.* He worried then for Ganister— *Surely he didn't know he was returning to my home to face a legion of Quag so large?* As things stood now, Magnus knew nothing of the fate of all those he cared for. The only thing that seemed certain was that he was still capable of travelling to Guame—albeit alone. Magnus recalled Ganister's instructions—*"Speak before the Authoritarium. They will afford counsel to the son of Bonstaph."* He hoped Ganister was right.

The night was a blur of events and emotions. Magnus had lost track of time. *Was it past midnight yet?* He felt light headed and unsteady on his feet. As he approached Kriser, he saw that Csilla was now standing with him. They were engaged in quiet conversation. Kriser was nodding in response to her words. Magnus shook his head and pulled himself together. He was desperate to know what Csilla knew about Catanya.

Csilla saw Magnus approaching and walked toward him. "Magnus—"

"Csilla, please," Magnus interrupted. "What do you know of Catanya joining the Priesthood?"

Csilla put her hands on her hips. Magnus gathered she was not used to been interrupted. But he was determined. She considered him for a moment then lowered her arms. "I apologise Magnus, I should not have broached the subject. It was neither the time nor the place."

"Well, you did," Magnus asserted. "Was it her parents' choice, or her uncle's?"

Csilla's eyebrows lifted. "I knew nothing of this before today, when I spoke with my sister. Prior to that it was my understanding she was always to marry you."

"She left for the Romghold this afternoon," Magnus countered. "With her uncle... On the back of a dragon!" Magnus was growing more and more frustrated. He took a breath and calmed himself. "Sorry," he said, somewhat ashamed of his tone.

Csilla stepped forward. Her face was almost touching his. Magnus looked at her closely. She did look like Alessandra, but even more so like Catanya. She was lean, but strong—the kind of strength that comes from hard work. Her demeanour was harder than Alessandra's. She had a thin scar beneath her left eye that trailed back to her ear. *As she said... 'Not a 'Ma'am' at all'*.

Csilla stared hard at Magnus. "Catanya loves you, you know that," she said. "She always has. And I can see you love her too. But... it seems her fate was chosen for her, a fate bigger than her. Like her uncle before her." Magnus was hardly appeased by her words. Nor had he learned any more of the truth behind Catanya joining the priesthood. "Tell me this—did you see the dragon?"

"Yes," Magnus said.

"When you've not seen one in a while you forget." Csilla paused as her thoughts trailed off.

"Forget what?"

"The power of their presence, the brilliance of their bronze scales... It makes these wyverns look like rats. No wonder they fled to the Corville Mountains all those years ago. I only wish they'd stayed there."

"Why are the dragons not coming to fight with us?" Magnus asked, accepting the conversation's change of direction.

Csilla looked away and shook her head. "Things have changed among the dragon realm. I do not know what it is, but something in the Romghold has changed. Perhaps with three breeds of dragons extinct at the hands of men, one can appreciate why they keep their distance."

"Was it not the Authoritarium that told them to leave?"

"No one tells the dragons what to do. But to dishonour them—dragons don't take that lightly. It will be a hard thing to undo." Csilla looked around, surveying the camp area. "We can only pray they are here before the end, when we need them most."

Magnus lowered his gaze to the ground. Somewhere in his heart he thought that maybe with all this turmoil, he could find Catanya and flee with her.

"Magnus." Csilla looked into his eyes again. "It may pain you hear this, but it is for your own good. Do not follow her. Not on your white horse, not in your heart." Magnus choked back his feelings. "Your destiny lies in another direction now." Csilla stepped back from Magnus and waved to a group of her men across the camp. "Where is it you plan to travel to?"

"Guame. Ganister asked me to appeal to the Authoritarium for aid."

"Someone ought to. You're more equipped for the task than any of us." She nodded to Breona. "Besides, I need all my men here. With Bonstaph as your father the reception may be prickly. But they'll no doubt be keen to hear what you have to say."

"I certainly hope so."

"Go now to Kriser. He wishes to speak with you about your friend. Come see me before you leave."

Magnus agreed, and with that, Csilla left with her comrades.

Magnus joined Kriser, who had waited for him.

"She respects you," Kriser said.

"Who? Csilla?"

"Aye. She does not give time to people without good reason." Magnus was not sure what to think of Kriser's observation. "Consider it a compliment. At times like this it is not easy to make friends."

Magnus smiled, then his thoughts shifted to Lucas. "Well, if you tell me Lucas is going to be okay, I'll consider you a friend of mine."

Kriser smiled for the first time since Magnus had met him. "Very well then." His expression turned serious again. "Wherever your journey takes you from here, you'd best continue alone. I have extracted much of the wyvern's venom from his body, but not all. His body will try to fever out what is left."

"But he will survive," Magnus insisted.

"I should think so. He has a strong disposition and there is much fight in him. But once on the other side of the fever, he will be too weak to journey for some time."

"Will you please look after him while I'm gone?"

"Csilla tells me your father is Bonstaph. And your friend is Ganister's son?"

Magnus nodded.

"Then you are brethren of the Fire Realm. We take care of our own," Kriser answered.

"Thank you. Wherever my fate takes me, I am indebted to you," Magnus said, shaking Kriser's hand. Kriser had not given a guarantee of Lucas's recovery but as close to one as he would get. He hoped the healer was a man of his word.

Magnus fretted as to whether he should leave and what he should tell Lucas. *If I tell Lucas I am leaving he may take it as a lack of faith that he will heal. But if I wait, I lose time... precious time... The sooner I get to Guame the sooner the Authoritarium can send help.*

Magnus realised what he had to do. It did not please him at all, but it would serve both him and Lucas. He looked to Kriser again. "How long will Lucas take to fight the fever?"

Kriser looked at him questioningly. "He should be through the worst of it by midday tomorrow. But like I told you—he will be weak."

"That's fine. May I speak with him now?"

Kriser hesitated. "You may."

Magnus marched back toward the healer's tent with Kriser close behind. Walt and the other healer moved to make room for him to sit beside Lucas again. Damp cloths were draped across his forehead to counter his rising temperature. Lucas began to shake. Magnus took a hold of his hand, feeling the hot sweat in his palm. His face had taken on a grey, clammy appearance that startled Magnus—his change in appearance had occurred so rapidly. Seeing Magnus, Lucas gripped his hand.

"Can you hear me Lucas?" Magnus spoke gently. Lucas forced a smile at his friend. Magnus did the same. "The healers say you must fight this fever tonight and if you do, you will be rid of it by tomorrow." Lucas had closed his eyes again. "Do you hear me Lucas?" Magnus spoke louder now. "Fight this tonight and tomorrow we will ride out of here together."

Lucas smiled again. "Aye," he stammered through chattering teeth. "W-wait for me Magnus!" A look of determination came to him.

Kriser moved in to speak but Magnus got his words in first. "The healers want me out of their way so they can help you. So I'll leave you now to fight this, Lucas. Fight through the night. Promise me that."

"Aye… I promise. Se-see you tomorrow."

Magnus bent down and hugged his friend. Lucas wrapped his good arm around Magnus. The vice of his grip told Magnus this was not a fight he was giving in to. Lucas closed his eyes again. Reluctantly, Magnus released himself of Lucas's embrace and looked to the two healers who sat beside him, thanking them in turn.

"We will look after him," Walt said with a smile.

Standing, Magnus left the tent and stood beside Kriser. "What time is it now?" Magnus asked.

"It's past midnight." Kriser stared at him.

"I'll be leaving immediately." Magnus lifted both swords from his back. He held them together, one in each hand, running a thumb over the pommel of each. He recalled Sarah's words. *"Remember you are as brothers…"* He took Lucas's sword with the bronze-coloured pommel and cross guard and handed it to Kriser. "Please see that this stays with him. Lucas is a brother to me and this is our bond."

Kriser nodded, smiling for the second time. He took the sword from Magnus. "You have imbued Lucas with the determination he needs in the dark hours ahead. I will see this does not leave his side."

"When his fever breaks and he is out of danger, he will ask after me. Tell him I shall return for him as soon as I can."

"That I will," Kriser said.

The two men shook hands. Magnus leapt upon Breona and Kriser directed him toward the quarry where Csilla was moving her men. After a ten-minute journey away from the Nuyan River, Magnus came upon the quarry road on which he had travelled many times as a child. Soon the road came to the deeply cut caverns of sandstone that disappeared into darkness below. Navigating the narrow, gravel roads, Breona travelled to the quarry's northern border, where they found Csilla. Seeing Magnus approach, she excused herself from her men and came over to him.

"You are leaving directly?"

"Aye," Magnus said. "The sooner I get to Guame, the sooner I return with help."

"It will be needed. I am sure the Quag will come in greater numbers soon enough. We have two thousand fighting men and women. Most of our numbers have moved to Realms End under Xavier's command at the frontline of attack."

Magnus thought of the abandoned posts along the Southern border known as Realms End. "Did Xavier order the posts to be abandoned yesterday?"

Csilla shook her head. "We do not know where the order originated. But as soon as Xavier found out, he knew it was pre-emptive of a Quag attack." Magnus nodded. *Perhaps this is why he wanted Catanya sent away.*

"Here at the northern borders, I have an archer placed every quarter of a mile." Csilla pointed to the east. "Beyond the quarry, scouts are positioned every mile for ten. I have passed word that a warrior riding an Astermeer will pass swiftly through the night and they must afford you safe passage."

"A warrior? On an Astermeer?" Magnus said, surprised. "Only the Rhydermere or Irucantî are so worthy."

"Aye. That got them talking. I don't think they take me seriously, so it will be entertaining when they see I speak truth. Furthermore, it lifts their spirits. If the Authoritarium respond, we could have ten thousand trained men here in a week. Most likely several hundred knights among them."

"I will travel as fast as I can for both our sakes," Magnus agreed. "I have left Lucas with Kriser. He has done much for him already."

"You leave your friend in good hands, I assure you."

"Thank you again for all you have done to help us. And for speaking candidly about Catanya."

Csilla smiled and gave Breona a pat on her side. "I'd wager you will reach Froughton Forest by sunrise. Follow this road to the east," she instructed.

"It will lead directly to Froughton Forest?"

"It will. I trust you know how to traverse through it?"

Magnus nodded, recounting Ganister's instructions about sticking to the Outer Rim and avoiding the Valley of Shadows. Magnus ventured to ask her a question, "How will I know when I am near the Valley of Shadows?"

A flash of fear crossed Csilla's face. "You will *know* you are near the Valley. It will chill you through. Keep your distance. Stick to the roads— always." She held a serious expression as Magnus acknowledged her warning.

"Aye, I will," Magnus said. Csilla had a look of doubt upon her face. "I will stick to the roads of the Outer Rim as you say, Csilla."

"Good. You will do fine. Be off now, son of Bonstaph." Csilla smacked Breona on the rump, giving both her and Magnus a start. "Farewell, Magnus."

"Farewell, Csilla."

Magnus turned toward the east. *"Let's go now Breona, to Froughton Forest and on to Guame."* Breona charged forward along the narrow quarry road and Magnus sensed she was relieved to be moving again. They moved quickly across the boundaries of the quarry and past the archers positioned every quarter mile. From here, they ventured out through barley fields split by a dirt road that undulated its way eastward. Breona galloped at a pace she could keep up for the hours of travel ahead and soon, several miles separated them from Lucas, the healers and Csilla.

With events of the first half of the night behind them, Magnus looked to the future and what he had set forth to achieve. From here on he and Breona were alone, but for the occasional Uydfer scout he spotted in the field who would charge his sword and wave as they passed.

THE ROMGHOLD

The journey across Allumbreve was not easy. *Anyone that wishes to ride a dragon is wasting wishes,* Catanya thought to herself. Every part of her body ached from holding on for dear life. *People were surely not meant for flying.*

Far beyond her homelands, Catanya flew over the vast expanse of Froughton Forest. The continual rising and falling and unexpected changes of direction made her nauseous. Austagia told her she would learn to *"master the effects of flying"* over time. This was one of the only pieces of advice he had given her.

Catanya asked Austagia many questions, such as why she was the *"one concession"* he spoke of—drafted into priesthood in the off year. Why was she chosen over all the would-be-warriors in the realm? She also had questions she dared not ask—*What will Austagia do if I refuse to train? What if I flee in the middle of the night and return home to Magnus?*

Austagia refused to answer any of her questions. "You have started your induction into the Priesthood," he said. "You should seek neither comfort nor conversation."

Austagia explained to Catanya she had entered what was known as a period of 'cleansing'. He also made it perfectly clear that from this moment on he was no longer to be considered her uncle. Catanya thought even less of her uncle after this. *First he takes me from my family and Magnus, now he denies any responsibility for me?*

Where the moon shone bright and they emerged from the clouds, Catanya was afforded the opportunity to study the creature that carried them through the night sky. She was huge. Catanya's legs were so firmly strapped into the saddle she could not move and they were splayed so far apart she was convinced she would split in two, such was the breadth of the dragon's long neck. Behind her, the dragon's wings seemed to span forever and beat every once in a while, thrusting them forward at an alarming pace.

The dragon's name was Rubea. *A fitting name,* Catanya thought, looking at her dark red scales sparkling even in the night sky. Her discomfort aside,

Catanya thought Rubea was the most beautiful creature she had ever seen. Her thoughts, it seemed, were being scrutinised by the dragon once again, only this time less aggressively. Rubea thanked Catanya for her compliments and shared her own thoughts with Catanya.

The two of them melded their minds together. The dragon seemed most curious about the strange new girl she carried over the lands. Soon enough Austagia interjected, suggesting Rubea leave Catanya to her cleansing. And so Rubea withdrew her mind from Catanya's.

"Fine then," Catanya had responded, not caring if Austagia sensed bitterness in her manner. It was not her who had chosen this path. Catanya was certain every time they met from this day forth she would see him as nothing more than the man who took her away from Magnus.

It was dark and silent when they reached the eastern border of Froughton Forest. The giant trees gave way to steep mountains. Rubea began to climb alongside the sharp, snow capped crags of the Romgnian Mountain range. As they climbed, the sweep of Rubea's wings sent tufts of cloud fluting out from fissures in the mountain. Catanya felt the bite of the cool mountain air as Rubea ascended toward Romgnia's highest peak.

They reached the summit and Catanya quickly forgot about her discomfort. She was awestruck by the sight before her. Upon the highest peak—as though it had grown out of the mountain itself—was a tall, grey-stoned castle. Its narrow construction towered up from the mountain peaks. Its shape was dominated by dozens of steeples that spiralled upward, each ending with sharp spires. An endless array of stone buttresses connected the construction, giving it an eerie, skeletal appearance. Not a single one of the hundreds of narrow lancets held a light. In fact, there was no sign of life about the whole structure or the surrounding mountain region. It looked like the most ominous, uninviting place in all of Allumbreve.

Rubea twisted out of her ascent and began to glide down toward the bleak-looking castle. She let out a roar that echoed off the mountain face. Catanya winced, letting go of the saddle horn to cover her ears as the sound tore through her. Once it had dispersed, the air between them and the foreboding castle began to shimmer, as though looking through a smooth sheet of water. A translucent wall revealed itself as a barrier extending as a dome over the castle. Rubea descended toward it and Catanya shuddered as they passed through the wall.

On the other side of the barrier, Catanya saw a different world. The castle was gone.

"Was it an illusion?" Catanya felt she was entitled to ask this one question.

"A deterrent to outsiders," Austagia answered. "What you see now is real."

On the other side of the deception, Catanya was able to see the real world of the dragons and the Irucantî for the first time—and there was no foreboding castle.

Surrounded by the snow-capped peaks of the Romgnian Mountains on all but the west side was a flat plain half a mile wide and at least as deep. Upon the plain were modest stone buildings that were neatly constructed and laid out along organised alleyways. Everything was perfectly symmetrical. To the northern border of the community was a temple that, despite its small base, was tall and proud. Catanya was struck by its perfect detail—with two small steeples toward the front of the building and two much larger ones toward the rear. The whole temple was constructed of a burnished black stone the likes of which Catanya had never seen before.

"The Temple of Fire," Austagia said, seemingly knowing it was drawing Catanya's attention.

Their approach was to the western part of the Romghold where a large, almost circular lawn area spanned from one side of the Romghold to the other. To its west, the perfectly manicured lawn dropped away down the mountainside. The clearing was gently lit by the soft, green glow of hundreds of small lanterns positioned around the field's perimeter. Rubea extended her large rear legs and touched down on the clearing with a dull thud. She sidestepped for a moment, folded in her large wings and drew in a deep breath that she forced out of her nostrils, blowing two matching rings of smoke into the night air.

Austagia helped Catanya unbuckle the straps holding her legs in place before leaping out of the saddle, falling ten feet to the ground and landing without a sound. Catanya was surprised at his agility for his age, considering he could not have been much less than fifty. She dropped herself from the saddle and as she touched the ground she fell to her knees, weakened and sore from the journey. Austagia helped her to her feet and she thanked him, a little embarrassed after his own impressive dismount. Looking to the ground, Catanya cursed under her breath. She was unsure what would come of her time here in the Romghold but swore she would not show her uncle signs of weakness again.

Catanya took a deep breath, pulled her shoulders back and looked at Austagia. He was standing beside another man who seemed to appear out of nowhere. Like Austagia, he was dressed in a hooded black robe that was a complicated folding arrangement of layers that looked comfortable enough, but uninspiring to Catanya. The only other clothing of note was the black boots they both wore, made of a combination of canvas and leather stitched lengthwise and diagonally with matching laces that crisscrossed over the front.

Austagia bowed to his companion, who did the same in turn, then stood as still as a statue. Even though his face was hidden beneath his hood, Catanya felt his eyes staring at her. She stared right back at him, into the dark space beneath his hood, refusing to be intimidated. She squinted slightly, intensifying her gaze. After a long minute, the man turned slowly toward Austagia and gave an almost imperceptible nod. Austagia pulled his hood up over his face then turned and walked away toward the temple.

Catanya maintained her gaze at the priest. She decided she would not back down unless he instructed her to. The priest took several steps toward her. At well over six feet tall he towered over Catanya. He drew back his hood revealing his face. Like her uncle, his head was close shaved and tattooed over the left side with the glyphic markings of Fireisgh—the ancient script of the Fire Realm. Catanya winced, wondering if she too was expected to have this done. His face was long and his jaw chiselled down to a pointed chin that matched his narrow, fine nose. The priest took a step closer.

"You have entered the realm of the Irucantî. Do you understand why?"

His voice was assertive yet he spoke in a calm manner. She was unsure how to reply. *Of course I know why,* she thought, but decided to heed Austagia's advice and remain silent.

"Very good," the priest said, as if he had gained the answer he was looking for.

Is he reading my mind? Catanya considered. She glanced briefly at Rubea who was lying restfully on the ground beside her. Rubea looked right at her. Catanya gazed into the fire-red depths of Rubea's eyes and as she did they changed colour—flickering between various colours and finally settling on a brown colour—much like her own eyes. She turned back to the priest who was still looking at her.

"My name is Joffren. You will call me *Semsdi*—Fireisgh for *teacher...* Come." He motioned for Catanya to follow him. She turned to look at Rubea once again who was fast asleep on her patch of soft grass in the middle of the field.

"Goodnight Rubea," she dared to whisper in her mind. No response came.

"The Romghold is our sacred ground," Joffren explained as he walked with Catanya beside him. "The temple is a place of reflection. Everything that surrounds it will be your training ground." Joffren stopped walking and turned to face Catanya once again. "Do you have any questions?" Catanya hesitated, unsure whether to talk. "You are free to speak. This place is new to you and so there must be much you wish to know of it and our ways."

"Yes, there is," Catanya said. "Do all the priests live here?"

"Many of our order are here in the Romgnian Mountains. Some close, some farther afield. Others still are elsewhere in Allumbreve serving in other ways."

Catanya decided Joffren was not a bad person and dared to speak a little more candidly with him. "Are you able to read my mind?"

Joffren was silent for a moment as if thinking about his answer. "To an extent. I find however, your body language speaks louder than your thoughts. Are you able to read mine?"

Catanya looked him in the eyes, trying to see if he was mocking her. "No," she answered, "I do no better at reading your body language." She was sure then that Joffren smiled ever so slightly.

They reached the edge of the green field. Joffren turned and looked over the field, waved an arm and said, *"Fara namon."* The hundreds of small lanterns surrounding the field dimmed gradually until they were extinguished, leaving Rubea to sleep in darkness. Joffren and Catanya walked off the field and onto a stone common with the temple to their left and a neat arrangement of small stone buildings to their right.

Catanya considered other questions. "Do the dragons live here?"

"They move throughout the Romgnian Mountains and far beyond, as we do. You will meet them as your training progresses and through this, you will learn much of their ways and wisdom."

They arrived at one of the small buildings. It had a small lantern hanging from a hook beside a wooden door. Joffren lifted the lamp free of the hook and handed it to Catanya. He then opened the door for her.

"You will stay here during your training. Sleep well, for you will need your strength tomorrow." Catanya had many more questions she wanted to ask but fearing the time to ask them might be short, she asked the most pressing one. The one neither her father nor her uncle had bothered to explain to her since being told she was to join the priesthood.

"What is my purpose here?"

Joffren looked at Catanya and considered her for a moment. "Beyond your training and vocation? I see righteousness." With that, he turned and walked away toward the large temple.

Righteousness? Catanya twitched her nose. *My purpose is righteousness?* She pondered the thought as she entered the small building, holding the small lamp ahead of her. The building was a small, single room that was completely empty aside from a small wooden table and chair at the centre of the room and a single small window beside the door. Catanya looked around the room, searching for something she must be missing. There was no bed, no bath and no eating facilities. She looked outside to where she last saw Joffren but he was gone. She scratched the back of her head, wondering how exactly she was meant to *"sleep well"*.

"Righteousness," Catanya said out loud. Sitting on the chair at the small table, she felt incredibly tired. Her whole body ached from the journey. She crossed her forearms and rested them on the table, laying her head upon them. Her mind drifted through thoughts of home and Magnus and she affirmed to herself that they would be together again soon. She wondered what Magnus was doing at that very moment. Holding the thought, she fell asleep.

FROUGHTON FOREST

Magnus peered along the narrow path that wound its way into Froughton Forest. He could only see a short way before the path was concealed by the darkness of the woods. After his desperate journey to get here, he froze with the realisation of what it really meant to be entering this forest. Both Ganister and Csilla warned him to be careful. *"On no account enter the Valley,"* Ganister had said.

The Valley of Shadows, Magnus contemplated.

As a child, Magnus often wondered if the stories of Froughton Forest were true—those of unknown creatures and demons lurking within its dark depths. His father, who was not one for such speculation, had told him to never assume anything one hears without evidence, but he made an exception to this rule with Froughton Forest. *"Assume the worst, hope for the best,"* he would say.

Breona was becoming skittish and shifted from side to side. He felt her fear wash over him, exacerbating his own. Looking to the right of the path into the forest, Magnus's eyes were suddenly drawn to a narrow break in the trees. With a gasp, he stared into a pair of pearlescent white eyes, shining against the darkness surrounding them. They were staring directly at him. A chill formed at the nape of his neck and tracked its way slowly down his spine. He froze on the spot. A long minute passed then the eyes turned and vanished into the darkness.

Magnus released his pent-up breath. Looking to the sky above, he saw the red glow of sunrise emerging above the tallest trees. *"We must move on Breona. We can travel safely within the forest, but it will test our bravery."* He leant forward, stroking Breona's white mane and waited for her response. Breona's feelings merged with his own.

"This will lead us to where we need to go? To find help for Alavia?"

"Aye, it will." Magnus waited for Breona to think it over. There was no point forcing her. She would never go against her will.

After a moment's reflection, Breona repeated, *"This is the way we need to go?"*

"It is the only way."

"So be it. I will enter that dark place with you, Magnus."

"So be it." Magnus held his breath again as they rode into the forest. *"We stick to this path, no matter what."* He sensed Breona's determination and mustered his own to match.

Magnus rode slowly into the darkness of Froughton Forest. Half a mile deep, the road narrowed and turned gradually northward until it ran parallel with the forest's outer perimeter.

"This is the Outer Rim," Magnus shared thoughts with Breona, daring not to whisper. *"So long as we keep to the path or to the left of it, we will avoid the Valley of Shadows."* Going by Ganister's instructions, Magnus gathered the path would eventually turn in a northeasterly direction and continue on before exiting at the northern most point, three days travel away. Here, he would find the Northern Road that would take him to Guame.

The air in the forest felt close and carried the damp, sweet scent of the ancient trees. The rising sun occasionally pierced the canopy above sending down yellow spears of light that hinted at the path ahead.

An hour's travel into the forest realm, Magnus heard the scream of a wyvern coming from the skies to the west. He spun Breona about and looked back, but the convoluted path blocked his view. He waited, motionless, for any sign of movement. *Have they tracked us this far?* He did not hear the wyvern again, nor was there any movement through the forest. Satisfied he was not being followed, he turned Breona around and continued along the path faster than before.

As the day progressed the sun rose higher in the sky yet the forest became darker and the air became thicker. Magnus felt confident they were heading the right way, but he was ever aware of the darkness to his right. *Somewhere through there,* Magnus considered, *is the Valley of Shadows.* Magnus's attention was drawn to the trees in this direction. As midday came, lethargy encouraged his imagination to wander and he began to see movement in the darkness.

"Did you see that?" Magnus's fears caused Breona to jump and lose her concentration keeping to the path. He apologised to her and kept his feelings to himself.

They were both exhausted and Magnus knew they needed rest. He encouraged Breona to stop, and dismounted. Breona foraged for grass while Magnus paced along the road for a moment, feeling the soft pine needles beneath his boots. He looked to the trees, observing how the large trunks speared upward, narrowing gradually as they reached toward the sky overhead without a hint of a curve. He marvelled at how tall they were compared to the Crescent Woods back home. He took several deep breaths to calm his mind. Magnus became aware of the silence within the forest that was broken only occasionally by the call of a bird overhead whose song would be answered by another far away.

Magnus looked around to be sure no one was near then returned to Breona. He removed the pack from the saddle that Sarah had prepared for him. He laid it on the ground beside Breona and unravelled the neatly bound blanket before kneeling beside it and taking inventory of what he had. He arranged the assorted foods neatly to one side. Magnus had enough food here for a tidy feast. He took a chunk of bread from the loaf and used a paring knife to cut off a piece of cheese. Knowing he had many days of travel ahead, he spared the rest. The package also contained a small hessian bag he had not noticed before, in which there were several carrots. He fed two to Breona, who crunched them in delight. He then drank sparingly from the flask.

Satisfied, Magnus rolled up his belongings tightly into the blanket once again and looked to Breona who was resting amongst the soft undergrowth beside the road. He decided she had the right idea—they needed rest. His only concern was how visible they were to the left of the road they travelled on. He had the enchanted blanket that Sarah said would afford him cover, but this would be of little help to Breona. On the far side of the road however, the forest was more than adequate to hide them.

Magnus walked across the narrow road and peered through the trees beyond. He could see a good fifty feet before the light disappeared altogether. He looked back at Breona then took a tentative step into the trees. Magnus considered—*I doubt the Valley of Shadows starts for many miles deeper into the forest than here, and who is to say where the Valley starts and ends?*

Magnus suggested to Breona that they find shelter amongst these trees.

"South is the Valley. It is darker and scares me."

Magnus appreciated Breona's honesty and understood her fears. Still, they could not afford to lie exposed to the elements where they were. He considered that they could take turns resting whilst the other was on watch but dismissed this idea, as they were both too tired to stay awake much longer. Breona was not altogether convinced but nevertheless moved cautiously across to the darker side of the road. Magnus decided they would venture no further than was necessary and would stick together.

In amongst the thickness of the trees, Magnus relaxed a little. It seemed less dark here than it did from the road and the trees here were thicker, many of them old oaks and a mixture of pine and ash. The undergrowth was thick with ferns and various other plants Magnus had never seen before. *Perhaps the Valley is not so bad after all,* he thought to himself.

Confident they were hidden from the road, Magnus put his blanket of belongings on the ground beside the thick base of a tall ash, then removed his sword from over his shoulder and lay beside Breona, resting the sword upon his lap. He looked around at the wildness of the forest and out from the trees to the path that weaved its way onward through the forest. At first he tried to resist falling asleep but as he looked deeper into the darkness of the Valley around him he wondered if there was a secret world beyond the darkness—a sanctuary where he could live happily ever after. Soon, exhaustion won him over and daydreaming gave in to sleep.

CREATURE OF THE VALLEY

The sun had shifted through the sky and sat low in the west when Magnus awoke. He was curled up on the ground beside the ash tree, using his rolled up blanket as a pillow. He sat up with a start. Looking around he caught sight of Breona who had returned to the other side of the road and was chewing on grass. Magnus scanned the area but there was no sign of anyone or anything about. Resting his head back against the tree he gathered his thoughts and glanced upward along the trunk of the tree. Only a few feet above him was a creature clinging to the side of the tree. Its eyes were locked on Magnus.

Magnus froze. The creature edged closer to him, maintaining eye contact. Magnus drew a deep breath, ready to scream, but as he opened his mouth the creature stopped, tilting its head to the side as if curious about what he was about to do. Magnus hesitated and looked the creature over in more detail. He was unsure where the tree ended and the creature began, for it was so perfectly camouflaged. In fact, Magnus was sure that if it weren't for its large, green, staring eyes he would not have seen it at all. It looked almost human-like. Its face seemed to be that of a young woman but the surface of its skin changed in complexion and colour as it moved slowly down the ash tree. Atop its head was an entanglement of twigs and leaves, spiralling shreds of bark and threaded vines, giving the appearance of voluminous, curly hair. Its body followed the same theme and Magnus found himself blushing as he observed the creature's naked, womanly shape resting against the tree.

As if reading his mind, the creature removed her eyes from Magnus, looking herself over before returning her attention to him with a subtle smile. She pushed out from the tree with her arms, revealing the shapeliness of her upper body. Her complexion changed to a human-like milky white colour. Her lower body however, remained camouflaged against the tree.

Magnus took some heavy breaths. "Wow…" he whispered, unable to take his attention away from the creature. She placed two fingers against her now red lips and kissed them before reaching her hand toward him. Magnus watched as her delicate fingers touched his face and warmth surged from her fingers through his whole body, making him feel relaxed and content.

The womanly creature whispered to Magnus in his mind. Her voice was the most soft and gentle thing he had ever heard. All urgency and fear vanished from thought and was replaced with her promise to completely satisfy him. Magnus thought of everything that made him unsure of himself. None if it mattered any more. He no longer felt the need to hope for anything, for the instant gratification she gave him made the need to hope disappear. There was no need to hope his parents were safe, no need to hope Lucas would recover, no need to hope he would see Catanya again...

No need to hope... Magnus thought to himself.

No need to hope...

A vision of his father came to mind. He dug deep into his mind where the beautiful creature was yet to infiltrate and thought of his father's words—

"Hope...

Hope for the best...

Assume the worst..."

Suddenly Magnus knew—he was being manipulated, his mind poisoned— just like the wyvern had tried to do. He pulled his head away from her and she smiled, reaching for him again. Magnus scampered back from the tree. Finding his sword, he unsheathed it and stood, pointing the blade at the creature. The smile left her face and was replaced with sadness. Magnus lowered the blade, feeling guilty for upsetting her. She moved away from the tree toward him. Her body's camouflage changed again. She was now completely human, naked and seductive. She smiled again, her green eyes sparkling and Magnus smiled back to her. Reaching him, she wrapped her arms around him, embracing him, and began to infiltrate his mind once again. Everything she shared with him was so appealing. Magnus felt as if he could live in this moment forever.

"Assume the worst..."

His father's words wrung through his mind again. Magnus tried to shake her free but she had a firm grip on both his body and mind. Her arms wrapped around him repeatedly, like fast growing vines would do to a tree. He peeled his eyes away from her seductive gaze and saw her limbs changing shape, taking the form of long strands of vine, wrapping around his body tightly. Twisting and pulling, he could not free himself. Her mind was frantically trying to dominate his, permeating through every thought and memory he had, trying to make him replace every belief with just one—*"You need me..."*

"Get away from me, you witch!" Magnus screamed with his mind, unable to speak with her vines wrapped around his neck. For a moment she withdrew and Magnus sensed that he had offended her. Seizing the moment, he thrashed his body about, trying to cut the vines with the sword he still held in his left hand, but she had him bound too tight.

Digging deep into his own mind, he muttered the Fireisgh spell his father had taught him,

"Fara gin parshin-ar!"

Instantly a flash of pure white flame shot down the length of his sword. He felt the heat sear through his leather pants, and the creature let out a high-pitched scream that echoed through the forest. She pulled back from Magnus and glared at him, her green eyes now threatening rather than seductive. She looked at her own body, still naked but with a long scar down her right side from Magnus's blade. Magnus raised the blade again, swinging it toward her. She glared and crouched to the ground. Magnus shouted angrily at her and swung the sword again. She backed toward the tree, turning her wounded side from Magnus and hissed as she looked at the sword.

The creature reached the ash tree and embraced it with one arm—still glaring at Magnus. She looked around, spotting his rolled up blanket at the foot of the tree. Lifting it up, she examined it, all the while careful not to look away from Magnus for too long.

"Damn it!" Magnus said, thinking he would lose everything that was neatly packed away in the folded blanket. Suddenly, she threw the baggage at Magnus with such might that it hit him in the stomach, throwing him back into an oak tree behind him. He struggled for breath, winded from the impact. Taking a grip of his sword again in one hand and his belongings in the other, he stood as quickly as he could. Looking back to the ash tree, he caught one last glimpse of the creature. She flashed her green eyes for the last time then closed them, blending completely into the tree.

Magnus fled back through the trees and across the road to where Breona was. She was still happily chewing on grass, oblivious to what had just happened.

"Shall we move on?" Breona asked, without a hint of concern.

Magnus looked at her closely then back over the road and into the dark woods beyond. *"Did you see that? Did you hear that, Breona?"* Magnus sensed some slight confusion from Breona but nothing more. It seemed that she was oblivious to his struggle with the seductive creature in the forest.

"We had best be off."

"Aye," replied Magnus, fastening his belongings onto Breona's saddle. They were barely a day into the forest and already he had nearly lost himself to a creature of the Valley of Shadows. Magnus felt stupid that he had fallen for the enchantments of the forest so easily.

He slung the belt of his scabbard across his back once again and climbed back into the saddle. "Hope for the best, assume the worst," he repeated to himself, vowing to be more focussed on his surroundings from now on. They set off once again along the road through the Outer Rim.

EAMON

Night came rapidly in Froughton Forest. Magnus cursed himself for sleeping as long as he had, for travelling in the dark was difficult. In the end he had to walk ahead of Breona to try and discern where the road lay. He dared not make a torch to light the way—other creatures of the forest would see him coming long before he knew of their whereabouts.

On more than one occasion they wandered off the road and wasted time backtracking. After several futile hours Magnus decided to stop, only this time to the left and away from the Valley on the far side of the road.

The quiet and still of the night left him alone with thoughts of the horrors of the previous night. The most haunting memory was the Quagman attacking him outside his burning house. In that moment, all his training with Ganister accounted for nothing. The dark warrior with his two black blades was not playing games. *He was trying to kill me... and I was helpless against him.* He pictured Ganister blocking the Quagman's heavy blow and finally driving his sword into the man's back. Magnus had never considered such brutal work in the act of swordsmanship. To him it had always been as much a show as anything else.

Magnus thought of his father. He had felt such disdain toward him. He shook his head in shame. *What do I know of my father's past and of the battles he's fought? What horrors has he seen? Who am I to judge him?* Magnus cursed himself then began to panic, thinking that he would never see his parents again. The Quag warriors wanted them dead—he was sure of it. And they wanted *him* dead too. *"You are Bonstaph's son."* Ganister's words troubled him. Had his father done something years before to elicit such an attack? *But what do they know of me?* Magnus wondered.

The night passed without incident. The morning sun found a small gap in the forest canopy to throw a single blade of white light across the dirt road. Magnus ate sparingly and gave the remaining three carrots to Breona before setting off again at a good pace that they maintained throughout the day.

As night fell on them for the second time in Froughton Forest, Magnus was convinced they had travelled a good distance. *"Another day's travel and we'll be clear of the forest."* He sensed Breona's pleasure in that. They soon came upon a small clearing that seemed an ideal place to spend the night.

Resting in the quietness of the forest, Magnus heard a sound. It came in waves—a humming passing between the trees so naturally Magnus could almost believe the trees themselves were singing.

"Hmmm, hmmm, hmmm," it sang. "Hmmm, hmmm, hmmm," it repeated with breaks suggesting a breath between each melody. "Hmmm, aaah, hmmm…"

Magnus hummed to himself quietly along with the tune. He recognised it somehow, as though it were something from his past long forgotten. It made him nostalgic, remembering his childhood. Magnus stood and stopped mid thought—*This is another forest enchantment. The forest tries again to seduce me.* He peered further along the road as best he could in the darkness. The humming still resonated throughout the forest. Walking down the road a little way, Magnus could see a faint, shimmering glow of light in the distance. *A fire? Has someone made camp in the forest?*

Leaving Breona to rest, Magnus checked his sword was still securely strapped to his back and dared himself to wander a little way along the road in the direction of the light. He reasoned that he would not be able to rest knowing someone was camped nearby. In truth, he knew it was curiosity that urged him on.

Further down the road, the melodic humming grew louder and the light could be seen through the trees to the north. In almost complete darkness, Magnus stepped through the soft pine needles of the undergrowth, heading in that direction. Feeling for the trunk of one tree after another, he directed himself onward, the glow becoming brighter and brighter and the humming more focussed.

Magnus judged he was no more than fifty feet from the source when he heard the sound of wood crackling in a burning fire. Still, the deep voice hummed the same familiar tune. *From where do I know that song?* As he drew closer he grew ever more curious.

"I wouldn't do that if I were you," a voice spoke. Magnus froze on the spot. "Yes… I'm talking to you." The voice was coming from the direction of the humming. Magnus was unsure how to respond. He slowly drew his sword. "That won't do you much good."

"Who are you?" Magnus called out.

"You need be only concerned with yourself." It was a man's voice—an elderly man perhaps. "Move around to your right. That way you'll keep both your legs," he continued.

Magnus thought of running but the harsh reality sank in—he had been caught. Conceding, he sheathed his sword and did as he was told, moving around to his right. After a minute's walk, Magnus arrived at the edge of a clearing. At its centre burned the fire that threw a yellow glow across the forest canopy. In the clearing there was an array of things—strings tied between trees with clothes hung upon them to dry, a camping tripod with a simmering pot suspended from it, a collection of books and scrolls resting upon a blanket. To the right of the fire there was a donkey, happily chewing on a collection of discarded vegetable cuttings—no doubt left over from the meal brewing in the pot. To the left of the fire, a man sat on a large fallen tree trunk.

Magnus considered the man for a moment as the man did him. His most noticeable feature was his weathered, short-brimmed hat that drooped lazily over his face. Sticking out from beneath it was a stout smoking pipe whose embers glowed when the man drew back on it and blew smoke into the air. He appeared completely relaxed, wearing what appeared to be his undergarments. He raised his chin up and folded the front of his hat back so that he could get a better look at Magnus and in doing so revealed his long, grey beard and long, grey hair.

"Good evening," the man said. He raised his hat above his head and held it there, waiting for a reply.

"Um… good evening," Magnus replied.

The man placed the hat beside him and looked back to Magnus, eying him up and down. Magnus guessed his age at about seventy but it was hard to tell with all the hair. He felt a little uneasy staring at a man in his undergarments, although he still wore leather boots leaving only his knobbly knees bare as he sat there.

"I apologise if I startled you before, but I've set a few traps about." The old man pointed in several directions. "You were headed right into one. Like I said—your legs."

"My legs?" Magnus was confused.

"If you'd walked into that trap, you'd have lost your legs. Make it hard to travel after that. Where are you headed?"

Magnus was not sure how to answer, so he remained silent.

"Hmph." The old man placed his pipe next to his hat and stood, grunting from the effort. "Ah, winter approaches... a curse on my bones." He walked over to the fire and held his hands out to warm them. He looked back in the direction Magnus had come from then back at Magnus. "Guame. I'm guessing you're travelling to Guame, yes?"

Not wanting to appear rude and satisfied the man meant him no immediate harm, Magnus decided to reply. "Yes, to Guame."

"Ah," the old man shuffled over to his pot of food and stirred it with a wooden spoon. "I'm also guessing you're not walking the whole way?"

"No."

"Well," he said, tasting the food from the pot and nodding in approval, "No need to abandon your steed to the darkness. You are both welcome to share the fire with Mr Overstreet and myself."

Mr Overstreet? Magnus could see no sign of another person about. Nevertheless he called to Breona with his mind. He felt a faint response and so he closed his eyes, concentrating his mind to tell her he was safe and she should come to him. She acknowledged him and said she would do so. Opening his eyes again, Magnus saw the old man was staring at him.

"Words with thought," he observed. "This should be no ordinary steed." The old man turned to his donkey. "What do you say, Mr Overstreet? Are you happy to share your supper with another?" The donkey was happy to ignore him and continue eating his scraps.

"Mr Overstreet?" Magnus queried.

"Aye. There's hardly a street in Allumbreve he's not walked over in his long life and I with him for the most part. Sometimes I wonder whom is older—he or I. That's in donkey years, of course."

"Of course," agreed Magnus, a little confused at the comparison.

"Well now, there's an impressive sight if ever there was one," the old man said as Breona walked through the trees, over to Magnus, her white coat shining in the light of the fire. Magnus waited to be questioned further about her. He realised he was conspicuous riding an Astermeer across Allumbreve.

The old man looked Breona over. He picked up a piece of cabbage that Mr Overstreet was most likely intending to eat and walked over to Breona, offering it to her. Breona stood tall and stared the man in the face, refusing the food. "Fair enough," he said, leaving the cabbage at Breona's feet. "Well then... introductions. You've met Mr Overstreet. My name is Eamon."

"I am Magnus." He shook Eamon's hand. "This is Breona."

"A pleasure to make your acquaintance. Come, rest and keep warm by the fire."

Magnus shared thoughts with Breona—*"Do your feelings tell you we are safe here?"*

"We must rest. Where we do, I leave to you."

"It will be nice to do so in the warmth of a fire," said Magnus.

Eamon took a bowl and filled it with hot food from the cooking pot. He handed it to Magnus. In turn, Magnus took his travel pack out and opened it, splitting what remained of his bread and cheese and offering it to Eamon. Together they shared a meal. Magnus looked about at the campsite, taking in further the neatly stacked books and well organised cooking provisions. It seemed strange to go to so much effort to make the surroundings homely when he was likely only going to be there for the night. Curious about many things, Magnus asked Eamon the most pressing question—"How did you know I was in the forest over there?"

Busy eating his meal, Eamon pointed to various locations among the trees. "Mirrors," he finally said, swallowing his mouthful. Magnus looked around at the trees and saw many mirrors of various shapes and sizes balanced between branches in the trees and hanging from nails high in the trees themselves. "They're all placed for good reason. That one there," Eamon pointed at a triangular-shaped mirror high in a tree behind where Magnus sat. "That is where I saw you."

Magnus nodded, appreciating the effort he had gone to. "I guess you can never be too careful."

Eamon gave a slow nod. "Having your wits about you is not enough in the dark parts of Allumbreve."

Magnus agreed and thought of the creature in the ash tree that seduced his mind and nearly took his life. The two of them sat and ate in silence. After a while, Magnus began to relax for the first time since his ordeal had started three days before.

"Where does your journey take you?" Magnus asked Eamon.

"I'm also travelling to Guame. I travel with the seasons and go where my interests serve me best. What with it being the end of the harvest season and winter now upon us, we will find cashed-up merchants who've come to make trade in the Capitol." Eamon reached for his pipe. "Many times I have passed through Froughton Forest. What of you, Magnus? I've not seen you travel in this mystical realm before."

"This is my first time," Magnus said. Eamon remained quiet, as though waiting for more of an explanation. Magnus was not sure how much to tell Eamon so decided to keep it simple. "I'm travelling as a messenger. To give word before the Authoritarium."

"Is that so?" Eamon was studying Magnus, looking him up and down then peering into his eyes. "Well then, it is imperative you get there in one piece. Come sunrise, the both of you are welcome to travel with Mr Overstreet and myself."

"Thank you," Magnus tried to sound appreciative. "But we must get there as fast as possible." Come sunrise he planned to ride Breona as quickly as he could.

"Of course. Urgency most certainly warrants haste. For now though, rest by the fire. Save your haste for the morrow." Eamon stood and refilled his bowl from the cooking pot, gesturing for Magnus to also have more. Once they had eaten all the food, Eamon rummaged through his belongings and pulled out a bottle of mead and two small cups. He poured one for each of them.

Eamon stoked the fire as he drank. "That should keep burning until morning. If you should rise before me, I bid you fair travels. If I should be gone before you rise, I bid you the same, and if we rise together, then we may bid each other as we see fit at the time. Good night, Magnus." Eamon pulled a blanket off the makeshift clothesline, then pushed aside the books that sat upon another blanket on the ground. He lay down, making himself comfortable.

Magnus still had the tune in his mind that Eamon was humming earlier. "Eamon..."

"Hmm," Eamon mumbled.

"That song you were humming before. Do you know its name?"

Eamon turned over, tucking his hands behind his head. "I *was* humming, wasn't I?" he chuckled. "It is an old Paragon song, sung in the Old-Words from the first age of Allumbreve, before the days of the realms. Before the days of dragons."

Magnus remembered then how he knew of it. Sarah often sang the old songs and quoted the ancient poetry of the Paragon era. *"Gypsy songs,"* Ganister would say. "It is a gypsy song—*Flo Ena',* meaning *'Move On'."* Magnus said.

Eamon sat up on his elbows. "Gypsy song?" his eyebrows raised. "Fair enough. It is only the gypsies who sing the old songs. Wise words nevertheless. And apt for a young man on the road as you are. *"Flo ena unna gwatter flemabee"*—move on and let the past be as it be."

Magnus looked at Eamon and smiled. He wondered where he was from and what he had seen in his many years. "Goodnight Eamon. Thank you for your hospitality."

"Think nothing of it," Eamon said, falling back into his blankets.

Magnus stared into the fire and let the dancing flames keep his thoughts away from pressing issues—issues he could do nothing about in the dark depths of Froughton Forest. Instead, he hummed *Flo Ena* quietly to himself as the fire burned bright.

CLEANSING

Catanya was sure she would pass out at any moment. Her legs could not carry her much longer and her throat screamed with pain from thirst. She licked her dry lips only to feel the abrasive texture of blisters and cracks scrape across her tongue. She had long since lost track of time. Days had passed—perhaps nights. No rest had come to her. All Catanya knew was the path she trod. She stumbled on and on around the training compound, following the yellow-green glow of the small lanterns around the field's perimeter. Her path was marked with her own blood, spilled from the welts upon her bare feet.

It all started her first morning at the Romghold. Catanya was woken by Joffren long before sunrise and taken to the large green field without explanation. Once there, he placed a small lamp in the centre of the field and ignited a glowing amber light within it.

"From this moment forth, as I said before, you will address me as *Semsdi*. It is the formal address of one's teacher. And you will be *Semsarian*—student."

"Semsdi… Semsarian," Catanya confirmed. She looked across the field, as much to hide her derisive expression as anything else.

"Today your cleansing truly begins," Joffren continued. "You are to run around the perimeter of this training field. Be ever mindful of the verity light. Under no circumstances are you to stop as long as the light still burns."

No, I won't do it. I'm going home. Catanya repeated the words over and over again in her mind, trying to muster the courage to say them to Joffren. Instead, she started around the training field, cursing under her breath.

Catanya ran clumsily at first. The crisp air at the mountain peak pierced through her and it took a while for her body to loosen up and warm to the task. She was still wearing her favourite summer dress that was not particularly suitable for running in. Her soft leather shoes worked their laces free as she ran. Afraid to stop to retie them, she soon discarded them and ran bare footed. Catanya found the soft lawn beneath gave cool relief to her feet.

As the sun moved across the peaks of the Romgnian Mountains, fatigue settled in and Catanya wondered when she might be permitted to stop. The amber lamp still burned strong. Joffren occasionally came over to the compound and provided her with a bowl of water. She would stop and drink of it, half expecting him to say "Enough", but he never did. She would continue running and Joffren would watch for a few moments, only to disappear into the temple once again. As the hours passed, fatigue turned to exhaustion. She began to feel dizzy and hungry, for she had not eaten since leaving the Uydferlands.

Night came and Catanya's running became more and more clumsy. She slowed to a shuffle and started tripping over the hem of her dress. Eventually, she tripped and fell.

"That's it. I am done with this."

She stood, rubbing her knees that ached from the fall and stormed off the training field. Out of the corner of her eye she saw Joffren silently watching from the front of the temple. Catanya ignored him and continued toward her room that she entered and slammed the door behind her. She sat in the chair and sniffed back tears before they got the best of her. Folding her arms across the table as she had the previous night, she lowered her head and fell asleep in moments.

"Catanya."

Catanya woke with a start. She sat up wiping her mouth and looked around the small room. Her heart jumped—someone was standing in front of the small window to her left. She rubbed her eyes to focus. It was Austagia.

"Are you here to take me home?" Catanya sniffed. She looked at the closed door. "Is Rubea waiting for us?"

Catanya mirrored Austagia's blank expression. Something had to come of her failure on the field and she was prepared to fail again and again. Sooner or later he would have to take her home.

"Are you ready to continue?"

These were not the words she expected him to say. "What do you mean?"

"Drink." Austagia handed her a cup of water. She took it and examined her uncle for a moment, then drank the water down.

"I failed the test." Catanya gathered he knew this.

"It is not a test. It is a cleansing."

"What's the difference?"

"You will keep going until the verity light is done."

"*I* am done. I am finished. I want to go home." Catanya stood and her legs seemed to scream at her in protest. She winced but kept silent. *Damn it!*

"There is no other way this ends."

"Why me? Why have I been chosen for this? Has our family not paid a great enough price losing *you* to the priesthood? Do you not know how much my father suffered without you there?"

Austagia crossed his arms. "You have been chosen to become an Irucantî. What do you imagine you *cannot* do as an Irucantî?"

Catanya thought for a moment. *What I "cannot" do? There would not be much I cannot do...* "I guess... I could do anything." Their eyes met. For a moment it seemed as if she was looking into her father's eyes. *No one tells an Irucantî to do anything. In time then, I can do as I please.*

Austagia stepped to the door. "It is the only way. Some things you cannot run from," he said. With that he turned from her and left the room.

Catanya stood in the doorway as Austagia walked along a pathway to the right before veering off behind a building. She looked back at the training field where the verity light shone bright.

Become the warrior, then do as I want, Catanya said to herself. She walked back to the field and started running again.

The day was half worn when Joffren came to her with a ration of water and a morsel of bread. She thanked him, ate the bread in as few bites as possible, chased it with the water and kept moving. As she came around the field again, she tripped on her dress as before. Joffren was still there.

"Remove your dress, it slows you down."

Catanya ignored him until she ran around the field once again and came upon him.

"Remove your dress." This time she realised it was an order. "Forget your vanity, this is your cleansing. Remove your dress."

Catanya cast Joffren a scolding look as she yanked at her dress, pulling it over her head clumsily and throwing it to the ground. She resumed her running and doubled her pace wearing nothing but a thin white slip that ended above her knees.

Catanya pushed on. By midday a cruel wind tore though the Romghold, whipping at Catanya's exposed body. She pushed through ever increasing exhaustion and as the second day of uninterrupted running passed, the verity light seemed to stare at her unblinkingly. Her run had slowed to a shuffle barely faster than a walk. Alas, Joffren's instruction ran through her mind—

Under no circumstance am I to stop. Many times she considered it but knew what Austagia said was true. *This is not a test—the verity light will keep shining.*

The wind finally calmed as the sun set to the west. Joffren came to the training field carrying a long item wrapped in a linen cloth. Catanya watched him as she stumbled around the field. He sat himself in the middle of the field and unwrapped the object. He placed it before the verity light and bowed before it, then picked it up again and walked to the edge of the field as Catanya shuffled toward him.

"Carry this. It is the talon of Balgur." He placed it upon Catanya's shoulders. She winced. Exposure to the sun and wind had left her skin sore and reddened. She felt the weight of the heavy object course down her spine.

"Wrap your arms around it," Joffren instructed, helping her to lift her arms behind the heavy object and wrap her forearms over the top as though she were carrying a log upon her shoulders.

"What is it?" Catanya murmured, trying to turn her head to the side.

"It is a dragon talon. You bear the weight of the most powerful dragon that ever lived. His name was *Balgur*. He was killed by the Quag King—Delvion. Feel the weight, understand his power and know the strength the enemy mustered to destroy him. Then you will know the strength required to face such an enemy. Know your enemy intimately and you learn more of yourself."

Catanya was too tired to argue. She stumbled on, carrying the heavy ivory talon with her. The dark of night foreshadowed the stars of the realms and the passing night saw the moon arc its way westward. To Catanya it seemed like weeks had passed. Balgur's talon began to weigh so heavily she struggled to breathe for the pain it caused in her back. The abrasive texture of the talon rubbed across her shoulders, cutting at her raw and blistered skin.

The night was half spent when Catanya dropped the talon. She had all but fallen asleep while walking. Joffren was there, placing it back on her shoulders, hoisting her arms up again.

"Keep moving, Semsarian."

Catanya continued to move. She had no run left in her so all she could do was trudge around the training field, glancing every once in a while at the merciless verity light that seemed set on killing her.

Hours later Catanya fell. Joffren was there again, pulling her to her feet.

"Get off me!" Catanya yelled, flashing a scathing look at Joffren. It did not seem to bother him.

Joffren lifted Balgur's talon and Catanya could see her blood smeared across its ivory surface. He placed it on her shoulders yet again. She continued her march around the training field. To cope, she tried to occupy herself with thoughts of Magnus, but her mind was spent and she felt as if she no longer had control over it. Catanya imagined she was carrying the dragon's whole body. She pictured Balgur as a giant among dragons, proud and strong, only to be slain by a king who she respected for doing so, for she would be relieved of her burden. Then she remembered the dragon slayer was Delvion and she felt weighed down by sorrow, for she had sanctioned the murder of a beautiful dragon and brought all of Allumbreve to ruin.

As the sun rose on her third morning in the Romghold, Catanya dropped Balgur's talon for the third time. It landed heavily on the ground and she stood where it fell, crying with all her heart. "I'm so sorry," Catanya called out to Balgur. She could no longer carry him. She looked herself over. Her olive skin was darkened and blistered from the sun. The slip she wore was stained with blood, sweat and dirt and hung off her like an old rag.

Looking across the compound to the temple, Catanya saw Joffren watching her. Anger boiled inside her and she screamed at him in a long, deep screech that pained her through even more. The anger made her more determined. She wiped the tears from her face, smearing blood and dirt across her cheeks. She bent to her knees, tore a strip of fabric from the bottom of her slip and used it to wipe Balgur's talon clean.

Picking up the talon and hoisting it back onto her shoulders, Catanya started moving again. She looked to the amber light and saw it was gone. It no longer glowed its relentless, cruel light that led the way to death. Instead now, Catanya led the way to death herself.

"You've forgotten how to light the way. Follow me, I'll show you." She broke into a run again, forcing herself on, summoning the power of Balgur to work with her to push her on and on and on. Soon she felt her pain begin to wane and in its place was a sense of ecstasy. Catanya kept running around the training field throughout the morning. She felt invincible. "Together, Balgur, we will find Delvion and destroy him."

As the sun reached its zenith, Catanya's deliriousness cleared and she thought once again of Magnus. She stopped suddenly in her tracks and dropped Balgur's talon once again.

"Magnus," Catanya whispered to herself. She turned and saw the blurred silhouette of Joffren walking briskly toward her, across the field. She looked then to the sky and gazed at the sun. Her vision faded to white and she fell deep into thoughtless oblivion.

SIX THIEVES

Magnus woke at sunrise, stretching his limbs out as far as they could go until he felt his spine pop. It felt good to rise from a good night's sleep, but even so, morning came with a familiar sense of urgency.

Magnus looked around. There was no sign of Eamon. The fire had been smothered, making it hard to tell there had been one at all. The cooking pot, books and scrolls, and clothing hanging from lines were all gone. There was nothing at all giving evidence that Eamon was not a figment of Magnus's imagination except for one thing—the mirrors in the trees. *But a passer by would likely not notice them.* It dawned on Magnus how clever Eamon was. He considered that the old man perhaps had several locations in the forest just like this one, each set up for his next return.

Magnus and Breona got back on the road through the Outer Rim immediately. It concerned Magnus that Eamon could have packed camp and moved on without him waking. *What if he had tried to harm me? I may have been killed in my sleep.* He scratched the back of his head, picking out several prickles from his hair.

The road was different to the day before. It curved and wound its way tightly through undulating terrain, giving little chance for Breona to get up a good pace. Magnus grew frustrated at the lack of progress they were making. By mid morning he began to speculate how far ahead Eamon could be. *Does he know a faster way through the forest? Surely we should have caught up to him by now?* As he considered such things, the forest finally opened up and Magnus could see a mile-long stretch of road lined with late autumn leaves from the tall oak trees that grew along its length. Its bare branches allowed thick sheets of sunlight through to light the way. Magnus thought it a glorious sight after the gloom of recent days. Sensing Breona's eagerness, Magnus encouraged her to gallop. *"Go, Breona!"* Breona charged ahead, sending the orange, red and yellow leaves spiralling into a trailing eddy behind her.

Halfway down the straight stretch of road, Eamon suddenly appeared from behind a tree. He leapt into the middle of the road and raised a hand, signalling Magnus to stop. Breona pulled herself up and slid forward sending the trail of leaves that had been following her wafting onward down the road past Eamon. Magnus looked at him for an explanation.

Eamon removed his hat with one hand and held an index finger to his lips. "Shhh," he whispered, "Follow me *now*." There was urgency in his voice. Magnus was quick to follow. Eamon led the way, trekking southward into the darkness of the woods.

"Should we not avoid the Valley?"

"Shhh…" Eamon interrupted. "That's the least of your worries. Get off your horse and have her lie low. *Now!*"

Magnus did as he was told, encouraging Breona to crouch low amongst a collection of large ferns. Mr Overstreet was there next to them, also hiding in the scrub. Eamon tapped Magnus's shoulder firmly and pointed further up the road. At first Magnus saw nothing, but soon the sound of horse hooves striking the road, accompanied by murmuring voices, echoed through the forest.

Eamon stroked his beard feverishly and mumbled incoherently under his breath. He turned to Breona, muttering, "Damn, damn, damn…" He crawled on all fours back to Mr Overstreet and pulled a large blanket from his luggage. He continued his crawl over to Breona and threw it over her. Her body was camouflaged, but more than that, her thoughts fell to silence in Magnus's mind. *An enchanted blanket*—Magnus realised—*like the one Sarah gave me*. Breona sat in silence and so Magnus assumed she did not mind.

"You can't hide a white horse in a green forest, not unless it be covered in winter's snow," whispered Eamon.

Magnus looked back to the road. A group of men were heading along the road toward them. "Who are they?"

"Dangerous men—thieves, scoundrels, villains." Eamon crouched low in the ferns. Copying his stance, Magnus did the same. "We must let them pass, then I will show you a safer route out of Froughton."

"Thank you." Magnus was grateful to Eamon, shuddering at the thought of how close he was to riding directly into their path.

As if hearing him Eamon said, "If you'd run into them, you'd be a dead man by now. Unless of course you're well skilled with that sword."

Magnus looked at Eamon and saw he was closely examining the fleu-steel sword at his back. He then looked at Magnus again with a frown across his face. Magnus knew Eamon had questions, but now was not the time.

The men approached. Peering through the trees, Magnus counted six of them. Their horses moved at a trot and were soon close enough for Magnus to hear their conversation.

"How many days travel?" asked a stout man with a bald head.

"Three through Froughton. The word is he'd be two into the journey by now." The answer came from a pale-faced man with a scruffy looking red beard.

"We should run into him any time today then," the stout man concluded.

"A knight from the west you say... on a fast horse... are you sure he's travelling alone? I don't wanna take on more than one knight at a time!"

A third man spoke as they travelled past a clump of trees. "There are six of us, Maldor. And yes, he was seen alone, so stop your fretting."

"Aye, I'm just sayin' it'd best be worth the trouble, Wilfred."

"Shut it, Maldor," a deeper voice boomed, making Magnus jump. "He's as good as a corpse when we find him. His horse will be worth fifty gold coins and whatever else he carries, we split even."

Just then Eamon nudged Magnus. "They're talking about you," he said. Magnus looked to Eamon who nodded, affirming his words.

The man named Wilfred continued. "Remember men—he's on a white horse and it's fast. So no hesitating when the time comes. We'll go a mile further where the road gets all bendy and hide in the Valley—wait him out. He won't be able to run fast through there."

"Aye," the other men replied, and they charged their horses onward and out of sight.

Magnus was confused. *A knight on a white horse—how could they know I was coming?*

"Who knew you were making this trip?" Eamon asked.

Magnus thought back. *What was it Csilla had told her men? "A warrior on an Astermeer."* The description had changed but the message was the same. He thought of the archers he passed when he rode through the Uydferlands. *None of them would betray me.* In truth, he had no idea who might betray him.

Magnus decided to explain things to Eamon. After all, he had shared his supper, refrained from killing him in the night and saved his life just now. *I at least owe him the truth.* He spared some of the details, telling Eamon only of the Quag attack on the Fire Realm and his mission to ask the Authoritarium for help. Magnus kept what had happened to his parents and to Ganister, and the attack on his home, to himself.

Eamon listened carefully. "That is grave news," he concluded.

"But how could these villains know of my journey so soon? I have travelled the fastest route through Froughton, have I not?"

"There are faster, but not necessarily safer. And certainly no route that these halfwits would dare take." Eamon pondered for a moment. "News and gossip on the other hand… yes… that travels as the crow flies. It has a speed all of its own."

"As the crow flies?" Magnus was confused.

"Yes… well… *swallows* mostly. Messenger swallows. They have better homing instincts. *Ahrona* swallows from the Clouded Mountains would be my guess… exceptional little creatures. Do you know them?"

Magnus stared blankly at Eamon.

"White bellies, yellow flash, blue wings?"

Magnus shook his head, wondering what the old man's point was.

"If a message be given to an Ahrona swallow nothing will arrive at its destination faster."

Magnus was trying to keep up with Eamon's ramblings. "It is safe to say then that someone would prefer I did not reach Guame?"

Eamon scratched his nose while he thought. He walked to Mr Overstreet and pulled his pipe out from his belongings, tapping its bowl against the palm of his hand before burying his little finger into the chamber to clean it out. "Considering the nature of these men," Eamon reasoned, "I'd say they weren't here to stop you, but to profit from your assets. These men are thieves, not bounty hunters." Eamon leaned toward Magnus. "You ride alone in the company of an Astermeer, carry an Icerealmish sword… why, that alone would net these thieves quite a profit *without* a bounty on your head. I believe the agenda goes no deeper than that."

"Yet they would still kill me to get what they want."

"No doubt," Eamon agreed.

Magnus let all the possibilities flow through his mind, taking stock once again at how his life had turned upside down so quickly. He was feeling overwhelmed. *"Flo Ena…"* he said to himself, trying to move on from his thoughts. "How much further is it to the northern border?"

"On this route? You will never get there." Eamon was stuffing his pipe with tobacco. "The northern reach is notorious for mischief such as this. I'm betting others may well know of your coming too."

"Then what is the alternative?"

"There is a lesser known path south of the Outer Rim. It exits a safe distance east of the main road."

"Through the Valley?" Magnus interrupted, "I've had a taste of that and wish for no more."

Eamon frowned at Magnus. "Then you've another plan, young traveller?" He placed the pipe in his mouth and mumbled a familiar spell—"*Fara gin parshin-ar.*" The tobacco sparked into flame. Magnus was surprised to see him using the Fireisgh spell.

"Are you of the Fire Realm?"

Eamon took a long draw on his pipe and blew the smoke from his nostrils. He seemed to Magnus to be considering his answer. Eamon shrugged. "I guess I'm a gypsy of sorts. I have my own brand of mischief," he winked. "And a good gypsy knows which way to go. If I were you, Magnus, I'd follow me." Eamon walked off leading Mr Overstreet deeper into the forest.

Magnus looked back at the road that led to Guame. It was barely half a day's travel to the Northern Road, yet if he believed what Eamon said, he would never get there. He knew he had no alternative but to follow the old man and be hopeful it was not to a dark and gruesome end deep in the Valley of Shadows. With reluctance, he led Breona and followed Eamon and Mr Overstreet deeper into the forest.

The more they moved through the forest, the more enclosed and suffocated Magnus felt. There was no path to follow and the dense undergrowth made progress slow and disorientating. He knew he couldn't possibly find his way back to the Outer Rim if he were alone. Hour after hour they pushed along. The thick canopy blocked the sun, leaving only a sombre haze of grey that gave Magnus just enough light to know he was still behind Mr Overstreet.

If Breona was feeling the same, Magnus did not know. She seemed to have completely cut her mind off from him. Whether out of fear or because she did not trust him, he could only speculate. Whatever the reason, he wished he had the courage to let her know she would be okay. *She would know I was lying anyway.* Just as Magnus thought he could take it no more, they stumbled onto an overgrown path. It appeared to be made of river stones.

"Yes, here it is." Eamon knelt to the ground slowly, grunting as his knees cracked on the way down. "Juniper stones!" With gnarled fingers, he tried to pull a stone from the path without success. He removed a small dagger from within his robes and dug in under it, prising it out. He dusted the stone off and handed it to Magnus.

Magnus studied the deep purple, pebble-like stone that filled the palm of his hand.

"Warm. Is it not?" Eamon smiled with enthusiasm. Magnus wrapped his fingers around the stone.

"Yes, it is warm." Magnus was curious. "As though it's basked in the sun all day."

"Dragon-fired stones. Fired from the flame of dragons. As hard as diamond they are. They once paved paths throughout Froughton Forest during the Second Age. In those days, the paths shone brilliant with Juniper stones and weaved throughout the Valley." Eamon pressed on the stone in Magnus's hand, "They say when the dragons forged them in fire the stones glowed hot for a hundred years before they cooled enough to walk upon. That last bit I'd wager is not true. Nevertheless, they still have their heat—you see?"

It was true—the heat did not fade as Magnus gripped the stone. He handed it back to Eamon, who shook his head. "It is yours to keep. Hold it at sunrise to bring you hope and at sunset to bring you peace. If what you say of the Quag is true, then you will be challenged at both soon enough."

Magnus tucked the stone away in the small pocket of his jacket and cast his eyes down the worn, overgrown road of Juniper stones.

"When did the Valley become so… inhospitable?" Magnus asked.

"At the dawn of the third age. A thousand years of peace in the realms changed in a moment." Eamon clicked his fingers. "The Quag invaded the realms. The first attacked was Froughton Forest—home to Earth Realm and unfortunately, the worst prepared. They were all but destroyed. Some say they cursed the Valley to protect it from invaders. I say codswallop to that. If you abandon a place as malevolent as this it becomes nasty of its own accord."

"Did they abandon the forest altogether?"

"Altogether?" Eamon seemed lost in thought. "No, Magnus," he said in a slow, drawn out way. "They will never abandon her. The ƟhUid clansfolk are a part of this earth, as are their dragons—the *Spindlefax*. Far deeper into the forest you must travel to find them. Deeper still than the Valley of Shadows. To *The Core* you must go."

"The Core?"

"The very heart of Froughton Forest. Seclusion is their key to survival. And the respectful fear outsiders have of the Forest."

"Yes," Magnus looked about. "Us outsiders certainly have that."

"Fear not, Magnus. We will be free of Froughton Forest by sundown," Eamon said. Magnus was pleased to hear it.

With a set path to follow, Magnus was glad to be back in the saddle. They were making good distance now and the pace set by Mr Overstreet impressed him. The donkey's small legs zigzagged beneath his well-loaded back, never faltering. Breona even appeared intrigued by the spectacle. *No wonder it took a while to catch up with them this morning.*

Little was spoken between Magnus and Eamon over the few hours that followed. Magnus was grateful. It gave him time to clear his mind and think about everything that had transpired and what was to come. The urgency in his manner had faded and he felt guilty because of it. He needed to get to Guame as quickly as he could and he still feared the worst for his parents as well as Ganister and Sarah. Still, it was pointless charging forth without rest or thought. He was only increasing the likelihood of placing himself in danger. Magnus began to think more about Catanya and the dragon priests and wondered if Eamon knew much about them.

"What do you know of the Irucantî, Eamon?" he asked the old man, who was riding a short way ahead of him. At first there was no reply and from behind, Magnus watched puffs of smoke bloom out from the side of Eamon's short-brimmed hat. He decided to leave his travelling companion be, for he was perhaps deep in thought himself. But just when Magnus had all but forgotten the question, Eamon answered him.

"An interesting subject you raise, Magnus. But if I may, I have one myself. It is pressing on my mind and is perhaps more relevant to our present environment. May I delay in answering yours for a spell?"

"Of course," Magnus said, curious as to what Eamon's question might be.

"Earlier, you mentioned that you'd had a taste of the Valley before and wished for no more."

"Yes," Magnus agreed, thinking of the seductive creature in the trees.

"Care to elaborate?"

Magnus described how he woke after sleeping by the ash tree and the altercation he had with the creature. Magnus blushed as he spoke of her seductive approach and how she entered the depths of his mind. He told Eamon how he wounded and scarred her with his sword. As he spoke, Eamon began to chuckle. The more he told of his tale, the more Eamon found it humorous. By the time Magnus concluded his story, with the creature throwing his travel pack at him before morphing back into the ash tree, Eamon was arching back, laughing so loud Magnus was sure every creature in the forest could hear him. When he finally regained his composure, Eamon apologised for his behaviour and looked at Magnus, whose face burned red. It was all too much. Eamon began to heave with laughter once again, nearly falling from Mr Overstreet and catching his hat as it fell from his head. After wiping his eyes with a handkerchief and blowing his nose noisily, he recovered.

"Well then... a wounded nymph of the woodlands! That would be a *meliae*. They reside in the ash trees. You'd best not go near her again," he giggled. "A woman scorned would have nothing on an insulted nymph. They are beautiful creatures no matter what form they take and are more vain than the prettiest of women. The more she dwells on her injury—not to mention your rejection—the more she'll curse your name. She'll make you suffer more than you could ever imagine should you cross paths again."

"I can imagine quite a lot. She was moments away from crushing me to death with her limbs, the way they were wrapped around me."

"A nymph will only hurt you where her seduction falters. Not that you'll have an option next time. Should you two meet again, she won't be out to seduce you, she'll be set to kill you—I promise you that!"

"I'll keep that in mind," Magnus said, trying to end the conversation.

The Juniper stone path came to a point where it turned sharply in a southerly direction. Magnus peered down the path that vanished into the darkness beyond. Eeriness seemed to leach back toward him. He shuddered and turned away.

"We shan't be going that way," Eamon said. "Through there is the *true* Valley of Shadows. We've being skirting its borders."

"Have you been that way before?" Magnus asked.

"Aye. That I have." A macabre expression washed over Eamon's face and he swallowed hard. "Don't be tempted to go there." He pointed down the path with a long, bony finger.

"I've no intention to."

"You may never come out and if you do, you'll not be the same person."

Magnus looked around. The trees were so densely packed together, there was no way Breona could squeeze through in any other direction. The southern road seemed the only option. "Very well, but I see no other path."

"There's always another path," Eamon insisted. He picked a long, thin stick from the side of the road and pointed it. "That way is north. Now watch carefully." He threw the stick with all his might toward several thick-trunked pine trees. The stick hit the nearest tree then fell to the ground. "Now you try."

Magnus alighted from Breona and stood on the juniper stone path. *I've been led into the middle of nowhere by a madman.* He put his hands on his hips and stared at Eamon.

"Do it!"

"Okay, okay," Magnus sighed and bent to pick up a stick of his own to throw.

"Not a stick, throw your Juniper stone."

Magnus pulled the stone from his coat pocket and felt its warmth. He stared at Eamon again, shaking his head.

"Throw it!"

He drew back his left arm, focussed on the widest of the pine trees in front of him and threw the stone with all his strength. The stone hurtled toward the tree. As it drew closer it threw a brilliant purple light until it made contact with the tree and vanished without a trace. In its place, a quivering purple glow danced across the tree's surface. Magnus stared wide-eyed, trying to understand what had just happened.

"That's our path—come." Eamon led Mr Overstreet toward the large tree. "Come Magnus, the gate shan't stay open for long."

Magnus watched as Eamon vanished through the tree just as the stone had. He turned to Breona, who backed away from the tree. Magnus reassured her as best he could and without hesitating, closed his eyes and walked headlong toward the large pine tree, pulling Breona's reins behind him.

By the time Magnus prised his eyes open again, he and Breona were on the far side of the tree.

Magnus felt his body over, making sure he was still in one piece then looked to Breona, who side stepped clumsily, disorientated. Magnus looked around and drank in their new environment. They were now free of the forest, standing in a shaded clearing a short distance from a paved road. Eamon was talking to one of many people who were busily moving about the roadside, packing horse drawn carts and talking amongst themselves. Magnus felt as though he had just woken from a dream. *Or have I just fallen into one?* He turned and looked back at the tree behind him and felt the rough surface of the trunk with the palms of his hands. A purple light danced momentarily across them before fading to nothing.

"Magnus!" Eamon called from across the clearing. The old man looked pleased with himself. He bid farewell to the woman he had been talking to and trotted back toward Magnus.

"Welcome to the Northern Road!" Eamon said. "We've come out of Froughton four miles east of the main road through the Outer Rim. No one will suspect you left the forest here. And we're only a day's journey to Guame. What do you think?"

Magnus nodded. He was happy they had made it yet still a little perplexed about the sudden change of scenery.

"Here, don't forget your stone. You'll need it for the return journey." Eamon handed Magnus the Juniper stone. Its purple glow had all but faded. "You've a good arm. I found it over by the roadside. You threw it a good hundred feet!"

"And through a tree," Magnus mumbled, shaking his head in disbelief.

"Yes, it's a kind of magic!" Eamon whispered with a wink.

THE HUGMDAEL INN

Over his shoulder, Magnus watched the last rays of sun sink beyond the western horizon. It thinned to a green flash before disappearing altogether, marking the end of autumn's days. Magnus longed to follow it over the horizon and be home again with his parents. He wanted to be with his father, mending the fences and ploughing the fields. He wanted to hand Breona's reins to his mother, having developed a greater appreciation for their relationship. Magnus wondered if he could have done something to make things any different, but nothing would have stopped the Quagmen attacking in the night. And nothing would have stopped the priest from taking Catanya away from him on the back of a fire dragon.

Magnus looked back to the east and the road where his journey would continue. *At least my path has been set. To have nowhere to go and no hope at all would be unbearable.* Neither Ganister nor Csilla gave any mention of travelling the Northern Road to Guame. It was to be the final leg of his journey before speaking before the Authoritarium. Magnus began to feel the burden of what he was about to do.

Eamon convinced Magnus he was best keeping off the road once night had fallen. "You must stay at the Hugmdael Inn. They have rooms that will keep you safe and warm and it will do you good to sleep in a bed."

Once they reached the Inn, half a mile along the Northern Road, Magnus insisted Eamon stay with him. "I will pay your way and you will eat a hot meal with me. I owe you that much and more." Eamon eventually agreed.

Magnus was reluctant to leave Breona in the stables at the far end of the compound behind the Hugmdael Inn, but Eamon did so with Mr Overstreet, leaving all his worldly goods neatly stacked in the corner of the stable. In the end he decided if Eamon felt safe to do so, then he should too. However, Magnus kept his belongings strapped to the saddle that was still on Breona's back. *"Just in case,"* he told her.

The front tavern of the Hugmdael Inn was dimly lit and littered with dozens of men in small groups mumbling into pewters of ale. The tavern stank of damp, stale beer and sweat. As Magnus and Eamon entered, all eyes fixed on them and soon singled out Magnus as the stranger none of them recognised.

Eamon led the way to the bar. A burly waiter with an unkempt crop of oily hair stared lazily as Eamon ordered two pints of beer. He handed them two pre-poured mugs, plonking Magnus's down in front of him and spilling its foamy head across the table before wiping the mess with a greasy rag he then threw over his shoulder. The waiter looked Magnus over, pushing his tongue under his bottom lip. "Eating?"

"Aye," Eamon replied.

The waiter grunted and moped to a room out the back. He returned with two bowls containing a grey gruel that Magnus could not identify as any known type of edible food. The waiter spilt half the bowls' contents across the table, again using the oily rag to clean the mess up. Magnus breathed through a wave of nausea and Eamon quickly handed the waiter two gold coins and took his mug and plate of food.

"Follow me," he said to Magnus.

They found a vacant table and sat. Magnus insisted, "I told you I would pay your way."

"Shhh," Eamon whispered. "Not here. These men are trying to size you up. If they think you have money, they will take an unsavoury interest in you."

Magnus looked around. While most had resumed muttering between themselves, they still cast furtive glances at him. "This is the hot meal I promised you?" Magnus said, quieter than before.

"Aye. The best you'll find in these parts. And the best drink," Eamon leaned in toward Magnus. "Wait till you see the accommodation."

Magnus tilted his bowl letting the sloppy grey contents roll around inside it. He tried to figure out what it was and how exactly he was supposed to eat it, as they were not given utensils of any kind. Glancing around, Magnus saw others scooping their food with their fingers or slurping from the bowl's edge. Soon enough Eamon was doing the same. Not convinced, Magnus took a tentative swig at his mug of warm beer.

"You asked me earlier about the dragon priests," Eamon mumbled, his mouth half full of gruel.

"Yes," Magnus whispered, not convinced this was the place to discuss the subject. "Should we discuss this later?"

"Baa, don't mind that. They could use an education." Eamon slurped his drink. "What is it you'd like to know?"

"What do you know of them?" Magnus fiddled with the crudely made handle of his beer mug. Eamon exercised his usual habit of pausing at length before responding, further frustrating Magnus.

"Battle-hardened," he finally said.

"Battle-hardened? When was the last time they fought a battle?"

"Hmm. Twenty years since the Battle of Fire. Before you were born. But they train hard—very hard. Fierce warriors, they are."

Magnus waited for further explanation, raising his eyebrows. "Anything else?"

"Well, I knew one once—an Irucantî. He received the calling. Once he joined the order, he trained and trained…" Eamon drank heavily of his beer. "Anyway, he was never the same after that. Are you following me?"

"I think so." Magnus was not at all sure though. He tried as he had before to see Catanya as a warrior.

"The priesthood is about shedding away everything that makes them who they were and becoming a committed warrior." Eamon raised his mug and knocked it against Magnus's. "Commitment!" he continued. "Well, I suppose a dragon is totally committed to being a dragon, so a priest should be totally committed to being a priest." Eamon raised his mug again. "Here's to commitment!"

"Commitment!" shouted a drunken man at the table nearest to them. He and Eamon knocked their beer mugs together and drank to their toast. More men joined the cheer, shouting and drinking with no apparent care of what it was exactly that they were celebrating.

At the height of the cheer the oak doors of the Inn's tavern burst inward and several men entered. The room fell silent. Magnus immediately recognised who they were—*Quagmen*. Every hair on his body stood on end and he struggled to breathe. He felt Eamon's hand grip his knee firmly under the table. He looked to his companion, whose expression had turned to stone.

"Say nothing," Eamon mouthed in silence.

There were four Quagmen in total and each wore the same dull, black armour as the man who attacked Magnus and Ganister back at his home. Each of them carried a black steel helm with collar spikes in one arm and a pair of sheathed black swords at the waist. In the light of the Inn they looked no less menacing than those Magnus had seen in the darkness of night.

A fifth man followed. The other four stood aside to let him through. He was younger and leaner by comparison, yet strong, nonetheless. His armour was more intricately put together with engraved panels on his chest and forearms. His face was not as broad as the other Quagmen and his pitch black hair was styled short but for a long fringe that fell across his face. His dark eyes scanned the room, looking at each man, and soon enough at Magnus, who couldn't help but return his gaze. After a pause, the Quagman looked away and walked toward the bar.

"Waiter!" he shouted, but the waiter was nowhere to be seen. He nodded to one of the other Quagmen—the largest of the group—who walked behind the bar to the back room and returned moments later hauling the oily-haired waiter by the collar. "Beer for my men," the young Quagman demanded.

"Sire," the waiter nodded nervously, pouring four pints of beer and placing them on the bar before the large Quagman, careful this time not to spill a drop.

"Two gold pieces for the beer, sire?" The waiter's voice trembled nervously and he held a hand out in waiting.

The young Quagman scanned the room once again, returning his gaze to Magnus. "Who will pay for my companions' beers?" No answer came from the soundless room. "Who will pay?" the young man demanded in a more aggressive tone. Still no answer came. "Briet. Pay the man yourself."

The large Quagman grunted and placed his half-drunk beer on the counter, glaring at the expectant waiter. Reaching behind his back he fumbled for a moment then paused. "I have your payment here," he sneered. As quick as lighting he drew a dagger from within his robes and brought it down hard, burying it into the palm of the waiter's hand, pinning it to the table. The waiter shrieked in pain and all in the tavern gasped collectively. Some patrons stood from their chairs, trying to move back against the walls, while others froze where they sat. The waiter continued to moan in agony.

Magnus looked at Eamon, who remained seated and held Magnus's knee firmly as if suggesting he do the same.

"Allow me to introduce myself," the young Quagman announced as his four men positioned themselves at the four corners of the tavern. The patrons shuffled about, trying to distance themselves from the Quagmen. "My name is Crugion, son of Delvion." Eyes widened even more than when the waiter was assaulted.

Magnus stared hard. *Delvion the Quag King... this is his son?*

"It seems time has not forgotten us after all," Crugion continued. "Alas, time does change things and change is coming to you—all of you. Some perhaps tonight, but soon all of you in one way or another will feel the change." He spoke calmly and deliberately, ignoring the wailing waiter who was trying desperately to pull the blade from his hand that was still pinned to the table.

"I have spoken before your Authoritarium this day past, bringing word from the South." He started to pace around the room again. "Would you like to hear what news from the South I bring?" The room remained silent. "Would you?" he shouted angrily.

Even through his fear Magnus felt it was strange that a room of so many men would so easily bow to the barking of one young man, even with the company he kept. Then he realised these people were mostly peasants—farmers, traders and gardeners. They had no knowledge of fighting. *Then where are the knights of the Authoritarium? Why do they allow five Quagmen to roam freely this far north?* His father's words haunted him—*"This is what comes of a dictatorship..."*

Crugion started to shout again—"Briet, shut that mewling man up." Magnus turned to look at the moaning waiter. His oily hair now looked more like a wet mop, bobbing around as he jerked frantically trying to pull the blade free. Magnus noticed the big man's hand was turning black where the blade had entered. The blackness was spreading slowly up—firstly to his wrist, then his forearm. The sight of the encroaching blackness was sending the waiter into fits of hysteria.

"Shut him up!" Crugion shouted. Briet gulped a final swig of beer and sighed loudly, clearly not impressed he had twice been interrupted while enjoying his drink. He placed the empty mug on the bar and took a firm grip of the blade's handle, studying the waiter's agonised face. As quick as he had driven it in, he pulled it free, spun the blade around in the palm of his hand and thrust it up under the waiter's chin, driving it into his throat and out through the back of his neck.

The silence in the tavern was broken by a collective gasp of horror. The waiter's face turned grey and black mist oozed from the wound in his neck. Thin dark lines started to spread across the dying man's face.

A cursed blade? Magnus wondered, growing ever more fearful for his own life. It reminded him of the poison Kriser drew from Lucas's body. The waiter's eyes turned black and he crashed heavily onto the bar—dead.

"*Black blades*," whispered Eamon. Magnus turned to him. "Say nothing," he mouthed once again.

Magnus heard the scrape of Crugion's armour and froze. He glanced to his right and saw he was standing directly over him.

"You are not from around these parts," Crugion said. Magnus said nothing, partly because he was told not to and partly because he was terrified. "Does your companion speak?" Crugion addressed Eamon.

"Neither one of us are from around here," Eamon said in the coolest of manners. "We are just passing through."

Crugion looked Eamon over with an expression of contempt. "You get around old man. I've seen you in Ba'rrat. That's your old donkey in the stables, is it not?"

"Correct."

Crugion's attention returned to Magnus, who looked to the ground, desperate to remain anonymous. He knew there was no greater enemy of the Quag clan than the people of the Fire Realm. It was *his* realm and *their* dragons that put an end to Delvion's attack on the realms years ago, and now they were attacking the Fire Realm once again. Magnus doubted he would leave this tavern alive if Crugion learned of his true identity.

"My companion here is a *Rhyderman*," Eamon said.

"Is that a fact?" Crugion stood so close to Magnus he was convinced he would strike him. "You're from the Ice Realm?" Magnus looked at Eamon who sat in silence. "What are you looking at him for? You can answer my questions yourself."

"Whilst at the stables, did you see the Astermeer beside my old steed?" Eamon asked.

"I did," Crugion asserted. "What of it?"

"No man beyond the Ice Realm rides an Astermeer, save for the Irucantî."

"So then you could be a dragon priest?" Crugion laughed and his men laughed with him. He raised a gloved hand in the air and the men fell silent.

Magnus's fear turned to frustration. He knew it would do him no good to confront Crugion but Eamon's suggestion to remain mute would not last much longer. He would be pressed into talking one way or another.

Magnus stood from his chair and faced Crugion directly. Their eyes were level. Crugion stared back at Magnus in silence as if waiting for him to make a move. The four Quagmen did not wait—they moved in swiftly, drawing their swords. Magnus looked at each of them. They all had extremely high cheekbones and low, wide jawbones making their faces appear square and somewhat beastly. Each of them had scars on their faces. The one named Briet had a scar that ran through his right eye and across his cheek. He looked to be blind in that eye. Crugion moved closer to Magnus so that their noses almost touched. They considered one another for a moment. Magnus did not flinch.

"You're not a Rhyderman," Crugion stated.

"Aye. That I am," Magnus said.

"Why is a Rhyderman in the company of an old merchant trader?"

"I choose my company as I see fit."

"What brings you so far from home?"

Magnus considered all manner of lies and half-truths as to why he was heading into Guame, but in the end decided to be as cryptic as Crugion was. "I bring news to the Authoritarium from the Ice Realm, as you do from the South. I believe you were about to tell us of your news?"

Crugion breathed heavily through his nose and clenched his jaw tight. Magnus stood his ground and thought of the waiter. *If I am going to die, this is surely when it will happen.* But then Crugion stepped away.

"The Rhyderman speaks a truth—I have allowed myself to be distracted. My people are moving northward as we speak in an attempt to... *integrate...* with the people of the realms." This drew laughter once again from the Quag henchmen. Crugion smiled, clearly pleased with his own wit.

Magnus's frustration was turning to anger. *Integrate?* He was fuming. *Is that what you call your attack on my home?* He ached to shout the words at Crugion but bit the inside of his cheek to hold them at bay. He tasted blood and wished for more—for the blood of Delvion's son. *What better place to start. If only I had my sword.*

Eamon kicked Magnus's leg under the table and flashed a stern gaze. Magnus glared at him. Eamon then stood and gave an over-exaggerated grunt that caught Crugion's attention. "My companion and I must be off now. It was good to make your acquaintance," Eamon nodded to each of the Quagmen, then finally at Crugion before motioning to Magnus to make a move to leave.

The four Quagmen moved toward Eamon, blocking his path to the tavern door. Eamon looked at the men and continued his casual façade. "Come now, I see no need for hostilities. We have a pressing engagement in Guame. The Authoritarium awaits." Eamon smiled. "We don't want to keep the Authoritarium waiting now, do we?"

"Anything you wish to share with the Authoritarium you can share with me, old man." Crugion was not smiling. "I have shared what news I have, now what do you bring from the Ice Realm worthy of my letting you pass?"

Eamon reached into two pockets in his coat and pulled out fistfuls of what appeared to be sand.

"Behold the answer to your inquisitive mind, son of Delvion!" Eamon shouted, casting large plumes of the glittering sand out and over the four Quagman as he mumbled a spell—*"Ligta illume!"*

The countless grains of sand exploded into flame as they fell upon the Quagmen and other surrounding people and objects. It brought chaos to the room as the flames took a hold of everything they fell upon, from the tables and chairs to the low ceiling above. One of the Quagmen fell to the floor screaming as some of the dust exploded in his face. Magnus glanced over to Crugion who was as bewildered as everyone else. Eamon cast more and more of the magical substance across the room, mumbling his spell over and over until the tavern was filled with flame, smoke and panic. The people began to riot, desperate to reach the doors and escape the madness Eamon had created.

Eamon grabbed Magnus by the arm and pushed him toward the exit. "GO!"

Magnus needed no further encouragement. He held tight to Eamon's arm, pulling him toward the doors. Only one of the Quagman was recovered enough to try and pursue them—Briet. They were ten men deep from the door but twenty men were trying to funnel into the line. The pushing and shoving made progress slow. Looking back, Magnus saw Briet sweeping men aside with his powerful arms, his gaze fixed on Eamon and Magnus as he worked his way toward them.

"Leave me Magnus! Go!" Eamon shouted. Magnus ignored him, tightening his grip on Eamon's arm so as not to lose him in the skirmish. He knew he could make faster progress if he was not dragging Eamon behind him, but he would be leaving him to his death. Pushing through the men as hard as he could, Magnus looked back again and saw Briet was growing ever more desperate, hacking away at people with his swords. Bodies fell and men screamed, inducing even more panic. Magnus knew something had to happen to clear the way to the door.

"Eamon, do you have any more of that dust?"

"No. I'm spent of it."

Magnus grunted, trying to think of another way to get through. His thoughts were interrupted by screams coming from either side of the room. Two of the other Quagmen came in from either side of the crowd, culling people with swords as Briet was and working their way toward the middle where Magnus and Eamon were now trapped in the desperate, pressing group of people.

Magnus and Eamon were five people deep to the exit, with many more pushing in from the sides—desperate to be the next in line to leave. Briet meanwhile, was fending off several men who decided to turn on him rather than be slain.

The door needs to be cleared…

We need to get to Breona…

Magnus looked to the door and realised what he had to do. *"Breona!"* Magnus called with his mind. Soon enough she responded. As always, he felt her emotions. At his panic, she seemed to panic herself. It was not what he wanted to induce in her, but moments later there was a new kind of terror at the tavern door— *"Breona!"*

Breona was furious. She reared up and filled the tavern with her screams, then pushed her way through the doorway, sending men tumbling back and scrambling out of her way. The effect made the remaining twenty or so men in the tavern shift back into the Quagmen, pressing them further away from Magnus and Eamon. Breona was soon in the tavern itself, rearing up and inducing as much terror as the Quagmen. Only a few feet separated Breona from Magnus and he pulled Eamon toward her, helping him into her saddle before climbing up himself.

Breona turned and charged out and away from the Hugmdael Inn at full speed. Eamon, sitting behind Magnus, tightly gripped his waist. They turned back to look at the scene behind them. It was madness. Men were tumbling out of the burning tavern and into the street and people from neighbouring homes had come out to see what the commotion was about, adding to the confusion. Crugion stepped out into the night air. His eyes were fixed on Magnus, watching him as he, Eamon and Breona charged along the Northern Road toward Guame.

GUAME

Guame - 2 miles

The two-mile marker, carved into a flat bed of stone on the roadside, indicated they were close to the capital city. *Finally,* Magnus sighed. Breona slowed to a walk. He stroked her neck and thanked her for her diligence throughout the night. It was now the early hours of morning and they were nearly there. Breona let Magnus know she was glad to have stretched her legs and distance herself from the trouble at Hugmdael and even more so to be free of Froughton Forest.

It came at a cost though. "I'm sorry about Mr Overstreet." Magnus felt terrible that they left him behind at the stables of the Hugmdael Inn, but knew they would never had survived had they tried to flee with him.

"We'll be together again soon enough," Eamon conceded.

"When my business in Guame is done, we shall travel back together and find him."

"That's very kind of you Magnus. But you've done enough for me already and I'm guessing from the moment you enter Guame's city gates you will have far more pressing issues than helping an old man find his donkey."

Still sitting behind Magnus in Breona's saddle, Eamon patted Magnus on the shoulder. "You're a good man, Magnus. You possess a rare breed of courage. You stood up to Crugion and held your ground."

"But I was terrified. There's not much courage in that." Magnus felt ashamed, yet was not sure why.

"Courage is not the absence of fear, Magnus. It is standing up for what is right in the face of fear. Remember that." Eamon's remarks made Magnus feel a little better about himself.

There was a gradual rise in the road and at its peak they stopped to take in the view. Just over a mile away at the bottom of a hill was the city of Guame. Magnus was awestruck by its appearance. It was a vast metropolis with hundreds of buildings made mostly of brown stone with thatched or tiled

114

roofs. Between the buildings were more rudimentary constructions of canvas tents and scaffolding ensuring every piece of land was being used. The buildings were laid out in formation around a central building of mammoth proportions. From this vantage point, Magnus observed its rectangular shape with spires at the four corners and a large central dome. The entire city was surrounded by an almost perfectly circular wall made of the same stone.

"See the cathedral at its centre?" Eamon pointed. "Under that dome is the Great Hall. That is where you will speak before the Authoritarium."

Magnus's stomach twisted at the thought. "Why would the Authoritarium grant audience with Delvion's son?" he wondered aloud.

"Now there's a question you could ask them while you're there," Eamon chuckled. It did nothing to settle Magnus's nerves.

As they neared the city proper, the Northern Road was lined with horse wagons and tables where merchants sold produce to people approaching the city. The merchants flittered about, determined to separate Guame's visitors from their coin even before they entered the city walls. Magnus and Eamon alighted from Breona and approached the city gates on foot with Magnus leading Breona.

"Pray tell, what is your business in the city, Eamon?" Magnus asked.

"Yes well, your business is yours and mine is mine. Best we keep it that way, young knight from the West," Eamon said, before turning to fend off a persistent merchant.

Magnus decided not to press the issue, but instead took in the sight of the wall surrounding the city. It seemed much larger than it appeared when viewed a mile back along the Northern Road.

They took themselves to the end of a queue at the city gates. Over fifty people were waiting to enter. Some were on foot, others on horses or in horse drawn carts. Many were with children. Most of them looked as tired as Magnus felt. He wondered how far others had travelled to get here and what their own reasons were for coming to the capital.

Magnus looked up at the parapet above the gates where four flags flew, each one depicting a dragon from its respective realm.

"Can you name them?" Eamon asked.

Magnus smiled. "I can. A *Jaat* dragon of the Air Realm, a *Spindlefax* of the Earth Realm, an *Ertwe* Dragon from the Ice Realm and, of course, the *Couldradt* dragon from the Fire Realm."

"The largest of course are the Couldradt dragons."

The subject raised a question for Magnus, "Do you think, Eamon, that is why the fire dragons have survived, where the others have perished against the Quag?"

"They certainly aren't afraid of a fight. I think their tenacity in battle has helped more than size alone. But I wouldn't be too hasty to write off the dragons of any realm just yet, Magnus. Three of the four may have spawned their *Electus*, but that's not to say we've seen the last of their dragons."

Magnus frowned. *Eamon thinks dragons of the other realms may still live?* It sounded a little far-fetched to Magnus. But the *Electus*? Eamon's tales were starting to smell of myth. There was no greater myth than the prophecy that a dragon from each realm would give their power to a chosen one whom they deemed worthy. *So their legacy may live on.* "You don't really believe that do you?"

"Believe what?" Eamon asked.

"That there are people walking the lands with the power of dragons," Magnus scoffed. "The *chosen few* who walk with dragon blood in their veins? *Please*, Eamon, spare me."

Eamon appeared taken aback. "I don't believe in blind faith anymore than you do, my young friend. But my old eyes have seen a lot more than yours. I've seen power corrupt. I've seen the desire for it drive a man insane. Your friend back there, at the Hugmdael Inn," Eamon pointed back up the Northern Road. "Did you know his father has killed newborns with the blood of a Jaat dragon then drank their blood to get it for himself? Entire family bloodlines have been wiped out for the same reason, all at the hands of Delvion. The most frightening of all, he slayed the greatest dragon that ever lived in the hope to gain its power."

Magnus was aware people were staring at him and Eamon. The old man was getting heated. Still, Magnus could not help himself. "You saw that did you? You saw Balgur getting slayed by Delvion?" Eamon went to speak but stopped himself short. Magnus knew he had taken it too far.

"I pray you'll never see half of what I've seen," Eamon retorted.

The queue moved along. They walked beneath a great archway that held an enormous iron portcullis suspended within a deep crevice in the stone ceiling overhead. At the end of the arch was a pair of iron-studded wooden doors that swung open on gigantic iron hinges revealing the city of Guame beyond. Four stately looking knights were positioned at the doors. Their attire was like Xavier's yet everything about them was meticulous and far more impressive. Magnus could not help but think how proud he would feel dressing like them.

Magnus, Eamon and Breona came to the inner gates and one of the knights approached them. He carried a sheathed longsword and silver kite-shaped shield. Magnus noticed the knight bore nothing to indicate which realm he was born to, but that his sword was sheathed to his left, suggesting he was right-handed. *We of the Fire Realm are left-handed...*

"What business do you have here in Guame?" The knight addressed Magnus and Eamon in a routine manner, without looking at either of them.

"Simon... it is me good man, let us through!" Eamon stated. The tall knight crouched a little and squinted to look beneath Eamon's hat. Eamon folded the front portion of the brim back revealing a somewhat comical smile.

"Ah! Eamon. Apologies. I did not recognise you there without your old mule."

"All is forgiven." Eamon started to move forward past the guard and Magnus followed. The knight stepped across their path.

"Who is your companion?"

"This is Magnus, he needs to speak before the Authoritarium." Eamon said as casually as possible.

"If it is business of the council it will need to be announced. Is it official?" The guard named Simon frowned as he unfurled a parchment and read over it.

"It is officially urgent—I can tell you that much. Magnus travels with haste and therefore faster than any precursor to his visit," Eamon smiled.

Simon looked Eamon over then did the same to Magnus. Magnus was unsure what to do to contribute to the conversation to persuade him to let him through.

"Urgent you say?" He looked at Magnus, awaiting further explanation.

"Such that I myself don't even know the nature of its urgency," Eamon explained. "I think it best left to the elders of the Authoritarium to—"

"Elders you say?" Simon interrupted Eamon then looked around to be sure no one was listening. He moved in closer to him and spoke quietly. "There are few elders *left* in the council of the Authoritarium."

"I have heard words to this effect," Eamon spoke sympathetically. "Who then holds representation of the realms?" Simon opened his mouth to speak again when another of the knights approached.

"Other people wait to enter the city this morning. What's the hold up?" He looked at Simon who addressed Magnus in a more formal manner.

"What is the nature of this urgency? The Authoritarium will want to know as much before granting an audience with an unannounced guest."

With both guards and Eamon now looking at him for a response, Magnus thought of the best way to explain things without announcing to the gathering mass of people behind them that the Quag had brought war to the Fire Realm. He decided instead to risk revealing whom he represented in order to gain credibility.

"I come as the son of Bonstaph of J'esmagd, under formal instruction of Ganister of Bowthwait, both former knights of Allumbreve. I come also as representative of the greater Fire Realm under instruction of Csilla of the Uydferlands. I bring word of urgency that cannot wait."

Eamon and the guards stared at Magnus without speaking. The guards then stepped away to speak among themselves. They stopped occasionally to look at Magnus.

Magnus turned to Breona and shared his thoughts with her. *"I guess this is it Breona, hopefully we get to speak before the Authoritarium and they give us the support we need."*

She seemed pleased with this. *"I hope they do."*

Eamon was still examining Magnus, like he was seeing a side of him he had not before. "Well, aren't you full of surprises. With news of this nature the guards have a duty to report to the Authoritarium and no doubt they will grant you audience."

Sure enough, Simon approached Magnus. "Your matter will be brought to the attention of the council. You will be notified if your request for an audience has been granted. Make your way to the Cathedral and enter via the main entrance."

"Very well," Eamon said. Magnus handed the knight three gold coins as payment for their entry into the city as Sarah had instructed him to do so.

"Much obliged," Simon said, stashing the money into a pocket in his tunic.

"What was that for?" Eamon asked.

"The entry fee into Guame—one gold coin each for you, myself and Breona."

Eamon chuckled. "That idea went out a long time ago. There is too much money to be made of the poorer folk within the city walls to discourage them with such things as an entry fee."

"But the fee is returned to a person on leaving the city, is it not?"

"Hmm, maybe that's where it failed. How often do you suppose coins were returned to their owner upon leaving?"

Magnus felt disappointed. Not that he'd given away three gold coins, but that a legacy his father started had failed. "It was meant to be a sign of goodwill, yet not even the knights guarding the gates could be trusted?" *If the knights would not uphold an example of honour then who would?*

"Whoever told you of such a fee has not ventured to these parts for a long time. Was it Ganister?" Eamon asked.

"Did you know Ganister?" Magnus asked in return.

"In a way. Your father—Bonstaph—certainly made a name for himself. If the old regime of the Council of Elders still stood, I'm sure he would be a representative of the Fire Realm by now. How is your father?"

Magnus was surprised at Eamon's knowledge of his father. "He is well," Magnus lied. He was not sure why he did so, but in this unfamiliar city with prying ears and eyes, it seemed wise to keep personal matters to himself.

Eamon seemed to respect Magnus's economy of words and charged forward, leading the way off the main street through the convolution of by-alleys. They weaved around the dizzying arrangement of stalls, taverns and markets that were jammed between the more permanent stone buildings of the city. Every plot of real estate was accounted for and people were everywhere, crowding the narrow streets and bustling for position at the merchants of their choice to get the bargains they came for. Eamon conversed with several of the merchants as they went. He exchanged sly winks, handshakes and in one case, a payment of coin. Soon Magnus and Eamon traversed their way back to the main street that ran from the front gates to the cathedral.

"Do you see how the street sinks deep into the ground at the centre?" Eamon asked. Magnus followed the arrow-straight street and indeed noticed how its surface was uneven, with a channel worn into the stones along its central axis. "It's from the heavy footsteps of dragons."

Magnus tried to picture a large dragon walking up the cobbled street toward the cathedral. "I'd wager the council afforded *them* time to have their say." He pondered this a moment.

Magnus was brought back to reality as they neared the steps of the cathedral. Before him was by far the largest building he had ever seen. The towering spires he had seen from a mile away seemed to ascend to the Gods, and the large central dome—the roof of the Great Hall—reached a similar height. He looked to Eamon, anticipating any last words of advice he may afford him.

"Well, this is it. You made it and I wish you well. I hope the council gives you both audience and empathy for your plight."

Magnus was surprised at his frankness. Of all the advice in all the situations they had been in together, surely Eamon would shine with invaluable words of wisdom at this moment. But all he was offering was a polite farewell. "Are you off then?" Magnus asked, failing to think of better words himself.

"I have business to attend to. No doubt our paths will cross again, if fate sees it fitting."

Eamon's words sounded deliberately distant, but Magnus noticed he was watching the streets around him, looking at some people carefully and avoiding the gaze of others. Knowing Eamon had his own concerns, he bid him farewell.

"Very well. It has been a pleasure and I am indebted to you, Eamon."

"And I to you, Magnus." Eamon smiled and flashed another of his sly winks. He then disappeared across the main street and down one of the narrow alleys.

AUTHORITARIUM

"I mean you no disrespect Breona, but this is the done thing and I don't want us to draw attention." Magnus tied Breona's reins to a hitching post. Breona was not impressed.

"I am no common, thick-witted horse," she protested. Magnus had never seen Breona tied up before and felt as uncomfortable about it as she did. She looked up at the cathedral and Magnus sensed her concern. *"There is a darkness within that place, Magnus."*

"I will return as soon as I can. With any luck, we will gain the help we need to find Mother and Father and return home in the company of knights."

Breona was drawing a lot of attention. Children were oohing and aahing at the sight of her and adults proclaimed, "Is that an Astermeer?" within earshot. Magnus patted Breona and shared his affection for her with his thoughts, before leaving her side to walk up the forty-two steps to the doors of the cathedral, counting as he went. All he carried with him was his sword, strapped once again over his right shoulder.

At the cathedral's entrance, four more knights stood in pairs at either side of two great doors that were finished in dark lacquer with an intricately carved tympanum over the entrance. The carvings depicted the four dragons of the realms. Each dragon carried the unique features of its breed and all four were connected in a symmetrical pattern filling the circle of the tympanum.

As Magnus approached the doors, he expected the guards to intercept him once again, but none did. In fact, the doors opened from within, revealing a young servant, who beckoned him to enter. "Good morning sire, my name is Dermot. May I take your coat?" he asked without looking up to see that Magnus was not, in fact, wearing an overcoat.

"No, thank you."

"Shall I take your sword for you, sire?" he continued politely.

"I'd rather keep it with me, if you don't mind," Magnus found himself deepening his voice, as though trying to sound formal and important. He cursed himself for sounding ridiculous.

"I'm sorry, sire. No weapons allowed in the cathedral." Dermot extended his arms to accept Magnus's sword. Reluctantly, Magnus obliged. "It will be kept safe in the armoury, sire, just ask for it as you leave."

"Thank you." Magnus felt uneasy without it, but appreciated he could hardly walk through to the great hall carrying a sword.

Following Dermot down a long corridor, he looked in fascination at the coloured marble floors and the tall, vaulted ceiling that finished in an arch at its peak. After several hundred feet, the corridor opened into a large hall. It was empty except for a large hardwood table off to one side and a collection of velour and leather covered chairs neatly lined up along the far wall. They walked across the hall and continued down another corridor that mirrored the first. As they walked the only sound was the echo of their footsteps striking the hard floor beneath them.

Magnus was beginning to think the two of them were the only people in the entire cathedral, but as they progressed along the second corridor, he could hear the murmuring sound of voices getting nearer. Half way along they came across two men who sat silently in wooden chairs. The servant stopped next to them.

"Thank you, sire," Dermot said, indicating that Magnus should sit in one of two vacant wooden chairs next to the other two men. Magnus glanced at the men then looked further up the corridor that ended a hundred feet further along. "Please be seated, sire, and someone will come for you directly." Magnus sat. The young servant bowed and turned, swiftly walking back the way he had come.

Magnus remained seated for what seemed like hours. At one point the other two men were summoned to follow another servant further down the corridor where, at its end, they turned off to the right. More time passed and Magnus guessed it to be mid afternoon. He stood and paced a short way along the corridor, stretching his arms behind his back. After a few minutes of pacing a voice called his name.

"Magnus of J'esmagd." The voice was formal. Magnus looked back up the corridor at a tall man with fine features and a closely shaved head of black hair. He wore robes that fell beyond his hands and feet, sewn from white layers of fine silk, embroidered in cream-coloured cotton with twirled patterns that appeared to depict gusts of wind.

An elder of the Air Realm, Magnus supposed.

"Would you come with me please?" the man asked with indifference, then quickly turned and walked away. Magnus ran to catch up. At the end of the corridor they turned to the right as the other men had, and headed down another. A little way along they came to the end of the corridor, where two more knights guarded a set of huge wooden doors.

Magnus's eyes were drawn to the intricate carvings on the dark mahogany doors. He was unable to understand what they meant but the doors were so grand he was sure they led to the Great Hall. "Enter," the man in white said in a formal, expressionless manner. The knights drew the doors open.

The room beyond the doors was dimly lit and it took a moment for his eyes to adjust to the light. What light there was came from two sources—a row of tall candles mounted in single candelabras positioned down the axis of a long, rectangular table, and shards of light that pierced through coloured stained glass windows far overhead within the Dome that formed the elevated ceiling. Magnus knew this was certainly the Great Hall.

Eight men were seated along each side of the table and an elderly man was seated at the head of the table to Magnus's left. The table itself was covered in scrolls and parchments, wine goblets and bowls of fruit. Most of the men appeared to be over fifty years of age. Within the hall there were four more knights, standing back against the four walls of the great room.

Magnus entered and the men at the table turned to look at him but remained seated. Several of them sniggered at the sight of him while most stared incredulously, but one man—fat, with a short white beard and neatly parted hair—shook his head in a dramatic fashion and waved a hand in Magnus's direction. He chuckled in a gargling manner that gave in to a cough.

"Sorry," the fat man said between chuckles. "I have no time for this." He coughed again. "This is a joke—correct?" He drank heavily from his jewel-encrusted goblet then stood, bidding the other men farewell. "I shall return when the light entertainment has finished for the afternoon." He pointed an accusing finger at Magnus as he walked toward the doors.

"Sit down, Frederick," said the elderly man at the end of the table. He pointed to the fat man's seat but said no more. After a moment of huffing, the fat man waddled back around the table and seated himself without further protest.

Magnus stood still, feeling nervous and out of place.

"Be seated." The elderly man pointed to a single vacant chair at the other end of the table to Magnus's right. Magnus walked over to it.

"Here?" Magnus asked politely, swallowing hard. The elderly man nodded once. He had a hollow, solemn look about him. His face was gaunt and his eyes sunk deep into their dark ringed sockets from where they stared out in a tired manner at Magnus. Upon his head he wore a small black felt cap to match his black robes and dark demeanour. Some of the men at the table had begun talking among themselves and so the elderly man waited until the room was completely silent before he spoke.

"You are seated before the council of the Authoritarium." He had a scratchy, controlled voice. "You bring news from the West?" Magnus nodded. "Speak." The old man called abruptly.

"I do." Magnus choked on his words.

"What brings you so far from home?"

The room remained silent and all eyes were on Magnus. During his travels he had not given thought to how he would deliver his message to the Authoritarium. Now that he was here he felt small and insignificant.

"Speak!"

Magnus jumped at the sharp tone of the old man's voice. He took a nervous breath and thought of Ganister's instructions back at the Crescent Woods. *Let them know the Quag have invaded our lands,"* he had said. *"They will mobilise their legions to Realms End."* After coughing into his fist, Magnus spoke.

"I come here with news from the Fire Realm, representing—"

"Yes. We know who sent you," the old man interrupted. "We know whose son you are and we know you speak for Ganister."

"As former knights of Allumbreve and protectors of our lands, they request support from the knights of the Authoritarium."

The elderly man leaned forward over the table. "Your father has no affiliation with the Authoritarium. But tell me, what is it you require the services of our knights for?"

No affiliation? Magnus stared at the old man at the far end of the table, stumped by his counter argument. "The Quag are attacking our lands, killing our people." Magnus looked around the room to the other council members. Most of them looked away when he caught their eyes. None seemed at all surprised by his news. The old man continued to stare at him.

"Carry on."

Magnus did not know what else to say. He wished Ganister were there, for he would know exactly what to do. He licked his lips, trying to replace the moisture that seemed to have left his mouth and taken refuge in the palms of his hands. He decided to elaborate on his previous statement. "The Quag have come with the support of the Corville wyverns, in large numbers. They have spread themselves throughout our realm. The Uydfer Clan are at war, defending their lands. My family and Ganister's have been overrun—our homes destroyed. Many of the good fighting men of our realm are not at their homes to defend them because of their sworn allegiance with the Authoritarium."

"And yet your father has not sworn such allegiance."

The conversation was not going at all as Magnus thought it would. He wondered why the old man seemed repeatedly concerned with his father's allegiance and paid little value to the predicament they were in. He imagined if his father were here the conversation would be far more aggressive than it was. Magnus drew on that thought for inspiration.

"My father was a knight back when they swore to defend our lands and protect the people. He fought those who threatened it. He was a Commander and other knights followed him."

"Your father," shouted the old man, waving an unsteady finger at him, "was asked long ago to swear an oath to the Authoritarium but chose instead to exile himself. And now, years later, he ignores these transgressions yet asks for our support? Has he made a formal appeal for clemency?"

Magnus felt the familiar feeling of anger well up inside him. After all he had been through, after all he had lost, it had all come down to this old man's game of tit for tat. He took a deep breath and decided to get straight to the point. "Will your knights defend our lands from the Quag attack?"

"That will be a matter for the council to decide." The old man turned to his fellow council members. The chit-chatter among them resumed as though Magnus was no longer present. Magnus sat in silence, wondering what else he could have said to help his cause. The talking became louder and Magnus could hear the conversations had nothing to do with the predicament in the Fire Realm.

At the end of his tether, Magnus stood at the table and thumped it with a fist as hard as he could. The table shuddered and several wine goblets toppled over, pouring blood red wine across the scrolls on the table. All the men in the Great Hall turned and looked at him. The knights stepped forward and grasped their swords.

"Council of the Authoritarium, I demand your answer. Will you help my people?" Magnus could feel himself shaking in anger.

The gaunt old man stood at the far end of the table and appeared to be as angry as Magnus. He pointed a finger at him again. "You stand before us as a beggar who demands payment where it has not been earned." The old man moved around the table toward Magnus, never taking his ghostly eyes off him. He stood close to him much as Crugion had the previous night. He grabbed Magnus firmly by the jaw, his long nails sinking into the flesh of his cheeks. "You have much of your father in you." He looked Magnus over, taking in everything about him. "His confidence, his arrogance." He continued to gaze at him, breathing noisily through his nose. Magnus's blood boiled, but he kept his anger in check. The man roughly released Magnus's jaw and addressed the men at the table.

"Councillors. Are any among you sympathetic to the plight of this boy?"

Magnus looked at each of the men, but none were keen to speak. After a pause, one man spoke out. "Perhaps a company could be sent to the West to assess the legitimacy of the claim?"

"Legitimacy?" Magnus said. "By the time you learn I speak the truth there will be no time left to send help."

"Perhaps," the old man said, having calmed down. "Perhaps the lands you speak of no longer belong to your people."

"What do you mean?" asked Magnus.

"Your people are the last realm with a living race of dragons. Yet even they choose to live far from their land of origin, hiding away at the peaks of the Romgnian Mountains." Magnus was unsure of the point he was trying to make. "Perhaps... Perhaps it is time for your people to also move on. Think of the Quag attack as a purging—a new beginning, if you will. It is time for you to move on, Magnus of J'esmagd."

A tear rolled down Magnus's cheek as his emotions spilled. Anger seethed from within him and any willpower that would stop him from choking the old man was gone. And so he did. Magnus grabbed him by the throat and choked him with all his strength. The knights fell upon Magnus and tried to peel his unrelenting grip free of the old man's neck without success. With every passing moment, Magnus's grip strengthened and he watched as the old man turned a satisfying shade of blue. Then Magnus felt a hard blow across the back, knocking the wind from his lungs. Another blow came to his legs making him fall and loosen his grip. The knights pulled the old man free and Magnus was struck a third time across his face with a fist of armour, sending him sprawling across the table, only to be dragged off it again and held firmly by two of the knights.

Magnus stared at the old man through the blood dripping down his face. He was seated again, doubled over coughing and wheezing, struggling to get his breath back. Colour started to return to his face and he sat up staring at Magnus. His eyes were now bloodshot and his face badly swollen, making his expression all the more frightening.

Struggling to his feet again, the old man turned to one of the knights. "Your sword, give me your sword!" he coughed. Hesitating at first, the knight drew his longsword and handed it to the old man. "Put him on his knees," he shouted. Magnus's legs were kicked out from beneath him and he was pushed down to his knees. His arms were wrenched behind his back until his shoulders felt as if they were being torn from their sockets. Magnus winced from the pain, made worse as one of the guards placed a foot on his back, pushing his torso forward.

"I have your answer now, boy. I will send your head in a bag of pig manure to your father. It will come with a message." The old man leaned over Magnus and spat at him. "The message will declare your head *fit payment* for his years in the knighthood and he will understand his son's death is of his own doing."

Magnus felt the cold steel of the blade rest upon his neck. He closed his eyes, shaking with fear, and waited for the inevitable. In a brief moment, he thought of the broken promise he made to Lucas, for he would not return for him as he said he would. He thought of Catanya, who promised him they would be together again. *How can it end this way?* He held his breath and waited for the end. But then Magnus heard a familiar voice speak from the far end of the room.

"Your message would be for nothing, Trager. His father is not there."

Magnus turned his head to the source of the voice only to be kicked in the ribs and pushed down again.

"What?" the old man questioned. Magnus felt the blade lift from his neck.

"His father has been captured… and his mother for that matter. Not four days ago by my men."

Magnus was dragged back up to his feet where he could see the source of the familiar voice. It was Crugion, standing with Briet and two other Quagmen.

"Is that so?" the old man named Trager asked.

"Yes, they're alive—for the time being," Crugion looked at Magnus. "They've been taken south with many other slaves. Soon they'll arrive at the coast, where I am sure my father holds a special role for Bonstaph within the walls of Ba'rrat. It is here they will be weighed and measured."

Trager let the sword drop to the ground and walked around the table to Crugion. "Why, pray tell, have you kept them alive? That man caused me more trouble than all the other knights under the old regime together.

Bonstaph—curse him! That sanctimonious bastard nearly caused an uprising against the council when he refused to swear his allegiance."

Crugion held a scowl on his face as he turned from Magnus to Trager. "My father has requested Bonstaph himself. Does your addled memory not serve you well enough to remember why?"

Trager stared at Crugion much as he had at Magnus. He ran his tongue across his lips as he thought. "Ah yes... of course... *he killed your brother.*"

Crugion stared once again at Magnus. Magnus did not know what to think. *Ganister said they would be looking for me—because I was Bonstaph's son—and this is why!* He imagined his parents in the hands of Delvion waiting for vengeance to be dealt.

"Boron was his name," Trager remembered. "After his death your legions retreated."

"My father was driven mad by Boron's death."

"Your father was mad long before that," Magnus contributed. Both Crugion and Trager looked at him. Crugion's face darkened.

"Then there's the matter of the mother—Bonstaph's wife," Trager said. "Are you aware of her heritage?"

"I can't say that I am," Crugion answered in a condescending manner.

"She is of the Ice Realm... of the Rhydermere. If her blood is spilt on your account, you will bring the wrath of the Rhyders of the North. You know full well how they dispense vengeance."

Crugion pointed a gloved finger at Magnus who was struggling to comprehend the layers of deception and scheming that pre-empted the attack on his family. "I see you speak half truths, *Rhyderman.*" He turned back to Trager. "Leave the boy with me."

"Why would I do that?" Trager insisted.

"With father and son in my keep, what would I *not* be able to get either to do?"

"Very well," Trager turned to Magnus. "You get to keep your head, boy. But I trust before the end you will wish I had cut it off."

The knights holding Magnus dragged him around toward the large doors of the Great Hall. The doors opened and Magnus struggled as best he could to free himself. He slipped one hand free and used it to punch one of the knights in the face. Both his arms were then gripped by the strongest of holds. It was one of the Quagman. Briet appeared in front of him, baring new scars upon his face. Magnus guessed it was from Eamon's fire dust. Briet drew one of his black swords and spun it so that its pommel faced forward and drove it into Magnus's forehead. Magnus felt immediate, blinding pain that stole his vision moments before he collapsed, unconscious on the floor of the Great Hall.

TRAINING

The aroma of scented oils permeated through the room and into Catanya's dreams. She breathed of it deeply, dreaming she was at home in the Uydferlands, walking through the barley fields and feeling the warmth of the summer sun on her face. Through its burning brilliance, Catanya squinted— something was soaring toward her.

"Catanya!" a voice called. The creature shielded the sun and she could see it was Balgur. *"Catanya!"* the voice called again. It was familiar and made her heart race. Balgur turned and Catanya could see he was carrying a rider. It was Magnus.

"Magnus!" Catanya shouted, reaching out for him. She gasped from the pain that seared through her body, waking her. She slumped back against the hard bed and groaned. The sound echoed back to her.

"Rest." A woman's voice came from behind her.

Catanya opened her eyes and looked around the unfamiliar room. The walls and ceiling were crafted of perfect white stone, each meticulously placed alongside the next. Small crevices in the stonework held candles that gave the room a mellow glow. She was in the middle of the room lying upon a white marble table draped with white cloth. Catanya sighed as the blissful dream faded from her mind.

"What is this place?" Catanya asked with a raspy voice. She arched her head back and saw a priest hidden beneath hooded robes at the head of the table.

"Be still." The priest moved towards her, standing over Catanya, where she placed her palms on her head and tilting it forward. She then moved to Catanya's side, drawing her hood back. Catanya studied her. She was taller and had fairer skin than Catanya. Her facial features were fine with dark, cat-like eyes. Her nose was long and thin and led her chiselled face down to a pointy chin. Her appearance was striking and she had a very controlled, serious demeanour about her. Her jet-black hair was pulled neatly back across the right side of her head where it was tied into a tight plait that flowed down her back then up and over her left shoulder. The left side of her head was shaven and covered in the markings all priests seemed to have.

"Your body has purged and now it rebuilds," the priest said. Looking down, Catanya saw that her body was entirely wrapped in white cloths that were soaked in oils. The priest leaned over her and wrapped an additional cloth around her right ankle. Catanya winced from the pain.

"The pain will pass. You have many wounds from your cleansing. But you heal well. Balgur smiles upon you." Catanya looked at the woman for further explanation. "You carried Balgur's talon beyond your cleansing. You accepted his strength. Balgur smiles upon you now. That is why you heal well."

Catanya closed her eyes for a moment. They hurt as much as the rest of her body. "What exactly have I *purged?*"

"All the rubbish," the priest tapped Catanya's forehead, "up here."

Catanya frowned and thought about the answer for a moment. "What then replaces it?"

"That is for you to discover. Your training will help with that." The priest took a palm-sized bowl from a small table behind her. She supported Catanya's head, bringing the bowl to her lips. Catanya was ravenous and the sweet, warm nectar surged down her throat and into her stomach making her body shake with vigour. She gulped at the bowl but too soon the priest took it away. "A little at a time."

Grateful for the food, Catanya's spirits lifted. "Thank you. What is your name?"

"Jael."

"Thank you, Jael," Catanya said. She wanted to know more about Jael but decided instead to respect her instruction to rest.

When Catanya next woke, she felt somewhat better. The stabbing pain of her wounds had lessened to dull aches. Sitting up on her bed, she swung her legs around and carefully lowered her feet, shivering as they touched the cold stone floor. Looking herself over she saw Jael had removed the cloths and replaced them with a silk robe draped over the front of her body. Catanya took the robe and wrapped it around herself, feeling how smooth her skin had become from the scented oils that helped with her healing.

How long have I been here? she wondered. On the small white table beside her bed were three single white candles—now the only light illuminating the otherwise dark room. On the table was a bowl of the sweet syrup she had tasted earlier. She took the bowl and drank of it slowly this time, savouring the intriguing flavours of honey, ginger, camomile and other more spicy extracts she could not recognise. Catanya replaced the empty bowl and noticed a small piece of folded paper beside it. She opened it, reading the single word written on it. "*Fleatermara*," she said aloud. She considered it for a moment, then recognised it as the Fireisgh word for *righteous*. She realised then Joffren must have left it for her.

Catanya paced around the room, feeling the blood course through her limbs and the pins and needles fade from her feet. She craved for two things at this point—a hot bath and a warm, hearty meal. Neither seemed likely at this stage. Yawning, she pushed her arms high above her head, clasped her hands together and stretched her palms until her knuckles cracked. She bent forward until her head touched her legs and pushed her knees back until they locked, feeling the stiffness in the back of her legs stretch out. Upright again, she twisted her body from side to side, pushing past the tightness in her back until her spine clicked free.

The only other thing in the room was a set of clothes at the end of the bed, neatly folded with a pair of boots sitting on top. Taken as a sign she was to dress when ready, Catanya did so and found herself clothed as the other priests were, in a black hooded robe that folded across her front, around her back and tied off to the side. The boots were made of a mixture of black canvas and leather that ended midway up her lower leg. They had black laces from toe to top and a series of leather straps that buckled across the foot, ankle and shin. She moved around the room and was pleased to find the clothes were comfortable. Catanya repeated her stretches once again then tied her hair back with one of the folded cloth pieces that remained on the small table, grateful to still have her hair. Then she found the door.

Before opening it, she reflected on the words Austagia had told her. *"What do you imagine you cannot do as an Irucantí? ... It is the only way. Some things you cannot run from."*

Catanya squinted in the midday sun. Her eyes soon adjusted and she looked back and saw that the door through which she had just exited was a small auxiliary door at the eastern side of the shining black temple. There were several other doors evenly spaced along the smooth wall. Catanya looked up, following the wall of the temple that vaulted ever upward and ended just below a thin wisp of cloud that moved swiftly across the perfect blue sky.

She followed a pebbled path that led to the front of the temple. Here she saw Joffren sitting cross-legged on stone steps leading down to the common. His eyes were closed and he remained still. Not wanting to disturb him, Catanya sat silently on a step a small distance from him. Assuming it was the appropriate thing to do, she crossed her legs and sat tall, enjoying the stretch through her muscles yet again. She felt the sluggishness in her movement and wondered once again how long she had been asleep in the temple.

After a moment, Joffren stood and walked over to Catanya. She too stood and looked to him.

"Hello, Joffren," Catanya said. Joffren stared at her without responding. "Semsdi," she nodded, using the formal address.

"Semsarian," Joffren replied. "Are you well?"

Catanya did not answer, wary that Joffren might have another terrible episode waiting for her. Joffren seemed to sense her trepidation.

"You're cleansing period is over. Come." Joffren led the way down the stairs, away from the temple. Catanya looked back toward the black temple doors. She tried to see inside the sacred building but saw only darkness. They walked across the wide common leading to various smaller buildings arranged neatly around the Romghold. Catanya peered to her right toward the training field where she had completed her cleansing. A chill ran down her back and she turned away.

"Jael tells me you have healed exceptionally well."

"I feel well," Catanya said, trying not to sound too self-assured. Joffren broke into a jog and she followed him.

"Semsarian, what have you gained from the cleansing?"

Catanya picked up her pace to remain beside the long-legged man. They kept jogging as Joffren waited for Catanya to answer his question. She pondered it a moment, recalling what Jael had said about her purging the rubbish from her mind.

"Be quick to answer Semsarian—what have you gained?"

"A clear mind," Catanya said, hoping it would satisfy Joffren.

Joffren considered Catanya's answer a good while before responding, "Very well." He increased his speed, turning sharply to his right between two buildings then left again down a narrow path. Catanya kept close beside him. Then Joffren broke into a sprint, running past the last of the buildings toward the eastern border of the Romghold where a steep mountain ascended like a wall to the sky. They reached the mountain face and stopped. Joffren stood at ease, placing his arms behind his back, showing no evidence at all of strain from the run. Catanya faced him, mirroring his position, trying to play down her breathlessness and the countless aches in her body.

"Now that your mind is clear, find your purpose. One that is greater than your self," Joffren explained. "Your calling as a priest is your vocation, but your reason for doing so is your own. Remember this. It will help you on your path to righteousness."

Catanya nodded in acknowledgement. She looked up at him, staring into his blue eyes and whispered back to him, "*Fleatermara...* thank you for your note, Semsdi."

Joffren looked back to her and nodded once.

A voice called out, interrupting their conversation. Catanya turned to see Jael running toward them from the direction they had come. She was coming fast—unnaturally fast to Catanya's eyes. She looked tall and poised and barely touching the ground. Her demeanour was fierce and she looked nothing at all like she did when Catanya saw her in the healing room. She was dressed as a warrior. Her shoulders, chest and legs were covered in polished armour of a dark, ruddy hue that clung taut to her lithe body.

"An Irucantî warrior..." Catanya said to herself.

"A *Ferustir*—if you will," Joffren corrected.

Jael pulled alongside Catanya and Joffren. "Semsame, Semsarian." she said, nodding to Joffren then Catanya respectively. "I travel west having been set to task and..." She paused looking at Catanya.

"You may break word with both of us, Semsame," Joffren assured her.

"I bring grave news. There is a wayward dragon youngling who has wandered into dangerous lands."

"That is indeed grave news," Joffren said with concern on his face.

"The High Priests have given me task to bring him back into the fold." Jael tightened a leather buckle across her chest that held some kind of weapon strapped to her back, together with a quiver of arrows and a bow. Catanya studied her, admiring her finely crafted suit. She pulled her shoulders back and drew her stomach in—emulating Jael's posture.

"Have you any knowledge of the youngling's whereabouts?" Joffren asked.

"The ΘhUid folk have seen him within Froughton Forest. He was last seen deep in the eastern arm of the Valley of Shadows," Jael sighed.

Joffren considered Catanya for a moment before addressing Jael again, "Let us accompany you as far as the Domult Lookout."

"Thank you, but I travel with urgency—"

"I will not hold you back," Catanya interrupted. "But if I do, go on without me."

Jael looked to Joffren.

"Agreed?" he said.

"Agreed," Jael conceded. She broke into a run along the base of the mountain with Joffren and Catanya hot on her heels. Catanya was excited and at the same time confused. She was happy to be part of something but still unsure of her commitment to her role as Semsarian.

Joffren glanced back to her. "So it is, then, your training begins."

After running several hundred yards, Jael vanished through a small crevice within the mountain face, closely followed by Joffren. Catanya ran hard and fast, determined to keep up with them. The crevice was narrow and the rock face either side went straight up as though the mountain here had split in two to allow them passage. It was close to a mile before they emerged at the far side of the mountain and turned a sharp left. Making the turn, Catanya caught her breath. To her right was a cliff face that dropped for miles below. She ran hard and fast along the narrow goat track, keeping her left shoulder brushing against the mountain face as assurance. She dared not look down over the cliff yet the view out beyond to the east was astounding. Catanya saw an eagle soaring high on the thermals where the mountain ranges ended giving way to the Neverseas beyond—an endless spread of blue that sparkled under a perfectly blue sky.

The run continued and Jael never let up. She would jump or somersault over any object in her path. Joffren mirrored each of Jael's movements and clearly had the fitness to match even though, Catanya supposed, he was twice Jael's age. The ground widened out to the right and Catanya was able to relax a little, realising she had kept her whole body tense as she ran along the cliff face. She took a few deeper breaths and re-routed all her energy into running.

Is this all they do—run?

Jael then released a loud wolf whistle. She repeated it several times in a pattern of four sharp sounds. Joffren copied the call himself and the two of them ran faster still down the path that seemed to go nowhere. Catanya looked ahead where the path ended at a drop-off.

We are running to a dead end! Catanya realised. Still, they kept up their pace while Jael and Joffren persisted with their sharp, four-note whistle.

"Where to now?" Catanya shouted at them both.

"Jump," Joffren called back.

"Semsdi? What did you say?" Catanya shouted back, confused. There was nowhere to go. Then the unexpected happened.

Jael reached the path's end and leapt off into the air with arms spread wide as though she intended to fly. Close behind, Joffren did the same. Catanya dug the heels of her boots into the dirt beneath her, sliding to a halt right at the cliff face. She watched in horror as the two priests plummeted through the sky toward the ground, miles beneath them.

"No way…" Catanya exclaimed.

With a sudden gust of wind followed by bellowing roars that tore at Catanya's ears, two enormous fire dragons came spiralling down from the mountaintop and dove down beneath Jael and Joffren. The dragons matched the speed of the falling priests allowing them to land gracefully upon their backs. Catanya watched in awe at the cliff face.

Next came a ground shaking thump directly behind her. A third dragon had landed and stood next to Catanya, looking at her, snorting loudly. It lowered itself and arched its head toward the saddle at the base of its neck.

"Okay," Catanya said. Not wanting to show any more weakness, she jumped up on the dragon's back, positioned herself in the saddle with her feet in the stirrups and pulled the straps tightly against her shins. She grabbed hold of the large, leather saddle horn just before the dragon leaped off the cliff. Gripping with all her strength, she squealed as the dragon tucked its wings in and fell into a spiral.

The dragon dropped straight down, picking up speed so fast that all Catanya could think was—*do not let go!* Soon, they caught up with the other two dragons and Catanya's dragon unfurled its wings slightly to reduce its speed until all three flew in formation, one behind the other with Jael leading.

Catanya sealed her lips tight, trying to hold a scream of excitement mixed with terror at bay. The three fire dragons were massive—much larger than Rubea—and in the cloudless sky their bronze scales sparkled brilliantly. Their dancing reflections shimmered against the rock face as they sped down the mountainside. Jael's dragon let out a guttural roar. The other two dragons followed suit. Catanya could feel the roar of her dragon vibrating through its body and her own. The sound loosened rocks on the cliffs and sent them tumbling down the mountainside.

For the first time, Catanya felt privileged to be a part of the priesthood and vowed to see her training through.

"Then next time, jump!" the deep, cavernous voice of her dragon replied in her mind.

Catanya grinned. *"I promise… next time I'll jump."*

The three dragons reached the northern side of the Romgnian mountain range and Catanya saw a break in the cliff face, out of which a flat bed of stone protruded. The dragons all swung wide, extending their wings, and landed one at a time on the platform.

Jael, Joffren and then Catanya alighted from their dragons. Catanya watched as Jael and Joffren walked to the front of their dragons, bowed and touched their foreheads against their dragons' noses. It was a gentle, intimate moment. The dragons closed their eyes and seemed to purr much as a cat would. Still shaking and breathing heavily from excitement, Catanya walked to face her dragon. It lowered its head to meet Catanya's and its eyes changed colour as Rubea's had done—settling on a brown colour just like her own. She placed the palms of both hands on its large nose, feeling the bristly texture of the tiny scales that formed its reptilian cone shape. Each nostril was a foot long teardrop that blew warm air across Catanya's body. She bowed forward, placing her forehead on its nose and closed her eyes.

From the moment they touched, Catanya felt warmth flow through her body. A flood of thoughts and emotions followed as she and the dragon formed a bond with one another. Catanya was hesitant to allow this creature to know about her hopes, dreams and fears but the dragon was embracing them without judgement and eager to share his own. She learned that his name was Brue and he was over two hundred years old. His favourite food was deer and those from the western borders of Allumbreve proved the most tender and therefore most to his liking. He liked the scent of Catanya's hair and noted it carried the aroma of jasmine. Catanya thanked Brue for his kind words and complimented him on his impressively long tail. She told Brue she hoped she could travel with him to the western border to hunt deer some time and thanked him for allowing her to ride him.

Catanya had disappeared into a strange, intimate world with the dragon when she felt a hand on her shoulder. She bid Brue farewell and lifted her head, turning to face Joffren.

"You've made a friend," Joffren said, releasing her shoulder. Catanya blushed and looked to the ground as Brue swung his tail around and admired it. Catanya stepped back and turned away, embarrassed at being seen in such an intimate moment.

"You should be pleased, Semsarian. In time you will get to know all the dragons of the realm, as will they know you," Joffren said. "You will of course have some thoughts you wish to keep to yourself. In time you will learn discretion as it suits you."

"Thank you, Semsdi." Catanya saw that Jael was standing at the precipice of the platform looking off toward the west.

"This is the Domult Lookout," Jael said without turning. "It gives a good vantage point down to the Traas River that flows from Froughton Forest." She pointed down, over the cliff. Catanya came forward and looked down to a wide river below that flowed from west to east and disappeared into the Romgnian Mountain ranges. From the lookout, Catanya could appreciate the vastness of Froughton Forest. For as far west as she looked, she could see nothing but tall trees that extended to the horizon, many miles away.

"Where do you start looking for the dragon youngling?" Catanya asked, wishing she could go with her.

Joffren joined them, appearing keen to hear Jael's response.

"We will follow the river upstream into Froughton," Jael said. "Then I'll go alone on foot through to the Valley of Shadows and into The Core. I will speak with the ƟhUid people and from here, pick up the youngling's trail. Two or three days and I should find him."

"The Core?" Catanya asked.

"The very centre of Froughton Forest," Joffren said. "The stronghold of the ƟhUid clan—the last people of the Earth Realm."

Catanya knew nothing of Froughton other than it was a place to be feared and avoided. She certainly knew nothing of people residing within its dark depths.

"There are many secrets within the realms, Semsarian," Joffren explained. "You are now privileged to know about the ƟhUid clan. It is the discretion of such knowledge that has assured their survival."

"I understand," Catanya said.

Jael reached over her shoulder and pulled a strange, two-foot long bronze shaft from its scabbard. Catanya had never seen anything like it before. Along the shaft were intricate carvings of exquisite detail that she recognised as Fireisgh insignia. The object blazingly expressed itself as an instrument of the Fire Realm.

"It is a *Ferustir's* lance," Jael said, seeing Catanya watching her inquiringly. She gripped the weapon tightly in her right hand and the engravings illuminated brightly in a brilliant amber that glowed through her fingers. The ends of the shaft shot out violently in length with a loud cracking sound to become a five-foot long double-ended weapon with razor sharp tips as formidable as any dragon talon. She spun the lance around with precision before the blades sank violently back into their handle, extinguishing their amber glow. Replacing the lance in its scabbard, Jael pulled a dozen arrows from their quiver and groomed the fletching of each one between two fingers, carefully removing any stray feathers with her teeth before placing them one at a time back into their quiver. Catanya was entranced by Jael's demonstration.

"Ready?" Joffren asked.

"Ready," Jael answered. She replaced her weapons and tightened the buckle again. She and Joffren embraced one another's forearm and said their farewells. Jael turned to Catanya and offered her arm in the same manner. Catanya embraced her in the same way.

"In my absence, train hard, Semsarian." Jael held a serious expression.

"Yes, Semsame," Catanya replied.

Jael mounted her dragon and strapped her legs into the stirrups. The dragon squatted and tensed its large hind legs before thrusting up and over the cliff face. It soared down the mountainside toward the Traas River below. Soon, Jael and the dragon had ventured out of Catanya's sight.

Catanya turned to Joffren for instruction. He was already seated on his dragon who arched his head back and released a long stream of fire from his open mouth that leapt out across the mountain sky and stretched on for close to half a mile. Satisfied, the dragon closed its wide maw with a snap and blew the last remnants of flame out of his nostrils. Catanya's legs went weak with shock. It was the most powerful expression of strength she had ever witnessed and yet it came so effortlessly from the creature. She was overcome with emotion, yet was not sure why. A tear rolled down her cheek as she tried to come to terms with the ferocity of this beast beside her.

"Come, Semsarian. Let us return to the Romghold!" Joffren shouted as his dragon leapt off the stone platform and started his ascent up the mountain. Catanya regained her composure and looked at Brue.

"Don't you do that, please," she pleaded and climbed into her dragon's saddle once again.

DECEPTIONS

Magnus sat in a prison carriage, pulled by two huge black horses. His hands and feet were bound together with thick rope that gnawed at his flesh. The carriage was open to the elements with steel bars forming the walls and roof, bolted through the floor. There was a horrid stink that festered inside. Magnus figured it was likely from one of the other prisoners who sat or lay beside him. He looked to the old, wooden floor. It was blood stained, some of it old and brown, and some of it crimson—evidently recent. His bleeding forehead contributed to the stains and pounded with pain. He could feel that several of his ribs were cracked, too, all thanks to the altercation in the Great Hall. He thought of how he could have played his part better in negotiations, but knew in truth, from the moment he stepped foot into the Great Hall, his fate was sealed. Neither Crugion nor Trager would have had it any other way.

He wondered why Ganister sent him to the Great Hall like a lamb to the wolves. *He knew of Father's history with the Authoritarium.* Magnus had no idea his father had caused them so much trouble. Then again, Ganister had no idea the Authoritarium had dealings with the Quag, or that they were indifferent to his lands being overrun. *At least,* Magnus conceded, *I may yet see my parents again in Ba'rrat.*

"Your travelling companion is quite a character."

Magnus turned to the voice and saw Crugion riding alongside the prison carriage that was now beyond the city walls.

"His story of you being a Rhyderman proved true. Well… a *half breed* Rhyderman perhaps… if ever there was such a thing." Crugion was smug. "Whatever you are, you have found yourself a trickster for a friend in that old man."

"He's a good man," Magnus mumbled, scratching at the ropes binding his ankles.

"Is that so?" Crugion laughed out loud. "I remarked to him just before how impressive your thoroughbred Astermeer was, for I could not catch the two of you on my steed—a purpose-bred warhorse himself. Before I knew it, your friend was bargaining with me to make purchase of her." He laughed again. "I intended to kill the man and he has the audacity to try and sell me your horse!" Crugion frowned. "Alas, the old man has many friends in Guame and of a braver sort than the folk in Hugmdael. Trager too, it seems, is not fond of violence within the city walls. We agreed to set hostilities aside."

"What is your point?" Magnus asked, tired of his gloating voice.

"An agreement was struck. You friend escapes with his life and I have a prize Astermeer in my keeping."

"You are lying." Magnus scowled. He turned away, trying to appear disinterested.

"See for yourself." Crugion looked over his shoulder. Magnus turned back and followed his gaze. At the rear of the carriage he saw Breona walking with a Quagmen riding either side of her. One of them was Briet. They each held a steel pole welded to a clasp locked around Breona's neck. Her hide was blood stained and scarred as though from a whip. Magnus's heart sank and, as he was becoming accustomed, it quickly manifested into anger.

"Leave her be and set her free. You have no quarrel with her,' Magnus pleaded between gritted teeth.

Crugion grabbed a steel rail of the prison carriage, pulling himself closer to Magnus. "I have no quarrel you say? I have quarrel with *all* of Allumbreve. And all shall fall to their knees before my people soon enough."

"I will kill you long before then, Crugion!" Magnus shouted.

"One thing is for certain, Magnus of J'esmagd, I find you very entertaining." Crugion's men laughed at the comment. "But this I promise you—you *will* have your chance. With my father's blessing, we shall fight one another in Ba'rrat's arena where the finest of our Quag warriors prove themselves against less fortunate scum like you. And your parents shall bear witness to your death. A fit form of revenge for my brother."

"You will die by my sword in front of your father come that day," Magnus shot back.

"By your sword? Do you mean this one?" Crugion drew Magnus's sword from the pack on his saddle and examined it. "A Rhyder sword of fleu-steel. You do have exquisite taste, I'll grant you that. I'll make you a deal. You arrive at Ba'rrat alive to be presented as a prize to my father and I shall return it to you for our meeting in the arena."

Magnus looked away from Crugion and back toward Breona. He tried to feel her emotions but just as he touched her consciousness his attention was drawn further back to the walls of Guame and the gates that divided them. He caught a glimpse of Eamon, who moved swiftly behind a group of travellers leaving the city.

Curse you Eamon, Magnus grumbled under his breath. *You led me right into this.*

Magnus slouched down against the side of the carriage, resting his throbbing head against the shaking carriage bars. Rubbing his bound and bloodied wrists he was surprised to feel Catanya's bracelet still attached. With everything he had been through, he felt pleased that her enchantment had held true and protected it from damage.

Within the carriage were three other prisoners. One was an old man dressed in rags who mumbled incoherently as he gazed off into the distance. Going by his state of cleanliness, Magnus picked him as the source of the dreadful smell. Another was a robust woman with frizzy brown hair. Fast asleep on the bloodied floor, she smelled of the wine spilled over her filthy dress. Finally, there was a middle-aged man with a short beard and bald head. He was looking at Magnus. Magnus turned away from him, not wanting to elicit conversation nor trouble. The man however, persisted with his gaze.

"In a spot of trouble are you?" the man said quietly. Magnus ignored him. He let his thoughts stray from his predicament for he knew there was nothing he could do to rectify it at this point. Instead, he thought of Lucas and wondered how he was faring with his recovery.

As time wore on the carriage moved further along the Northern Road, back the way Magnus had come that morning. He continued to think of Lucas. He pictured him healthy and smiling as he was before all this trouble began and wished they were back in the Crescent Woods hunting rabbits or scaling the cliffs of the western coast. They were always able to get themselves in and out of dilemmas they never thought they would get away with. The thought sparked enthusiasm in Magnus. He imagined he and Lucas were in the prison carriage together, figuring out a way to escape. *There is no way Lucas and I wouldn't be able to escape from something as simple as an old prison carriage.* Magnus imagined the conversation he and Lucas would have—

"Okay Lucas, there are four Quagmen on horseback… and Crugion makes five. This carriage is being towed by two more horses… and then there's Breona—we need to free her and ride her once we have escaped."

"Is that it?" Lucas responded. *"We could do that blindfolded!"*

"Well, our hands and feet are tied, so that makes it interesting," Magnus thought in response.

"Interesting, but not all that much harder, Magnus! So who else is in here with us? Anyone who could help?"

"There's a crazy old man, a drunk woman and another man watching us." Magnus cast a cautious glance at the bald man, who now seemed to be studying the floorboards of the carriage.

"Excellent. He'll be of help then. What about Breona… are those shackles really going to keep her from going free?"

"Not for long I imagine. At least, not once she knows we have a plan to break free."

Magnus cast another quick glance at the bald man, then to Breona who was staring right at him. He knew the answer to escaping rested with these two. Breona breaking free of her shackles would create a distraction and he just needed to enlist the support of the bald man. Magnus searched for Crugion and saw he was now leading the carriage. *Good.* He extended his thoughts to Breona but in return he received a muddled selection of mixed emotions ranging from fear to despondence. He needed her to understand he was working on getting them out of this predicament.

"You've got something brewing in that head of yours?" the bald man asked quietly without turning to face him.

"Aye," Magnus replied in the same manner. "I need to convince my horse back there to break free."

"I can be of help," the man said.

"Aye, it will take us both to break out of this carriage," Magnus confided.

"You are Magnus of J'esmagd. I heard the man say so. I knew your father. He is a good man. My name is Barron. I am a resident of Guame."

Magnus gave Barron an affirmative nod. Barron continued to study the floor of the carriage.

"You've an idea yourself?" Magnus asked. Barron shuffled a little closer to Magnus and looked to the other two prisoners, who seemed content in their states of incoherence.

"The floor is rotten through. One good blow, maybe two and it'll give way for sure." Barron looked away from Magnus as one of the Quagmen rode to the back of the carriage. Once at the rear, he relieved Briet who took his place at the front with Crugion.

Magnus lifted his legs and let his heels land firmly on one of the central boards of the floor. Sure enough, it gave way a little.

"Termites," Barron whispered. "The five middle planks and possibly under the old man. Your side seems intact."

"Are you a builder?" Magnus asked.

"Blacksmith. I have built the frames for many of these carriages. And I built the collar around your horse's neck. I can have her free of that in a moment." Magnus nodded in acknowledgement. "Best we wait till dark," Barron suggested.

"Very well. My horse can carry us both. They won't be able to catch us."

"Much appreciated," Barron said, then moved away from Magnus and continued to peer out into the afternoon sky.

As the last of the day's rays faded, the prison carriage turned off the Northern Road and into Froughton Forest. They were further east from where Magnus had left the forest two days prior, so their journey through it was set to be longer than before.

For several hours now, Magnus had been working his way through the tangled labyrinth of emotions that crippled Breona. He knew she must have gone through a terrible ordeal at the hands of the Quagmen to be broken to the point where she was not breaking herself free of her shackles. She was far stronger than any common horse the shackles were designed for, and yet, for the first time ever, she had yielded to the will of others. Magnus needed her to reclaim her resolve.

Finally, he had her attention, but even more than that, he had her focus. She set aside her feelings and listened to Magnus.

"What are you, Breona?" Magnus began.

"I am an Astermeer of the Ice Realm."

"From where does your bloodline come?"

"From the Ice Seas of the North and from the Ertwe Dragons of the seas."

"To whom are you sworn?"

"Beautiful Alavia—Rhyder of the Ice Realm, daughter of Hasledom."

Magnus could feel her sense of dignity returning to her. He continued, *"Do you still trust me, as Alavia's son?"*

"I do."

"And together, what is our task?"

"To find her and to protect her."

Magnus felt Breona's new sense of determination. He looked back to her again in the fading light of dusk and her demeanour had changed. She foamed at the mouth and the muscles of her shoulders and neck were flexed with anticipation. At any moment she could cause mayhem.

"What in all of Allumbreve is going on here? What damnation has me locked in this pig-squalor with these prisoners? I demand an explanation!"

The drunken woman had woken and was standing up, stumbling about the carriage. Her legs were tied but the ropes had worked their way loose.

"Shut your mouth you senseless beast!" one of the Quagmen from the rear shouted at her.

"Don't you tell me to shut up, you son of a rodent, I've seen men of better stature wearing nappies and feeding off their mother's bosom!"

Magnus could see things were going to dissolve into violence. They had to put their plan into action immediately. He looked to Barron who shuffled over to Magnus. He had freed himself of his ropes and started to feverishly untie Magnus's wrist and ankle ropes.

"At least she provides distraction enough for me to free you," Barron said.

His rope ties removed, Magnus looked Barron in the eyes. "You take care of the floor boards, I'll ask Breona to break free."

"Come here you Quag filth!" The drunken woman shook at the bars of the carriage and stomped her feet. The rotten floorboards creaked and cracked beneath her. One of the Quagmen from the front of the procession rode back level with the sides of the carriage. Magnus cursed under his breath.

"Lady, you are drunk and your words are painful to my ears." This time it was Barron. "Now!" he grunted to Magnus. The woman turned and stumbled toward Barron.

Magnus concentrated on feeding his thoughts to Breona. *'It's time for us to leave. Breona, break free of your shackles. You are an Astermeer from the Ice Realm, you are not meant to bow to anyone. Especially those who also hold Alavia captive!'*

Magnus shifted to avoid Barron and the woman who were locked in a standing wrestle. *'NOW Breona. Free yourself!'*

Magnus looked at the woman, who swung a punch and caught him clean in the jaw, knocking him off balance and onto the bloody floor. He stood again quickly and caught a glimpse of the old man who had started to shout incoherently.

"Breona!" Magnus shouted out loud. Finally she reacted. She reared up, pulling a Quagmen from his horse and sending him falling to the ground. He let go of the pole. Free now on her right, Breona charged to her left and barrelled into the horse on that side, sending it tumbling and taking the other Quagman with it.

The carriage suddenly pulled to stop. Seizing the moment, Barron grunted loudly and pushed the drunken woman forward. Magnus extended his legs behind her, causing her to trip and fall backward. She fell hard and all the more so for having Barron on top of her. She landed squarely in the middle of the rotten floorboards, crashing straight through to the ground beneath, cushioning Barron's fall. Still on top of her, Barron was quick to reach back into the cart, offering a hand to Magnus who took it and threw himself down through the hole.

The Quagmen at the side of the carriage had shifted away in reaction to Breona's outburst. She was behaving so ferociously even Magnus was concerned. She charged forward, dragging the two poles connected to her neck with her, launching herself from side to side like a raging bull. One of the poles broke free of the collar but she came toward the carriage with the other flailing about to the side.

Magnus and Barron were still under the carriage, using the dark of night for protection. Magnus saw Crugion charge around to their left, holding a lamp in search of trouble. There was a violent shudder as Breona slammed into the back of the carriage. Magnus and Barron ran out to the right side to avoid Crugion and back to Breona, who was still in the throes of fury. Crugion would soon realise Magnus and Barron had escaped. They had to be quick.

"*Breona, stop!*" Magnus cried out with his mind. He reached her and grabbed her by the muzzle, pulling it to his face in the hope she would recognise his familiar scent. Within moments she settled, but her body heaved and shook uncontrollably.

"*Breona, you must carry us both and we must run, like never we have before.*"

Barron was beneath Breona, working the neck shackles free and within seconds, they fell to the ground. He kicked the remaining pole away from under her. Magnus leapt on top of her bare back, cursing the Quagmen for removing her saddle. *Or was it that traitor—Eamon?* Reaching down, Magnus took Barron's hand but as he did, Crugion was upon them. He swung his sword, slicing it across Barron's back making him arch backward in pain. He released Magnus's hand.

Breona took off. She charged forward as fast as she could and without any reins, Magnus leant forward, gripping fists of Breona's mane. He looked back just the once and saw Crugion swing his blade around and drive it down into Barron's back.

"I am so sorry, Barron," Magnus lamented.

Unperturbed by the lack of light, Breona ran. The road through this part of the Outer Rim was wide and Breona took advantage of its worn, smooth surface and charged faster than ever before. Her ears pricked back as if expecting to hear a Quagman's whip snapping at her side. They disappeared into the darkness of Froughton Forest once again and Magnus could hear the fading sounds of the Quagmen shouting curses after him. He knew it did not matter—they could not catch him.

The road through the Outer Rim this close to Guame ran shallow into the forest. To his right Magnus could see occasional lights on the Northern Road less than a hundred feet away. Breona's pace seemed to quicken with every passing moment and never let up. A horn sounded from behind. Again and again the ominous tone rang through the forest. Magnus wondered what it was for, but then Breona spotted something.

"Riders approach from ahead."

At first Magnus could not see anyone, then through the darkness he spotted numerous torchlights approaching from the opposite direction—no doubt answering the call of the horn. They were turning off the Northern road, carving their way through the forest, and would soon intersect them.

"We need to move into the Valley, Breona."

Breona slowed her pace as they tried to find a break in the forest wall wide enough for Breona to fit through. Alas, there was none. The forest here was dense—so dense in fact that beyond the ancient trunks was pure darkness. *Perfect for hiding... If only we could get in.*

A little way ahead, the Quagmen on horseback broke through the forest to the road through the Outer Rim. Magnus was trapped. He looked to his left, desperate to find a break. Breona pulled to a halt then skittered about, unsure which way to run.

"They come from both directions," she stressed.

Magnus became aware of a focussed spot of warmth in his chest. *The Juniper stone!* He prised it out of his jacket pocket and held it firmly in his hand, feeling its warmth radiate through his palm. He looked toward the largest of the oak trees and pitched the stone at its trunk. Just as before, the Juniper stone glowed bright and flew straight through the tree, leaving a trace of violet light shimmering across the tree's surface. Breona needed no encouragement—she ran straight at the tree. They emerged on the far side amongst thick vegetation and pure darkness.

Magnus alighted and crouched beside Breona, pulling her down onto her haunches into the undergrowth of ferns. She was breathing heavily and shaking. Magnus could feel her fear permeating through his mind. He wrapped an arm around her as reassurance. He was not able to see back out to the road and hoped the Quagmen could not see him. Moments later he heard the two groups of horses approaching from opposite directions. With the sound of crackling gravel and hooves slipping across the road, the groups met directly in front of the tree Magnus and Breona had gone through.

"Where did they go?" It sounded like Briet, but Magnus couldn't be sure.

"They must have turned off the road," said another Quagman.

"To where?" the first voice spoke angrily this time. "Where do you think they disappeared to? They rode right past you, you useless sacks of horse—"

"He was *your* prisoner, Briet, ya halfwit. What… you just let him get on his 'orse and ride away?"

The two men were drawn into an altercation with one another, and the sound of a sword being drawn from its scabbard rung through Magnus's ears.

"Hahaha! You wouldn't dare!" shouted the second Quagman. He continued shouting obscenities until Magnus heard the blood-curdling sound of a swishing blade meeting flesh. It was followed by a dull thud.

There was silence among the Quagmen for a moment, then—"Anyone else have words to share?" Briet bellowed. "We must find the boy or Crugion'll have *our* heads. He must've gone into the Valley. Find a break in the trees. It'll be close. There's nowhere else they could have gone."

Magnus heard the horses start to move again, spreading out across the road. He waited in silence with his arm still embracing Breona who was still shaking. The familiar, eerie silence of the forest fell upon him as the Quagmen spread out along the road. Magnus went to push up off the ground when his heart jumped as Briet spoke again, still close on the other side of the tree.

"Can you hear me boy? I know you're there. You think you're smart hiding in the darkness, don't ya boy. Well let me tell ya something… There are worse things than me in the Valley. And I'll tell you something else… I *will* find you. And your horse. And this is what I'll do to you both."

Magnus heard Briet shuffling about. A moment later something rustled in the trees over Magnus's head. He looked up. In the darkness he could see little, but then from between a fork in the tree an object fell, landing with a thud before rolling back and settling right beside Magnus. It was a Quagman's severed head.

Magnus's stomach heaved. He covered his mouth to mask the sound of his own retching. Breona remained still, but her shaking grew worse. Magnus shared thoughts with her. *"Be still Breona, a few more moments and we will be free of this man."*

They waited in the dark for some time and still there was little sound or indication that Briet had moved. Then Magnus heard a horse let out a snort.

"Shhh," Briet whispered.

Magnus froze again. *He's cunning.* He realised he may be playing a waiting game for some time. Minutes passed and a single horse came galloping from the east, pulling up near the tree.

"Crugion wants to speak with you, Briet. He's sent some men back to Guame to find that old man. I reckon he's got a beef with him." Briet grumbled in reply. "Are ya going to keep him waiting?"

"Are *you* going to keep annoying me, Wilfred?"

"Not if I'm gonna end up like this sorry sod," Wilfred laughed.

"Have the men regroup on the Northern Road, and that means your boys too," Briet ordered.

Wilfred... Magnus remembered the name. *He was one of the men trying to find me two days ago in the forest.* It began to seem as though all of Allumbreve was working against him—*Wilfred and his thug friends, the Quag* and *the Authoritarium.*

Magnus heard two horses leave, heading eastward back to Guame. He breathed a sigh of relief but then it dawned on him—*What of the dead man's horse? Where is it?* There seemed to him to be a horse unaccounted for. If Briet sent the dead man's horse with Wilfred as a decoy, then he could still be standing behind the tree in waiting. *"Keep silent Breona, just a while longer,"* he begged of her.

After an infuriating wait, Briet eventually spoke. "Until we meet again— son of Bonstaph." With that, Briet rode back toward Guame.

THE YOUNGLING

It was mid morning the following day when Magnus was awoken from blissful sleep by a sniffing nose and warm breath. Hidden in the Valley with no sense of direction or purpose, sleep seemed like the only thing to do. "Let me sleep, Breona," he mumbled. He resented opening his eyes and having to face the day ahead. But when he did, he found himself staring straight into a pair of large, fiery eyes with thin slits for pupils. It was definitely not Breona.

Magnus leaped back into a cluster of ferns and took in the rest of the creature before him. Its large head shimmered with bronze-coloured scales that grew in size along its serpent like neck and body. The curious creature snorted loudly and blew rings of smoke through its nostrils, slowly moving closer toward Magnus, prodding him with extended claws.

A dragon!

Magnus looked the beast over, trying not to make any sudden movements. Pulling himself free of the ferns, he tried to stand but the dragon pounced on him, pinning him back to the ground with its front paws. It sniffed loudly and licked his face with its rough, forked tongue. Magnus stretched his thoughts toward Breona.

"Where are you, Breona?" An explosion of thoughts came back to him, but it was not from Breona. It was far more direct and raw, and foreign to him. His heart pounding, Magnus looked deep into the dragon's eyes, only inches from his own, and watched as they changed colour. What started as an intense, burning amber changed through a multitude of colours before settling on a blue colour—just like his. *Is it mirroring me?* Magnus wondered.

"Breona?" Magnus called again, but felt no response. The dragon persisted with its sniffing and licking and Magnus guessed it was being inquisitive rather than aggressive—much like an excited puppy. He decided to treat it like one.

"Stop it!"

The dragon paused, drawing its long tongue back into its mouth with a watery snap. It stared at him, tilting its head to one side. Magnus thought it far too small to be an adult dragon. But with its bronze-coloured scales and smoking nostrils it was definitely a fire dragon.

He risked a quick scan of the surrounding forest but Breona was nowhere to be seen. *What a time to wander off… Perhaps the dragon scared her away? But then surely she would have made a scene to warn me first?*

"What have you done with Breona?" Magnus asked the dragon. "Have you eaten her?"

The dragon pushed away from Magnus and sat up, craning its long neck back, revealing an underbelly covered in much larger scales of a paler hue giving the appearance of large plates of armour, two of which formed the width of its breast and about eight or ten from neck to groin. It stood at about eight feet tall—or about the size of the wyvern he had fought trying to protect Lucas.

Magnus felt the abrasiveness of the dragon's thoughts again as it scanned the forest, locking its focus on something in the distance. Then a deep, drumming growl that seemed to start at the pit of its stomach rose up its long neck to its throat, echoing out through the forest. Still lying down, Magnus could feel the ground tremble with the noise. The dragon fell silent again and crept forward, slowly at first, then broke into a run, heading off through the trees and away from Magnus. Its powerful hind legs stomped across ferns and mosses leaving a path of destruction.

A dragon youngling, Magnus decided. *What is it doing here in Froughton Forest?* They were a long way from the Romgnian Mountains. He could not make sense of it. The dragon took a sharp left turn and disappeared into the darkness. Just as quickly, Breona charged out from between the trees with the dragon close on her tail. Magnus sprang to his feet and ran after them.

"Magnus!" Breona called. Magnus heard her plea for just a moment before the gruff consciousness of the dragon overshadowed the gentler touch of Breona's. Breona turned and faced the dragon, rearing up tall and neighing. The youngling responded with a bellowing roar. Magnus was in awe at the sight of them upon their hind legs in a brilliant flash of white and bronze, hoof to claw, as two mythical creatures would be in combat.

The dragon shifted back and started dancing around Breona making her spin about, trying to keep track of its whereabouts. The dragon seemed to have the better of her when it became distracted, twisting and turning about itself. Magnus saw a bright blue butterfly dancing around the dragon's head and realised it was the source of distraction. The dragon bounded off after the butterfly, deeper into the Valley and out of sight. Magnus and Breona were left in silence, bewildered by the playful episode.

"Are you okay?" Magnus asked, running to Breona.

"He was very annoying," Breona responded. Magnus shook his head and smiled, his heart somewhat lightened by the unlikely experience.

Magnus and Breona carved a path through the Valley of Shadows. It was painstakingly slow without existing trails but Magnus had no choice. Heading directly west would take them back to the Outer Rim where Crugion's men might be scouting for him.

They travelled in complete silence except for the occasional rustling from deeper within the Valley. It was sometimes a bird, sometimes a rabbit, but the dragon youngling seemed to have vanished. Magnus did however have the constant feeling that they were being followed. It was as though the forest had eyes and was ever evaluating their whereabouts, watching and waiting for the right moment to get the better of him or Breona.

Near the day's end they stumbled across a flowing river. Magnus drank greedily from it and speared several good-sized trout with the sharpest stick he could find. He risked building a small fire to cook the fish upon, mindful to extinguish the flames once done for fear the smoke may tell tale of his whereabouts. As he settled down to enjoy his meal with a selection of blackberries that grew alongside the river, Magnus found his stalker.

On the far side of the river, a short distance away, was an oversized maple tree. The surrounding ground was red with fallen leaves. Staring out from behind the tree was a dark creature that was eerily familiar to Magnus. Its pearlescent white eyes were the same he had seen days ago before entering Froughton Forest. It stared at him without blinking or moving.

Magnus chewed slowly on a few blackberries, hoping his casual behaviour may disinterest the creature after a time. But it did not. Its relentless stare never faulted as time slowly passed. Magnus grew more concerned and found it difficult to turn his eyes from the eerie creature.

Half an hour passed without change until Breona sprung from her resting spot and stared into the woods to the left of the black creature. A moment later Magnus heard the source of her concern. The familiar growl of the dragon resonated through the woods. Magnus jumped to his feet and stood close to Breona. The black creature also turned its gaze in that direction. Its eyes widened as the dragon youngling hurled itself out from the darkness and grabbed the creature with its jaws. It shook it to and fro like a rag doll.

Magnus covered his ears as the creature let out a high pitch scream that lasted a few moments before the dragon killed it. Sniffing its prey, the dragon discarded the carcass, flinging it into the scrub. It then rubbed its open mouth with its front paws, finally electing to go to the river's edge and drink, it seemed, to rid itself of a foul taste in its mouth.

Once satisfied, the dragon walked over the river to where Magnus and Breona were standing and tentatively sniffed at the two remaining cooked fish Magnus left resting on a bed of leaves beside the ashes of the smouldering fire. Carefully, Magnus leant over and took one of the trout and reached toward the youngling. It was hesitant at first but soon came forward and snapped the fish from Magnus's hand, gulping the fish down its long neck before licking its chops with its long, sharp tongue.

Apparently satisfied with its meal, the dragon laid itself upon the ground right beside Magnus. It curled itself into a ball and spread one of its wings out like a blanket over its serpentine body. Magnus was dumbfounded. Looking at Breona for her perspective on the matter revealed she too had found contentment and decided to lie down and rest again.

And so, with no known destination and no idea of what his future would bring him, Magnus laid himself to bed in the Valley of Shadows in the company of a horse and a fire dragon.

RUBEA

It was another crisp, cool morning in the Romghold. Catanya expected an early morning start but instead of Joffren, it was Rubea who greeted her.

"Brue told me you had trouble jumping yesterday," Rubea shared her thoughts with Catanya, who thought back to the previous day when Jael and Joffren soared off the cliff and landed on the backs of dragons. *"Yes, that was it."* Rubea was obviously reading her thoughts.

Catanya smiled at Rubea. *I really must learn to keep my thoughts to myself.*

"We can practice if you like," Rubea said. Catanya could see the dragon was much more excited at the idea than she was.

"I'm sure Joffren has training for me to do, Rubea." Catanya looked across the common for any signs of her Semsdi, hopeful he would rescue her from this situation.

"It were his idea, Semsarian. We shall train together this morning."

Catanya tried to look pleased. Rubea was sweet and Catanya did not want to give her any attitude and besides, she knew there was no way out of it. *"What do you suggest we do?"*

The excited dragon strode over to the training green. Catanya saw this as a bad omen but followed Rubea anyway. Sure enough, Rubea led Catanya to where the lawn dropped away at the cliff edge. Catanya peered over the cliff and down. It dropped for a mile then disappeared into cloud. She turned and looked into the dragon's big eyes.

"I will catch you before you hit the clouds," Rubea assured Catanya.

"You want me to jump?" Catanya said aloud.

Rubea touched her nose against Catanya's forehead. As it had with Brue the previous day, Catanya's mind became flooded with the dragon's thoughts. Rubea was excited to be training with Catanya, but at the same time mindful that she had to take care of her. *"I will catch you, Semsarian. Trust me."* Catanya tried to hold back thoughts of her fears but they manifested more so in her emotions and even more than that—*"I can smell your fear, Semsarian. But you will see, all will be fine."*

154

Catanya slowly withdrew from Rubea's mind and turned to the cliff face again. "This is insane," she mumbled. She knew though, that here in the Romghold, failure was not an option. *If I don't do this now I will be made to do it later.*

"*Are you ready then?*" Catanya looked at the dragon. Rubea's fiery eyes stared into her own.

"*Yes!*" Rubea replied. Her eyes flickered through a myriad of colours before settling on a familiar brown colour. Catanya knew then that Rubea was truly with her.

Rubea drew back her wings and stood at the cliff edge. Catanya stepped back toward the middle of the training field, giving herself the distance needed for a running start. She took some deep breaths and ran for the cliff, but stopped just short of it. "*Sorry... that won't happen again.*" She stepped back again and took a second run at the cliff. This time she jumped.

Catanya was alarmed at how quickly her dive over the cliff became an out-of-control plummet down the mountainside. It felt as though the wind were trying to tear her to shreds. She wanted to scream but the rushing air forced its way into her open mouth, so she closed it again.

"*Spread your arms wide.*"

Rubea's words shot through her mind. Catanya did as told, throwing her arms out. It levelled her out and stopped her tumbling but she was facing upwards. From this view, Catanya could see the fire dragon diving toward her. Wisps of cloud started to appear around her, so she knew she was approaching the bed of clouds below. Catanya dared not shift her position but had no idea how to land on the dragon the correct way about.

Rubea spread her wings and twisted herself about such that her back was facing Catanya. Catanya reached forward and grabbed for the horn on Rubea's saddle. "I've got it!" she shouted.

Rubea turned over, gliding away from the mountain face, right at the top of the clouds. Catanya felt her backside slam into the saddle's seat. Not bothering to fasten her stirrups, Catanya leaned forward and held on for dear life. Slowly, Rubea climbed the mountain and landed softly on the training field.

"We did it!" Catanya said through laboured breath. Her heart felt like it was pounding out of her chest.

"*Excellent! This time, spread your arms and legs wide when you first jump. You can control the fall better,*" Rubea said.

"This time? You mean, jump again?" Catanya climbed from the saddle onto the field. Rubea walked toward the cliff edge again and waited.

Catanya's second jump was more controlled than the first. She fell face down, arms wide, watching the clouds speed toward her. Rubea swept beneath her and tapered her speed so that Catanya could take a hold of the saddle horn and pull herself into the seat. This time she fastened the stirrups and Rubea dove into the clouds, emerging beneath them, yet still a mile above the ground below.

For her third dive, Rubea had Catanya fall *through* the clouds before catching her. The wet clouds slapped against Catanya's body and face making it impossible to see but when she finally emerged, she saw Rubea punch through the clouds to her right and glide beneath her as before.

"I think you've done well, Semsarian," Rubea said.

Catanya was glad to hear she was satisfied. She relaxed a little in the saddle as Rubea glided slowly toward the ground below. Catanya could see a river running between the border of the mountains and Froughton Forest. From high above, the river appeared red and weaved like a trail of blood along the landscape of green toward the Corville Mountains.

"What is that river?" Catanya asked.

"It was once called the Little Traas River. Now it is known as the Red River," Rubea shared. *"The Battle of Fire was fought here."*

Catanya regretted asking, remembering that Balgur was slain during this battle. She looked again at the river as they descended, finally landing on the riverbank. Catanya alighted. She was glad to have her feet on solid ground again. Behind her the Romgnian Mountains towered upwards through the clouds and on the opposite side of the river, the eastern border of Froughton Forest sighed gloomily in the morning breeze.

Catanya knelt beside the river's edge and examined the water flowing southward. It was the water itself that was red. She felt she should not ask why, but Rubea seemed comfortable talking about it.

"You wonder at the colour, Semsarian?"

"Aye." Catanya looked at Rubea.

"For twenty years it has run red... since Balgur was slain," Rubea explained. *"Shall I show you where?"*

Catanya nodded and climbed back into Rubea's saddle. She flew downstream where the forest finished and the southern plains began. A mile further on, Rubea landed.

"It was here."

Catanya alighted again and walked a little way. The palms of her hands brushed over the tall stems of grass. The place had an eerie feel to it. Wind blew through the grasses, whispering gently to her, as though it were telling her secrets she would rather not know. Catanya turned to Rubea who seemed to be lost in thought, for her mind seemed distant and her thoughts aloof.

"Do you know how it happened?" Catanya asked.

The silence between Catanya and Rubea broke, and Rubea explained, *"I was not here. My role was to look after the younger of our kin and I was quite young myself. Perhaps then, it is easier for me than others to return here and listen to the winds speak to me of the past."*

"You hear that too?" Catanya was glad she was not the only one.

"Aye. Many unrested spirits live here. Many lives were lost in the battle." Rubea looked into the depths of the narrow river. *"It was a confusing battle. Ba'drohm warriors came down from the Cloud Mountains, ꙨhUid warriors from the forest and the Rhydermere from the North. They were each led by an Electus. None brought dragons. My kin knew they had fallen to the Quag warmongers. But we fire dragons do not fall to anyone... at least, not until this battle."*

Rubea continued. *"A fire-sword lost its master and found the bloodstained hand of Delvion. Whether by chance or skill I do not know, but Balgur fell. In the aftermath, the Ferustir named Steyne took claim to the sword. Many felt him responsible, but who can be held responsible for a single tragedy in a battle where so many perished?"*

Catanya remembered the name—*Steyne*—as the priest who took Austagia away to join the order of the Irucantî. She tried to imagine what he must have been like. *"It's no small thing to have the death of a dragon on your hands,"* Catanya said, feeling Steyne was perhaps judged harshly.

"I think perhaps Steyne judged himself harsher than anyone else did," Rubea said. *"In the months to come, Steyne disappeared."*

"Where did he go?" Catanya was intrigued that a priest had walked away from the priesthood.

"I don't think anyone really knows." Rubea's thoughts came across as a murmur. Catanya figured the dragon was thinking things over much as she was.

"And the river?" Catanya asked.

"Balgur fell upon the river as he died. He bled out from his wounds and the river has run red ever since, from its start at the Traas River through what is now called the Red Pass, dividing the Romgnian and Corville Mountains." Rubea arched her long neck up and peered off to the south. *"Some people say the river is cursed whilst others*

drink or bathe in it hoping to gain the power of the Electus for themselves. People are strange, don't you think?"

"*Yes, we are strange.*" Catanya smiled.

"*For my kin, this is a place we rarely come to, except on the anniversary of Balgur's death.*" Sadness seemed to wash over Rubea's thoughts.

Catanya let her words sink in and she thought about how ferocious such a battle must have been—right here at the foot of the Romgnian Mountains. *"Tell me of the Electus who came to fight."*

"*It was the first time our people had heard of such a thing. Us dragons thought it to be possible. In all ways, the Electus of each realm were more powerful than all other warriors—even the Irucanti. Each had the power of a dragon within their small bodies. Their strength, their mastery of the magic of their own realms... they were a great asset to the battle. Each of the three Electi who came to battle was a child of the chosen ones, proving the powers could be inherited. It opened Delvion's eyes. It was a power he wanted from then on, though he has never had it.*"

"*Thank the Gods for that,*" Catanya said. "*A man as mad as him slayed a dragon—he is powerful enough.*"

"*Aye,*" agreed Rubea. *"Let's hope he gains no more."*

The wind blew erratically for a moment and Catanya looked about, spotting another dragon circling above. By the long tail, she could tell it was Brue. He came in toward them and landed. Joffren was in the saddle.

"*How did you fare?*" Joffren shared his thoughts with Catanya and Rubea.

"*Your Semsarian did well, Joffren,*" Rubea answered.

Joffren looked to Catanya. "Excellent."

"Quite a start to the day, Semsdi," Catanya said, wondering what was next on Joffren's agenda.

"Indeed," Joffren said in a distant voice, squatting beside the river. He reached for the red, flowing water with outstretched fingers but stopped short, curling his hand into a fist and standing again. He tilted his head, peering up the vertical mountainside, then glanced back at Catanya. *"Shall we return to the Romghold?"*

"*Aye.*" Brue and Rubea both answered.

"*We shall see you back there, then.*" Joffren waved to both dragons. They took flight and started their steep ascent. Catanya and Joffren were left standing alone by the Red River.

"Shan't we be needing them?" Catanya queried.

Without answering, Joffren pulled a large drawstring bag from over his shoulder and placed it on the ground. He dropped to one knee and rummaged through the bag, pulling out several objects and handing them to Catanya without looking up from the bag. First came a pair of steel spiked frames with leather straps that Catanya thought resembled rabbit traps. Then came a pair of short, wooden poles with spikes attached to them. Joffren removed another set of the same objects. Seating himself, he took the first of his spiked frames and began strapping it to the bottom of his boots.

"These are crampons," Joffren explained and then pointed to the spiked poles, "and those are climbing axes."

"*Climbing* axes?" Catanya repeated.

"Yes. We should reach the Romghold by nightfall…"

Catanya sat beside Joffren without saying another word and began to strap the spiked crampons to her feet. She could feel Joffren looking at her, but kept all her thoughts guarded, just in case Joffren was reading her mind. Instead, she glanced up the mountainside. She could only see as far as the clouds a mile up. *We're going to climb the mountain…* Catanya let it sink in. *So be it…*

CONFRONTATION

Magnus heard the dragon youngling wander off during the night but was unaware it had eaten the last fish Magnus had cooked the evening before. Slightly bothered that his breakfast was stolen, Magnus walked to the river's edge to wash before moving on.

Looking at his reflection in the water, Magnus was surprised to see how drawn and haggard he looked. His face was thin, his eyes deep set and his forehead marked and bruised. What little amount of facial hair he had looked patchy and unkempt, matching his scruffy hair. He removed his jacket and white shirt, placed them by the riverside and dropped into the cold water to wash. He brushed his hair back with the palms of his hands and examined the bruising over his ribs.

Breona wandered down to join Magnus and he took the opportunity to look closer at her wounds. They were mostly from the Quagmen's whips but some were from the scratching of thorns and other spikey plants scored in the Valley. *"Aren't we a matching pair?"* Magnus scooped water with his hands and poured it over Breona's body, cleaning the blood from her hide. Breona's injuries were not as bad as they first seemed and with the blood removed from her pure white hide she looked her usual radiant self again. Telling her as much, Breona thanked him with a hint of pride.

Setting off for the morning, Breona shared her desire to keep looking for Alavia. Magnus knew she would have it no other way, which suited him. He thought, too, of his promise to return to Lucas. He desperately wanted to know if his friend had recovered. Returning to the Uydferlands would also allow him to warn Csilla of the Authoritarium's support for the Quag attack. The journey westward would however be treacherous. Crugion and his men would be expecting Magnus to make a run for home, or would they think him bold enough to search for his parents in Ba'rrat? *Then there's the issue of the scouting wyverns…*

No, Magnus decided. They would continue to the southern border of Froughton Forest and find a way over the Corville Mountains to Ba'rrat. *"It is there we will find my parents, Breona."* The thought came to him reluctantly. He dared not try to comprehend the journey ahead. Instead, he would take one step at a time.

By mid morning they descended into a deep gulley that was filled with chattering birds. The air became cool and still. A creek trickled its way through the forest at the lowest point of the gully. On the far side of the ravine, the forest rose steeply once again.

Magnus decided to follow the creek upstream, hoping it would guide him westward enough to get closer to the Outer Rim where he could assess how safe it was to travel that way. They followed the creek that gradually widened as several other creek divisions converged upon it. After several hours, a broader river began to take shape and Magnus began to notice purple irises growing along the riverbank, reminding him of the Nuyan River. He picked an iris, imagining he was waiting for Catanya to meet him by the river. *Was it six, seven or more days since I last saw Catanya?* He drew in the flower's delicate, earthy scent and made a wish on it, hoping Catanya was well and safe.

He held the long stem of the flower between his fingertips then threw it, watching it glide down over the flowing river, where it landed upon a thin stream of red blood coursing its way down the river. Magnus followed the blood trail up stream. It led him to an outcrop of rock on the southern bank atop which a discarded arrow rested. He walked to the rock where the flowing river was washing blood from the rock's surface into the river. Magnus looked intently at the arrow. It was black with crudely crafted black-feathered vanes and a broadly angled steel tip. Breona walked over and sniffed at the bloody rock.

"Dragon blood," she concluded. *"The youngling is wounded."*

It was then that Magnus became aware of the deathly silence of the gulley—that the chattering of the birds had fallen silent. The silence was soon disturbed with a guttural roar that echoed through the gully. They heard it again. To Magnus it sounded like a roar of pain.

"It is the dragon youngling," Breona said.

Magnus reached over his shoulder, grabbing for his sword that was not there. "Curses!" he muttered under his breath. *"Can you hear his thoughts?"* he asked Breona.

"He has fallen silent," Breona answered.

Magnus sensed her anxiety and was surprised at her concern for the dragon. With trepidation, they started on and up the southern hill face. Minutes later they reached the top of the next rise and peered down to

161

another gully and a clearing beyond it. It seemed at first there was little to see, but soon there was movement.

"Over there, beyond the trees." Magnus pointed to the bottom of the gully where he could make out the dark figures of several men partially hidden by the trees. They were moving around excitedly. The dragon's roar came again and was followed by the eruption of laughter.

"Again, again, go for the leg!" shouted one of them. There was a pause followed by another roar and more laughter. Magnus lay flat on his belly, trying to catch sight of the dragon youngling.

"They are torturing him!" Breona's thoughts were sharp with anger. Magnus looked at her, standing tall on the top of the rise making no effort to conceal her whereabouts.

"Breona, they will see you there. Get back."

Breona dug at the ground with a hoof and snorted angrily. *"They are hurting the youngling as they did me. He may be annoying but he is of sacred blood."*

"Breona!" Magnus tried to settle her, but it was too late. She charged down the embankment toward the gully below. Not knowing what else to do, Magnus ran after her. Her emotions were overloaded with anger, even more so than when she freed herself from the Quagmen's shackles. Magnus knew there was no reasoning with her now.

Down and down they went, slipping their way down the steep descent that soon tapered out to level ground where Breona broke into a gallop, weaving around the trees and thrashing through the undergrowth with little regard for her own safety.

"Breona!"

Magnus watched as she crashed through the last of the scrub and out into the clearing. Magnus followed her, running hard, until he came to a halt at the edge of the clearing. Sure enough, a Quagman was poised with an arrow aimed at the dragon while several other Quagmen looked on. None seemed to have spotted Breona yet.

"Take it down!" one of them shouted, gesturing towards the dragon youngling.

Breona ran over to the archer and knocked him flat to the ground. Relentlessly, she stomped on him—again and again and again. Magnus recognised the three remaining Quagmen. It was Briet and his accomplices. They stood back in alarm.

Arrows were embedded in the youngling's shoulders, legs and neck, where his scales gave less protection. He favoured his right front leg and was guarding his injured left foreleg where an arrow cut deep. His bronze scales glistened in the sun that shone through the clearing.

Breona trampled the fallen Quagman to a bloody pulp. His helmet and armour did little to protect him from Breona's rage. Looking back to the men, Magnus saw Briet move in with his sword, ready to attack Breona. Thinking fast, Magnus spotted the fallen man's bow and a single arrow lying just a few feet from him. He ran to it as fast as he could, making Briet hesitate in his advance. Gripping the bow and loading the arrow with fumbling fingers, Magnus pointed it at Briet, drawing back the arrow with as much tension as he could muster.

"Stop!" Magnus shouted. Breona settled herself down but still shifted about angrily.

Briet raised his eyebrows in surprise. It was soon replaced with a grimace that swept across his face as he advanced once again. Magnus dropped to one knee, tilted his head and peered down the shaft of the arrow, aiming straight at Briet's head. Briet grunted and stood his ground.

"Not one step further," Magnus shouted. The two other men drew their swords and moved around the edges of the clearing. Soon, one was positioned to his right and one to his left, with Briet in front of him. He could feel the dragon behind him breathing heavily and Breona jumping around in a state of anger.

"You kill me boy, what next, hey?" said Briet.

The man to Magnus's right stumbled as he walked. Standing again, he removed his helmet and stood swaying as he drank sloppily from a large jug, spilling red wine across his face. Magnus could smell the alcohol and, now that he looked for it, noticed Briet seemed unsteady on his feet, too.

"So long as I kill you Briet, I'm happy." Magnus replied.

'You kill him, ya dead!" the Quagmen to his left grunted, advancing slowly toward him. The dragon roared, making Magnus's heart leap in his chest. The man to his left backed up a little. Breona moved to Magnus's immediate left and reared up, screaming in support of the dragon. The man to Magnus's right shouted and charged at him. Magnus turned to him and released his arrow. It sank deep into his forehead. As he watched the man fall, Magnus was overcome with searing pain as an arrow tore into his left thigh. It was Crugion, who walked into the clearing from the trees behind Briet, holding a crossbow that he was reloading. Magnus looked at his leg. The black arrow had sunk deep and protruded from both sides.

The sound of another arrow whistling through the air drew Magnus's attention. It embedded itself into Breona's chest. She released a high pitch scream and sank to the ground. Struggling for breath, she was full of fear and pain that permeated through Magnus's mind.

"No!" Magnus cried. Seeing her fallen, Magnus was overcome with anger and dove for the sword that belonged to the dead man to his right. He had lost track of who was where and so wielded the sword around like a mad man.

Briet came to him with his black swords drawn, swinging them about with all his strength and fury. Magnus caught the blow of both with his own blade but could not match his strength. Briet pushed hard against him, grunting and spitting between gritted teeth. He smashed against Magnus's Quag blade again, grated down to the hilt and across Magnus's left forearm, cutting deep to the bone. Magnus dropped his sword. Another blow from Briet came fast, but the dragon leapt at him faster, releasing another bellowing roar even louder than before. Its anger pierced through Magnus's mind like the blade through his arm as it shared its emotions with him once again. The claws of its foreleg tore the sword from Briet's arm and sliced through his flesh.

The remaining Quagman leapt to Briet's defence, stabbing at the dragon's underbelly repeatedly. A further thrust of Briet's second sword tore through the dragon's already injured foreleg, bringing the dragon crashing to the ground. It clawed desperately to right itself but its strength was waning and it could no longer stand.

Breona came to the dragon's defence again, pushing her full weight against the other Quagman. They fell together, Breona crushing him as she fell. The Quagman wailed then coughed as he struggled for breath through his broken body.

Crugion was still standing a good distance from the altercation. He launched another arrow at Breona that sank deep into her neck. Magnus howled at the sight of her.

Briet backed away from the dragon, examining his injured arm. He spat at the ground, threw his robes aside and drew his notorious black dagger from his belt. He advanced toward Magnus again.

"Briet! Back down!" Crugion shouted. Briet ignored him, flipping the blade about its tang until his thumb pressed firmly on its butt.

"Briet. I said back down," Crugion warned again. Briet cursed in frustration, holding the blade hard against Magnus's neck. Crugion came over and placed a gloved hand on his kinsman's shoulder. "He is mine."

Briet stood and stepped aside, spitting at the ground and cursing. Magnus watched as Crugion discarded his crossbow and held aloft a sword, still in its scabbard. It was Magnus's sword. He threw it to him.

"I told you I would return your blade to you in the arena. You've wasted enough of my time. *This* will be your arena." Crugion gripped the pommels of his own two swords, then released them again. "I'll give you a moment to catch your breath, *Rhyderman.*" He turned his back on Magnus and walked away toward Briet who had stormed off in anger to the far side of the clearing.

ELECTUS

Magnus glanced over to Breona. Life was draining from her, but she was looking at the dragon youngling, who looked back to her. They seemed to be sharing thoughts, both breaking occasionally to look at Magnus.

"You have your mother's heart, Magnus." Breona's thoughts were weak. *"There is none more deserving."*

Magnus pulled himself to his feet and limped over to Breona's side, dragging his injured leg behind him. He fell upon her and embraced her head in a hug, sobbing.

"Tell Alavia we will meet again... beyond the Ice Seas..."

"I will tell her," Magnus lied, sure he would be joining her very soon.

"Go now, chosen one." Breona said. Her struggling breath ceased and her mind distanced itself from Magnus's. Magnus willed himself to go with her but his body was not ready to die.

Magnus turned away from Breona, tears coursing down his face. He pushed himself up to face his fate but stumbled and fell. He lay on his back with outstretched arms. The dragon youngling was fast to pin his right arm to the ground with its wounded left paw. Magnus felt the talon at the heel of its paw pressing firmly into his wrist. He tried to pull free but the dragon persisted, pressing harder and harder until Magnus felt the talon break through his skin and wedge its way between the two bones of his forearm.

"You're hurting me!" his mind yelled at the dragon, worried it didn't know friend from foe. The pain seared through him, stealing his breath away. It was unlike any pain he had ever experienced—even more so than the arrow embedded in his thigh. He looked over at Crugion, whose attention was on fastening his gauntlets, readying himself for their fight.

Then the dragon youngling spoke to him—*"I am spent and so I grant you my strength."* The dragon clenched his paw, drawing his front claws into a fist and thrusting the heel talon deeper still into Magnus's wrist. *"I give you my blood, I give you my life."*

166

Magnus felt heat build in his wrist. It grew and grew until the heat felt like acid burning so mercilessly he was sure it would cause his arm to burst into flames. Then the pain began to spread up his arm toward his shoulder. Magnus looked to the dragon. *"Why are you torturing me?"* It did not stop there. The pain spread through his whole body. His heart began to pound hard and within moments he was consumed with unyielding heat and unbearable pain.

Magnus grabbed the dragon's foreleg with his wounded arm and felt its hard scales beneath his hand. The dragon had ironclad strength and would not yield. But the attack was not over. The youngling started to invade Magnus's mind, filling it with thoughts and memories that were not his own. He saw all of the dragon's memories. The dragon's name was *Thioci*. He had lived a life of fifty years—too short for a fire dragon. But there was more to come. Magnus saw memories the youngling had inherited from its forefathers and theirs before them. Memories of the bond shared between father and son, of love for the people of the Fire Realm and of the bond that people and dragons shared. He saw memories of the disintegration of a thousand years of peace among the four realms of Allumbreve. Finally he saw the will of the God of Fire. He saw the fierceness of his nature and the truth of his plan. Above all—he wanted peace among people.

Magnus stopped resisting and allowed the pain to have its way with him— there was nothing more he could do. Soon enough, the pain subsided but the heat remained. Magnus looked the dragon in the eyes. They were blue. Slowly, they changed back to amber.

"You are worthy of my blood, Magnus. Breona of the Ice Seas has shown me. You are the chosen one. You are the Electus."

Thioci withdrew his talon from Magnus's wrist. He felt the warmth drain from the dragon's paw. Before his eyes, the dragon's radiant scales began to fade and its eyes lost their fire. Thioci rested his head upon the ground and slowly closed his eyes, heaving slow, weak breaths.

Magnus stood up, feeling the heat in his body surge through him with each beat of his heart. He saw that Crugion was now layered with thick black Quag armour and wore a spiked black helm on his head. He drew his two black blades and broke into a run toward Magnus. Magnus knelt down with his injured leg forward. The heat in his body shifted. It throbbed about his injured forearm and the arrow embedded in his leg. Magnus gritted his teeth and watched as the ends of the arrow ignited into flame then burned to ash that floated to the ground. The pain was gone. Likewise—his forearm were healed. Crugion stopped in his tracks, ripping the helm from his head.

"What's this?" he asked, his face contorting as he looked at Magnus's leg.

Magnus picked his sword off the ground and pulled it from its scabbard, the white flash of the blade shimmering down its length. He twisted his head from one side to the other making his neck crack and pop. He drew his shoulders back, lifting his chest, and his bruised ribs seared with heat for just a moment before fading away, leaving them healed. Magnus felt almost invigorated. Then he advanced toward Crugion and took first charge, slicing his sword at him at a rate that alarmed even himself.

Crugion moved fast, blocking Magnus's move with both blades crossed in front of him. He spun about and brought the left blade down across Magnus's face. Magnus arched back, averting the blow by a hair's breadth before thrusting forward with a stabbing blow, just missing Crugion's chest. Crugion danced around Magnus with a grin on his face, apparently enjoying the sport of the event.

"Finish him off!" Briet shouted. Magnus glanced over at Breona lying dead beside the fallen dragon. Anger and grief wrestled within his heart for supremacy and anger won out. He leaped at Crugion and attacked him with all the skill of his swordsmanship. Crugion was on the defensive with no chance for a counter attack. Finally Magnus landed a blow across Crugion's face, the fleu-steel of his blade slicing deeply through his right cheek and upper lip.

Crugion reeled back and Magnus stopped, watching the Quagman's shocked reaction. Crugion retaliated with fury. He forced Magnus back as he worked both blades with precision, delivering more blows than Magnus could counter. A blow struck Magnus across his chest, another his abdomen, and finally Crugion thrust a blade deep beneath Magnus's ribs, just below his heart.

Magnus fell to his knees. He was spent. Blood flowed from his wounds and his vision was failing him, replaced instead with hallucinations of the mind. He became a spectator watching reruns of the blows dealt to Breona and the dragon that brought them to their ends.

Thioci... Magnus thought of the dragon youngling. *His name is Thioci.* The sun hitting Magnus's face felt warm and inviting until Crugion's shadow blocked it. He crouched down to Magnus's level and grabbed a lock of his hair, bringing their faces together much as he had when first they met. He licked his wounded lip and glared into Magnus's unfocussed eyes.

"You are *done*, son of Bonstaph. Go to the halls of your ancestors and wait just a little while, for your father shall join you soon enough."

Magnus heard the words but barely comprehended them. He was hanging onto life's final thread, his breath spent and his body bleeding profusely. Crugion spoke again but it came to Magnus as a distant drone, fading in volume and void of meaning. Magnus felt himself fall to oblivion but he was seized by the presence of another. It was Thioci.

Thioci was speaking with his elders, telling them what he had done. *"I have chosen Magnus,"* he told them. Magnus sensed deliberation from a source of power far more ancient than the living. It came from the ancestors of dragons. The voices were old and wise and they asked Thioci to explain his choice. Thioci told his elders what had come to pass. He told them of Breona—the Astermeer who carried the blood of the Ertwe dragons who gave her life to protect him. It was she who showed Thioci the virtue in Magnus and how Magnus had fought to defend them both.

After consideration of Thioci's judgement, they agreed Magnus was worthy of choice. He was to be the *Electus*. It was then that one among them spoke with authority. His name was *Balgur*.

"I will show you the way to the salvation of your people. Your time is not ended. You carry the legacy of the Fire Realm."

Magnus did not know what Balgur meant, but his body was overcome with convulsions of pain that took the place of any questions. Magnus's mind fell into darkness but the pain in his body turned to fire, pulling him from the darkness, breathing life back into his lungs and pouring blood back into his body. Magnus began to course with new life but Balgur warned it came at a cost. An obligation. A fate had been thrust upon him.

INAUGURATION

Training with her Semsdi was relentless. Catanya had spent three days running, sparring and pushing herself beyond anything she ever believed herself capable of, yet Joffren always expected more.

"What is training if not to further your abilities?" Joffren had asked. "You must not allow comfort and familiarity to be that which you seek. You must continue to grow, Semsarian."

"Yes, Semsdi," Catanya replied as always, careful to conceal her resentment. In fact she had gone further than that—she had learned to dismiss any inklings of anger toward him or offense taken as it arose, knowing everything Joffren put her through was a step closer to becoming a dragon priest. *Once a priest, I can do anything I want.* This had become her personal mantra.

As the days passed, Catanya appreciated sleep more than ever before. She spent the nights in her room where she had earned herself a bed with a pillow and blanket, together with a washing bowl that she was able to replenish each evening and morning with hot water and fresh washing cloths.

Meals were taken twice a day at midmorning and evening in a common kitchen at the northern side of the Romghold. Joffren seemed to time their meals such that they ate when no other priests were present. Not that it made much difference, for the priests ate mostly in silence with only the slightest of murmurs heard in conversation or from those who worked in the kitchen.

On the evening of her second day of training she found a red, leather-bound book placed on the table in her room. The book itself was written entirely in Fireisgh. Catanya struggled with this at first, but she soon recalled the language she had been taught the basics of as a child. It told stories of the history of Allumbreve—the changes the lands had struggled through leading to the coming of the Second Age that brought the four realms and their dragon guardians. She learned of the feuding that led to war and the defeat of the other three realms of dragons. Catanya found the book interesting and would have liked to spend her days reading it. She would always start her reading by feeling the texture of the book and rubbing her thumbs over the embossed gold lettering on the red cover that spelled the words, *"Murata Fara"*—*Heart of Fire.*

She soon realised the small book made Joffren's life easier, for each time she asked him a question about dragons or the reason behind certain beliefs or rituals the priests adhere to, he would simply answer— "Read your *Murata Fara*," or where Joffren wished to make a specific point, "Page one hundred fifty eight, paragraph two." Catanya would always follow up on his direction, spending the evenings reading the recommended passages and contemplating their meaning.

On the fifth day following her cleansing, Catanya woke to the attractive smell of soup. She turned over in her bed and saw steam rising from a bowl set beside a cup of herbal water on her table. It was the first time she had taken food in her room. She sat at the side of her bed and scratched her temples in a vain attempt to alleviate the confusion. Then she spotted a small wooden box sat upon the table.

Catanya sampled the soup. It was a delicate flavour of celery, carrot and fennel with more of the mysterious herb and spice she was becoming accustomed to. She finished the soup and wrapped her hands around the warm cup of herbal water, sipping lightly from it as she considered the box. Almost immediately she became distracted by something else. Hanging on the inside of the door to her room was a new robe. It was strikingly beautiful. Forgetting the box for a moment, Catanya walked to the door and ran her fingertips down the delicate fabric. She removed it from its hanger and laid it upon her bed.

The robe was pure silk of black, burgundy and white. Gold stitching separated the colours and matching gold embroidery weaved through the sleeves in patterns depicting vines climbing a tree. It seemed to Catanya to be a formal piece of attire and feeling the fabric, she believed it to be newly made.

"Hardly practical for training," she said to herself. She put the robe on and felt its unexpected weight rest on her shoulders and flow to the ground, covering her boots. The robe had a matching hood that fell behind her back. Its gold embroidery followed the hood's rim and continued over her shoulders and down the length of the robe.

There was a knock at the door. Catanya pulled on the steel latch and opened it. It was Joffren. He too was dressed in a formal robe similar to her own. His was predominantly black with ruby-coloured embroidery flowing throughout its silken threads.

"Are you ready, Semsarian?" he inquired in his usual formal demeanour.

"Ready for what, Semsdi?"

"Today is your inauguration." Joffren nodded toward the box upon the table.

Catanya sat at the table and reached for the wooden box, turned the circular brass catch and lifted its lid. Within, were three items—a small steel blade, a palm-sized stone dish and a vial containing an amber liquid of some sort. Catanya considered the items for a moment. Then it came to her. Every hair on her neck and arms stood up at once and her breath was caught.

"This is to shave my head," she declared.

Joffren walked over to her without saying anything and took the vial of fluid, removed its cork and poured it into the dish that he placed before Catanya on the table. Catanya could smell the scent of lavender. He took the blade from the box and ran his index finger gently across the blade, testing its sharpness. He looked at Catanya.

"Really? Why did you not tell me of this earlier?" Catanya asked, dropping her usual, formal politeness. She realised then that she knew this moment would come, even though she allowed herself to hope it wouldn't, or at least not so soon.

"Such things are for you to know when you must and come only when they are meant to come."

Catanya struggled to grasp the reality of what was about to happen. All the years of her mother plaiting her long flowing hair, and of Magnus stroking it lovingly. All that was about to change. Catanya thought hard about whether her playing along with the training had gone too far. *Should I have fled the Romghold before now?*

Catanya pulled herself back into the moment. *It's nothing, really*, she told herself. *This won't change a thing. I know what I want. I know who I am.*

Joffren walked to Catanya's side. She sat upright and rigid with tight fists resting on her thighs.

"Jael would have liked to be here. She would have made touches to your presentation in ways that elude me. Alas, she seems waylaid with her task in Froughton Forest. However…" he stood back and examined her, "I did this for Jael when her time came. I am sure I can prepare you just the same."

Catanya appreciated Joffren speaking in a more familiar tone for once. She forced a weak smile and took a nervous breath, releasing it again through pursed lips.

"Very well then."

Catanya freed her loosely tied ponytail and let her hair flow freely down her back and across her shoulders. Joffren gently tilted her head to one side and used the blunt side of the blade to form a part line above her left temple. Catanya felt the muscles in her thighs tense. The part of her that wanted to flee was working feverishly to make her do so. But there was another part of her that kept calm. Was it a naive, trusting part of her? Or perhaps it was a new side that wanted to know more about this life she had been thrust into. Regardless, Catanya steadied her legs with her tight fists, letting just her feet squirm beneath her chair.

Brushing the hair below the part line with the back of his hand, Joffren then used the blade to cut these lengths of hair short. Catanya fanned her fingers and felt the strands of hair fall over them. She bit her bottom lip as Joffren dipped his fingers in the dish of lavender oil and smeared it across the side of her head until it soaked into her scalp. Finally, he used the blade to gently shave the hair from Catanya's left temple. His touch was so gentle that Catanya was confident he would not hurt her, but she still struggled with her thoughts about the sudden commitment she was making to the priesthood. When he was finished, Joffren took Catanya's washing cloth and wiped the side of her head clean. Catanya shivered at the sensitive touch against the clean-shaved portion of her head.

"There," Joffren concluded. Catanya stood, letting the hair fall from her lap to the ground.

"How do I look?" Catanya felt the side of her head with the tips of her fingers, alarmed by the foreign sensation of smooth skin.

"You look the part," Joffren risked a smile. He walked around Catanya, brushing away any remaining bits of hair from the robe. As a final touch he pulled the robe hood up over her head. It fell across her face leaving her little vision beyond her feet.

"Will you do the tattoo yourself, Semsdi?" Catanya asked, lifting her hood to look at him. Joffren briefly touched the side of his own head.

"It is not really a tattoo as such, Semsarian. You will see for yourself. Come—let's go." Joffren walked out the door, holding it open for Catanya. Her mouth had grown dry and so she grabbed the cup of herbal water from the table and gulped down its remaining contents.

"Okay, I'm ready," she affirmed, stepping out the door. Pulling her hood up again, she was greeted with a most unexpected view. From directly outside her room there were two lines of priests—at least twenty in each—forming a passage for her to walk down that led to the temple. They each wore similar but unique formal robes with their faces concealed beneath hoods as they bowed their heads. Catanya was speechless and began to feel dizzy. It was as if she had only now realised this was all a ridiculous dream and that it was time to wake up.

"Joffren," she whispered, not knowing what she should do. "Where did they all come from? Why are they all here?"

"They have travelled from far and wide for your inauguration. This is your day, Semsarian." He took her arm and led her to the start of the pathway where the first of the dragon priests bowed further, throwing a pink gladiolus flower at her feet. Catanya began her walk toward the temple, one step at a time. Each of the priests in turn bowed before her and laid the pink flowers at her feet.

"*Gladiolus*... the flower of strength, faithfulness and honour," Joffren explained.

Catanya thought of these three virtues but could only really see herself abiding by the first one. *Faithfulness and honour? I'm not so sure...*

She was glad the hood of her robe covered her face, hiding how awkward she felt. Catanya climbed the steps of the temple where fire dragons stood at either side of the temple doors. To the left was Brue, standing tall and proud and to the right was Rubea—smaller but equally proud. They both shared their thoughts with Catanya.

"*Welcome to our family, young warrior,*" Brue shared.

"*I am glad you are with us, Catanya,*" Rubea added, excitement in her thoughts.

Catanya thanked them both, trying to think of flattering words in return when a sudden roar came from the training field. She drew her hood back from her head, disregarding the etiquette of the occasion. There were six dragons standing in the field, with more approaching from the west, from the north and from the east. *Nine, ten, eleven...* Catanya counted them, gliding toward the Romghold. Their thoughts saturated her mind, giving more praise in the fashion of Brue and Rubea. Catanya counted twelve in all as they formed a row across the training field and pointed their heads to the sky. They then released a collective roar and filled the morning sky with jets of flame. As the flames extinguished, the sky above the temple was left with hanging, oily black smoke that gradually permeated through the drifting clouds. Catanya found it hard to breathe. Joffren supported her, holding her arm.

"It is time to enter the temple, Semsarian."

For the first time, Catanya walked through the arch of the portico leading to the tall, narrow doors that opened into the temple. Following Joffren, she entered the temple's narthex before going through a further set of doors leading to the nave. This central chamber was void of all furniture except for an altar positioned in the centre of the floor, finished in the blackest, shiniest stone Catanya had ever seen. It was draped in burgundy fabric with gold woven scripture around its sides.

At the very back of the nave sat a broad stone plinth centred on the polished black marble floor. Towering above the plinth was a gigantic statue of a dragon carved from contrasting white marble. A bronze plaque at its base bore inscription too small for Catanya to read from the far end of the nave, except for the first line that read, *Balgur Qewrum Fara*—Balgur King of Fire. Catanya examined the immense size of the statue—it was far larger than any dragon she had encountered. Looking at the dragon's large talons, she recalled the one she carried during her cleansing. They were of similar size.

"Was Balgur really that large, Semsdi?" Catanya asked.

Joffren whispered into her ear. "Look to the front right middle talon. That is the one you carried. The statue is true size, Semsarian." Catanya felt humbled.

As if by contrast, the main room of the temple was smaller than Catanya had imagined, yet the vaulted ceilings seemed to climb forever. There were no separate rooms above the nave and so Catanya could see directly up through the numerous narrow steeples above. The room's perimeter was lit with a multitude of small spheres of burning fire that were attached to nothing, but hovered above the nave, moving occasionally and by their own volition. The lights extended up through the steeples but not so far as to illuminate the ceiling, giving the impression of a limitless dark void that gave Catanya chills.

As she stood and took in the ambiance of the ancient room, the priests moved into the temple behind her, maintaining their two lines along the eastern and western walls of the nave. Above them soared the narrowest of windows—twelve on each side—finishing at sharp points and cast in stained glass of a dull purple hue. Catanya considered how the temple would appear less dreary if someone swapped the glass for a more radiant palate. She soon withdrew herself from the thought, realising she was losing focus on the proceedings and pinched her thumbnails into her forefingers, forcing herself back into the moment.

Once all the priests were assembled, Brue and Rubea entered the nave. Their talons clattering against the stone ground as they positioned themselves either side of Catanya and Joffren. Finally, two priests entered the chamber from a discretely placed door in the northwest wall of the nave. Catanya noticed there were many of these doors. Against the far eastern wall there were four such doors, and she calculated the third would lead to the healing room where she recovered from her torturous cleansing ritual.

The two priests who entered were dressed differently. Their robes were pure black with detailed embroidery of the same black colour that was hardly visible, leaving Catanya to wonder why whoever made them had bothered at all. The two of them stood at the front of the large statue of Balgur and drew their hoods back, revealing their familiar shaved heads, yet their tattoo markings were unique. Rather than being tattooed across the temples, their markings covered their entire face and head.

"The High Priests of our order," Joffren said. Catanya felt uneasy again, thinking she had made a bad decision not to run when she had the chance. The congregation of priests fell to one knee and bowed before the High Priests. Catanya went to do the same, but Joffren held her arm, stopping her and shaking his head.

"Not us, Semsarian," he whispered. "We stand."

Catanya noticed Brue and Rubea stood tall and proud, and so she did too. The High Priests waited, and after a minute's silence, Joffren led Catanya to the altar, indicating she should lie down. She did as she was told, wishing Jael were there for reassurance, although she did not know why. Once settled, Rubea walked forward and positioned herself to the left side of the altar. Brue remained where he was and Joffren returned to his side.

"There is nothing to fear," Rubea told her. Catanya was not convinced. The two black-robed priests moved to her right. One of them took a hold of Catanya's hands and placed them crosswise over her chest. In this position, she felt like a sacrificial lamb waiting to be slaughtered.

Whatever it is I'm about to go through, Catanya feared, *I've got a feeling it's going to hurt.* She took deep breaths, trying to resist the urge to pull her arms down and leap off the altar. One of the High Priests moved around in front of Rubea and inspected the freshly shaved flesh on the side of Catanya's head. He nodded approvingly before stepping aside, allowing Rubea to move close to Catanya.

"What are you going to do?" Catanya asked the dragon, not even trying to mask her fear.

"You will be fine. I'm going to gift you with the marking of the Irucanti. I am very excited—it is the first time I have done so."

Catanya could sense Rubea's nervousness and anticipation. But then one of the High Priests imposed on her conversation.

"It is time for you to give the mark of the priesthood," the High Priest said to Rubea.

Catanya stared at the priest. His demeanour was so disciplined and his face so expressionless she found it hard to get a measure on him. She found his voice unnerving. It had an air of authority but was tainted with an unpleasant, condescending tone.

Rubea remained enthusiastic and so Catanya decided to focus on her, watching as she lifted her left forefoot and gently placed her heel talon against the delicate flesh of Catanya's temple. Catanya winced, anticipating pain. Soon enough, it came.

It was faster and far worse than she could ever have imagined. Rubea pushed her talon harder. Heat seared through the side of her head as if hot oil had been poured over her and was burning off her flesh. She drew a sharp breath at the sudden sensation but relaxed as it subsided. The priests moved close and looked her in the eyes. Catanya looked to each of them, wanting an explanation for what had just happened. The priests then looked to Rubea who once again brought her talon toward her head.

Oh... not again! Catanya thought, gritting her teeth.

Rubea pushed her talon harder into her head this time. Heat burned through her with greater strength and continued across her entire head, down her neck, her arms and across her chest. From here, Catanya felt the searing heat shoot down the length of her body like a jolt of lightning. The speed of the shock made her body leap from the surface of the altar for a moment. Just as quickly, the heat was gone—all except for a persisting sharp sting across the left side of her head.

Catanya lay motionless on the hard stone altar. The High Priests stood over her again and prised her eyes wide open, studying them closely. Catanya looked at them both. Her vision was tainted with a reddish hue as though she were peering through coloured glass. The priests examined the left side of Catanya's head before looking to one another, nodding their approval. They turned to the other priests and likewise nodded to them.

The temple filled with chanting as the priests moved toward the altar. They formed a line and Joffren was first, helping Catanya to sit up. One at a time the other priests drew back their hoods and congratulated Catanya. They kissed their closed fist, touched it on their own forehead then placed their palm against Catanya's forehead. They were all eager to give their blessing.

Catanya was speechless. After days of having little to do with anyone except Joffren, she was now the centre of attention. Eventually, when all of the priests had touched her forehead, given blessings and left the temple, Catanya was left alone with Joffren and the two dragons. She wanted to ask Rubea what she had done to her but when she opened her mouth, she retched violently and vomited on the floor.

"Well done, Semsarian," Joffren said, seemingly oblivious to her sickness. She heaved and was sick again.

"I don't understand…" Catanya muttered breathlessly.

"Come, you must rest. You have entered the cycle known at *Anunya*. It is the transformation process as your body accepts—"

"What have you done to me?" Catanya demanded, looking at Rubea, her stomach churning.

"I have blessed you, young Irucanti. We are as sisters now!"

"You have received the sacrament of the Fire Realm," Joffren explained further. "A blessing of the powers bestowed unto our dragons."

"I have? Me?"

"Do not be alarmed," Joffren said. "We all receive this blessing. Your blood is still your own, but you have a bond we all share. You should be proud."

Joffren helped Catanya stand but she was too weak to walk unaided. "You keep finding ways to try and kill me," she mumbled, retching once again. She felt a fever begin to take hold and her head continued to throb with pain. Feeling the side of her head with her fingers, she winced at her own touch. The smooth flesh she had felt before was replaced now with rough markings that covered the side of her head, over her temple and back behind her ear. "Ouch!"

"Alas, you survive and are ever the stronger because of it." Joffren smiled again. "And now, *you are an Irucanti.*"

AWAKENINGS

In the clearing in Froughton Forest the weather had turned and it was raining hard. The ground was waterlogged and the soil beneath the grass had turned to mud. The three dead Quagmen's bodies were gone but those of Breona, Thioci and Magnus remained where they had fallen. Unlike the Quagmen, two of them were still alive.

The dragon's body twitched and its lungs heaved begrudgingly with a sound like bellows blowing wind on a fire. The gleam of its scales had faded like a fire's last embers. Not ten feet from the fallen dragon lay Magnus. He had not moved since succumbing to his injuries.

After two days of lying motionless, Magnus woke from his dream state. He sat up in the thundering rain and the darkness of night, broken only by the continuous flash of lightning. In the white flashes he saw Breona's limp body and Thioci's sodden wings draped sadly over the muddy ground. Magnus's entire body throbbed with pain—no part of him was immune to the agony—yet his body showed no evidence of the wounds he had received from Crugion's blades.

Resting back on his arms, he clenched his hands into fistfuls of the mud beneath him. He screamed as loud and long as his lungs could bear.

"This is not right!"

"This is not natural!"

"This is not fair!"

The storm fell calm for a moment and so did Magnus. *Was it all a dream?* In a silent flash of lightning he saw the ground surrounding him awash with the redness of his blood, yet the rain had washed it free of his body. The only scar he bore was the one on his right wrist made by the dragon's talon.

"What's happening to me?" Magnus said out loud. His stomach heaved and he vomited. He began to shake with fever.

"Anunya," a voice whispered as a thought.

"Who's there? What have you done to me?" Magnus's body was overtaken by convulsions.

"Your body takes my blood. You are purged of your own. It is 'Anunya'."

Magnus looked at Thioci. A weak eye peered from beneath a heavy lid.

"You?" Magnus cried between violent shudders. *"You did this to me?"*

Thioci's lungs heaved. *"Anunya."*

"Anunya… What is that?" Magnus's fever worsened and his vision blurred. Shaking, he lay back down on the sodden ground and curled himself into a ball. The rain showered upon him and drenched him through, yet he felt no cold. He lay in the mud sweating as the sickness gripped him.

By morning the rain had shifted to the south and Magnus had recovered from the sickness. He stood, slumped, and walked to Breona. He checked her over to see if there were any signs of life but found none. Magnus felt the softness of her face for a moment, searching for reason within the violent episode that led to her death. Unable to find such reason, he turned away from Breona.

He went to the dragon youngling and sat beside him. Thioci was still alive yet hung to the thinnest of life's threads. Magnus touched the dragon's mind delicately and found himself immersed in the dark labyrinth where the youngling had retreated, waiting for its time in this world to pass. But Thioci recognised Magnus and was grateful for his presence.

"You are well?" Thioci whispered thinly, like that of rustling autumn leaves moments before they fall from the tree. All his strength and rawness had passed.

"I am healed of my wounds, thanks to you."

"Then why such sorrow?"

"You traded your life for mine. Why did you do that?"

"My wounds were beyond healing. But yours I could repair. My role in this life is complete. Yours has just begun."

With each thought, Thioci faded further from Magnus's mind. He tried desperately to stay with him. He needed to know more. He needed to know why. There was no sadness in the dragon's mind. He was content. But as it was with Breona—where Thioci was going Magnus could not follow.

"Thank you, Thioci," Magnus said, wanting the last thing the youngling heard to be his gratitude. Thioci's mind trailed off, beyond his reach, and so Magnus withdrew from the darkness into his own mind. Here, he felt a stranger in his own world. He looked upon the youngling one more time, holding its paw and examining the talon in its heel. A smidgen of Magnus's

blood still stained its tip. The scar on the back of Magnus's wrist was testament to how real everything was—this was not a dream.

Magnus sat back against the dragon's body and felt the rising sun warm his face. He breathed deeply as the life of the forest surrounding him entered his chest and permeated his body. He knew then it was time to move on. He knew not why, but if there were a purpose to this fate, it was not to be found in Froughton Forest.

Magnus spoke the peculiar chant that Catanya had when she placed the bracelet upon his wrist—"*Shalla boyowa muto evavar.*" The words were awkward for Magnus for although they were Fireisgh, they were of a dialect unique to Catanya's family. But it worked. They broke the spell and he was able to remove the bracelet. He wrapped it around Breona's left foreleg, whispering the chant once again to ensure it stayed with her. He found comfort knowing a part of him would stay with her in the forest.

Magnus scouted about, soon finding his sword lying a short distance away. He reunited it with its scabbard, slung it over his back then bid farewell to his fallen companions.

With the Quagmen gone, and a sense of having nothing to lose, Magnus trekked westward for a day until he reached the Outer Rim and the familiar road. Night came but he felt no desire to rest. In fact, he felt a restlessness that needed to be vented. He started to run. Air filled his lungs and his heart pounded with new strength. Magnus began to feel whole again, although not entirely himself. The more he ran the more he pushed. Morning came and still he kept the pace up, no more tired than he was the previous day.

What was not so assuring was how strange everything felt to him. He could feel the pulsating veins in his limbs—they looked more pronounced than ever before. His muscles seemed toned as though he'd done a day's work in the fields, but without the fatigue.

By midway through the second day he came across an area familiar to him. It was where he had encountered the tree nymph—the *meliae* as Eamon had called it. He stopped and looked around, astounded that he had travelled so far in so short a time. He listened to the forest for a while and heard the silence differently than before. Magnus peered down into the Valley. Not far away was the ash tree he had foolishly let himself rest upon not so long ago. He stood and he stared, deep into the darkness. He knew *she* was waiting for him. He knew she was hoping he would return and part of him longed to feel the tenderness she had offered him.

"She'll make you suffer more than you could ever imagine should you cross paths again." Eamon's words came back to him as a timely warning. But he resented having to acknowledge the value of the old man's wisdom. *Why did he offer me such guidance only to betray me?* The paradox played on his mind as he moved swiftly through the Outer Rim toward the western border. *Did he have a change of heart or was there an agenda from the very beginning?* Either way his conclusion was the same—*Eamon was not to be trusted.*

Night came and Magnus reached the end of the road and the western border of Froughton Forest. Nearly two weeks had passed since he had entered at this exact same spot. Little had been achieved and yet he felt a greater sense of purpose. He realised he may be the only free person in Allumbreve who knew the truth of the Authoritarium's alliance with the Quag.

Magnus reflected on his options once again and decided there was only one. With the Quag thinking he was dead, he would enter Ba'rrat and find his parents without Crugion looking for him. With newfound vigour, Magnus vowed to find a way into Ba'rrat. He would head south along the border of Froughton Forest and navigate the southern plains as he saw fit.

He stretched his arms above his head, intrigued with how malleable his body had become. With each stretch he felt heat course through his limbs, leaving him invigorated. But something was not right. The heat began to turn to fever once again and the nausea and blurred vision returned. Magnus lay on the ground, shaking from the sickness as before. *"Anunya,"* he remembered Thioci saying. *How long will this sickness last?*

It was still night when he regained enough strength to stand again. By the moon's shift through the clear sky, he must have been out for several hours. *This is not good.* He vowed as he headed south toward Ba'rrat to keep close to the forest border so if he were to fall ill again he would hopefully have enough warning to hide himself away in the woods.

Through the rest of the night Magnus ran southward across the grassy fields with the forest to his left. As before, it seemed with every passing hour his strength increased and the muscles in his legs thrived on the abuse he dealt them. *Nothing can stop me now.*

JAEL

It took Jael three days out from The Core of Froughton Forest to pick up the youngling's trail. His movements were irrational and that frustrated her. Frustration was not a quality she accepted in herself so she was pleased when she finally came upon the remains of a small deer that had been eaten almost entirely except for its entrails.

Dragon's have no taste for offal, Jael reflected. Furthermore, no other creature in the forest capable of devouring an entire deer—bones and all—had such discerning taste. From here, the youngling's trail was easy to track.

He appeared to have entered the Valley of Shadows further west than she had suspected. He then continued in a northeasterly direction. His trail kept clear of established routes but for a brief period along one of the Valley's ancient Juniper paths. It made it easy for Jael to track the destruction through the forest and yet, even after a day following his course, no definite reason for his journey came to her.

He seems to have picked up on a scent of some kind.

In the afternoon on the second day of following the trail, the youngling's course seemed to come to a sudden halt. Here, Jael found tracks of both human and horse and traces of blood belonging to both. She was relieved no trace of dragon blood was found. The following day she had found a campsite with the ashes of a three-day-old fire beside a flowing river, and further traces of both human and horse blood. Most confusing to Jael, it appeared as though the youngling had rested with the human and the horse for the night. On the far side of the river, Jael found the carcass of a slaughtered black-skinned creature. It was about four and a half foot tall and had the most ghostly white eyes.

A worgriel… foul creature. Why has it wandered this far from the caves beneath the Corville Mountains? Jael grew concerned for the strange goings on within the forest realm.

From here the youngling's course seemed to backtrack. On her fourth day of tracking, Jael crossed the Nuyan River and discovered the black Quag

183

arrow together with the congealed blood of the dragon youngling. She moved to higher ground south of the river and drew her lance from its scabbard, holding it at the ready. Jael traversed down the embankment then through the trees and ferns to the edge of the clearing beyond. Here, she saw the fallen dragon youngling, together with the body of a white Astermeer.

Gasping for breath, Jael fought to keep herself from panicking. She closed her eyes and controlled her breathing, utilising her skills as an Irucantî to bring herself back into the moment and evaluate the situation critically. First, she needed to ensure this was not a trap, enticing her to run into the clearing. She canvassed the area until she was sure neither person nor any other living creature was within a half mile of the clearing. Satisfied, Jael approached the fallen dragon. By the time she reached Thioci she was sobbing and fell upon him, trying desperately to find some sign of life.

Soon enough, she accepted the inevitable—the youngling was dead. Jael sat back and looked at him, his scales cold and grey. It made no sense to her.

A dragon's scales should shine for a thousand years, even after they have died.

She walked over to the fallen Astermeer, trying to make sense of the situation from a different perspective.

"So this is the horse you were tracking in the Valley," Jael sniffed, wiping tears from her face. "I can see why—she was beautiful."

Jael thought about the track marks she had been following. There was someone missing from this scene. "Astermeers never leave their foresworn, so where is yours?"

Jael examined the puncture wounds in the bodies of both creatures made by arrows that had since been removed. She estimated they had been dead for several days and feared they would soon draw scavengers from the forest seeking an easy meal. She cast a spell to protect Thioci's remains, putting a small but effective shield over his body.

Something unusual then caught her eye. She crouched by the white horse's foreleg and took in her hand the leather-plaited bracelet fixed upon it. She tried to remove it only to discover it was protected by an unusual enchantment.

Leaving the horse's side, she turned her attention to the youngling once again, examining him in further detail. Her eyes soon found the talon on his left heel, stained in dried blood. Jael smeared some of the blood onto her forefinger and tasted it.

"Human blood." Jael stood back and considered the situation again, looking from one fallen creature to the other. It was in that moment she knew. "The dragon has bonded with a human." Jael looked back to the bracelet on the Astermeer's leg. She knew it held the answer to whom the dragon youngling had bonded with.

As the truth came to her, Jael became aware of the sound of masked movement in the forest surrounding the clearing. It was coming from several directions and seemed to be closing in.

Jael worked feverishly to decipher the riddle of the enchantment bonding the bracelet to the Astermeer's leg. As she did, she was aware the movement in the forest was becoming more widespread. It was taking her much longer than she anticipated. The enchantment seemed to be Fireisgh, but of a peculiar dialect she could not decipher. Sweat beaded across her forehead. Whatever was in the woods was now moving across the clearing from all directions.

Jael kept her focus. In desperation, she whispered a powerful spell in an Airisth dialect to override the enchantment. It was a turbulent spell she swore never to divulge and she knew could have side effects, but she was desperate, and it worked.

The bracelet fell free from the Astermeer's leg and into the palm of her hand. Jael fastened it to her own wrist. She whispered another potent enchantment of the same tongue to secure the bracelet once again—the bracelet that would reveal the identity of the one who inherited the power of the Fire Realm, the one who would shape the history of Allumbreve and the war with the Quag. "The *Electus*."

With the encroaching sound almost upon her, Jael spun about to face a most horrific sight—a sight she knew meant she had made a dreadful mistake. She stood fast and ignited her lance. A large pack of worgriels stared at her with their ghostly, pearlescent eyes and then, screeching their dreadful cry, lunged at her.

SOUTHERN PLAINS

The southern border of Froughton Forest came at last and with it, Realms End.

"Finally."

Magnus slowed to a comfortable walk. He was twenty leagues from the Cliffs of Overpell and the border of his homelands. It was the dawn of a new day and Magnus could see across the southern plains to the Corville Mountains. At their centre was the break known as the Corville Pass. Through here, Magnus hoped to pass into the southern wastelands.

"There has to be another way through." Magnus scratched his head. He looked at his nails and examined the dirt lodged under them, prising it out with opposing thumbnails. He kept walking while he was thinking, listening to the chirping wrens and robins making their dawn call from the outer reaches of the forest. A different sound began to emerge from around the hill to his right where a road from the Uydferlands led to the junction where he stood. At first he heard voices but as it got closer to the foot of the hill he could hear the striking of horses hooves and cracking of whips.

Magnus ran and dropped behind a small group of boulders at the base of the hill a short way back from the road. He watched as a slow moving convoy of Quagmen on horseback moved into view. Magnus peered through a thin slit between the rocks. Behind the Quagmen came a procession of six prison carriages. They were filled with prisoners. Their clothes were torn, and many of their backs were bare and bloodied from whips. Most had their wrists and ankles bound together, with the exception of five pairs of prisoners behind the last carriage who were chained to one another and forced to walk. At the rear of the procession were more Quagmen on horseback and two wyverns that snarled at the heels of the walking prisoners.

Magnus looked at each one of the people in the carts. On the one hand he hoped not to see anyone he knew, but on the other, he was curious to see if he would. And then, he did. At the rear of the final carriage, almost hidden among the many expressionless faces, was Sarah. Her curling locks of blonde hair covered half her face, but it was unmistakably her. She wore the same purple dress she had worn when last Magnus saw her, although it was now as torn and tattered as her companions' clothes. The entourage trundled past heading south for the Corville Pass.

"Think Magnus, *think*…" he muttered. There had to be a way to help Sarah. *Perhaps hide beneath one of the carriages,* he thought. But the more he thought, the more futile the idea seemed.

Unless—Magnus had an absurd idea—*perhaps I could turn myself in?* He knew it would have nothing but negative consequences. But the alternative was challenging the dozen or so Quag guards and the wyverns that had now grown to four in number. That could only result in his death. But giving himself up? If they took him prisoner, rather than killing him, he would have passage into Ba'rrat and even, perhaps, into the prison where his parents were being held. It was a truly absurd option—that much he knew. *But*, he realised, *I have no other choice.*

Magnus removed his sword and scabbard. Aside from his clothing, the sword was the only thing he possessed and the only thing of value to him. He slid it carefully into an opening between two large rocks, knowing no one would find it without deliberately searching for it. Then he walked out into the open field, behind the four wyverns. His heart raced. He waited for one of them to turn and spot him. However, something was not right. Magnus's vision became shaky and his body hot. He began to sweat and nausea came over him worse than it had the previous night.

"No… not now," Magnus mumbled. He turned, knowing he had to get back to the rocks and hide himself again while he still could. But it was too late. Two of the wyverns at the rear of the train had spotted him and were immediately upon him, hissing and spitting. Magnus fell to his knees shaking and just before he passed out, the wyverns' awful screeches pierced through him.

"Magnus!" a voice whispered sternly. The sickness for him was bad this time. He still shook with fever and struggled to see straight. "My boy, you're burning up." The whispering continued. It was Sarah.

"Sarah…" he replied weakly.

"What on earth were you thinking? I hardly recognised you at first. You've changed… put on weight if anything… what in all of Allumbreve?" And then her voice fell silent. Magnus felt her grab his right wrist, rubbing his scar with her thumb. "Oh my…" she exclaimed aloud.

"Shut it!" one of the guards shouted. Magnus tried to sit up but Sarah held him in her lap.

"Stay where you are," Sarah whispered again. "You'll avoid the whip if they think you're too weak to stand."

"I said, shut it woman, or you'll take to walking."

"Sorry," Sarah replied politely.

Magnus grimaced as waves of heat and nausea worked in unison, twisting and turning through his body more so than before. It was as though this sickness of *Anunya* was getting worse. *No wonder the dragon made such a point of it.* He held tight to Sarah, welcoming the comfort of her touch. Everything about her seemed wonderful—her familiar smell, her reassuring voice… It all seemed to meld into his feverish dreams and he let himself imagine they were safe and sound back home at the western margins. She had always been as a second mother to him and so he allowed himself to rest in her company for perhaps the last time.

The carriage rolled on all through the day and into the night that followed. Magnus's sickness never abated and Sarah never let him out of her arms. On the occasion that he awoke, often only for minutes at a time, she would whisper in his ear. Her words were always of reassurance and never told of the nightmare they were facing. At one stage during the night he woke and saw they were passing through a deep, narrow ravine with cliff walls hundreds of feet tall.

"The Corville Pass," Sarah had explained.

Finally, some time during the second day of travel, Magnus's fever broke and he was able to see clearly again. He was wet through from perspiration, yet craved no drink. He had not eaten since he shared fish with Thioci many days past, yet craved no food. Magnus looked at the people in his company who were faring far worse than him. All of them were suffering from exhaustion, hunger and thirst. Most of them were Uydfermen and women, with their characteristic olive complexion, dark hair and brown eyes. There were a few others that Magnus could not place—most likely people who lived on the outskirts of the Fire Realm, like he and his family.

Looking about, Magnus saw they had travelled far beyond the Corville Mountains and were deep into the southern wastelands. The four wyverns had taken position at the front of the prison train, forming a buffer against the sand storms that blew mercilessly. Visibility was poor and Magnus shielded his eyes and mouth with his arms from the assaulting sand. Still they pushed on southward.

Magnus was yet to be bound like the other prisoners. He gathered the Quagmen thought he was too sick to pose a threat. Shifting closer to Sarah, he removed his leather jacket and used it to shield both their heads from the wind. Sarah looked exhausted. Her cheeks had lost their plumpness and her eyes their cheeky sparkle. She smiled a deliberate smile but he could see there was no joy in it. He was not sure how to explain what Lucas had gone through, yet knew she would be dying to know.

"Sarah, when last I saw Lucas he was fine. I left him with the Uydfer clan, near the northern border." He knew his words were half-truths, for he was yet to learn that Lucas had recovered from the wyvern's poison.

"I am glad to hear that," Sarah replied, staring at Magnus. He knew she was sizing him up, deciding if what he said was true. Magnus questioned his decision not to return to the Uydferlands to find his friend.

"Look at yourself, Magnus," Sarah spoke quietly beneath the jacket. "Despite the illness, you're the picture of health. I have known you a long time and you are not the same. Something stirs inside you and going by the scar on your wrist I believe I know what it is. But I'll not speak of it here."

Her words trailed off as a Quag guard whipped her through the bars of the prison carriage, catching her across her upper back. She arched back with the pain before slumping forward into Magnus's arms. Magnus scowled at the guard who pointed his whip at him in return.

"Speak again boy and you'll be flogged far worse." Magnus gritted his teeth and looked away.

Night fell again, the winds died down and the carriages drew to a halt. The guards dismounted their horses and helped themselves to food and drink. The wyverns skulked about, sniffing the ground in search of prey. Magnus looked at the people in the other carriages who were all starving and thirsty. Many of them were children. In the carriage ahead was a young boy of about eight who began to whimper. The guard with the whip shouted at him to be quiet. The boy stopped, fear written across his face, and his mother comforted him all she could. Magnus saw red with anger and envisioned himself breaking down the carriage bars and attacking the guards with his bare hands. The guard then turned and came toward his carriage, immediately spotting Magnus.

"I see you have recovered from your illness," he scorned. "You can come join your kinsmen and walk." Another guard opened a door at the leading end of the carriage, grabbed Magnus by the hair and dragged him out. Magnus did not object, but Sarah did. She shouted obscenities at the guard only to be silenced by the whip once again.

"Leave her be! If you have a grievance, have it with me," Magnus shouted.

Several of the guards whooped in excitement.

"Hahaha, yes!" the guard with the whip revelled as Magnus was deposited at his feet, his shirt torn from his back. The guard raised his whip to strike when a Quagman astride a wyvern approached.

"What goes on here?" the wyvern rider asked.

"This one is in need of a lesson."

"Then give him a proper one and learn one for yourself," demanded the wyvern rider. "Smaggard—give the boy one of your swords."

The guard who pulled Magnus from the carriage grunted, drew a black sword and handed it to Magnus. "Get up," Smaggard shouted, forcing Magnus to take his sword. Magnus looked to the guard with the whip, who looked as confused as he was.

"If you're gonna teach the boy a lesson, teach every other slave scum the same," the rider shouted so that everyone would hear him. "If you answer back to a Quagman, you face death, not just a whipping."

The surrounding guards laughed with approval.

"Very well then," the first guard replied, throwing down his whip and drawing his two black blades.

Magnus eyed the Quagman who stepped toward him. The now familiar feeling of heat coursed through his body. His vision sharpened and the blade felt light within his grip. He recalled his fight with Crugion—how he had landed a blow across his face. He was much stronger now—Thioci had seen to that.

The guard came to him swinging, but with predictability and not nearly the skill he himself had learned under Ganister all these years. Magnus sidestepped the attacker's falling blade, making the Quagman overextend himself. His comrades laughed loudly, embarrassing the Quagman.

Turning back to Magnus, he came again and swung his blade crosswise. Magnus caught the blow with his sword firmly extended and with lightning reflexes he twisted his blade free and swung it sideways directly at the Quagman's neck. Magnus leapt back, unsure of the effect of his blow. The Quagman fell to his knees, dropping his swords to his sides and stared in shock at Magnus. He then fell forward to the ground, choking as his neck bled out.

There was absolute silence. Quagmen, slaves and wyverns alike were staring at the dead Quagman. But the silence lasted for just a moment. Every Quagman drew his sword and came at Magnus.

"Enough!" yelled the wyvern rider. "This one stays alive." His fellow Quagmen stopped and looked at him, as did Magnus—keen for an explanation. "With skills like that, I know someone who'll pay handsomely for him in Ba'rrat."

"What happened to *'facing death for answering back'?*" Smaggard spat, holding his one remaining sword. Magnus gripped hard to Smaggard's other sword, waiting the final decision. He was seething with anger. Smaggard was closest to him, so he decided he would go for him first if the fight continued.

"He's worth more than half of these slaves together. Killing him profits no one." The wyvern rider eyed Magnus. "Drop the sword and you'll live this day." Grumbling in protest, the Quagmen backed down. Magnus dropped the sword.

Five guards brought Magnus to the ground and bound his hands. He was taken to the back of the last carriage and chained in line with the other prisoners. Magnus was grinding his teeth, tensing his muscles and burning with rage. *It has to be the dragon blood...* Magnus could think of no other reason for his aggression. He imagined a dragon would feel the same under these circumstances. He thought of Thioci, brimming with anger at the Quagmen even when death was certain.

Once he calmed himself, Magnus could think a little clearer about what had just passed. He could not believe he bested the Quag Warrior. Even though he was chained up with little chance of escape, hope had returned. *If I can best one I can best them all!*

The carriages started moving again and he looked to the other walking prisoners. He wondered where and when they were captured. *Have Xavier's men lost to the Quag in the South? Has Csilla held fast to the lands in the North?* He hoped they were well and Lucas was safe with them.

Magnus saw Sarah watching over him like a hawk. He smiled back, wanting her to know he was unharmed. The carriage moved at an infuriatingly slow pace. Magnus never lost his footing nor protested and so avoided the guard's whip. However, his companions did not fare so well, with many receiving a beating past the point of recovery, at which point they were thrown into a carriage and another took their place.

There was one among the prisoners walking beside Magnus who seemed able to keep pace. He was about Magnus's age, tall and wiry with curly black hair. He looked to Magnus frequently.

"Do I know you?" Magnus whispered, after one of many such looks, leaning toward the other prisoner as discretely as possible.

"Aye," the man responded with a whisper but dared say no more. Later, the guards behind them were distracted in conversation among themselves and so the man spoke further. "I am Walt. I am a healer and understudy to Kriser. I helped your friend purge the wyvern poison." He spoke fast and nervously. Magnus thought back, remembering Kriser's two helpers in the healing tent.

"You healed Lucas's broken arm." Magnus remembered.

"Aye." Walt smiled.

"Is he well?"

"He is *recovered* if that's what you mean, but *well?* That's a matter of perspective." Magnus stared at Walt, waiting for him to elaborate. "Did your friend have…" he took a breath, considering his words carefully. "What I mean is, did your friend have an aggressive personality as you knew him?"

"Aggressive?" Magnus shook his head. "Not at all."

"Once Lucas was recovered, he fought alongside Csilla and her men. He fought well and bravely. But as days passed, something changed. His temper began to get the better of him and he began bickering and fighting with our people. The men could do nothing to appease him and eventually called for him to be banished. Csilla intervened, asking Kriser to examine him in case the wyvern had poisoned his mind. But before he got the chance, Lucas disappeared."

"Disappeared?" Magnus asked.

"Aye. About four days ago," Walt concluded.

Magnus opened his mouth to speak but the Quagman's whip came down upon both their backs—first Magnus and then Walt. They both fell under the sting of its bite but were fortunate enough to only receive one lick each. The Quagmen rode closely behind them from here on making further conversation impossible.

Lucas is alive, but something is wrong… Magnus wondered where he would have gone. *Perhaps he tried to follow me to Guame, or travelled back home to find Sarah.*

Magnus looked to Sarah, who had fallen asleep in the back of the carriage. He felt all the more sorry for her. He considered Walt and wondered what circumstances led to him being captured. Magnus had so many questions for him and hoped he would have the opportunity to ask them.

BA'RRAT

It was mid-morning the following day when the sandy wastelands gave way to hard granite. The granite itself soon ended at a cliff top with a spectacular view across the southern coast.

"The Black Cliffs of Ba'rrat," one of the prisoners walking beside Magnus murmured in a raspy voice.

"Out of the carts, all of you," a guard ordered.

The steel doors to all six of the carriages opened and the prisoners spilled out under the constant shoving and threat of the guards. Sarah was slow to move but shuffled herself out when prompted. Magnus and the other walking wounded were freed of their shackles and shoved into ordered lines with the other prisoners. They were herding all prisoners toward the cliff edge. Some of them began to cry, fearing the worst. A Quagman atop a horse rode between the prisoners and the cliff's edge.

"Stop your wailing. Do you think we brought you this far to throw you over a cliff? Make your way down the stairs and keep yourselves quiet, else we'll find a reason to do just that. Now move!"

As the line of nearly a hundred shuffled against their will to the edge of the cliff, Magnus realised, *If these are the Black Cliffs of Ba'rrat, then…*

He cast his eyes down over the foreboding expanse of the city of Ba'rrat. It was beyond anything he had ever seen before and was easily twice the size of Guame. The entire city was made of black granite, carved from the cliffs he now stood upon, leaving the cliff face a surface of smooth, shimmering black that cloaked the city in its hulking shadow. Ba'rrat stood at the ocean's edge as if in defiance of the waves that crashed against a great sea wall made of the same black stone. The city's outer walls ran for miles around the labyrinth of buildings and streets within. The entire city was covered in a salty ocean mist.

Magnus was pushed firmly in the back, snapping him out of his dream state. He moved in line and followed the other prisoners who were advancing down the stairs carved into the sheer wall. The stairs were narrow and zigzagged their way to the bottom, about five hundred feet below. The coast winds blew hard making progress slow, always threatening to pick them up and throw them down the cliff.

Walt was directly in front of Magnus and the nearest guard was at least ten people away to the front and as many to the rear. "Walt," Magnus whispered. "How did you get yourself captured?"

"I travelled to the South to help the wounded," Walt whispered over his shoulder. "They were overrun within days. The North holds strong though. Csilla maintains a strong defence there."

"Any word of her family? Of Xavier?" Magnus asked.

"I hear Xavier pulled his men back to protect Nuyan. They've been able to protect our lands from Nuyan to the quarries in the North. It was his daughter who met with the best of fortunes. What timing—she was taken into the fold of the dragon priests."

"Aye." Magnus hid his personal association with Catanya.

"Alas, there has been no sign of the priests or dragons coming to our defence."

"Aye," Magnus repeated. He recalled Csilla's words about the matter. *Things have changed among the dragon realm.*

"If there was ever a time we could use their help, it is now," Walt added.

Magnus drifted away from the conversation and looked again over the ominous city. He considered his parents and possibly Ganister who were being held captive within its borders. *My parents are down there somewhere…*

"You see those ships at sea?" Walt continued. Magnus did not really want to continue his conversation with Walt—it seemed every topic they discussed brought bad news. Nevertheless, Magnus cast his eyes over the Neverseas and saw three large ships with billowing sails making their way toward the coast. The huge waves of the impenetrable ocean were merciless—crashing rhythmically over and over again. But there was a narrow strip of ocean where the waves were tame and infrequent. *The Southern Gap,* Magnus supposed. It was here that the ships could pass safely toward shore and the foreboding black city.

"They're for us," Walt explained. "Most of us, anyway."

"What do you mean?" Magnus asked, reluctant to probe any further.

"I hear slaves fetch a better price beyond the lands of Allumbreve. Those ships will carry many of us to the Otherlands, through the Southern Gap and over the Neverseas."

Magnus felt a sense of panic. *I cannot be made to leave Allumbreve.* He needed to get into Ba'rrat and find his parents.

As they progressed their way down the stairs, Magnus spent time looking over the city, knowing it was the one chance he had to evaluate it from above. The streets seemed to span out in all directions from a central axis off-centred slightly to the south, with many narrower lanes interconnecting the streets. Magnus thought the pattern was much like a spider's web. The streets were lined with densely packed buildings, all made of the same black granite. Unlike Guame, whose buildings were joined with makeshift canopies and stalls, Ba'rrat's buildings butted up against one another. *This city was built to last...*

At the axis of the city was a massive, circular structure divided into quadrants with tall towers. *Ba'rrat's arena... as Crugion spoke of,* Magnus recalled.

It took over an hour to descend the cliff face. Magnus, all the while, kept an eye on Sarah, six people in front of him. She glanced back at him occasionally, as if checking he was still there. *Should I tell her what I've learned of Lucas?* He did not want to say her son had disappeared and lost his mind, at least not without knowing for certain himself.

The descending stairs ended at a narrow, steel barred gate. The prisoners were made to wait whilst the slower of them came down the stairs, the guards chastising them for their tardiness. Once assembled, the barred gate began to thump and grind and the heavy steel bars ascended, revealing the innards of the city. From within, Magnus could hear the low drone of a horn being blown over and over again. The line of prisoners began to move forward through the gate and into Ba'rrat.

Magnus kept his position in line. As he got closer to the gate he could hear cheering from within the Capitol. It grew louder as he neared the gate. Magnus's stomach fluttered and his heartbeat quickened. He could hear the cheers accompanied with laughter and jesting snipes backed up by the incessant horn that sounded the same single tone over and over. No sooner had Magnus entered through the gate when an apple hit him square in the face. A crowd of a hundred people were teasing and taunting the new prisoners. The Quagmen who had travelled with them smiled proudly to the people as if bringing Magnus and the other prisoners into the city somehow made them heroes or conquerors.

Magnus wondered where the city folk came from. Were they all Quag clanspeople? Were they outcasts from the North who had taken up residency here? Or had they travelled from over the Neverseas to help conquer the lands of Allumbreve? Aside from those involved in the mockery, the townsfolk appeared to be going about their business much like the people Magnus saw in Guame.

The last of the prisoners entered the city and the gate closed behind them. *There's no escaping now.* He took a deep breath. They were led down a straight, cobbled street. It was several metres wide with tall buildings either side. The continuous walls of buildings were broken only by the smallest of windows and locked doors. Occasionally, Magnus caught a glimpse of peering eyes behind drawn curtains or peeping from cracked doors. The road opened into a wide, paved square. The prisoners were instructed to stand across it in single file.

The square was walled in on all sides with buildings. Each corner of the square had a tower with a city guard positioned at the top holding a crossbow pointing to the people below. The uniforms of the city guards were more uniform than battle attire, and each carried just a single longsword. Magnus thought they looked more like hired soldiers than bloodthirsty warriors.

Magnus looked at his companions. Most of them were so exhausted they could barely stand. Some murmured among themselves and the youngest of the children whimpered. Magnus shuffled for position beside Sarah and took her arm, supporting her. She fell onto him, barely able to maintain consciousness. Magnus held her tight, fearful for what the guards may do if they saw her so frail.

By contrast, he still felt as rested and alive as ever. He stood with a deliberate slump so as to blend in. As he held Sarah close he could still feel the heat of the dragon blood course through his veins like molten steel pouring through a long channel. His heart pumped hard, struggling to keep up with the demands of the new, foreign blood that ruled his body. *"I give you my blood..."* Magnus recalled Thioci saying. He clenched his fists and felt the strength in his forearm, the blood throbbing in his fingers.

The drone of the horn finally ceased and a trumpet sounded in its place. Several horses approached the square. Magnus winced, hoping to all the Gods it was not Crugion, nor Briet, nor any Quagman who may recognise him. It was none of these, but as four horses rode into view, the leading black horse caught Magnus's eye—*Tameror!*

It was Ganister's Wardemeer—immediately recognisable by the small flash of white that ran diagonally across his nose. Astride him was a large Quag warrior dressed in full armour with a black sword strapped to either side of his saddle—*Ganister's saddle.*

Magnus looked into the man's characteristic deep-set eyes and wondered if he had killed Ganister. The other horses were not warhorses at all and likewise, their riders were not warriors but were overdressed in exotic fabrics, the likes of which Magnus had never seen before. He looked at Sarah, who struggled to remain awake. She was yet to recognise her husband's horse.

"So this is it then." The Quagman astride Tameror spoke with a husky, forced voice. "This is all the Fire Realm has to offer in defence of your lands." He drew one of his swords and reached forward from Tameror's saddle, pointing it at a prisoner down the line to Magnus's left. "Tell me, where are your priests? Where are your dragons?" He waited for the prisoner to answer, but they did not. "Have you even called them to your aid?" Still, no answer came. "Then tell me this—do your priests and your dragons even exist?"

A voice called out from the far end of the line. It was the small, squeaky voice of a child. "They exist you horrible man. And when they come they will kill you all!" The guards laughed and the Quagman astride Tameror sheathed his sword and alighted, walked over and kneeled in front of the child.

"Come child," he held his hand out but the child refused to come forward. "Come!" The child's mother sobbed as she pushed her son gently toward the warrior. Magnus ground his teeth together once again and squeezed his fists into tight balls. The child walked toward the Quagman. He was no more than six years of age. Magnus looked to the nearest guard, spotting the sword that hung from his left hip. He shifted his weight between his feet. Magnus could see all the other prisoners held their breath, watching the interaction play out. Magnus knew that if the boy were killed, the Quagman would have to face an angry mob.

The Quagman placed one of his gloved hands on the boy's shoulder. "You are a brave young man, speaking out as you did. It's a pity your people don't share your courage. If they did they surely wouldn't be standing here now." The guards laughed once again. Then one of the well-dressed horsemen called out.

"Fifty for the boy."

The Quagman let the boy return to his mother and turned to face the man. "Fifty?"

"I count a dozen children here under the age of ten. I call it five hundred darna for all of them." Magnus looked at the man in disgust. He was by far the fattest man he had ever seen with a large round head and a long moustache that hung down over his belly, which was covered in yellow silken fabrics. His accent was foreign to Magnus.

"Very well," the Quagman replied. "A deal is struck."

The other horsemen started to speak out. They shouted offers of purchase for other prisoners in the line up. One middle-aged man with tanned and tattooed skin dressed as lavishly as the fat man but in his own unique way, took a liking to the women.

"A thousand for the best five women here." He pointed in turn to the five he preferred. Most of them were no older than Catanya. Magnus was glad she was not there.

Magnus suddenly felt his forearm being gripped tightly as if caught in a vice. He looked down and saw Sarah was holding onto him, white knuckled and shaking. Her eyes were wide and fixed on Tameror. *Oh no, she's seen him.* Magnus stroked her hair with his free hand, trying to calm her, but knew it was futile. She lifted herself up and shrugged herself free of Magnus.

"Sarah, no…" Magnus pleaded, but it was to late.

Sarah marched forward toward the large Quagman who stood beside Tameror. The guards did not anticipate such defiance and fumbled for their swords. Sarah moved briskly, hitching her billowing, tattered dress up as she went.

"Where is he? What have you done with him?" she shouted at the Quagman, who was conversing with one of the traders. He looked up to see what the commotion was about.

"Where is my husband?"

The guard nearest Magnus ran at Sarah and kicked her square in the back, sending her toppling forward. Her face slammed into the stone ground at the guard's feet and she let out a cry of pain. The guard came at her, his sword raised to strike.

Magnus plunged at the guard as hard and fast as he could, throwing his full weight at his back and tackling him to the ground. He seized his fallen sword. The guard lifted himself from the ground and came at Magnus who drove the sword through the guard's chest, pulling it free again and leaving the guard to fall to his death. Magnus blinked—it had all happened so quickly. He stood over Sarah, ready to face his next opponent. He looked to his left then his right, evaluating the approaching guards and calculating who would reach him first.

Directly behind him was the large Quagman. Magnus spun quickly to face him. His right hand reached for his weapon, but he hesitated for a moment as

Magnus threatened with his raised sword. To his left, a guard came upon him clumsily and Magnus moved quickly, allowing the guard's blow to swing through the air without purchase. Magnus swung his blade across the guard's neck—much as he had done to the Quagman in the wastelands—killing him instantly.

The next guard came faster and parried several blows with Magnus, drawing blood from his right forearm as it cut deep into his flesh. Magnus grunted as he returned in form, swinging the large blade again and again until he forced the guard off balance. He fell to his back with Magnus driving his borrowed sword into the man's stomach.

Magnus leapt back to Sarah and stood over her again. The guards in the towers each had their crossbow pointed at him. The large Quagman warrior had not yet drawn his sword but held a raised hand above his head. Magnus knew in an instant he would signal for the tower guards to release their arrows and then he and Sarah would be killed.

I may have time to kill this Quagman, Magnus considered.

"Kill him, Magnus!" Sarah spat and glared at the Quagman through her bloodied face.

"Wait!" a voice called. "Don't kill him, Daxton." Magnus glanced to another of the riders in the company—a weathered man of about sixty years with a long silver goatee hanging from his chin and short hair combed stiffly to the front.

"I will make purchase of this boy," he continued.

"A *boy* you say," the Quagman responded. "He's just killed three of my men!"

"And for that I will pay a thousand darna."

"I'd pay twice that to see him dead, Carlo."

"Then you'll see half the day's profits wasted." Carlo alighted from his horse and walked toward Magnus. "Lower your sword," he said.

Magnus thought only of Sarah, still crouched on the ground beneath him. He kept his sword raised and every muscle in his body as taut as the strings in the crossbows still pointed at him. Carlo looked at Magnus, then to Sarah.

"You are most protective of this woman," he said. "Who is she to you?"

"My mother," Magnus answered, hoping somehow it would protect her.

"I will pay fifteen hundred." Carlo took a step toward Daxton. "No more. For that I will have the woman as well."

Daxton considered the man's offer for a moment longer then agreed with a nod.

"Very well. And you…" he pointed to Magnus, "I'll see you dead in the arena soon."

The Quagman signalled with a wave for the guards to stand down. Looking to the towers, Magnus saw the men lower their crossbows and the guards beside him sheath their swords. Magnus looked to the man who had bargained for his life—the man named Carlo. He was not at all tall but was of a strong build and presented as a battle-hardened man even though he was dressed well.

"Lower your sword and you'll both live the day out. Do not, and both your lives will be forfeit." Magnus did as instructed. The guards promptly seized both him and Sarah, binding their hands with rope.

Twice now Magnus had killed Quagmen and both times his life had been spared. He was beginning to think there was value in this practice. As he and Sarah were led away from the other prisoners and the large courtyard, Sarah turned and shouted once again at Daxton who had mounted Tameror again.

"Tell me, did you kill my husband?"

Daxton considered his answer for a moment. "I didn't need to, woman. Men like him die at your feet without provocation!" He laughed.

Sarah fell into Magnus's chest, sobbing. Daxton turned back to the business of selling the prisoners. Magnus looked to the others. A few were still looking at him but most were dealing with their own grief now that guards moved in to separate people from their loved ones and children from their parents. Magnus wondered how many would be taken beyond the Neverseas to live the life of slaves far away from their homelands as Walt had said. He caught Walt's eye for a final time and nodded to him. Walt nodded in return. It was a sign of farewell. They both knew it was the last time they were likely to see one another.

FERUSTIR

Catanya had been sick on and off for three days.

Joffren insisted she continue her training during periods of wellness, but it would always be interrupted with Catanya having to stop to deal with the cruel side effects of *Anunya*. "It is a process we have all gone through, Semsarian." Joffren's words, as usual, did little to encourage her and it was the last thing she wanted to hear when she was in the throes of fever and another episode of vomiting.

"Why is this happening to me?"

"Your body tries to reject the blood of the dragon. It fevers it out like poison in the blood. But it soon yields... it learns it cannot defeat it. It is far too powerful."

Catanya was not at all impressed. She was certain had she known her training led to this she would have certainly fled. But she did not know at all—none of the priests did prior to their inauguration. Catanya learnt that it was the greatest secret of the priest order. It was the secret to their superiority as warriors.

Joffren had told Catanya in the temple her blood was still her own.

"Then what will the chosen one—the *Electus*—receive that I have not?"

"From what we have learned from the other realms, the chosen one sacrifices themselves for the will of the Gods," Joffren said in the formal voice that he always used for such discourse. "They inherit the blood of the dragon in place of their own, and the absolute power of that realm." He then dropped his formal manner. "Can you imagine, Semsarian, having such power at your fingertips?"

Catanya was surprised Joffren spoke in this way. "Should we be craving such power, Semsdi—being the serving priests that we are?"

"Not at all. But it does no harm to wonder."

Catanya looked at Joffren for a long moment, wondering about his history and what circumstances brought him to the priesthood. She wondered then what the *Electus* could mean to her people.

"Will the chosen one turn the tide on the war with the Quag?" she asked.

Joffren nodded, "Yes, Semsarian, I believe they will."

"Then who, Semsdi, is worthy to receive the blood of the fire dragon?"

"In time we will know. The *Electus* will present themselves to us when the time is right." Joffren spoke as though he had read it straight from his *Murata Fara*, but Catanya could see he truly believed what he was saying. Having experienced the bond she had formed with Rubea, she was beginning to appreciate his faith.

"How will we recognise them? How will we know for sure they are the chosen one?"

Joffren paused and looked Catanya in the eyes. "We will know, Semsarian. They will not be able to hide from who they are…"

Nights had been the worst for Catanya's *Anunya*, tainted with strange dreams, often with visions of Magnus. They were always much the same as the dream she'd had after her cleansing—with Magnus riding to her on Balgur. In her dreams, Magnus was tall and proud and he smiled at her with confidence as though everything was right in the world. Catanya would wake wondering if the elders were playing mind games with her, maybe testing her loyalty to the priesthood. She resolved to never speak to Joffren of her dreams, nor her love for Magnus. At least, not until the time was right for her to leave.

On the fourth morning Catanya's fever broke for the last time. She left her room at sunrise feeling tired but was relieved the sickness was finally over. Peering across the grounds of the Romghold, she saw that the green training field teemed with activity. People were moving to and fro, setting up tents and tables and laying out chests and packages of all shapes and sizes stacked in rows beside and within the tents. The people themselves, both men and woman, were clearly not priests but dressed as artisans, mostly in neat white attire with sandals upon their feet. They moved with purpose. It was as though they were on a mission. Catanya was curious.

As she walked slowly toward the field, a priest exited the temple and came walking toward her. As he approached, he drew his hood back.

Austagia… Catanya stared blankly at him.

"Semsarian," Austagia nodded politely, offering his hand in greeting.

Catanya was not sure how to feel about him. She still resented him but so much had changed—so much about *her* had changed—since last they met.

She stood tall and kept her hands behind her back. She gave a slight nod but said nothing.

Austagia withdrew his hand and turned so that he stood beside Catanya and faced the commotion on the training field. "Congratulations."

"Thank you," Catanya replied, feeling she had taken her rudeness far enough.

"Have you recovered from *Anunya*?"

"I have. I don't want to experience that again." Catanya winced at her informal manner. She was not sure how to talk to him and it felt strange to be in his presence again. "You were not at my inauguration," she stated.

"I intended to be. Alas, I was waylaid in Froughton Forest."

Catanya immediately thought of Jael. She had been gone for weeks now, on a journey she said would be a measure of days. "Do you know of Jael's whereabouts?"

Austagia shook his head. "No. I only hope she has not met ill fate."

Catanya grew worried. "Is there really much in Froughton Forest that could threaten a Ferustir?" Catanya peered up at Austagia, shielding her eyes from the sun. He returned her gaze.

"There is, Semsarian. Do not go there. I will not let them send you there. That is something your parents would never forgive me for allowing."

Catanya was surprised to hear Austagia make mention of her parents. It seemed so out of place in the Romghold. She thought perhaps her uncle deserved more credit than she had given when travelling to the Romghold with him weeks ago. Maybe, Catanya thought, amidst all the hard training she had emerged a more compassionate person.

"Semsarian," a voice spoke. Catanya turned to see an elderly priest named Trax standing beside her. "Come. It is time for your fitment."

Catanya pointed a thumb at herself. "Me?"

"They await you, Semsarian. Come."

Catanya looked back at Austagia, but he was gone—already moved out of sight.

"Come, Semsarian," Trax insisted, leading the way to the training field. Catanya ran to catch up.

"What are they fitting me for, Semsame?"

"Why, your Ferustir suit, young Irucanti!" Trax smiled.

Catanya smiled back and skipped a step as she walked. "Yes!"

"Semsarian?" Trax enquired.

"What I mean is, yes… yes they are," she grinned back at him.

For the first time, Catanya was excited to step foot on the training field. The perfectly manicured grasses always looked soft and inviting but her *cleansing* had tainted that pleasure. Now she had a whole different reason to be there.

"Semsarian, this is Delik." Trax introduced Catanya to a perfectly dressed man with the most exquisitely sculpted hair—both facial and on his head— she had ever seen. "He will be your chief tailor. He will oversee everything through design, construction and completion of your Ferustir attire." Trax turned to the tailor, a serious expression on his face. "Anything less than perfection, Delik, will *not* do."

"Very well, Semsü." Delik bowed to Trax and did the same to Catanya. "It is an honour, Semsü." He turned to the gathering of people behind him.

"These are my seamstresses—Kael, Ivy and Susannah." The three women looked nervously at Catanya and bowed before her. Catanya smiled and looked to each of them, which seemed to accentuate their nervousness.

"And my fellow tailors, textile workers, armoury men, blacksmiths, healers and sorcerers." Delik cast a hand toward fifteen other men and women who stood to attention and bowed formally.

Sorcerers… Catanya wondered what their purpose was in all of this. She turned away for a moment and whispered to Trax.

"All of this? Just to make my Ferustir suit?"

"Yes, Semsarian," Trax whispered back. "They are the finest in all of Allumbreve. You will see."

"And what is *Semsü?*" Catanya questioned quickly. "He addressed us as *Semsü.*"

"It is the formal address to one of our order, from that of another."

"Shall we begin?" Delik asked.

Catanya was led into the first tent. Delik left her with the three seamstresses who began the painstaking task of measuring and writing down every conceivable dimension—arm length, inseam, neck circumference and length of each individual finger. It went on and on. "Why so much detail?" Catanya enquired.

"Everything must be perfect," said Ivy, the eldest of the women. It was the only thing any of them said to Catanya during the hour-long ordeal.

When finally all was measured and noted, Delik returned and led Catanya to the second tent where she was seated in a comfortable leather chair. A young man sat to her right and an older man to her left. They each took one of her hands and began to examine them closely. They twisted knuckles, flexed fingers and used an arrangement of tools to take further measurements. Each of them were handed a small scroll of paper that the seamstresses had written measurements on previously. Both men examined and carefully re-calculated each of her finger, hand and wrist measurements and adjusted the notes accordingly. Relaxing into the role of being doted on, Catanya glanced to the young man to her right and caught him looking at her. He began to blush.

"What is it?" Catanya asked, curious as to what made him so uncomfortable. The young man shifted in his seat.

"It is nothing Miss Semsü, it's just…"

"Talk, Dale!" the older man interrupted. "If you've something to say, son, speak your mind." This seemed to make the young man blush even more.

"What?" Catanya asked again.

"It's just… I've never seen an Irucantî so… I mean…" he stopped to swallow.

"So…?"

"So beautiful," he said quietly. Catanya looked him in the eyes. He seemed to be drinking in the sight of her for a moment before he turned away, more red-faced than ever. "Father, I am finished."

"Go then, set up the lathe. I shall meet you shortly." The father finished with his own calculations and looked at Catanya. "I apologise for my son." Catanya looked at the man in silence. "He is becoming a fine blacksmith. But even a lowly craftsman must take pause once in a while for the finer things in life."

Catanya smiled at the older man. "There is nothing lowly about a craftsman."

"It is certainly not as noble as the calling of the priesthood."

Catanya wanted to reply that the *"calling of the priesthood"* was not of her choosing, but decided it was neither the time nor place to express her lingering bitterness. Instead she probed for information. "What is it you craft as a blacksmith?"

"For you? Weapons. A bow, arrows, throwing knives… and the more rudimentary parts of your lance." He was looking closely at Catanya's thumb. "But the latter takes far more skills to complete than I can do alone."

"Is that why you measure my hands?"

"Precisely. Each knife, for example, will be weighted to suit you. They will feel as an extension to your hand. And your lance will feel as one with you."

"That is certainly one of the finest things I've ever heard of," Catanya said.

The older man smiled at her and considered her for a moment. "I can see what my son sees in you, young Semsü. You are truly unique. Perhaps in another time and place, fate would have seen you as suitor to Dale and a daughter to me."

Catanya smiled. It had been a long time since she was paid such a personal compliment. She wanted to say, *"In another time and place I have been spoken for,"* but again, thought it inappropriate. Instead, Catanya politely thanked him.

Delik soon returned and took Catanya to a third tent where she was bled for a sample of her blood. The droplets were carefully tipped into a glass dish where one of the sorcerers cast spells to protect the valuable substance from contamination. Delik explained to Catanya how her blood would be unified with the fire-bronze used to manufacture her Ferustir's lance whilst in liquid form.

"Once completed, your lance will ignite for none but you, Semsarian." It was Joffren. "I will accompany you for the next stage."

Delik led Catanya and Joffren to the fourth tent. "Please Semsü, be seated."

Catanya sat in a reclined chair, but kept herself upright as she saw the two remaining sorcerers take position either side of her. She looked to Joffren who stood behind her—even closer than the sorcerers were.

"Joffren... What are they here for?"

Joffren nodded to Delik who stepped in to explain proceedings. "At any stage of your life, until this moment, it is possible you have encountered or been encumbered with spells or curses. Shale and Delmar will search your body and mind for such impediments and clear them. This allows you to fulfil your role of Irucanti untainted."

"Impediments? Untainted?" Catanya looked at one sorcerer then the other, then turned about and looked to Joffren. "What is your role in this?"

"I will be watching proceedings closely. There will be no mistreatment of *my* Semsarian, that I promise you." His face was stern. Catanya was convinced he would not let the sorcerers go astray.

"My memories. My past. What of those, Delik?"

"They will not be touched. You will remain the person chosen to fulfil the role of Irucantî, Semsü," Delik replied.

"Very well." Catanya lay back in the chair.

The sorcerers came closer and immediately got to work. Catanya found the elusiveness of their touch on her mind unsettling. It was so subtle that, without prior knowledge, she would not have been aware of their presence at all. Joffren, on the other hand, knew exactly what they were doing.

"They tread carefully so as to not interfere with your mind," he explained. "It also gives them the point of advantage should they come across something untoward."

An hour passed and the sorcerers were finished. They silently withdrew from her mind. Catanya felt a sense of relief wash over her.

"Did you find anything?" she asked.

"Not at all, Semsü," the dark-skinned woman named Shale explained. "You have some gentle enchantments made when you were an infant by a blood relative—more than likely your mother. These protect against illness and harm and have become a part of you without hindrance. We felt it best to leave them alone."

Catanya looked at Joffren. "That is all they saw, Joffren?"

"That is all," Joffren confirmed.

Catanya entered the fifth and final tent after parting ways with Joffren. Delik also bid farewell. "I will leave you here with my healers. Please, stay as long as you like. It will take some time before we require you for your first trial fitment."

"Thank you, Delik," Catanya smiled. Delik raised a hand toward one of the three women in the tent who came to Catanya and touched the still tender skin over her left temple.

"We will repair your broken skin, Semsü," she said, showing Catanya a piece of flaking skin that came away from her head where the markings were made.

Catanya wrinkled her nose at the sight, wondering what she must look like with her broken skin and dishevelled, partially shaved hair. The Irucantî always presented so perfectly yet Catanya had given no thought to her appearance since the *Anunya* process started. All she was concerned with was getting over the sickness.

"Oh!" Catanya exclaimed.

"Do not worry, we will make you radiant," the sprightly little healer said. She led Catanya to a tall bed. The other two motherly looking healers waited beside a table of assorted creams, oils, wraps and herbal mixtures. Catanya lay on the bed and closed her eyes as the healers weaved their magic, exfoliating her skin, massaging her tight muscles and tending to her face and hair.

In the decadence of her treatments, Catanya slept. When she woke some time later in the healer's tent, night had fallen. The tent was illuminated with lanterns and candles giving a peaceful light that supported her rested state. The table beside the bed was now cleared except for a square mirror facing her. Catanya examined her own reflection. She gasped and covered her mouth, then slowly pulled her hand away. The woman in the reflection was hardly anyone she knew at all. Her skin was flawless, her hair perfectly sculpted in a spiralling braid pulled neatly away from her left temple, over and across her right shoulder. The left side of her head shone with the soft oils that worked to accentuate the now-almost black markings that Rubea gave her. There were no doubts now—Catanya knew she looked like a dragon priest. And through the shocked expression on her reflected self, she saw the smallest of smiles come to her face.

Finding her usual priest robe draped across the bed end, Catanya dressed and left the tent, walked across the training field and back to her room. She settled into her bed for the night without any desire for supper. Within moments she was asleep, dreaming once again of Balgur and the handsome rider upon his back.

In the days that followed, Catanya resumed her training with Joffren with an emphasis on learning how to embrace the enhancements Rubea had gifted her.

"You will see now how your abilities expand," Joffren had said. Catanya did not understand at all and told Joffren as much. "You will come to see as your training progresses."

Training continued and Catanya experienced improvements in her strength, her speed and ability to focus. She was not sure she could attribute it to her *enhancements,* but each day she was noticeably better than the last.

Over the next week, her training was interrupted several times by Delik summoning her for trial fitments. No two fabrics they draped over her body were the same. With each fitment the shape of the material seemed to be more bizarre and unrecognisable. At one point, a sorcerer was required to remove several enchantments from a hardened, fibrous fabric to allow it to be moulded in numerous sections over her body, only for the sorcerer to reapply the spells once the shape was refined.

It was ten days since it all began when Catanya was summoned for the last time. She had just completed sparring with Joffren where she bested him once after a hundred bouts, but not without receiving a sword cut through her right upper arm. Joffren applied a small bandage to the cut and accompanied her to the training field and into a separate, large pavilion.

Inside, Delik was waiting with the seamstress named Ivy and the sorcerer, Shale. Delik stepped over to her and presented her with a neatly folded and completed Ferustir suit.

When she saw the final result, Catanya was lost for words. It was magnificent. Dressing in it, she found it form fitting. Her extra training over the past ten days had made her taut and toned and the suit sculpted firmly to her body's shape. Her personal Ferustir suit had hardened plates of armour made of a material she was not familiar with. It was smooth with a shimmering black finish but with a tightly woven burgundy pattern through it. The material was as hard as steel but when she tapped it with her fingers, it sounded dull like wood. It protected selected areas of her chest, shoulders, abdomen, back and upper thighs, with separate pieces of armour for her forearms and lower legs. The rest was left unadorned, allowing her to feel light and agile. Catanya was able to twist her torso from side to side, forward and back, the suit proving as nimble as she was. The more she moved the more the firmness eased until it felt as comfortable as any outfit she had ever worn.

"Perfect," Catanya said, looking at Delik. "Thank you… all of you." She looked to Ivy and Shale who smiled in appreciation. Ivy, meanwhile, had removed the old, tattered black laces from her boots and replaced them with new ones she had fashioned out of thin strips of burgundy leather that matched her suit. Catanya smiled, laced up the boots and pulled the leather straps back into place. She was glad to be wearing the one familiar piece of clothing that had served her well to date.

"Come," Delik instructed, taking Catanya over to a table that was neatly arranged with her own, newly crafted Ferustir weapons. "The weapons of a priest, Semsü." He had a look of pride on his face. Catanya saw that he was looking toward the rear of the pavilion and followed his gaze where Dale and his father were standing, peering around the entrance flap.

"Come in… please," Catanya insisted. The two men walked hesitantly toward the table. The father looked Catanya up and down.

"Semsü, you look magnificent."

"Thank you." Catanya looked at Dale, who was avoiding her gaze. "Dale, please explain to me what you have created here."

Clearing his throat, Dale walked around to the opposite side of the table. "Firstly Semsü, your bow. And a slim, tapered quiver holding five arrows. They are light and will not hinder you." He pointed to the bow that appeared to be made of the same black material as her armour along its limbs with a crafted grip of hardwood. Lifting it, she was amazed at its lightness. The strings of the bow were plaited twines of three strings that attached through three separate nocks at the tips. Replacing the bow, Catanya observed the beautiful, leather-crafted quiver that she lifted and placed over her right shoulder. She awkwardly tried to adjust the fastening buckle. Dale moved around the table.

"Please, allow me." He removed it and shifted it over to her left shoulder. "You are left handed, so you will draw with your left hand," he explained. He fastened the buckle so that its diagonal strap sat neatly in purpose made grooves in her suit. Satisfied, Dale moved back around the table. "Your throwing knives. Five in total once again." Dale pointed to the five, slim black handled knives whose blades were almost white. "Small, yet strong, the blades are made of Icerealmish steel. The only steel that can be milled so finely and keep its strength. The blades will never dull."

Catanya picked one of them from the sheet of white cloth they rested on, surprised by their lightness and balance.

Dale came back around the table again. "May I?" he asked. Catanya nodded, letting Dale take each knife individually and slot it into a small pouch built into the left thigh of her suit. Catanya moved her leg about once all five knives were in place. She could not feel them there—they fit perfectly.

"Finally, your lance," Dale said. He stepped back allowing his father to approach Catanya.

"Thank you, Dale," his father said. He stood beside Catanya with his hands behind his back, looking at the last object on the table. "This is your lance, Semsü. It is *bound* to you. It is of your blood. It will not yield to the will of another."

The lance rested on another white cloth. Its cylindrical shape was about a foot and a half long and was the usual bronze in colour. The engravings in the metal work, cut clean through its outer casing, were so fine and intricate that Catanya could not imagine a tool capable of carving with such precision. Through the carvings, a dull red light moved about like a small lurking creature within, waiting to be unleashed.

Catanya reached for the lance. Just before she touched it, the blacksmith spoke again.

"We have breached new ground with your lance, Semsü. The sorcerers have worked to bind it with a more potent mix of enchantments never used before."

Catanya hesitated for a moment then reached forward and held the lance at both ends with her fingers. The swirling red glow increased its speed a little. She shifted her left hand over its centre. Wincing, she held it out before her and gripped the lance with a fist.

"Tighter, Semsarian," Joffren whispered.

Catanya tightened her grip and the lance ignited with a loud cracking sound and a violent jolt as the two blades shot out—it was now a five-foot weapon. A flash of brilliant red light burst out in all directions and the engravings illuminated with such intensity they splayed shards of light between her fingers. The lance settled itself into a constant glow, shooting occasional rings of crimson light down the shafts of each blade. It was just as Catanya had seen when Jael ignited her own.

"It will take a while to settle into itself, Semsü," the blacksmith added.

Catanya twisted her wrist about and flexed her elbow, turning the lance over itself in a figure eight. It seemed to Catanya to be a living entity. She loosened her grip again and the blades retracted, sending a sharp jolt up her arm. Her extinguished weapon lay dormant in her hand and the red light faded to its former dull glow—swirling within the engraved handle.

Joffren stepped forward and looked the lance over. He smiled at Catanya, who smiled in return.

"Thank you," Catanya said to the two blacksmiths. She turned to face Delik, who now had his entire staff gathered behind him, watching the proceedings. "Thanks to all of you. What you have done here, in Dale's words, is beautiful." There was a collective sigh of relief from the artisans who all turned to quietly congratulate one another. Dale buried his head in his hands. His father smiled, giving him a pat on the shoulder.

Catanya continued. "I am honoured to be the subject of all your hard work, your years of combined skill that produced... this." She stood with her arms wide. She saw that Joffren was a little uncomfortable with her informal gratitude, but it never occurred to her to leave the pavilion without thanking the people for their efforts. Catanya turned to Delik for the last time. "Thank you, Delik. I hope I can honour you by putting my suit and weapons to good use."

"That, Semsü, I'm sure you will. May I?" Delik took the lance from Catanya and fitted it into a purpose made scabbard in her suit over her left shoulder, adjacent to her arrow quiver. "And thank you for your gratitude." Delik bowed then turned to instruct his staff to move on.

Catanya and Joffren were left alone in the pavilion. Joffren looked Catanya over in silence.

"Well, Semsdi. Have you nothing to say?"

"You are now a priest and a warrior, *Semsame*. An Irucantî and—when the need calls—a *Ferustir*."

Catanya bowed approvingly.

"Shall we put your new attire to the test?" Joffren suggested.

"Yes… most definitely!" Catanya agreed.

THE ARENA

Carlo peered through the bars of the prison cage. Mounted above the door with rusted twists of wire was a steel number '6'. His eyes were locked on the young prisoner he made purchase of nearly a fortnight ago.

"Has he spoken yet?"

"Not a word," the guard said.

"Two weeks..." Carlo mumbled, gripping the bars of the cage. "You there... Brutus," he addressed the large, powerful slave who shared the cage with Magnus. "Eaten? Has he eaten?"

"No, not really."

"And yet, Brutus, his plate is empty of a morning."

"He does not object, so I eat it myself. It gives me strength to fight."

Carlo shook the bars of the cage violently for a moment. Magnus was lying curled in a ball at the back of the cage. He sat up, wiping matted hair from his face—dirty from lying day in, day out on the damp, filthy floor. He was still shirtless, wearing only the pants and boots he inherited from Lucas. He stared blankly at Carlo.

Carlo snorted then looked at the two guards nearest him.

"Clean him, then bring him up top." He looked again at Magnus and back to the guards, "Did you hear me? Clean him then bring him up to the arena. I want him there in ten minutes."

The guards nodded and Carlo left the dungeon.

"Your time has come boy. You weren't going to be left here forever," Brutus laughed.

Magnus had not seen Sarah since Carlo's guards took them away. They were forced to walk down dark stairwells and passageways beneath the city and separated midway through the journey. Sarah did not stop wailing at the news of Ganister's death.

Somehow, Magnus did not believe it. Something about the way the Quagman joked about Ganister—*"dying at his feet without provocation"*—was misplaced. *Daxton... his name was Daxton.* Magnus vowed to remember the

Quagman's name, hoping he would chance upon him again to avenge Ganister whether his story were true or not.

Magnus was dragged deeper into the depths of darkness along a confusing arrangement of corridors he would never remember. When finally he reached the dungeon that held Carlo's collection of slaves, he was thrown into cage six.

For two weeks Magnus learned nothing of his reason for being there. Cage six held five men, including himself, when he arrived. The number reduced to two within a week. For two weeks now Magnus had seen Brutus, together with men from the five other cages built into the dungeon, taken away by guards one at a time. Some came back, bloody and beaten. Others never returned at all. As he learned from Brutus himself, of all the men in the six cages, only he had lived to see three months in the arena.

So far, Magnus had not been chosen to fight. He was relieved at first, but soon he grew weary of the waiting and thinking about what might become of him. Nevertheless, Magnus was grateful for one thing—he had not left the shores of Allumbreve. To what end he was not sure, but he was glad to be closer to his parents. He hoped beyond all measure that Crugion spoke the truth— that his parents were somewhere in the depths beneath Ba'rrat.

When the guards were busy or absent, Magnus spoke quietly to Brutus. "Do you know these underground passages well?" he had once asked.

"I believe so. For several months I have been marched to and fro through them. There are many divisions of prisoners beneath the city. Some are slaves used for fighting, others for labour, others await their execution and others— in the darker, deeper reaches—have been long forgotten and bide their time till the end. All considered, I think we get the best deal, the quickest death."

"And so, if I were to try and seek out a slave?"

"You'd best forget about them," Brutus chuckled.

This answer would not do. Magnus vowed to find Sarah, his parents and Ganister. *I just need to live long enough to do so.*

"Who do you fight up there in the arena?" Magnus asked.

"Whoever they give me. Most times other slaves, sometimes volunteers wishing to prove themselves. Today was something special—I faced a Quag warrior! Full of bravado he was, determined to show the crowd what a true warrior was made of. Twas the last mistake he'll ever make!"

Magnus let his companion consume his ration of the grey, oily gruel they were given each day. It reminded him of the food he was served at the Hugmdael Inn. It had pleased Eamon well enough at the time. *And was all he deserved.* In this case, his prison mate was perhaps gaining an edge in the arena thanks to his extra helping.

"Your appetite pleases me!" Brutus would say every time he tucked into Magnus's food.

Magnus could not account for his loss of appetite, or for his ability to remain alert having not eaten since his bonding with the dragon. The days blended together, with nothing to determine night from day other than when the other prisoners fought or slept. Magnus however, rarely slept, but at times the sickness returned with fevers and nausea and dreams of the dragon—*Balgur.* They were never as vivid as when he first bonded with Thioci, but Balgur's presence was always there, always with him.

The rattling of the oversized iron key in the lock marked the return of the two guards to cage number six, only this time it was Magnus who was summoned to leave.

One of the guards barked his well-rehearsed command. "Up top."

The other guard threw a bucket of water in Magnus's face.

"You're cleaned up, now get up top."

Magnus stood and wiped the water from his eyes.

"Stay alive *J'esmagdman,* no matter what," Brutus instructed.

"Why?" Magnus was pulled from the cage.

"I want to share your food tonight!" Brutus's voice trailed off and the last Magnus heard was his deep laughter. The guards placed his legs and hands in shackles and marched him awkwardly along a series of corridors turning to the left, then the right, then right again, then up a flight of stairs and along another series of corridors before finally climbing a second, longer flight of stairs. At the top, he was pushed through a gate and into the brightness of day.

Magnus squinted as the sun threatened to burn his eyes from their sockets. After a moment, his blurred vision came back into focus and he took in the vast size of the construction before him. There was no mistaking it—he was standing in the great Ba'rrat Arena. Its flooring was black stone spanning over two hundred feet across, where it met a high perimeter wall on all sides. The seating was arranged atop the wall into four distinct wings to the north, south, east and west. Each climbed higher than the tallest building in Ba'rrat. Behind each wing were parapets that towered even higher.

The seats around the arena were completely empty, but standing in the centre of the arena was Carlo. He was instructing two other men who were training with swords, practicing sparring techniques not that different to how he had trained under Ganister's tutelage since he was a child. Carlo turned as the guards marched Magnus over to him.

"Unshackle him," Carlo instructed. The guards did as they were told then stepped back from Magnus. Magnus rubbed his wrists and within moments felt heat pulsate through the abrasions made by the shackles. He was alarmed at how quickly his body responded to the minor injuries.

"It's been over two weeks." Carlo kicked a pebble and watched it bounce across the ground. "Two weeks I have given you to eat, sleep, rest. Yet my guards tell me you choose not to eat and they are yet to see you sleep." He walked to Magnus, standing close to him. "Tell me boy, do you feel rested?" he asked.

"Rested enough," Magnus replied.

"Very well. What is your name?"

Magnus knew he could not give his real name. He still feared Crugion would find out he were alive and make his parents suffer as he originally promised. Instead, he said the only other name he could think of.

"Lucas."

Carlo folded his arms across his chest. "*Lucas*. Very well. Do you know why you are here, Lucas?"

The answer seemed obvious to Magnus. He kept his silence all the same.

"Let me explain my situation to you. In the hours before you and your fellow slaves arrived here in Ba'rrat, I received word that one among you had bested and killed a Quagman on the wasteland fields. The man killed—whilst notoriously a wretched fool—was also a notable swordsman. So good in fact that he wouldn't fall easily to one of his own kinsmen, let alone a starving slave. *This*, I was told, was a slave I needed to invest in." He leaned toward Magnus. "You are that slave, yes?"

"Yes," Magnus said.

"So tell me. As I figure it, you'd travelled for days without food or water yet you still had the strength to kill three of the city guards once you arrived here." Carlo paused as if waiting for Magnus to explain himself.

"If you'd not called off the guards, I'd have killed more than that," Magnus retorted. The two men training with swords stopped sparring and turned to Magnus, interested in the conversation.

"Keep practicing," Carlo barked at them. "I'll tell you when to stop!" The men resumed their sparring. "You've got spirit boy, I'll give you that. But where did you learn to fight like that?"

"My father. He taught me."

"Hmm…" Carlo considered. "What I really want to know is, will you fight like that for me in the arena?"

"To what end? Will you set me free?" Magnus asked. He pulled his shoulders back as if to emphasise his stance on the matter. The guards moved in to retaliate, but Carlo raised a hand to stop them.

"There is no freedom for you. Just death. One way or another."

"So then, why should I fight for you? Why would I bother if death is certain regardless?"

Carlo spoke quietly to one of the guards who nodded in reply, turned and disappeared back down the stairs. Carlo turned his attention to Magnus again.

"You would better understand your position, Lucas, if you appreciated two things. Firstly, I *own* you. This means what I ask you to do, you do. You see these two men?"

Magnus looked to the two sparring men. Both had strong builds and scars from fighting. To Magnus though, only one of them seemed to have any real skills in swordsmanship. Magnus recognised them as the two men who resided in cage number three. The better of them had managed to survive several weeks of fighting.

"Those men do what I ask them to do. Those that *do not* aren't here to tell tale of it."

Magnus was growing tired of Carlo's speech. "And the second thing I am supposed to appreciate?"

Just as Magnus spoke, the guard returned up the stairs dragging Sarah with him by the hair. She squealed from the pain and tripped as she tried to keep up with the guard's brisk pace. Magnus started toward them, but the guard held a sword to Sarah's neck.

"Stay where you are," he warned.

"The second thing you should appreciate," Carlo continued, "is your mother. Every day you fight in the arena and survive, so too will she. She will be fed. She will not be harmed. But should you refuse to fight, or should you die in the arena, her life will be forfeited."

Magnus realised just how clever Carlo had been—purchasing Sarah was the perfect leverage. He regretted calling Sarah his mother. *Any fate would have been better for her than this…*

"Let her be," Carlo commanded and Sarah sank to the hard stone ground of the arena. Magnus ran to her. He held her in his arms. She looked far weaker than when last he saw her.

"Can you hear me, Mother?" he feinted, not wanted to compromise his identity. But Sarah was barely conscious. Magnus sighed. *I need to protect her, no matter what.*

Magnus thought about the Quagman he killed so easily, so too the guards in the city. Thioci told him he had inherited his power and Balgur told him he carried the legacy of the Fire Realm. Perhaps he really did have the strength to do as well as Brutus in the arena. *So be it.* He spoke to Carlo in his most confident voice.

"You feed us well. You protect my mother. I see her each evening to ensure her safety. And I shall kill every man who stands before me in the arena."

"Very well," Carlo clapped his hands together. "You fight tomorrow."

Magnus was afforded time in Sarah's prison cell. It was not a shared cage like his accommodation, but a four-walled cell with a steel braced, hardwood door in a dungeon deeper beneath the city. Sarah was in complete darkness but for a small sphere of light induced by her spells that hovered a few inches beneath the damp ceiling. Her cell was nowhere near his own, but he believed with repeated visits he would soon memorise the route. *At some point I'll be able to get her out of here.*

As Carlo agreed, Magnus and Sarah were fed a meal consisting of wholesome food—cooked lamb, fruit, cheese and watered-down wine. Magnus could not believe Carlo was so agreeable on this matter. *He must be investing a lot on my success in the arena.*

Magnus took care to feed Sarah. She ravenously devoured half the quantity of food before falling asleep. Magnus then began to eat for himself for the first time in as long as he could remember. It did not take long to recall his appetite and he ate every remaining morsel of food before him, finishing off with the wine. With a belly full of food and his appetite rediscovered, his spirits lifted.

Magnus paced around Sarah's room, feeling elated he had achieved a small win for himself and Sarah. His body coursed with the combined warmth of food, wine and dragon blood. He began performing exercises, squatting with his arms crossed in front of him for a count of one hundred. He then lay face down and pushed upward for a further count of one hundred. As he finished he saw Sarah had woken and was watching him, without saying a word. Magnus smiled at her.

"Do you remember back home when you said to me, 'There is good yet to come of this'?" Magnus asked. "You called it 'gypsy's intuition'. Remember?"

Sarah nodded. "Aye. I underestimated how long the good would take to come." Magnus explained to her how their fates were tied together. "What a curse I have brought on you, Magnus." Sarah hung her head low.

"I brought this on myself, Sarah. And for that I am sorry."

They both fell to silence and Sarah cast a spell so that a second light appeared, hovering at the ceiling, giving the room more illumination. She stood and looked at Magnus, holding his face in her mothering manner. She examined his eyes then the rest of his face before checking him over from head to toe.

"I am fine, Sarah," Magnus assured her.

"No Magnus, you are not yourself."

"I feel good Sarah. I feel fit and strong and…"

"I can see that, but you are not yourself. Look at you Magnus… your strength has grown in a way unnatural for a mortal man. No magic I know of could bestow you with such a change. Two weeks in the dungeons and you bear not a scratch. Every wound you have heals over, except this one here…" Sarah held his right wrist and rubbed her fingers over the scar that Thioci gave him. "This mark will never fade, nor will its significance. You have received the blood of a dragon, haven't you?"

Magnus was silent. It was something he did not want to reveal to anyone, especially here in Ba'rrat.

"I smell its ashen scent in your sweat. I feel its heat radiating from you. I have known your energy and presence since I held you as a baby. They have changed. They are not your own. Since I held you in the prison carriage… I knew."

Magnus did not know what to say. He felt ashamed for keeping it a secret from Sarah, but it was hardly a secret if she knew all along.

"Do not fear this, Magnus." Sarah squeezed his wrist tightly. "It is a gift of fate. You have been chosen for greatness. There is nothing more for you here. Escape while you can and before your power is discovered. You know who rules over this place. He will never let you live if ever he found out."

Magnus smiled at Sarah. He felt good to have someone to confide in. "Mother and Father are here in the city, Sarah. I have been told as much."

Sarah sat herself down again with her back against the wall and sighed. "I see. That is why you allowed yourself to be brought here."

"It was the only way."

Sarah looked around the room as she gathered her thoughts. "It seems we are stuck here for the time being," she said. "The least I can do is spend it teaching you some useful magic—Gypsy magic that is. It will help with the story of my being your mother and possibly help you in the arena." Magnus thought it a good idea. "Aside from that, I can tell you about your parents—particularly your mother. She is a reserved woman but she has always confided in me. I think you would appreciate a broader understanding of her people... of her former life in the Ice Realm."

Magnus was grateful for her offer. "I would like that very much."

"Very well then. You come here every evening as Carlo agreed and I will have a schedule worked out. It will be your training." Sarah smiled the way she used to smile.

"Magic and history!" Magnus said.

"Yes, magic and history."

The guards opened the door and grunted at Magnus to clear out. Before he did, he gave Sarah a kiss on the cheek.

The following morning, Magnus had lost none of his fervour and stood at the ready when the guards came for him.

"Fight strong, Lucas!" Brutus boomed encouragingly.

"I shall see you soon," Magnus replied.

Magnus was taken to an armoury room that looked out to the Arena where a battle was taking place. One man wielded a dull, poorly made sword and the other a long spear. Magnus could immediately tell the man with the spear would win, for the swordsman appeared inexperienced and looked tired and beaten. Within minutes the fight was over, ending as Magnus predicted. A wave of anxiety passed through his stomach as he realised he was going to be fighting for the same prize—his life.

With the squeal of rusty hinges, the gate to the armoury opened, snapping Magnus out of his reflective state. Carlo entered from the arena.

"Useless," he scorned. "A hundred darna he cost me and not one fight in him." He looked at Magnus. "Lucas, I trust you and your mother enjoyed your meal last night?"

"We did," Magnus spoke flatly, not wanting to sound too appreciative.

"Well, make your choice." Carlo cast a hand over a table holding a selection of badly made weapons. There were swords, spears, a triton, daggers, a mace and several other things Magnus did not recognise. "I trust a sword will be to your liking? You've killed enough of Delvion's men with one to know it suits." Carlo picked one from the table and handed it to Magnus. "Our fine swordsmith—Dougal—sharpened them all himself. He died two winters ago." Carlo scratched his forehead.

Magnus wished he had his fleu-steel sword with him. It would never have needed sharpening thanks to the wards protecting the blade and hardness of the steel. *That would certainly make my job easier.* In lieu of it, he swapped the sword Carlo handed him for another, longer sword with parallel sides ending in a dull point. There was a broken full-length mirror beside the table that he glanced at. He was taken aback by his own reflection. The man before him had a short, dirty beard and unkempt hair. His leather pants were weathered. His chest and arms were strong and toned—hardly the body he knew as his own.

"When you've finished admiring yourself boy, there's a fight waiting for you."

Magnus stepped out into the sun-drenched arena. It was a completely different spectacle to the day before. The grandstands held hundreds of spectators filling the rows in each of the four wings that surrounded the arena. There were men, women and children of all ages. To the north, shaded by large black sails, were the seats of the more noble folk, going by their attire and the surrounding guards separating them from more common folk who sat or stood about in a more chaotic fashion. They cheered and leered as Magnus walked out to the centre of the arena. Then came colourful swearing and spitting in Magnus's direction with some even throwing scraps of food as insult.

It dawned on Magnus all at once that Sarah's life would be forfeit that day if he should be killed. "That will not happen…" Magnus repeated the words to himself as a mantra.

The arena was silenced when trumpets blared to announce the start of the fight. Magnus turned in circles, looking for his opponent, when seemingly out of nowhere something hit him hard in the chest, sending him barrelling to the ground. Winded and shocked, he wondered where the man who attacked him came from. He clambered to his feet, still holding his sword as the man charged at him again. He was very short, with long auburn hair that grew down from the back and sides of his head surrounding a bald top. He came at Magnus fast, leaping high and throwing a net over his head.

Magnus tugged at the netting, trying to free himself but the more he did the more entangled he was. Panic set in. He tried desperately to struggle free.

He was reminded of the meliae in The Valley of Shadows and how she tried to strangle him. The crowd cheered as the small man—no higher than Magnus's chest—waved his arms around encouraging excited screams from the crowd. The little man then picked up a trident from the ground and charged toward Magnus.

Magnus crouched to the ground. He slowed his breathing and curled himself into a ball giving the net enough slack that he could shift his sword about and cut through a strand of the rope. Just as the small man reached him, his sword cut free. The man jumped again and threw his trident as one would a spear. Magnus leaned just enough to let the trident glisten past him and spun his body around, catching the small man as he landed, driving his long sword deep into his stomach. His opponent fell to the ground. The crowd fell silent.

Able to relax, Magnus pulled himself free of the net and walked over to the small man who lay gasping for breath, his stomach bleeding out. The wound was fatal. Magnus looked back toward the gate of the armoury, where Carlo began to shout and cheer with delight. The crowd soon joined him and the trumpets sounded once again.

Beckoning him to return, Magnus walked over to Carlo who slapped him encouragingly across the shoulder.

"Good job, Lucas." Carlo was grinning. Magnus held tight to his sword.

"Have you another?" Magnus asked. Fire coursed through him again and Magnus felt as though he could take on all of Allumbreve.

Carlo cheered again. "Another fight? Not today. You have given the crowd a taste and they will return to see more. Even more so, they will want to know your name. What shall we name you for the crowd, young Lucas— hmm?"

Magnus could not help but feel a little encouraged by Carlo's enthusiasm. He thought about his question, thinking of a name that would suit. A name that would pay tribute to the Fire Realm and his people. A name that would pay tribute to the dragon realm that bestowed him with his strength. He thought again of the pride of the Couldradt fire dragons.

"Well, what of it? What shall we name you?" Carlo beckoned.

"*Balgur.* I shall be *Balgur.*"

BAD TIDINGS

6 months later...

"Do you think you are ready?"

"I do."

"Very well then."

Since her Inauguration, Joffren rarely questioned Catanya. He treated her as equal, addressed her always as *Semsame*, yet continued with her training for another gruelling six months. Catanya appreciated this quality in him for it reinforced her own confidence in her abilities. This time she was not so sure though—the *Tenuura of the knives* was considered the hardest test for a young Irucantî to pass.

It seemed Joffren sensed her apprehension. "We have rehearsed this for months, Semsame."

"I am ready." Catanya knelt and retied her laces. They did not need to be any tighter, it just gave her a moment of reflection and had become her little ritual before she began a test.

The first of these tests was the *shardo bu evorth*—pairing of the swords. Here, Catanya had to spar against Joffren until she was able to separate him from his sword and take it for herself—thereby be in possession of a pair of swords. It took twelve hours of straight sparring before she bested him just once. She was humiliated, exhausted and required two days healing from the lacerations she received during the ordeal.

Next was the *trusul diev*—trust dive. She was paired with a beautiful female dragon named Liné. Strapped into the saddle, Catanya rode with Liné as she dove deep into a ravine, far below the eastern cliff face and pulled up before hitting the bottom only when Liné sensed Catanya's fear or desire to do so. Liné repeated this stunt over and over again, each time they got closer to the rocky creek bed before Catanya was gripped with fear. They had repeated the dive over fifty times in two days before Catanya learned to trust Liné's judgement and free her mind of fear. Liné insisted they complete a successful dive many times over to ensure Catanya's trust. At the completion of the task, Catanya had nightmares about the ordeal for three nights.

The *Tenuura of the knives* was the most dangerous challenge of all and was the last of nine. Catanya first learned about it in her *Murata Fara*. To succeed she would focus her mind, allowing her to perceive the trajectory of a knife thrown with lethal intent. She must catch the knife and dispose of it into an offside target. As was tradition, a residing priest would take the role of *Tenuur*—thrower. Unfortunately for Catanya, a priest named Demi was passing through the Romghold. She was renowned for being the most competent wielder of knives in the priesthood.

"Is she really that good?" Catanya had asked Joffren.

In reply, Joffren had rolled the sleeves of his robe up and shown the half dozen scars across each arm she had dealt him during a sparring session. "She is the best, Semsame."

Her laces tied with double-knots, Catanya stood upon the training field and took a deep breath. She was wearing her regular priest's robes—her Ferustir suit was stored away for battle attire only. *Is this not battle worthy?* Catanya pondered, wishing for the protection of her battle suit's armour. Sitting on a podium fifty feet away with her legs crossed, back straight and eyes closed was Demi. In her right hand she held a sheath with eight throwing knives partially drawn and splayed apart for easy retrieval. She licked the tip of her thumb and rubbed it over the top of each blade's handle in turn. Demi's absolute focus intimidated Catanya. She took a breath. *So be it—my final test.*

Four targets stood each side of the fifty-foot distance between Catanya and Demi. Each target was an apple perched on top of a six-foot high pole. These were the targets Catanya had to hit *if* she caught the knives thrown by Demi. Demi never missed her target—that much Catanya knew. If she were to survive the ordeal it would be up to her to stop the blades—all eight of them.

Catanya walked cautiously toward Demi. She slowed her breathing as Joffren had taught her. His words resonated through her mind—*'Feel the heat of the dragon within you. Do not fight it. Let it clear your mind and give you the power you need. Whether you win or lose depends on this faith.'*

Demi allowed Catanya to settle into herself before she threw the first knife. When it came though, Catanya was alarmed at the violent speed of the blade. Whistling through the air with pinpoint accuracy, Catanya raised her arms and clapped her hands firmly together, feeling the blade's sting. It slipped through her hands, but Catanya turned and grabbed it, before hurtling it off to her right side and burying the blade into the first apple.

A nasty smirk crossed Demi's face. The second knife came faster. Catanya was more focussed this time, watching it hurtle toward her. She reached out and grabbed the knife by its handle. Her other hand was ready for the third knife that was already half way toward her. With both knives caught, she threw them simultaneously at respective targets, placing one perfectly through the centre of the apple, but the other twirled past its target, missing it by half an inch.

Catanya took several deep breaths and Demi allowed her a moment to recover.

Two out of three. I must get six of the eight to pass the test...

Demi held the next knife up, twisting it between her fingers revealing to Catanya that she in fact held two. Catanya felt the familiar sensation of heat searing through her body and her heart pounded. *"The heart of the Ferustir,"* Joffren called it. The world seemed to slow and she watched as the two blades came at her, only an inch from one another as they reached her. Catanya caught one by the handle and the other by the sharp blade itself, slicing through her right palm as it slithered to a halt. Blood ran freely through her fingers. Ignoring the pain, she threw both blades and each successfully hit their respective targets.

Pain gripped Catanya again as the sixth blade sliced through Catanya's left earlobe, almost severing it. She had not anticipated Demi throwing it so soon.

Cupping her good hand over her ear, Catanya reached out with her injured right hand and caught the next blade that Demi must have hoped would catch her off guard. Catanya carefully threw the blade into its target.

One knife to go... I must get the sixth target. Demi sat motionless, waiting for the opportune moment to throw the last of her blades. Catanya let go of her ear and could feel the warm blood run down her neck. She tried to ignore the pain from both injuries.

Demi waited. She was giving Catanya way too much time to think things over. Catanya was only twenty feet from Demi and wondered for a fleeting moment what the priest would do if she threw the last knife back at her instead of the target. She quickly dismissed the idea, knowing Demi would return it to her with such deadly force it would likely kill her.

Demi leapt to her feet and threw the last blade with far more ferocity than before. Catanya struggled to see the blade, but she relaxed, closed her eyes and listened. She heard the blade whistle toward her, closing the gap between

Demi and herself. She raised both hands and clapped her palms together on the blade of the knife. *She caught it.* Catanya twisted it in the palm of her bloody hand. She looked at the knife between her red-stained fingers and then at Demi, who stared back with a sour expression on her face and arms crossed in front of her. Catanya sank it into the last target to her right.

In the healing room, Catanya was surprised to see Demi arrive to help with her wounds. She applied an ointment out of her own travel satchel to Catanya's hand and ear, before whispering a spell of some kind that made her ear lobe twitch and sting as it healed over.

"You'll have a scar there," Demi said coldly.

"That's fine," Catanya replied respectfully.

Demi stopped what she was doing and frowned at her. "Why is that *fine?*"

Catanya was caught off guard, not knowing exactly why she said it was *fine* other than to be polite. "It's fine because you could have killed me with that blade, had you chosen to."

Demi pouted her plump, red lips that matched her round face. Her eyes were large and seemed to do her thinking for her. "Joffren told me not to kill you."

Catanya thought it sounded like a warning and so chose not to say anything more. Demi was a renowned killer. Catanya had heard other priests talking about her as such. She wondered if Demi's cold manner was simply a facade to back up her reputation. Regardless, she found it harder to warm to Demi than she did to Jael. She imagined in years to come her own persona may be somewhere between these two.

The droning *bong* of the temple bell rang out. It was familiar to Catanya but something was different—it was ringing at a fast and furious tempo that seemed to alarm Demi. It was the first time Catanya had seen a shift at all from her usual cool manner. She packed her ointments back into her satchel and ran out of the healing room. Catanya followed.

Outside, the bell was much louder. All the priests of the Romghold were walking briskly through the courtyard. *Something is wrong!* Catanya thought. Demi and Catanya came around to the front of the temple and looked to the training field.

In the centre of the field was the dragon Liné. She was standing over another dragon—a youngling—that lay motionless. Slumped in Liné's saddle was Jael, who appeared to be moments away from collapsing. She suddenly slid off the dragon, landing heavily on her side, unconscious.

All twenty priests who looked upon the tragic scene simultaneously sprinted to the training field. Catanya broke into a run as well and from the far end of the courtyard she saw a priest running as fast as he could toward Jael, easily outpacing the others.

Austagia! Catanya recognised him. As he reached Jael, she woke and feebly pushed herself upward, only to fall again. Austagia caught her and lifted her into his arms. He placed a palm over her forehead and whispered a spell. Jael gasped for breath. Her eyes opened wide and she stared at Austagia. Catanya stopped and cupped her hands over her mouth, in shock at the sight of Jael—she looked terrible. Her body was battered and bruised with cuts, welts and scars all over. The remains of her Ferustir suit clung to her body in tatters.

Jael whispered words to Austagia as other priests approached and so Catanya saw fit to do so herself. Demi however, turned and walked briskly toward her private room. Catanya got a closer look at the young dragon that lay protected beneath Liné. Its scales were a dull, greying colour unlike anything she had ever seen before. The poor creature looked to have been dead for some time but even so, its appearance contradicted the words of her *Murata Fara* that said the scales of a dragon should hold their colour for a thousand years. Joffren appeared beside her.

"Semsame," Catanya said. Joffren nodded in reply. He looked as disturbed as the other priests and altogether unsure of himself. Catanya had questions she dared not ask. The other priests formed a half-circle around the two dragons and began discussing the situation. They made room for Austagia, who carried Jael off the field, walking briskly toward the healing room from where Catanya and Demi had come. Catanya desperately wanted to follow them—to be sure Jael was okay and to offer Austagia help—before considering it was not her place to do so.

Turning back to the dragons, Catanya reached out with her mind to share thoughts with Liné. All she could glean from her was a great sense of sorrow and the knowledge that she was the youngling's mother. Then Liné blocked Catanya's mind out completely. All the priests took a step back from the dragons simultaneously and so Catanya gathered Liné had blocked all of them at once. She was clearly not interested in conversing with people. Out of respect, Catanya turned her mind away from her.

There seemed to be much confusion among the priests, as if they did not understand how this could have happened to the youngling. But Catanya sensed there was more at play here. The two High Priests moved in over the dragon youngling and began examining him as a healer would a sick patient.

They mumbled to each other in Fireisgh as they lifted his eyelids, opened his jaw and felt the dull sheen of his gleamless scales. Then the High Priests examined the youngling's talons and recoiled as if in shock. They conversed feverishly between one another then stood back in silence.

One of the High Priests hurried back toward the temple. The other addressed the crowd. "We will gather at midnight in the nave. Be rested and prepared," he commanded. "Trax—call all brethren to the Romghold." The elderly priest nodded and took off quickly toward the temple. The rest of the Irucantî began to disperse. There were some whispers between them but most moved away in silence. Not sure what to do, Catanya looked at Joffren.

"Return to your room and prepare—as Ferustir," Joffren said. "Dress as if for battle, Semsame."

"For battle?"

"We will surely be set to task this night. To what end I'm not sure, but soon enough we shall know."

"What is wrong, Joffren?" Catanya whispered as they walked from the training field back across the courtyard.

Before more could be said, the sound of the temple bell ceased and was replaced by the blaring drone of a horn. Catanya blocked her ears but it did little to stop the sound resonating through her entire body, threatening to shake her apart. Atop the temple in the highest parapet, Catanya saw Trax, blowing into a horn that wrapped itself around the tower like a giant serpent, ending at ground level in a large open bell that visibly vibrated, sending its droning sound across the Romghold and beyond the mountains.

"Go to your room," Joffren shouted over the immense sound. Catanya nodded and ran toward her room. As she opened the door and entered, she turned back and looked over to the healing room on the eastern side of the temple, wondering if Jael would recover.

The horn continued to blow as dusk approached and the winds carried the drone far off into the western skies as if chasing the setting sun. Catanya did her best to rest but found it impossible. The horn was a call—the High Priest had ordered it. She knew more dragons and Irucantî would arrive at the Romghold this evening. But to what end?

The approaching midnight call to the temple would no doubt answer her questions, but what would happen? What were the repercussions for the death of a dragon?

Catanya unpacked her Ferustir suit from the blanket she kept it in under her bed. It had been months since she had last worn it, and she quivered with excitement to wear it once more. It was even firmer fitting than before, but Delik assured her its materials were designed to mould to her shape. *Just as well.* Six months of training had robbed Catanya of much of her womanly curves and replaced them with a leaner figure with muscles in areas she never knew a woman could grow them.

Midnight finally arrived and the drone of the horn stopped to be replaced with the more familiar calling of the temple bell. Catanya folded her black robes and laid them on the end of her bed, then sorted through her weapons. She placed the throwing knives in their leg pouch then placed her lance into its scabbard in her suit.

There was a knock at Catanya's door. She left her bow and quiver of arrows on her bed and went to open it. To her surprise, Jael greeted her. Catanya stared wide-eyed in disbelief. Jael wore a long, loose fitting gown that wrapped around her body, and a hood drawn back enough for Catanya to see her battered face. Her lower lip was split through its centre and her right eye was bruised black.

"Jael, I—" Catanya began before being interrupted.

"Do you know where Austagia's quarters are?" Jael asked with a hoarse voice. Her expression was serious. Catanya was taken aback. She wished to offer her sympathy or condolences or something to show she cared but… "Go there now. He is waiting for you," Jael said sternly and waited for Catanya to respond.

"Very well, Semsame." Catanya stepped into the night and shut the door behind her. She headed eastward toward the wing of buildings where Austagia resided, turning just once to see if Jael was still looking toward her, but she was walking slowly back toward the cleansing room. A dozen or so other priests—all in Ferustir guise and armed to the teeth—were on the move toward the temple, running swiftly like a leash of foxes. Catanya moved against the flow, turning down a corner to her right and across a narrow pathway to the room she knew was her uncle's. As she took the steps towards it, the door opened. Austagia was expecting her.

"Come in," he said. His tone was imperative rather than welcoming. Catanya entered without saying a word. She glanced around, noting that the room was almost identical to her own, and yet, for such a sparse room, it somehow seemed more meticulous. A lamp burned in the centre of his table, its shimmering light giving life to Austagia's shadow on the wall behind him.

There were two chairs at the table. He indicated that she should sit. But before she did, she felt the need to ask after Jael.

"Jael, is she—"

"She will be well soon enough. Sit, Catanya."

Catanya... She had not heard him use her name before. Strangely though, she did not like him doing so—it seemed to her he was exercising his authority as her uncle when he had relinquished that role when he drafted her into the priesthood. He sat opposite her in the second chair.

"I need to ask you some questions." Austagia stared at Catanya, as though he might glean the answers from her without needing to ask for them. After a pause he continued, "Jael found the dragon youngling—deceased—over six months ago."

"What? *Six months* ago?" *What on earth has happened to her since then?* Catanya's mind spun.

"Two things of interest were noted at the site where the youngling was found. I assume at this point you have no idea what either is?"

Catanya did not understand his point. *What do I have to do with the dead dragon?* She shook her head.

"Beside the fallen dragon, there was a fallen horse—an Astermeer."

She thought about this for a moment—*A white horse of the Ice Realm...* She had seen two of these during her time in the Romghold, ridden by priests who were passing through. The only other one she knew of was Breona. *But she belongs to Magnus's mother.*

"There was no sign of a rider?" Catanya asked.

Austagia looked at her but ignored her question. "The second thing of interest was this." Austagia placed a brown leather bracelet on the table in front of Catanya. She recognised it immediately—it was the bracelet she had given to Magnus.

Catanya stared at the bracelet. The world seemed to close in around her, stealing her breath. Tears welled in her eyes as she stared, unblinking, at the bracelet. Her heart seemed to rise as though it were trying to leave her chest. She did not know what to say and dared not look into Austagia's judging eyes. With shaking hands she reached for the bracelet, but at the last moment withdrew, daring not to touch it. *This is a trick. Austagia is testing my strength of mind.*

"Jael struggled to unfurl the enchantments binding this to the Astermeer. Enchantments whose remnants I know to be of our family's dialect. And the braiding of this bracelet—your mother taught you this, did she not?"

Catanya's mixed emotions twisted into anger and she directed them at Austagia. "*Our* family? What family? We *have* no family thanks to you!" She couldn't help herself.

"I was there, Catanya. The day you gave this to your companion. The one named *Magnus*."

Catanya remembered back to the Nuyan River, when she placed the bracelet around Magnus's wrist and whispered her spell—"Bound forever, forever mine…". Austagia was indeed there, waiting to take her away. She scowled at Austagia. "Where is he?" Catanya stood, kicking her chair back hard against the wall. "Where is he?" she yelled again. Austagia remained seated and composed. "He wouldn't have killed the dragon. He *couldn't* have killed the dragon." Catanya shook uncontrollably. All her training to remain calm and at peace accounted for nothing in this moment. Just now, she was Catanya again.

"Be seated, Semsame," Austagia instructed. After a moment she calmed herself enough to retrieve her chair. Austagia continued. "Time is short and matters are urgent. Listen to what I tell you. There is enough evidence that Quagmen killed the dragon youngling. But that is not of concern to our brethren." Catanya did not understand. "What will concern the priesthood is this." He picked the bracelet up off the table, showing it again to Catanya. "Whoever this belonged to has received the bond of fire."

Catanya stared into her uncle's eyes. She finally understood what he was getting at. *The bond of fire… the chosen one… Magnus?* It still made little sense to her. *What was he doing there—in Froughton Forest?*

"Then shouldn't we be trying to find Magnus?" she asked. "I'm sure whatever he did was not intentional," she said in his defence.

"Did the Astermeer belong to him?"

"It was his mother's. Breona was bonded to her, not Magnus. What of her then?"

For the first time, Austagia looked away from Catanya. She sensed there was something he knew but was not telling her.

"What is it?" she asked.

"Much has happened since we left the Fire Realm. The Quag army have attacked our lands and many of our people have been taken prisoner. Your friend Magnus is likely among them."

"Then why are we not defending them? Is this why we gather in the temple? To plan our attack against the Quag?" Catanya paused for thought.

There was more. There was *something* she was missing. "That is not their intention is it? They are not going to protect our people."

"No, they are not." Austagia's shoulders slumped ever so slightly and for the first time, his voice carried emotion. "The High Priests made the decision some time ago—there will be no defence of our people."

Catanya racked her brain looking for reason in Austagia's words. "If not to defend our people, what purpose does the priesthood serve?" As the words left her mouth, she understood. "The High Priests—they want the bond of fire for themselves."

"They believe it to be their right." Austagia hung his head, as if in shame.

"And if the bond is given to Magnus, who is not of our order..."

"They will want him dead." Austagia took the words from Catanya's mouth.

"Are *you* not involved in this decision? What is your part in this?"

"Not all of us support this movement."

The door to Austagia's room opened and Jael entered. Outside it had started to rain heavily. "The rain will hide her tracks. We must go now before they wonder where we are," Jael said to Austagia, looking then to Catanya with concern on her face.

"Fara Namon," Austagia whispered, extinguishing the flame in the lamp and cloaking them in darkness.

"Catanya, this may seem a strange question now that you are an Irucantî," Austagia spoke in a gentle manner. "But, Magnus...who is he to you now?"

"If not for you, I would marry him," Catanya replied curtly.

"If not for me, you would likely be held captive in Ba'rrat with many of our kinsmen. That is why you are here. Your mother wanted you protected."

Catanya slumped in her chair. *My mother? She wanted this?*

"Semsame, we must go," Jael insisted. She hugged her robe closely. To Catanya she appeared far from well enough to be moving about.

"Just a moment. Catanya must know the truth," Austagia insisted.

Catanya tried to understand the gravity of what was happening. "My mother knew this war was coming?" she asked.

"I warned her. The Quag armies had been amassing, positioning themselves for attack for some time."

"Why would you confide such a thing in my mother?"

Austagia was slow to respond. He walked to the door, peering out into the rain soaked night that drove a cold draft of wind into the room. "We are family Catanya—first and foremost. I could not sit idly by and do nothing to protect my family. There is much for you to learn but time calls for urgency. For now you must understand this. Your friend Magnus is in danger— perhaps more so than he faces as a prisoner in Ba'rrat. Tonight the priests will descend on Froughton Forest in search of the one who possesses the bond of fire. They will track him down, one way or another. You must get to him first if you wish to save him."

Jael spoke then. "Our brethren do not know who the youngling bonded with. Only Austagia, myself and you share that information."

"What of Joffren? Is he in support of this movement?" Catanya found it hard to believe Joffren of all people would think this way.

"Jael is better qualified to answer that question," Austagia said. "She was Joffren's Semsarian once. I do not share such intimacy with him."

"I am not sure where Joffren's loyalties lie," Jael answered curtly, looking at Austagia.

"We will no doubt find out soon enough," Austagia countered.

Catanya looked at them both, wondering at their relationship and how such a bond of trust formed between them. Austagia handed Catanya a folded parchment of paper small enough to fit in the palm of her hand. Catanya took it and felt the warmth of his touch as he cupped his hands around hers.

"This will give you directions, Catanya. For now, take the eastern road until you reach the start of the Dormiul Path at the top of the cliffs. Follow the path down to the coast. A dragon named *Färgd* will find you there. He is the oldest and wisest of the Couldradt dragons. He will take you southward along the coastline, then westward as it turns to the coastal town of Brindle. It is as close to Ba'rrat as he will dare go alone. Wait for us in Brindle. We will find our way there when we can. This parchment will give you further instructions for when you arrive. Once there, you need to go into hiding."

Catanya was speechless. The whirlwind chain of events of the past few minutes came to a head. She now needed to trust in the person she resented most in her new world and flee from her Semsdi—the man she had trusted the most.

"Take this," Austagia placed the leather bracelet upon Catanya's wrist.

Jael looked on as Catanya whispered her enchantment once again, binding it so it would not fall into the wrong hands again.

"It is a good enchantment. And you are a fine Irucantî," Jael said.

Catanya was still not aware of what Jael had been through over the months she was missing. Not knowing only added to her confusion. There was no time to ask, so instead she said, "Take care and heal well Jael. I will see you when you are strong again."

"Thank you, Semsame."

Catanya stepped out of Austagia's room and into the pelting rain. *Jael said I am a fine Irucanti.* She turned and saw that Jael and Austagia were still looking at her. *But I am no priest.* She turned away from them and broke into a run, heading toward the Dormiul Path in search of the man she knew she should never have left by the Nuyan River all those months ago.

ONE HUNDRED

The sun beat at its highest and hottest since Magnus had arrived in Ba'rrat.

Summer Solstice—the longest, hottest day of the year.

On this day, the fearsome warrior *Balgur* would fight his hundredth battle, and a crowd larger than ever before had assembled to watch the spectacle. It was an hour after midday—the hour of the Solstice. The heat aggravated the crowd. They shouted and cursed at the two contestants impatiently.

One hundred battles… One hundred men dead at my sword… Magnus walked to the centre of the arena barefooted and dishevelled. He had given his shoes to a fellow slave in greater need than he was, for his wounds healed where others did not. On numerous occasions he had left the arena with wounds that should be fatal and yet he healed, just as they had when he fought Crugion. As he healed, Magnus would wonder if a part of him was truly dying, and that he became more dragon and less man with each passing day.

The part Magnus was most sure had died was his heart. Where once there was love there was anger. Where once there was fear was now hate.

Is this what it is like to be a dragon? What sort of life is this?

Magnus was beyond caring for his appearance. His hair was long over his shoulders and his face was hidden behind a scruffy beard. Carlo tried to encourage Magnus to shave and be proud in the arena but he cared nothing for it, nor for Carlo.

At one stage Sarah had fallen sick. Magnus pleaded with Carlo to release her or provide her with medicine, but he would have nothing of it. Magnus tried to bargain with Carlo. "I will fight every day, twice a day if you will tend to her. She needs daylight to heal—please, Carlo." But the man would not relent.

"You need to know your place, slave. I take neither orders nor suggestions from you. Our deal is struck. You fight, she is fed and you visit with her. Beyond that your desires have no meaning to me."

In the end, after a week of fevering and being nurtured by Magnus in the deep, dark cell in which she resided, Sarah recovered. But she was no longer the high-spirited gypsy he had grown up with who could talk all day long and still have plenty to say. Her words became fewer and were spared for only the most pressing subjects. Both of them spoke little of the loved ones lost. Sarah still knew nothing of what happened to Ganister, just as Magnus was no closer to finding his parents. Magnus had pressed Carlo for information, lying about his affiliation with them, suggesting they were distant relatives, but he was not forthcoming. Magnus did however tell Sarah he had learnt that Lucas recovered from his sickness of the wyvern poison. He was sure however that she knew he was hiding some truth from her.

Magnus reached the centre of the arena. He raised his gaze to his opponent—a man almost twice his size carrying a spiked mace and shield with his chest covered in armour and his legs bare but for leather boots. Instinctively, and in barely a moment, Magnus had sized the large warrior up—*Deep scar to the shoulder of his mace arm that he guards with a high shield. Another to the left knee that he favours over the other—his right leg is weak. He is a warrior of experience but he is old, worn and slow. He will be cunning but vulnerable to a fast attack—particularly if distracted.*

The warrior charged at Magnus, led by a war cry. Magnus sighed—*Here we go again.* He was twenty feet out when Magnus used a gypsy spell of illusion Sarah had taught him during their nights together—their nights of *magic and history.*

"*Gana mish deevway…*"

Magnus's body shimmered slightly, making his opponent think he was shifting from side to side when in fact he was not. The man hesitated bringing his mace down, unsure where exactly Magnus was in order to land the blow. The pause gave Magnus more than the moment he needed to deal a lethal stab to the man's chest with his sword and so, barely a minute into the fight, his one hundredth challenger fell to his death.

Magnus turned and walked from the arena giving no acknowledgement to the people in the crowd and avoiding Carlo's gaze of disapproval.

"You could at least make a scene for the people, *Balgur*. A true warrior relishes the fight and the win!" Carlo lifted his arms in the air for emphasis. Magnus gritted his teeth. Carlo always liked to offer Magnus advice after a fight.

"I am no warrior. I am your slave, remember?" Magnus looked at Carlo briefly then walked past him, throwing his sword across the weapons table.

"Slave! Look at me!" Carlo bellowed. Magnus stared at Carlo with indifference. "What would you say if I told you there will be no more visits to your mother until you clean yourself up and put on a grand show for the crowd in the arena?"

Magnus walked casually back toward the weapons rack and picked up the sword again, "Then I will kill both your guards here, followed by you." He pointed the sword to the two guards and then to Carlo and continued to hold it, waiting for Carlo's response. The guards shifted uneasily, waiting for Carlo to give them orders, but he stroked his chin and squinted at Magnus.

"I thought as much." Carlo looked to the guards. "Take him to his mother... *again*."

Magnus had no appetite that evening. *One hundred battles in the arena. To what end?* His despondence was palpable and he could feel Sarah's eyes burning a hole through his forehead.

"What is it?" he asked her.

She placed her food back on her plate and stood up from where she was sitting against the wall. She came over to Magnus and sat directly in front of him cross-legged, resting her hands in her lap. "You grow more despondent every day Magnus. Good is still to come of this. You must maintain your faith."

Magnus shook his head lazily. "I do not see it."

Sarah shuffled about making herself more comfortable. "Come, let me tell you a story. I promised you magic and history. I believe we have covered enough gypsy magic for the time being, but we are sorely lacking in history."

"Why is this so important, Sarah?" Magnus did not feel at all in the mood for tales.

"You have a fair understanding of your father's way of life—of the Fire Realm and the customs within the realm you grew up in. However, unlike my boy Lucas, your mother did not raise you with teachings about her people's ways. This is true?"

Magnus sighed and thought about this for a moment. "She would discuss some things, occasionally. It was usually in moments of sadness when she seemed to be missing home," he recalled.

"She told me it pained her too much to go back there," Sarah said. "In her mind and in her heart."

"Have you ever travelled north to the Ice Realm?" Magnus asked. To him, the Ice Realm was an enigma. He had never really given much thought as to why his mother spoke so little about it. It had simply always been that way.

"I have… twice actually. The first time was with Ganister and your father when he ventured north to ask Hasledom—your maternal grandfather—for Alavia's hand in marriage. Ganister and I travelled with him as far as the Ice Breach—two days travel into the Ice Realm. The lands from there were well guarded. Only your father was allowed to go further north into the Rhyderlands.

"And what happened?"

"Your father obviously got what he wanted. He returned a week later with your mother. She was the most beautiful woman I had ever seen."

"And the second time?"

"The second time…" Sarah's thoughts trailed off and a sombre expression crossed her face. "The second time was less than two years later." Sarah explained. "Lucas was a baby and stayed behind with Ganister. Your mother was with child. This time we travelled beyond the Ice Breach together into the most spectacular lands I have ever seen. You must promise me you will see it someday, Magnus—white snow-capped mountains against bright blue skies. It took two more days to traverse through the mountain ranges and then finally, the mountains sloped away to the north coast where pristine white beaches abutted the Ice Seas. Seas of crystal blue, home to the Ertwe dragons and their blood brethren—the Astermeers. You should see them Magnus— wild Astermeers running the beaches at sunrise. And this is where the Rhydermere live—your mother's people—along a stretch of coast spanning endless miles."

"What was your purpose of travelling there?"

"Your mother sought her father's blessing for you—her unborn child. But what she found was sorrow beyond her worst nightmares."

"I thought this story was meant to cheer me up!" Magnus scoffed. He immediately regretted saying it, seeing the still-sombre expression on Sarah's face. "I am sorry, Sarah, please continue."

"Hasledom had fallen to Quag assassins months before. In retaliation, his father—your great grandfather whose name eludes me, although I know he was the youngest of four sons—travelled with Alavia's brothers and attacked a band of Quag camped at Realms End near the three-realm border of Ice, Fire and Earth. It was a trap. The Quag knew they would seek revenge and were waiting in great numbers. They were all killed in the battle. Your mother's entire family was lost."

Sarah fell to silence. Magnus felt great sorrow for his mother's loss. There was nothing he could think to say or ask of Sarah that would resolve the sadness of her story.

"The Rhydermere retaliated with fury," Sarah continued. "They sent forth a legion of Rhyders to run them down. Two weeks later they caught them at the northern entrance to the Corville Pass. They killed every one of the Quagmen north of the Mountains." Sarah hung her shoulders low. "Your mother never got her wish of Hasledom's blessing. Her people pleaded with her to stay and live among them, but there was nothing left for her. She wished to return to her new home with you and Bonstaph. As a parting gift she was given a beautiful Astermeer foal—the only to ever leave the realm other than those sworn to the Irucantî."

"Breona…"

"Indeed. They were bonded for life. And so back in the comfort of our homes with our husbands and young children I watched Alavia change as the years passed by. Her sorrow eased and gave way to love. You, Bonstaph and Breona were all she had—her everything. To this day she loves you, Magnus, and there is *nothing* she would not do for you."

"Mother never returned to her people again?"

"Never. Not in the seventeen years that followed. At times I would ask her if she'd like me to accompany her back to the North to visit her people. *'Never again.'* That was always her response. But her people never forgot her. They would occasionally send gifts, such as the fleu-steel used to make your sword and Lucas's. So the connection was always there. But she never returned."

Magnus and Sarah shared what time they had left together in silence. As the bolt to Sarah's door slid from its lock, Magnus gave Sarah a hug.

"Thank you, Sarah," he said.

WAITING

As Austagia had told her, the dragon named Färgd was waiting for her at the bottom of the steep descent that was the Dormiul Path, where the eastern coastline met the foot of the Romgnian Mountains. The unrelenting rain suited Färgd. He told Catanya it provided him camouflage and masked his scent to the wyverns that patrolled the coastline further to the south. Nevertheless, as they flew together, rounding the southern reaches of the mountain, and changed their course to a westerly direction toward Brindle, they encountered a pair of the black creatures.

Catanya spotted them first. Through the darkness and rain their black, dull hides stood out for a moment in the brilliance of a lighting strike. They were closing in on Färgd fast, but with Catanya's warning, Färgd attacked with ferocity. He grabbed the first with his powerful rear claws, pulling it forward and into his open jaws, tearing it in two. The second, Catanya dealt with. She ignited her lance and stood in Färgd's saddle, her legs firmly strapped into place. Catanya struck the creature across its face with her lance, leaving it wounded and vulnerable. Färgd finished the wyvern off with a lethal jet of flame that engulfed it. The searing heat singed Catanya's hair and left her face sore. Färgd apologised and recommended an effective spell Catanya could use to prevent such mishaps from occurring again.

No further mishaps occurred, and as the new day dawned, they landed on the pebbled shore several miles east of Brindle. Catanya dismounted and stood before Färgd, touching her forehead to the dragon's nose. She shared thoughts and thanked him for his help.

"Your feelings suggest you face a great predicament, priest-girl," Färgd observed. *"Is it anything I may help you with?"*

Catanya was not sure what to say. She was uncertain whom she could trust and was even questioning her own beliefs. *"Thank you, Färgd, for your kindness and concern. But I think I am yet to learn all there is about the priesthood."*

"Very well, priest-girl, but if I may give one piece of advice before we part ways—it is to be true to yourself."

"True to myself?"

"Before any other principles or beliefs, yes." With that, Catanya saw Färgd's eyes flicker through a myriad of shades from her own brown to his usual amber. He bid Catanya farewell and spread his immense wings, taking once more to the skies.

Catanya walked the remaining three miles to the outskirts of Brindle. Along the way she unfolded the parchment Austagia had given her. He had written directions to an abandoned chancel that she could use for accommodation during her stay.

Mindful not to go too close to it before she determined it safe, Catanya found a position atop a rise half a mile away that gave her a clear view of the old chancel and the surrounding areas. For the rest of that day and the night that followed, Catanya stayed there, watching and waiting.

By the second morning she was confident no one was moving in or out of the chancel, nor that anyone was watching it. She was certain too that no one had followed her to Brindle. Satisfied, Catanya moved into the abandoned building.

For the first few days, Catanya cast her eyes and thoughts back to the east, waiting for Austagia or Jael or perhaps a hostile Ferustir on a mission to kill her. None came and so she began to venture out and explore the coastal town. She found an old brown robe within the chancel that she wore to conceal her Ferustir suit, and pulled her hair over to cover the bald side of her head and its telltale marks. In the solitude of her time alone, she allowed herself to sink deeper and deeper into regret over leaving Magnus. She wished they had fled earlier and found isolation together, away from the violence and deception of their world.

Catanya wondered how Joffren reacted to her disappearance and concluded that he probably thought that she fled for home and no longer wanted to be a part of the priesthood. It was considered blasphemy, but surely a lesser crime than working against the will of the priests. *Besides...* Catanya considered. *Steyne had fled the priesthood many years before without a death mark placed on him.*

After a week, Catanya grew agitated. *What if something has happened to Austagia or Jael?* She tried to keep the thoughts from her mind by reciting memorised passages from the *Murata Fara*. Translating the Fireisgh words into the common tongue, Catanya recited a passage she recalled from the last pages of the *Murata* about the bond of fire—

"The fourth of four realms,
The last to bring bond and the power of fire,
May give over to one of their choosing,
Whose progeny shall forever inherit the power of the
realm of fire…"

"Of *their* choosing… the *dragons'* choosing," Catanya re-evaluated. "Not of the priests' choosing." There was no promise to the priests themselves.

Catanya realised that if the priests had developed a false sense of entitlement, their retribution to an outsider receiving the bond would be deadly. *Austagia was right.* She recalled his words—*"They will want Magnus dead".*

On the thirteenth night of waiting, Catanya slept uneasily in the makeshift bed she had created at the rear of the chancel. She slept each night with one hand on her lance and the other on her sheath of throwing knives. Past midnight, her eyes became heavy and she replaced her sense of vision with a focus on hearing. She heard a cockroach scuttle across the stone floor. It was the same one that came out each night at this hour. But then she heard a foreign sound—that of a partially dried iris petal being broken under foot.

Each evening before Catanya retired to her bed she chose six petals from a dried iris for such a quality that *she* would hear an intruder step upon it, yet they themselves would unlikely discern the feeling underfoot, nor register the sound unless they were looking for it. She distributed the petals at each of the three possible entry points to the chancel, with more positioned closer to her bed. This was the first night it had been used to good effect.

Her eyes still closed, Catanya concentrated on slowing her breathing. With her thumb and forefinger, she silently drew a single throwing knife from its sheath, all the while gripping her lance with slightly less tension than was required to ignite it. A moment later, a second, closer iris petal was compromised. She knew by the direction and sound that the intruder had entered through a broken window along the eastern wall of the chancel and was now ten feet to her left from where she lay.

Catanya pounced.

She sat bolt upright and threw the knife. The blade pirouetted through the air and buried itself into the wall behind her target. The sound of another blade whistled back toward her. She tilted her head and it missed her scarred ear by a hair's breadth. The thumping-crackle sound of two lances igniting simultaneously pierced through the stone chancel.

In the glow of light emitted from her assailant's lance, Catanya could make out a face beneath a black hood—*Demi…*

Catanya thought that of all the priests sent to kill her, at least they had sent the one she was least fond of. *It will make it easier to kill her*, Catanya conceded.

Demi did not hesitate for a moment. She came hard and fast, swinging her lance at Catanya, who somersaulted off the bed, pulling her lance overhead as she landed. Her blade scored across Demi's, sending red sparks scattering across the floor. Demi came at Catanya again and again. Every strike was meant to kill and forced Catanya into a defensive position. If there was one thing Catanya had learned to hate, it was being on the defensive. Too often Joffren had held the upper hand, and she had worked hard over the months to learn how to reverse that position. But this was different. Demi was far more aggressive and gave Catanya little room to negotiate or make a counter attack.

Unexpectedly, Demi extinguished her lance, sheathed it, and drew two throwing knifes. Catanya waited. Her eyes were fixed on Demi's dark silhouette illuminated by the moon that peered through the long, narrow window behind her. Not a word was spoken between them.

Demi threw both blades at once. Catanya deflected one with her lance, sending it upward, embedding it in the ceiling. The other hit her firmly in the abdomen, burying itself into the armour of her Ferustir suit.

Catanya moved in, now on the attack. Demi reached for her lance but Catanya gave her no time to retrieve it so she had to resort to hand combat. The vambraces covering her forearms deflected the sharp blades of Catanya's lance with skill. She knew how to absorb the blows to minimise injury. However, Catanya knew the weak points in Demi's armour, for it was similar to her own. Her lance made purchase twice at the wrists and again under her left armpit, severing tendons and blood vessels each time.

'*Boe'l fara gin parshin-ar!*' Catanya shouted, creating a small ball of fire that hung above their heads, illuminating the room so she could better see her opponent. She continued the attack, giving Demi little time to draw a weapon.

'*Fara gin paroosha!*' Demi shouted back and the ball of fire exploded, throwing Catanya to the floor. Startled and singed from the flames, Catanya still managed to hold tight to her lance so it maintained its blaze. Demi reached for two more throwing knives but let them slip to the floor, her hands weak from wounds and slippery with blood. Still lying on the ground, Catanya was quick to throw a knife of her own that speared Demi's throat.

Demi's large eyes grew even larger with shock. She reached for her lance, squeezing it with both hands, but it failed to ignite. Catanya knew what this meant.

"The life of the fire drains from you," Catanya said. She knew that once a priest was fatally injured, their lance no longer recognised their life force. Catanya was back on her feet, ready to attack in case Demi had any surprises left. But she didn't. Instead, she chuckled and smiled a bloody smile.

"You are good, Semsame," Demi gargled then coughed. "You are good." She fell to her knees. Catanya dropped her weapon and lunged to Demi, catching her as she fell. As much as Catanya was not fond of her, it seemed wrong to turn her back on a dying priest.

She held Demi in her lap and they stared into one another's eyes. "I know who the *Electus* is," Catanya said, knowing her secret would die with Demi.

"We know you do," Demi struggled for her last breath. "That is why we need you dead." She smiled again, but Catanya saw this time it was different—there was sympathy in her face.

A moment later, Demi died in Catanya's arms.

The westward road toward Ba'rrat was bustling with peasants, traders and slaves. The relentless heat of summer made movement arduous and everyone was well sheltered from the sun in cloths and shawls covering their faces. A hot, dry wind from beyond the Neverseas scalded the people mercilessly like the torching flame of dragons. Any one of them could have been a cloaked assassin seeking their target, and one among them—dressed in a hooded robe—was a priest.

Catanya had fled the chancel in Brindle after killing Demi and ran the twenty-mile journey to the outskirts of Ba'rrat by sunrise, slowing only when walking afforded her anonymity among the crowd. She could not risk waiting for Austagia and Jael when her position in the chancel was obviously compromised. Catanya had buried Demi's lance beneath a tree at a mile marker ten miles short of Ba'rrat. She did not want it falling into the wrong hands. Demi's throwing knives, however, she stashed with her own in her Ferustir suit. Demi also had on her a leather pouch of gold coins that Catanya kept for herself.

The presence of Quag guards this close to the looming mass of the black capitol made her nervous. It was the first time Catanya had laid eyes on the infamous warriors. From the sight of their black armour, their black blades and their menacing demeanour she knew they would not back away easily in a fight. If any one of them pulled the robe from her back, she would present as an instant threat. *A priest is the sworn enemy of the Quag,* she deliberated. Catanya knew getting into Ba'rrat would require some ingenuity.

Walking slowly and loitering deliberately, Catanya considered her surroundings and assessed her options. She scanned the movements of everyone in her vicinity, looking for inconsistent behaviour, but knew any assassin would be too smart for that. *But who would be my assassin? Joffren? Austagia?* She had to consider every angle. *The deception came from somewhere… how else would Demi have known I was waiting in Brindle?*

A horse-drawn cart carrying bags of potatoes trundled slowly toward the city walls, accompanied by what looked like a father and son driving the horses forward. Catanya watched their progress carefully as they passed a guard check point where a snooping wyvern sniffed around the cart and the produce within it. After a brief argument, the father reluctantly made payment for passage to the second checkpoint further on, where the process occurred one more time. From here, the cart travelled just a mile more to Ba'rrat's southern city gates.

Further back along the road, many more carts lined the street, slowly trundling toward the gates. *It is the only way in…* Catanya determined. She considered each cart in turn—looking for an opportunity she could take advantage of. Each one carried goods for trade. Many carried food and produce, others livestock, chickens and fowls. Some carried more exotic things like garments, gems and jewellery.

There was one cart among them that had pulled over to the roadside. It was loaded with sacks and burdened with a broken wheel. The owner, most likely a farmer, struggled in the heat trying to repair the damage. He was travelling alone and none offered to help him with the task.

Catanya wandered over to the farmer. "Let me help you, sire," she offered.

Looking her over, the farmer dismissed her and laughed. "This is no job for a woman and besides… I have no coin to pay you with," he snorted.

"I ask for no payment," Catanya said, and set about moving large stones from the roadside in order to prop the cart up so the broken wheel could be removed. It was something she had helped do at the quarry back home when the sandstone wore heavy on the traders' carts. The farmer was intrigued with her efficiency and progress and in the end got to work, helping her until the cart was well supported and he was able to work the wheel free for repairs. Within the hour it was fixed and mounted back on the cart.

"Thanking you, kind lady," the farmer said, tipping his leather hat respectfully. "Much appreciated and ever the more so on this cursed hot day of Solstice. But like I said—I have no coin to pay you."

"I ask for no coin. In fact, I will pay your fee into the city in exchange for free passage." Catanya discretely deposited Demi's leather pouch into the man's hand then held his wrist firmly. "Are we agreed?"

The farmer prised open the strings of the purse revealing the gold coins within. His eyes widened and he nodded. "Agreed!"

After helping him move the stones away from under his cart, Catanya sat herself next to him at the front of it. The farmer leaned toward her and whispered, "I shall enjoy myself in Ba'rrat's taverns this evening!"

Catanya smiled. The farmer drove the cart over to the first checkpoint, paying without dispute, then onward to the next and toward the gates of Ba'rrat.

CARLO

The two guards escorted Magnus down the corridor toward the armoury. It was always the same two guards. Magnus wondered how they could stand doing this every day of their life when they were free to do as they pleased. *Living everyday the same,* Magnus considered, *is not living at all.* On this day, however, one of the guards halted halfway along the corridor and turned to Magnus, pinning him against the wall.

"Who are you really, *Balgur?*" he asked, pressing his forearm against Magnus's throat.

Magnus did not care for the guard's aggression and he knew he could overpower both him and his accomplice with his bare hands should he need to. Besides, Carlo valued his life far higher than any two of his miserable guards. Indeed—rumours had reached Magnus of the change in fortune and prosperity Carlo was experiencing thanks to Magnus's exploits in the arena. And so Magnus stared blankly at the guard and said nothing.

"Well, have you nothing to say?" The guard spat in Magnus's face. Still, Magnus stared back at the man, showing no signs at all of retaliating.

The second guard laughed. "That's ten darna you owe me! I told you he wouldn't flinch."

"Shut your gob," the first guard sneered at his kinsman. He released Magnus and pushed him on toward the armoury. Carlo was waiting for him as usual whilst watching another one of his slaves lose their life to a better fighter in the arena.

"Damn them all! I don't know why I even bother, Lucas. I should have you fight every battle here for me. No need for any other slaves." Magnus did not reply. He kept a strict policy of not conversing with Carlo any more than he had to.

"I have something for you," Carlo continued. He handed Magnus a long, bound package. Magnus lay it upon the weapons table, pushing the crude swords and spears aside to make room for it. "Open it!" Carlo insisted. Magnus folded back the cowhide wrapping to reveal two black blades. They were freshly forged and similar to those carried by the Quagmen. Looking at them brought old memories back.

"I had them made especially..." Carlo said.

... They were dark memories Magnus had all but forgotten...

"The right size for a swift attack..."

Magnus was not hearing Carlo's speech, for his mind was elsewhere.

... He was fleeing from his burning house. The large Quagman set upon him with his large black blades trying to kill him...

"These will take you to new heights, *Balgur*. You will be invincible..."

... Then the Quagman was set upon by Ganister, who saved his life and sacrificed his own to protect his family...

"Will you fight with them, *Balgur*?" Carlo was growing frustrated at Magnus, lost in his own world. Magnus thought of Sarah's story of his mother's loss—of her father and brothers, slaughtered by Quagmen in their own lands.

"What?" Magnus grunted.

"Don't give me attitude, boy. Remember your place if you wish to maintain your..."

Magnus interrupted him. "I'll fight with your blades, but give me someone worth fighting. Give me your guards, or better still, have Delvion give me his Quagmen and I'll show him that a man of the Fire Realm is thrice the man they are."

Carlo fell silent for a moment. Magnus could see he was deciding how to respond to this outburst.

Magnus concluded, "You make me fight to live. So give me a fight worth living for, Carlo."

After further contemplation, Carlo nodded. "Yes, very well then. It is time to raise the stakes. So I tell you what. You make a spectacle out there today and I'll see what I can organise for the morrow."

Magnus said no more. He marched out of the armoury and into the waiting arena. His opponent stood at its centre, waiting for the infamous *Balgur* to appear. It was a man who called himself *Shadow*. He had grown notorious over the past month for the spectacle he made in front of the crowd and they had quickly grown to love him. Magnus's battle with him today was long called for by the folk of Ba'rrat and was highly anticipated. Both *Balgur* and *Shadow* had their supporters and the crowd cheered heartily as Magnus walked to his opponent, swirling his blades through the air to please them.

Shadow's game was always to delay his first attack and focus on making a mockery of his opponent by avoiding their ill-attempted blows. Once the crowd were amused, they would shout and encourage their hero to strike. Shadow would bow to the crowd and defeat his opponent, as though the audience had taken ownership of the battle. *The perfect showman,* Magnus conceded. *This will not happen today.* Magnus wanted to shock the crowd—he wanted to shock them and silence them and have them understand he was not to be beaten.

And so the battle began…

Magnus walked to the centre of the arena, stopping fifty feet short of Shadow, where he knelt on one knee. Magnus brought his left blade to his face and ran his tongue along the length of it, feeling the sharpness of the steel cut the surface, releasing a stream of blood from his mouth. The crowd released a collective gasp as blood spilled down his chin to the ground. Even Shadow grimaced at the sight. Magnus was getting the response he wanted. He remained still as the dragon blood within him seared through his face, healing the deep wound in moments, yet the power of such healing was hidden within his closed mouth. He repeated the spectacle with his other blade, moving the crowd to silence at the peculiar exhibition.

Magnus remained on one knee as the crowd began to cheer, encouraging Shadow to move in for the kill. It was not his style at all, for he relished the counterattack. But *Balgur*—who they knew was named after the greatest fire dragon of them all—waited, bathing in the heat that coursed through him and filled him with strength and fury.

Against his better judgement, Shadow broke into a run, charging at Magnus, wielding his long sword above his head. He swung it down upon his foe with all his strength. Magnus leapt up off the ground with a speed Shadow did not expect, twisting his torso to avoid Shadow's attack and completing the movement by whipping his own blades about in an arc. The first blade sliced through Shadow's chest, the second his neck. Magnus's opponent fell dead to the ground.

The crowd were silenced. Magnus returned to the centre of the arena, raising both swords in a 'V' high above his head. He held a snarled expression upon his bloodied face. *Balgur* looked like a wild beast—much like the dragon whose name he bore. To complete the spectacle, he let out an angry roar. When he had finished, he addressed the crowd.

"Bring no more helpless slaves to fight me in the arena!" Magnus shouted as loud as he could, turning to be sure all the crowd were listening. "I Balgur—King of Fire—challenge Delvion's men to fight me, if they've the courage to do so. Fight me! Prove you are worthy of your King. And may the best of you step forward first."

Just as Magnus hoped, the crowd reacted with glorious cheers and screams. He walked from the arena to the armoury where Carlo was sitting with his face buried in his hands.

"No, no, no…" Carlo muttered. "Do not do this to me."

"Let us see how full the arena is tomorrow," Magnus said, spitting the last trace of blood from his mouth.

Carlo stormed over to the weapons rack, throwing the swords and spears across the room in a rage. "Who do you think you are? Now I will have every Quag warrior in all the land challenging you!" Magnus said nothing, letting Carlo blow off steam. "What am I to do with you dead? Hmm?"

"You have nothing to fear," Magnus assured, a smirk on his face. "From what I have seen, most Quagmen are cowards. It is likely none will rise to the challenge."

One of Carlo's guards took exception to Magnus's comment and drew his sword, cursing under his breath as he charged toward him from across the room. Magnus walked to face him with his new blades raised. At the last moment, the guard faltered, his eyes twitched and he backed away, lowering his sword.

"You see?" Magnus said. "Cowards!" He knew he was stirring a hornet's nest and that every guard in the city would be lining up to prove themselves *the man who bested Balgur.* All Magnus had to do was watch his back until then.

"Guards!" Carlo shouted. His face was red and veins pulsated across his forehead.

Three more guards burst into the armoury. Five in total stood to attention. For a moment Magnus thought they might attack.

"Have him spend the night with that woman he calls his mother. He's safer there. And I want no less than the four of you at the door at all times. If anyone so much as lands a finger on him, you'll all be sold into slavery."

Magnus was unsettled by Carlo's comment about Sarah. *Does he know the truth about her?* He considered him for a moment, wondering how much more Carlo knew about him than he realised.

"Wait… Leave us a moment," Carlo ordered his guards, who moved out of the armoury, leaving Magnus and Carlo alone together. Carlo paced up and down the room, looking to the ground. He had one hand behind his back and the other stroking his silver goatee. After his third time back across the room, Carlo stopped in his tracks and rested his index finger upon his lips, frowning.

"Why are you here, Lucas, if that really is your name?" Carlo asked.

Magnus could not understand why he was being asked such a question. "Because you made purchase of me."

"No, no. Why are you here in Ba'rrat? Is it that woman? Sarah? She means something to you, that I can see. But she's no relative of yours. Being captured by the Quag guards? I don't see it. There's more to know and you're going to tell me."

"There's nothing more to tell."

"I've completely run out of patience with you, boy." Carlo thumped a table with a strong fist, making Magnus shift uneasily on his feet. Carlo pointed an accusing finger. "You're strong, unnaturally strong. Some twisted work of gypsy magic and a decent education in swordsmanship keeps you in good stead. But if push comes to shove, I will kill you myself, do we understand one another?"

Magnus realised he was going to have to come up with a more convincing story, but he needed to at least challenge Carlo's accusations. "Who are you to say she is not my mother?"

Carlo grabbed a pair of small wooden stools, handed one to Magnus and sat on the other. "Sit," he instructed. Magnus did as told, sitting beside him. Carlo spoke softly, "I have spent my life sizing people up. I know what gives one warrior strength and another speed. These are different traits typical of each of the realms with few exceptions. This woman Sarah is a gypsy—through and through. You bear no resemblance to her. She is short, you are tall. You have fine hair, long limbs and an objective demeanour—those are the attributes of people from the Ice Realm. These would be from your *real* mother. Your fighting style and sword skill is somewhat refined but brutal in execution—not from the North at all, but, I warrant, from the Fire Realm. Taught by your father no doubt. Correct me where I'm wrong."

Magnus was left without words. The bravado he felt moments ago was gone and replaced with a deep sense of insecurity. Carlo had summed him up perfectly. All he had to do was name his parents, reveal his true identity and turn him over to Delvion and his wretched son. But there was more—he could feel it. There was a point to Carlo's revelation.

"This woman you are so protective of. I see you know each other well. But there is more. You owe her something."

Magnus felt the need to emphasise her importance to him. "I owe her my life. She and her husband saved my life."

"Her husband you say. This is one of the men you asked me of, whose horse is ridden by Daxton?"

"Aye, it is," Magnus said.

"Would it appease you to know this man—together with another I will assume is your father—is still alive? For now, at any rate."

Magnus was stricken with shock. He leapt to his feet and held one of the black blades to Carlo's throat. Carlo responded with a dagger of his own pressed to Magnus's breast above his heart. Neither budged from their position.

"What do you know of my father?" Magnus wanted to slaughter the man with every fibre of his being, but for the ache in his heart that so desperately wanted to know more.

"Both are captive here in Ba'rrat, under the King's guard. I tried to make purchase of them when they arrived the week before you did. Thanks to Delvion, they can't be bought at any price."

They are here. Magnus tried to hide his relief. He removed his blade from Carlo's neck. In turn, Carlo withdrew his own blade.

"It seems he has taken an interest in them, particularly since word has spread of Delvion's son exacting revenge for his brother's death—a death your father was responsible for." Carlo looked Magnus over, as though seeing him in a different light for the first time. "Unless you have a brother, you were the son Crugion is supposed to have slayed?" Carlo asked. Magnus nodded in confession. "There is just the minor problem of you, the supposedly *dead* son, drawing so much attention to yourself just now. The best of Crugion's men will no doubt wish to prove themselves against you in the arena. Tell me *J'esmagdman*, will they likely recognise you?"

"Crugion certainly will. And another—Briet."

"Ah, Briet. A savage warrior that man."

"You know of him?" Magnus asked.

"Aye, I do. And if it's him you face in the arena, you'd best fight with everything you've got. He's killed every man he's ever faced—in the arena *and* on the battlefield. Including many of my men."

Magnus looked Carlo over to see if he was serious about Briet. His bitter expression confirmed it. All the pieces of the puzzle seemed to be falling into place in Magnus's mind. All but one—where was his mother? He wanted to ask Carlo about her, but thought it best to keep something to himself. After all, he had no idea where Carlo's loyalties lay.

Carlo sheathed his dagger and let out an exasperated breath. "Well, if we're having you fight Delvion's guards we can't have you looking like a filthy slave anymore. The crowd see you as a warrior and so a warrior you shall be. Dine with your companion as you always do then return here. I will have a smithy fit you for appropriate armour including a helmet to aid in your disguise."

Magnus nodded in appreciation, more so for Carlo's discretion about his identity than the offer of armour. Before Carlo called in his guards to take him away, Magnus asked Carlo a final pressing question.

"When all this is over, what of Sarah? What will become of her?"

Carlo nodded. "I tell you what. You have fought well and longer than I anticipated in the arena. Give me a month more with the stakes raised as they are and she is free to go."

REPERCUSSIONS

Magnus shared what he knew with Sarah that evening. Relief mixed with desperation washed over her face.

"One more month, then Carlo will free you."

It was not soon enough for Sarah, who made him promise to escape when he could. He did so, knowing he would do no such thing until Sarah was safely away herself.

After his supper, Magnus returned to the armoury where a smithy was shaping a set of armour for him.

The smithy was a man of few words, which allowed Magnus to think over his predicament while he was fitted with various steel plates for size. Sarah wanted him to break free to try and find Ganister and his father as soon as he could. Yet if he did so without taking Sarah with him, Carlo would certainly kill her. Furthermore, he still had no idea where Delvion was keeping Ganister and his father, but was sure it would be the most guarded of prisons. There appeared to Magnus to be no solution, and yet he was so close. There was a solution at hand—he could feel it—but could not put his finger on it. His thoughts were broken as Carlo entered the armoury.

"It would seem your antics in the arena today have brought what you requested." Carlo handed Magnus a piece of paper. The paper was folded and addressed to Carlo. It had a broken wax seal, stamped with the Quag coat of arms consisting of a cross and two curved swords angled through the cross. Magnus folded back the letter and read the inked inscription within.

Carlo Dresenga,

It has come to my attention that you attempt to bring the abilities of my warriors into disrepute. Within the realm of Ba'rrat this is punishable by death. However, in light of your contribution to Ba'rrat's arena and the games within, I forward two of my men. Should your entrant into the games die, you have been proven wrong and your life is forfeit. Should both my men die, your point is made and I shall spare your life and pay the sum of 50,000 darna for ownership of your champion. The games will be held in the arena at dawn.

Delvion, King of Allumbreve.

Magnus's mind spun. He sat to avoid falling and reluctantly looked to Carlo whose expression was blank.

"You will kill these men or I will see to it that every person you know dies an agonising death. *Including* Ganister and your father. Do you hear me?"

"Yes," Magnus murmured.

"Do you hear me?" Carlo shouted.

"I do," Magnus said, nodding. Carlo signalled to the guards who pulled Magnus to his feet and dragged him out of the armoury.

Magnus shouted after Carlo, "What of Sarah? What will happen to her?"

Carlo stared blankly at Magnus as he was dragged away. He was taken back to the dungeons, rather than to Sarah's room for the night as was planned.

Locked as usual in cage six, Magnus sat cross-legged in the back corner of the room. Brutus was no longer in there with him and was nowhere to be seen within the other five cages. Magnus knew this meant he had lost his life in the arena. He shook with fear as to the ramifications of him losing the following day. All his worries came to a head at once.

'What if I fail?" Magnus mumbled to himself, shaking his head. He knew Delvion would send nothing less than his best men into the arena. *What was I thinking… was I thinking at all?* He fought to keep thoughts of those he loved from his mind for fear the pain would make him go mad. *Can a madman win in the arena?* He clenched his fists as tightly as he could until his knuckles turned white and his nails dug deep into the palms of his hands.

The harder he clenched, the more the dragon blood within him coursed through his arms and into his tightly bound fists, until he felt as if they would burn from the heat. But the feeling helped dull six months of pain. Gritting his teeth, Magnus stared at his fists, focussing to maintain the tension to see just how much of the heat he could bear. *There must be a limit.*

But what was beyond that limit? How was he to master this *gift*—this blessing of being the *Electus*—if he did not truly know what he was capable of? In the flash of a moment, the heat reached a climax and, straining to keep himself from screaming, his fists burst into two balls of flame.

Magnus leapt back, releasing his fists and spanning his fingers outward. The pain was gone, but the flames remained. He shook his hands, trying to shake the flames free but they clung to his flesh. He stared in shock. His hands were now completely engulfed in fire, yet there was no more pain and it did not burn him.

Awestruck by the spectacle, Magnus brought his hands together, then as he separated them a large ball of fire formed between the palms of his hands. He shook one hand free, leaving him holding the crimson ball within the palm of one hand. A grin crossed Magnus's face and he spoke the spell his father had taught him—*"Fara gin parshin-ar."*

The ball of fire exploded outward, filling all the cages in the dungeon with a flash of light. The other prisoners screamed in terror and Magnus heard the footsteps of the guards approaching. But as they entered the dungeons, the light had vanished and all that remained was a trail of smoke wafting toward the ceiling.

Magnus lay to sleep, facing away from the guards. His heart raced. Hope returned and as the night passed, he began to feel tired and drifted off to sleep, smiling and feeling more confident of the battle he was to fight in the arena the following day. At least that was one thing whose outcome he was now certain of.

BREAK IN

After passing into Ba'rrat without any trouble, Catanya spent the afternoon weaving her way through the throng of traders, trying to garner whatever information she could about where the prisoners were kept. She asked a question here and a question there, but was careful to never ask much of any one stranger, fearing it could cause suspicion.

At first her venture proved fruitless. The best she got was from a young farmer's wife who pointed to a gate. *"Many a prisoner is taken through there, but once underground, only a guard of the city knows of the labyrinth that weaves beneath."* Further inquiries suggested there were countless gates like this one, all servicing networks of underground tunnels. Catanya knew she needed more information than this.

As the day grew old and Catanya grew impatient, an eruption of excitement exploded from the direction of the arena. Catanya moved to the centre of the city and came upon throngs of people leaving the arena through its numerous gates. They were all talking about the warrior who had just battled a notorious slave by the name of Shadow and defeated him easily. The warrior's name was *Balgur.* This got Catanya's attention. With the people of Ba'rrat so distracted, Catanya dove in with questions.

"Tell me about Balgur!"

"Where is he from?"

"What does he look like?"

"How long has he been fighting in Ba'rrat's arena?"

All the descriptions seemed to fit, but one—*"He is built like a true warrior!"*

Magnus? Built like a warrior? Catanya tried to imagine it, but could not. Then she remembered Magnus laughing at the thought of her becoming an Irucantî—*and yet here I am… and if Magnus is the Electus…*Catanya was sure then that the warrior named Balgur must be him.

Heeding the words of the farmer's wife, Catanya knew she needed to find a guard to take her to Magnus. But not just any guard. It would have be one that worked for whoever claimed ownership over him.

"That would be Carlo Dresenga," a well-dressed trader shared with her. "His fortunes have changed since Balgur entered the arena."

As night came, Catanya retreated from obvious sight and studied the toing and froing of the guards of the city. They frequently moved in companies of two, three or four and crossed paths with other guards as they went. But as the hours passed, their numbers dwindled and many—particularly the younger ones—retreated to the taverns dotted around the southern end of Ba'rrat. Catanya decided it was one of these guards who could be persuaded to help her find Magnus.

As Catanya watched on, she thought more about Magnus and how he had remained captive for such a long period of time. *Surely if he has the strength to fight for so long in the arena, he has what it takes to escape. What keeps him here?* She was sure she would find out soon enough.

As the hours went by, Catanya chose a well-frequented bar close to the city's gates. Here, she spotted the old farmer who had helped her into Ba'rrat. He seemed to be enjoying himself, draining his purse of gold coins in exchange for ale and wine. By midnight, guards started to spill out of the tavern, drunk and disorderly and in no condition to put up a fight should Catanya pose a threat. But she waited in the darkness of shadows, hidden from the street lamps and rising moon, watching in silence.

As the hours passed, the tavern's patrons became louder and more intoxicated. They were leaving in fewer numbers and in worse condition. Two of the guards left the tavern and stumbled into the street, arguing.

"Fifty darna says Balgur defeats Delvion's men," slurred one of the guards.

"I don't care how good he is, there's no way a slave can best two Quag warriors," his friend argued.

"It's a bet then." the first guard tripped over his own feet, his friend steadying him.

"Aye. It's a bet." The two men shook hands.

Watching them, Catanya pulled back her hood, swept her hair across the left side of her head to conceal her markings and loosened the top of her robe. It took her little effort to present as an attractive young woman rather than a deadly Ferustir. She strode out in front of the guards, who were quick to notice her. "Good evening, my beauty!" one of them shouted. "Would you join us for a drink?"

"Perhaps," Catanya answered. The guards cheered with excitement. Catanya flashed a glance at their swords—each carried a single, heavy longsword that would be slow to draw in their inebriated state.

'Come then, join us back in the tavern!" the second guard encouraged.

"I've a better idea," Catanya spoke pleasantly. "Follow me." Much to their excitement, Catanya led the guards back up the narrow street. When they were out of sight of the tavern and away from the street lamps, she stopped and turned to them. The pungent scent of wine was on their breath.

"Do you know where I can find Carlo?" Catanya asked.

"Carlo? Carlo who?" the first guard replied.

"Carlo Dresenga."

"Nay, but stupid Stubert here does. He works for him." He pointed to the second guard, who struggled to walk at all, making his friend laugh. "What do you want of Carlo that you cannot have of us, my lady?"

Catanya ignored him and addressed Stubert. "You work for Carlo? Do you know where he keeps his slaves?"

"Of course, what of it?" Stubert said.

The first guard reached for Catanya. She brushed his arm away, still focussing her attention on Stubert. "Is Balgur among them?"

"Aye. You've got a sweet spot for the dragon warrior, have you?" Stubert said. "I'm not sure Carlo would approve of conjugal visits. You're best saving yourself for one of his men, pretty lady!"

Stubert made a clumsy lunge at Catanya. She stepped back and the other guard jumped at her and wrapped his arms tightly around her. His face was right at the back of her head. Catanya was quick to react. She threw her head back, breaking his nose. With a yell, he let go of Catanya, who pulled a throwing knife from beneath her robe and thrust it into his throat. She pushed the struggling guard to the roadside where he fell, gasping for breath. Retrieving her knife, she turned quickly to Stubert. She pulled her lance and pressed it to the guard's face. "You will take me to Carlo's slaves."

His eyes widened at the sight of the weapon held against him. The lance was unlit, yet its red glow moved about beneath Catanya's fingers. Stubert looked from Catanya to his friend, whose struggle for breath was weakening. "Who are you?" he stammered.

"No more talking." Catanya squeezed on the lance's grip and it ignited. The explosion of light and sound startled the guard, who yelped in fear. "Take me to Carlo's slaves *now*."

With encouragement by way of her lance, Stubert led Catanya through the deserted city streets. Twice the drunk guard stumbled, but Catanya dragged him to his feet, pushing him forward. She soon extinguished her lance and held instead the bloody knife to Stubert's throat as they walked.

They neared the city centre and turned a sharp left. Stubert spun about quickly, shoving Catanya in the chest, causing her to fall backward. She allowed herself to fall into a roll and sprang forward again with lightening reflexes. Stubert struggled to free his sword from his holster as Catanya swung her knife and severed the tendon at the back of the guard's heel with a *snap*. Stubert grunted in pain and half fell before Catanya yanked him to his feet again. She drew the longsword from his side and threw it back down the street.

"Do that again and you die, do you understand?" Catanya's eyes were wild. Stubert nodded. "Do you *understand?*" Catanya repeated. She swept the hair from her face, inadvertently revealing her Irucantî markings. Stubert stared at her, wide-eyed.

"You... you're a Ferustir!"

Catanya could see the fear in his face. *Good...*

They continued down a final street with Stubert hobbling awkwardly in pain, and arrived at a wall with a wrought iron gate set in a thick stone arch.

"Is this the way?" Catanya asked. Stubert nodded frantically. "Open it," Catanya insisted.

"I don't have the key," Stubert stuttered. "It can only be opened from the inside."

"Really? So the prisoners can free themselves?" Catanya pushed her knife into his cheek. "Open it now!"

"The guard... *inside*... has the key." Stubert's drunken eyes were rolling about. Catanya hoped to the Gods he would not pass out. She buried her foot into the guard's wounded heel, making him drop to the ground. His face contorted in pain but his eyes had regained their focus.

"Call the guard to the gate *now*."

"He will not hear us, lady. He'll be down in the dungeons."

Catanya grunted in frustration. She was so close. There had to be way through the gate. Leaving Stubert to nurse his wounded leg, she held the thick bars of the gate and pulled. Nothing happened—not so much as a rattle. The gate was impenetrable without a key.

Catanya peered through the gate and down the dimly lit flight of steps. She looked at the lamps that disappeared into darkness then whispered a spell. It was the same one her sister Hannah shared with Magnus when last she saw her. "*Fara mi parina.*" All the lamps flared for a moment, allowing Catanya to see to the bottom of the stairwell. In a few moments, they faded again. She looked then at the lamp closest to the gate. It appeared to be within arm's reach.

Catanya grabbed Stubert's collar, forcing him to stand. She pulled him over to the gate. "Stay here and don't move," she commanded. Catanya pushed her arm between the iron bars of the gate and stretched her hand toward the nearest lamp. She was less than a finger width short of reaching it. *Damn.* Turning to Stubert, she saw his eyelids were getting droopy. "Stubert!" she said sharply. His eyebrows lifted, but his eyes remained unfocussed. Catanya slapped him and his eyes widened again. "I need you to get that lamp for me." Stubert looked up, straining to focus on where Catanya was pointing. He used the gate to pull himself upright. Catanya put her knife to his throat again. "Reach through and get it for me."

Stubert nodded and reached through the bars. He took a hold of the thick candle and pulled it off the sconce on which it sat. The melted wax dripped over his hand.

"It's hot!" Stubert complained.

"Be quiet," Catanya said through gritted teeth. She looked about but there was no one around. Stubert pulled the candle through the bars of the gate and Catanya took it from him. She placed the still-burning candle on the gate, using her hands to mould the hot wax around the lock, careful to keep it alight. Taking three steps back, she whispered a second, more powerful spell—"*Exploda fara gin mara.*" The candle exploded, splattering hot wax over Stubert who was still holding himself upright against the gate. It also buckled the right side of the gate, destroying the lock. The door swung outward slightly on its squeaky hinges. Catanya smiled.

"What's going on here?" A loud voice boomed from behind Catanya. She spun about, drawing her lance. Two guards stood motionless, looking from Catanya to Stubert, who was rolling about, plucking wax off his burnt face and hands. The guards drew their longswords.

Catanya threw a knife at one of them, spearing his heart. He fell to his knees. His companion came at Catanya who turned and ran through the open gate to the landing at the top of the stairs. The guard followed and came through the gate with his sword swinging. Catanya shifted quickly to avoid his blow and ignited her lance. She thrust it toward the guard and speared him in the armpit. His good arm still free, the guard swung his blade about and down at Catanya. She caught the blow with her lance then drove her knee between the guard's legs. He buckled over and Catanya swung her lance across his head. The guard fell forward and Catanya helped with a kick, sending him tumbling down the stairs where he impaled himself on his sword as he hit the hard ground at the bottom.

Catanya took a breath and ran back out the gate and over to the dead guard. She retrieved her knife, sheathed her weapons and dragged the guard's body over to the gate. It was slow going, but she did not want to leave a trail of bodies for other guards to follow, knowing it was likely to be the way she would return. She looked to Stubert, hoping to garner his assistance, but he was sitting with his back to a wall, pulling wax from the backs of his hands.

Finally, Catanya had the guard at the gate. With a final heave she pulled him through to the top of the stairs where she pushed him over to join his colleague at the bottom. Catanya then grabbed Stubert. He struggled up once again, more willing than before, his face marked with burn marks and mounting fear. Catanya closed the gate behind them then marched Stubert down the stairs. It was slow going with an injured, drunk man dragging her down, but she needed him to show her the way.

"How far to the dungeons?"

Stubert did not answer, but stumbled onward down one corridor after the other, favouring his better leg. He finally came to a narrow archway off to one side of the corridor. "Through here," Stubert said.

Catanya looked at him. "What will I find through there?"

"Another corridor leading to the prison cages—six of them. Balgur is in the sixth cage."

"How many guards?"

"No more than one at this hour." Stubert sniffed and looked away.

Catanya was certain he was lying. She pushed Stubert through the archway and followed close behind, drawing a knife and holding it ready.

Suddenly, Stubert stopped and his body jolted. "Keep moving," Catanya said, but Stubert stood still. He then began to fall back and Catanya caught him. Holding him up, she looked over his shoulder and saw an arrow protruding from his chest. Further down the poorly lit corridor, Catanya could see four guards looking at her. One had a crossbow aimed at her head. The other three had swords drawn. The swordsmen each held a flaming torch. Catanya held Stubert's body in front of her as a shield and whispered her now favourite spell once again—"*Exploda fara gin mara!*"

BREAK OUT

In the dead of night, Magnus's eyes popped open as he heard the sound of keys connecting with the lock in his prison cage. His attention was drawn to the slow, delicate way the lock was being turned. *Someone is sneaking up on me...*

Magnus remained motionless, feigning sleep. He considered how he'd aggravated the guards earlier that day. *Anyone of them could want me dead.*

The cage door opened with the slightest of groans from the rusty hinges—not at all like the usual grinding clunk that came when the door was thrown open against its steel stop.

Magnus readied himself to pounce when the soft touch of a hand on his right shoulder startled him. He turned quickly, scrabbling backward on all fours from the stranger before him, cloaked in a dark robe. Magnus squinted in the darkness. The hooded stranger knelt down and drew the hood from their face.

"Magnus?"

The voice was a thing of beauty to him—all at once familiar, yet impossible. "Catanya?"

"Yes, it's me... it's me, Magnus," the voice whispered. She moved closer to him, placing a hand over his. Magnus saw before him the face of the woman he loved.

"Impossible!" Magnus exclaimed. She looked familiar yet so different. Her face was more chiselled, her hair was different and she bore the marking of an Irucantî across her bald scalp. With the speed of a cat, Catanya leapt at Magnus and embraced him in a desperate hug. She clung to him as if she never intended to let go. Magnus's heart melted with familiar emotions. All bitterness, fear and hatred were gone. He wrapped his arms tightly around Catanya. Her body felt so different. In place of her familiar gentleness was a hard, lean body that seemed to be that of another.

Magnus pulled her away and stared into her eyes. "Catanya!"

"Come Magnus," she whispered. "Let us leave this place." She pulled Magnus by the hand toward the cage door. As quick as a flash she led him out of the dungeon and along a dark narrow passage where they stepped over the bodies of the four guards who were posted to protect him. They all had severe burns.

"Did you do this?" Magnus could not believe was he was seeing.

"I tried to reason with them... actually that's a lie... I never tried to reason with them. Come!" She pulled Magnus further down the passage and came across another body. Magnus recognised the young guard. His face was burnt and his foot badly injured. But Magnus could see it was the arrow protruding from his chest that killed him.

They kept moving but a little further on, Magnus stopped. "Wait."

"What is it?" Catanya turned to him. A lamp illuminated her face. Magnus drew a breath at the sight of her, as she did at seeing him.

"You look so different," Magnus said.

"You have no idea what I've been through since we last saw one another. Looking at you though, I'm guessing you've been through worse. What happened to you?" She rubbed her hands along his upper arms that had nearly doubled in size since last she saw him. Then she stopped as she considered herself and blushed. Catanya turned away, but Magnus pulled her back to him and kissed her. For a moment they embraced one another, until Catanya pulled back.

"We must go," she said, trying in vain to hide a smile.

"I can't," Magnus confessed. "My fate is bound to others. If I leave, they will be executed." With every fibre of his being he wanted to flee with her and leave the nightmare behind. But he couldn't.

Catanya considered Magnus and then paced the corridor before turning back to him. "It is true then? You have bonded with a dragon?"

Magnus was dumbfounded. *How in all of Allumbreve could she know that?* Catanya held her wrist up to Magnus's face, showing him the leather bracelet.

"You left this with Breona. She died in the company of the dragon youngling."

"She did." Magnus felt a fool for leaving the bracelet. "She died protecting the dragon. She died protecting me—they both did." Magnus buried his face in his hands, fighting back emotions. It was the first he had talked of the ordeal to anyone.

"The dragon youngling chose *you* Magnus. Do you know what that means?" Catanya shook Magnus by the shoulders.

"Tell me. Tell me what it means? What am I to do?"

"You are the *Electus*. You hold the power of fire. It is *you* who will change the world. *'And your progeny shall forever inherit the power of the realm of fire'*... It is written in the *Murata*."

Magnus shook his head. "I don't know what the *Murata* is, Catanya. And I don't know what all this means. All I know is this—if I leave, Sarah will die. As will my father and Ganister."

"They are here?"

"Sarah is. My father and Ganister are elsewhere, being watched by Delvion. But all of their lives hang in the balance. I am to fight in the arena at dawn and the outcome determines whether we all live or die."

Catanya paced the corridor once again. "How did this happen?" she asked. Magnus shook his head—he was at a loss for words. The two of them remained silent for a moment. Magnus thought of how to best deal with their predicament.

"I cannot go Catanya. This battle is something I started. I must finish it." He could see how frustrated she was. There was a strength to her presence that Magnus had never seen before. She was an entirely different person now—no longer the girl in the white dress daring to cross the river to pick irises. She was a dragon priest, a *Ferustir*, breaking into dungeons beneath the most formidable place in Allumbreve with more certainty than he had ever seen in her.

"I heard the guards talking. You're to fight Delvion's men?" Catanya asked.

"Aye."

"You know he'll send his best? Or worse—himself!"

"Aye. I do," Magnus sighed. He did not know how to resolve the situation further. But then he had a thought—"If I show you where Sarah is, do you think you can get her out?"

"I could. But what then?"

"When I win in the arena tomorrow, Delvion promises to make purchase of me. No doubt he will want to meet me in person. Then I shall kill him and free my father and Ganister." Catanya raised her eyebrows. She went to speak but no words came out.

"It's the only way," Magnus concluded.

"Alright then," Catanya agreed. "Show me where Sarah is, I will get her to safety and I will meet you beyond the southern gates of the city, tomorrow night. No later."

Magnus ran with Catanya close behind, twisting through the dark and musty corridors that led to Sarah's small, isolated cell. Along the way they passed many doors to similar cells.

"Are there prisoners in every cell?" Catanya asked.

"I believe so."

Magnus ran as fast as he could with Catanya right behind him. He was surprised at her agility. As they approached the final corner, they heard the echoes of guards' boots striking stone. Magnus clenched his fists tightly as before. In moments the familiar heat charged through them and they ignited. He clasped his hands then separated them producing a ball of fire that he held aloft in his left hand. As the guards rounded the corner, Magnus flung it at them. The flames struck one of the two guards, slamming his body against the wall.

Catanya leapt across the wall to Magnus's left. He watched as she drew a strange weapon that released a loud cracking sound with an explosion of light. Holding the long, lethal lance, she quickly dispensed of the other guard. She turned to face Magnus, her weapon still holding its blaze. They looked one another over, breathing heavily from their efforts.

"Amazing!" Catanya said.

"I'll say!" Magnus replied. Smiling, he pointed to a door. "This is Sarah's cell."

Catanya nodded. "Go now, Magnus. Before you're discovered missing. They won't think you killed the guards if you're locked in that cage."

Magnus placed a hand upon her temple, feeling her markings. She took his hand and placed it over her heart. "Nothing has changed here."

ESCAPE

The steel bolt securing Sarah's prison door glided into the granite wall and Catanya pulled the door open. Sarah was sleeping against the wall on the hard stone floor to the right side of the room.

"Sarah?" Catanya watched the curly haired woman turn and sit. She squinted trying to focus her tired eyes. Catanya spoke gently—"Come, it is time to leave." She helped Sarah stand up and together they made for the door. Once free of the cell and under the lamp in the corridor, Sarah stopped and peered at Catanya's face.

'I know you."

"Aye—you do," Catanya whispered, hurrying to the next prison cell along on the opposite side of the corridor. She slid its bolt free also and took one step into the dark room before whispering the spell—"*Boe'l fara gin parshin-ar*". A small but intense ball of light ignited and floated at the centre of the room, momentarily blinding the thin, malnourished man who resided within. His sight returning, he looked at Catanya with wearisome eyes that lit up as though he'd found an old friend.

"*Ferustir!* Dragon warrior!" he exclaimed. "Do my eyes deceive me?"

"They do not. Come quickly."

As soon as the man stumbled out of his cell Catanya gave him orders. "Open the door opposite this one and free them as I have you. Have them do the same to the next door and so forth. Then keep behind me."

"Aye!" the man beamed a toothless smile and did as told. Within a few minutes, Catanya was leading seventeen prisoners through the complication of tunnels deep below Ba'rrat. All the while she had a firm grip on Sarah's arm, directing her forward.

"Priest, I am able to support myself," Sarah insisted.

"You do not leave my side. Not while I live," Catanya asserted, re-strengthening her grip on Sarah's arm.

"For what reason do I warrant precedence?" Sarah asked.

"Because I promised Magnus—I will free you tonight."

Sarah smiled as she ran, looking at Catanya. "Aye. I know now… you are Catanya. You have given Magnus reason to live all these months. I see now his love is well placed."

Catanya held fast to her emotions as she directed her entourage along corridors and up twisting stairways. Fifteen minutes after leaving Sarah's prison cell they passed the two dead guards at the bottom of the final set of stairs and climbed to the gate she had broken through less than an hour before. Catanya looked out to the street beyond, finding it empty.

"Keep to the shadows," she instructed. They moved in single file out of reach of the moonlight beneath the eaves of the buildings that lined the streets. Halfway to Ba'rrat's southern gate they entered a courtyard. At its centre was a guardhouse where one sleeping guard presided over an armoury rack that housed a collection of swords and shields. Catanya threw a single knife, dispensing with the guard, and the prisoners made their acquaintance with the weapons.

With over half of the escaped prisoners armed, they made their way further south toward the gate, keeping to the shadows. Soon the gate was in sight and Catanya turned away from it, down a narrow alleyway where several market carts and horses rested. She recognised the cart belonging to the farmer with whom she had entered Ba'rrat. His cart was now empty of sacks and in their place were bags of manure purchased to fertilise his crops back in Brindle.

Knowing the farmer was most likely still at the tavern, Catanya set her escapees to work. While Sarah petted the farmer's horses, she pulled back the large tarpaulin covering the cart and had them remove half the stock of fertiliser. They then hid amongst the foul-smelling stuff that remained.

"Cover yourself in manure. You must mask your scent from the wyverns who patrol outside the gates," Catanya instructed. Without hesitation, they did as told.

"Should I join them?" Sarah asked.

"No. I need you up front with me," Catanya said. She tied the tarpaulin down again and handed Sarah the farmer's coat and hat that lay on the seat of the carriage. Sarah donned the disguise and tied her hair up into the farmer's hat. Catanya pulled the hood of her brown robe over her head. "All must appear as it did when this cart arrived."

Catanya pulled on the horses' reins, setting the cart trundling slowly toward the city gates. As they got close, a single guard approached. He appeared somewhat annoyed at being risen so late in the night.

"Late is the hour for your departure, old man."

Sarah turned to Catanya and whispered, "Let me deal with this." Catanya held firm to her hidden lance as Sarah leaned forward and spoke to the guard in a deep voice. "I carry goods too unpleasant to spend the night within the city walls. A fellow colleague of yours insisted we take our leave."

"Oh?" the guard exclaimed, moving in closer to Sarah. "What are your goods then that be so unpleasant?"

Sarah reached behind her, burying her hand beneath the tarpaulin and pulled forward a large clump of the steaming horse manure. "Here, you see!" she exclaimed in her deep voice, shoving it under the guard's nose.

"Ah! Get that away from me. What is that filth?"

"Aye! It's filth! Too good for the fine folk of Ba'rrat!" Sarah enthused. "But wonderful for the crops back 'ome!"

The guard wiped his face with a sleeve and cursed. "Open!" he shouted to the gatekeepers as he stood back from the cart. "See if I don't double your fee next time you enter the city gates!"

Catanya moved the cart forward once again as the iron gates divided, allowing her, Sarah and the sixteen other escapees to leave the city of Ba'rrat. The checkpoints beyond the gate had no interest in people as they left the city, and the one wyvern lurking about in the night seemed to pick up the scent of their goods from afar and kept its distance.

Catanya smiled to herself, for she had expected far worse of the ordeal. But it was not over for her yet. *Now to get back into Ba'rrat...*

DELVION

By twisting his wrist and fiddling about with the lock, Magnus was able to secure cage number six from the inside. He pulled the rusty iron key from its lock and wedged it between the stone wall and lower bar of the prison cage.

Magnus lay down, closed his eyes and waited.

It did not take long to be visited by a group of vengeful guards. He knew they were there to punish him for the death of their kinsmen and so Magnus braced against their assault, resisting a counter attack. He and his fellow prisoners had been warned too many times that the penalty for attacking a guard was death. Magnus had come too far to forfeit his life for such a thing.

The beating seemed to go on forever before Carlo arrived, by which time Magnus was injured worse than he had ever been in the arena.

Carlo was furious.

"You all but kill the only person able to keep me alive beyond today!"

Magnus had not paid thought to this. *If I die, Carlo dies... At least there will be some justice in that.*

"Can you stand?" Carlo asked, concern in his voice. Magnus nodded, struggling to get up. His body flooded with heat— the healing had begun. The guards had broken several ribs and possibly his jaw. His right forearm was broken and his left knee had given in. After a moment limping about Magnus started to feel sick and fevers started to take hold of him. He had not had this sickness in months. *Why now?*

"*Anunya*," he mumbled.

"What was that?" Carlo asked.

Magnus threw up and doubled over, succumbing to the rigors that accompanied the sickness. "Just give me a while," Magnus grunted through chattering teeth.

"Damn it!" Carlo directed his anger at the guards. "You delinquents should each receive five lashings of the whip for this. Do you think if he killed the guards and freed all the prisoners he'd still be in his cage? It's more likely one of you drunk bastards left doors unlocked and they freed themselves!"

All the prisoners… Magnus smiled through his shakes. Catanya had been clever. *No better way to hide Sarah as being the primary target than to free other prisoners as well.*

"Clean him up as best you can," Carlo barked, then spoke directly to Magnus. "It seems Delvion has been alerted to the prisoners escaping. Between that and your actions, he has taken an unpleasant interest in my affairs."

Magnus wiped blood from his mouth. Sitting up as best he could, he stared at Carlo, showing deliberate contempt for the man. He could see fear in his face—he looked like he had aged ten years in one night.

"I've just spent the best part of an hour reasoning with the man. I've not grovelled like that since I was a boy."

Magnus tried not to laugh.

"Delvion now wishes to meet with *you*,' Carlo said. "Not so smug now, hey?" He stormed out of the cage but turned back. "You just remember our agreement."

One of the guards threw a bucket of cold water over Magnus's body. He gasped from the shock, but it seemed to help with his sickness. Another bucket followed and then a third.

"Like the big man said—we're cleaning you up," the guard sneered.

Magnus paid no attention to him. His blurred vision came back into focus and he found himself staring at a small white pebble embedded into the black stone wall at the back of his cage. He had never noticed it before. After all the days spent in the dark dungeon underneath the arena, he had never seen this one little pebble. He glanced around the cage, looking for any more detail that he may have missed over the past six months, for this was the last time he would ever see it. *Perhaps it wouldn't be so bad spending the rest of my life in this cage.* He knew the cage. It was predictable and it was always there at the end of the day's fighting in the arena.

A guard threw a towel and a clean white shirt into the cell. "It's time to go," the guard said.

Magnus wiped the water from his body. The fevers had passed quickly and his nausea was fading as well. Mindful of his still-healing ribs and arm he gingerly put the shirt on, buttoning it up at the front. Even through the pain it felt nice to have the clean shirt against his skin. It was the first time he had worn a shirt at all since arriving in Ba'rrat. The guards took amusement at his awkward appearance, wearing a clean shirt over the tattered remnants of his brown leather pants and dirty bare feet. Again, Magnus ignored them. He was thinking of his forthcoming meeting with Delvion.

It was a long walk down passageways Magnus was unfamiliar with. After half a mile following indirect and meandering passages the guards led Magnus upward and out into a small walled-in courtyard. From inside it, Magnus could hear the echoes of an excited crowd. *They're gathering already…*

There were at least twenty Quag warriors standing guard around the perimeter of the courtyard. They all fixed their eyes on Magnus. *They've all heard of my challenge to them.* Magnus eyed them closely. It had been a while since he had seen a Quag warrior. Whilst they certainly looked tougher than city guards, Magnus found them far less intimidating than he once did.

It was still dark and Magnus guessed about an hour before dawn—and an hour before his battle in the arena. He looked to the sky and drank in the stars for the first time in too long. To the northwest he recognised the Couldradt constellation. It seemed to shine bright, like the God of Fire was watching him, reminding him where he was from. Magnus smiled. He thought of Thioci and Balgur. He thought of the powers he unleashed the evening before and of Catanya—right there in Ba'rrat with him. Everything seemed to have its place. And now he was facing Delvion.

Several of the Quagmen came forward, relieving Carlo's guards. The Quagmen shackled Magnus's hands behind his back and placed others around his ankles. A final shackle was placed around his neck, reminding him of the one Breona was forced to endure. A Quagman either side of Magnus and another to his rear held tight to chains fastened to each shackle. It was almost impossible for Magnus to walk, let alone free himself. Nevertheless, he was pushed across the courtyard, through a doorway and, with the noisy clattering of chains, walked up another staircase.

The top of the stairs ended at a great passageway that reminded Magnus of the corridor leading to the Great Hall in Guame where he waited before his meeting with the Authoritarium. Here, at the opposite end of Allumbreve, he was about to meet the other great power threatening the freedom of his people.

Magnus observed the walls either side, lined with an ornamental array of weapons. There were swords and shields, spears and flails, maces, knives and more. Magnus took particular notice of the swords. There was a collection of steel swords from the Fire Realm, bronze swords from the Earth Realm and others not familiar to him. He noticed a single Icerealmish sword. Magnus thought again of the Quag attacking his mother's family, slaughtering them all. The weapons here were a crass testament to Delvion's domination of the four realms.

Magnus's progress was slow and awkward with the Quagmen dictating his movement, pulling on his shackles as if they wanted him to walk in several directions at once. The final sword mounted before a pair of tall doors at the end of the passageway caught his eye. It was bronze, but a paler colour than was usual. It was long and curved and its construction was fine and precisely made. It bore the glyphs of the Fire Realm. Magnus guessed it was a fire-bronze sword—the likes of which were only forged by artisans for the priests in the Romgnian Mountains. Magnus recalled the tale of the Battle of Fire and how Delvion slayed Balgur with a fire-sword. *This must be the sword*, Magnus realised. A chill ran down his spine at the thought of facing a warrior capable of slaying the greatest of dragons.

The Quagmen marched Magnus to the doors, which opened inward.

"Enter," a voice commanded from within.

Magnus was dragged into a wide, rectangular room. The far wall held eleven tall arched windows that looked out to the southern ocean beyond. A full moon threw thick, blue beams of light through each of the windows. Standing in front of the middle window were three men, hidden in shadow. The man in the middle stepped forward. A candelabrum at the centre of the room shed light across his face. Magnus stared at the man. He was tall—perhaps six foot five. Bony brows and high cheekbones framed his intense, staring eyes. The rest of his face was slender with a prominent chin accentuated by an underbite. His demeanour was too calm for Magnus's liking—a bit like a snake assessing its prey. He licked his upper lip slowly with a dry tongue.

"Do you know who I am?" he asked.

"Yes," Magnus said. His palms began to sweat.

"And now that I have you before me, is there anything you wish to say?"

Magnus shook his head.

"In the arena yesterday you certainly had a lot to say—words directed at me."

"My words were directed at your men."

The Quag guards pulled violently at Magnus's chains, thrashing his body to and fro.

"Enough," Delvion said calmly. "Leave us."

The four Quagmen left without a hint of hesitation and closed the doors behind them.

Delvion addressed Magnus again. "I understand you call yourself *Balgur* in the arena."

"Yes, I do," Magnus said.

Delvion pointed to the doors behind Magnus. "Did you see the last sword to your right as you came in?"

"I did."

"It is a fire-sword. It once belonged to a priest who was kind enough to relinquish it so that I may kill the great fire dragon—Balgur. That was twenty years ago. Unless you are he reincarnated, I am guessing you have another name."

Reincarnated... Magnus was intrigued by Delvion's choice of words, for he spoke a greater truth than he seemed to realise. As for his real name, Magnus felt it best to remain silent. It seemed Carlo had not turned him in. *I guess he needs me to fight in the arena to save his skin.*

"You are quite the accomplished fighter. *Warrior* is the term bandied amongst the people of Ba'rrat. Do you call yourself a warrior?" Delvion asked.

"Every bit as much as any Quagman. Perhaps more so," Magnus winced internally at his audacity, waiting for Delvion's retort.

Delvion lifted a hand and his two companions hidden in the shadows stepped forward. A hot flush of fear shuddered through Magnus. The man to Delvion's left was Crugion—bearing the scar across his cheek Magnus had given him months ago. He glanced with contempt at Magnus then let his sights wander as he crossed his arms, clearly not recognising him. The second face made Magnus gasp in horror.

It was Lucas.

Lucas's face was pale and drawn. His eyes were tired and grey and void of the spark they once held, but most of all, they did not recognise Magnus. Delvion turned to his son and whispered to him. Crugion nodded in reply.

Magnus flashed a glance at Lucas, wondering how he came to be under Delvion's control. Was it a spell? Was it some curse? Was it the wyvern poison? *That must be it—the wyvern poison... Oh no, Lucas...*

Lucas looked at Magnus and then, captured in the candlelight, Magnus saw a single tear fall from his friend's right eye, tumbling down his cheek. It was the only sign that Lucas was still present somewhere inside the shell of his former self.

Delvion finished talking with his son. "Be off with you then," he commanded. Crugion marched toward the door. Lucas turned and followed him. Magnus took a deep breath.

Alone in the room with Delvion, the Quag King looked Magnus over. "You have lasted longer than most in the arena, and yet, you seem to have kept your spirit. You may not be a warrior yet, but you certainly have the makings of one." Delvion walked to the window, his back to Magnus. "Unfortunately, when you enter the arena today, you go to your death."

Delvion turned back to the candelabra at the centre of the room and looked at the flames. Magnus silently muttered—*"Fara mi parina."* The flames of all eight candles flared momentarily. Delvion shifted backward a step. He glared at Magnus who pulled his shoulders back and glared in return.

"Before I send you to your death, I have an offer for you." Delvion walked back to Magnus. "I offer you the chance to become a warrior, but you must swear a binding oath of allegiance to me that cannot be broken."

Magnus was dumbfounded. "You know nothing of me, yet you offer this?"

"I know a strong man when I see one. The people of Ba'rrat see it too. If you show your allegiance to their king, they will follow you."

"When I win, they will follow me regardless of my allegiance." Magnus saw what looked like a twitch in Delvion's eye.

"Do you seriously think you can defeat two of my best men?" Delvion asked in a pompous tone. Still, Magnus thought perhaps Delvion was worried about the outcome.

"I think you are concerned I will."

An unpleasant smirk came to Delvion's face. "I see you have given this much thought." Delvion paused for a moment then paced the room, wringing his fingers in the palms of his hands. Finally he stopped and raised a finger. "Here is what I propose. I will send two men as promised. The first you will kill, of that I am certain. The second you will battle, but on my command, you will *yield.*"

"You mean, surrender?"

"Precisely. Then before the people of Ba'rrat you will swear an oath of fealty to me."

Magnus stared at Delvion. He could not believe what he was hearing. *Why would I swear allegiance to this madman?*

"Why would you want my allegiance?"

Delvion smirked again. "Because—*Magnus*—there is no greater vengeance against the man who killed my son than to win the allegiance of his own."

Magnus reeled. Delvion knew the truth after all. *That is why he has Lucas under his control—to spite Ganister. Now he wants the same of me.*

"And if I defeat both of your men?" Magnus asked.

"Then your father's life is forfeit."

"How do I know you've not killed him already?" Magnus strained against his shackles. "And Ganister?"

Delvion pointed a long, bony finger at Magnus. "You will yield in the arena tomorrow at the sound of the Quag horn." He drew a seething breath through his teeth. "Or witness Bonstaph *and* Ganister die in the arena alongside you."

Magnus thrashed at his shackles. He had no power over his situation—he never had—and realising that now only frustrated him more.

Delvion called for the guards, who returned and dragged Magnus away. Before he was taken from the room Delvion called after him.

"Know this, Magnus of J'esmagd—all virtuous beings eventually come to desire power as you have. But not all are destined for it."

DAWN

An hour later, Magnus was escorted up the all-too-familiar network of corridors and stairs that led to the arena. All the way, the four guards accompanying him spewed insults.

"You'll not last two minutes against Delvion's warriors…"

"Your mother fled to find a more worthy son…"

"Do you have any last words before you're cut to pieces?"

By the time Magnus climbed the second flight of stairs to the armoury, the last of his ailments—his injured knee—was healed. But the heat within him still raged. Magnus desperately wanted to kill Delvion, but in his absence, the guards would have to do.

Magnus spun about and kicked one of the guards square in the chest, sending him tumbling back down the stairs. His body hit the landing with a dull thud and the sharp crack of a leg bone snapping. The guard howled in pain. The remaining guards shuffled back, out of Magnus's reach.

"What did you expect?" Carlo scolded his guards as he met Magnus at the top of the stairs. "The man's a warrior. Can't say the same of you lot."

Carlo seemed in good spirits, which grated on Magnus no end.

"A *man* you say. No longer a boy?" Magnus asked.

"I think we can move beyond *boy* now." He winked at Magnus in the most condescending manner. "How are you feeling? Not too beaten up I hope?"

"I'll be fine. The wounds were mostly superficial," Magnus lied.

"Hmm. I call it gypsy magic." Carlo frowned. "Speaking of which, do you find it strange that your dearest friend would abandon you after such loyalty on your part?"

Magnus could see Carlo was searching for signs of his part in Sarah's escape.

"I'm happy for her. I've been telling her for months to flee if she got the chance."

"And why would you say a thing like that?" Carlo questioned.

"Sarah and I both knew I'd be killed someday. And then you would kill her, was that not the promise?"

Carlo mumbled to himself but said nothing coherent.

They arrived at the armoury. Magnus sniffed at the familiar scent of blood, sweat, steel and dust and was pleased it would be the last time he would ever have to be there.

The smithy was waiting with the completed suit of armour. It lifted Magnus's spirits to see how well it was finished. It seemed to have been re-crafted out of Quag armour. All the pieces of black armour had been burnished and beaten back to their natural copper hue. A chest and back plate were fitted with three thick leather buckles either side that the smithy tightened firmly, then loosened a touch to give Magnus breathing space. Next, he fitted greaves to his shins and thighs, rerebraces to his arms and vambraces to his forearms. Finally he handed Magnus a full-face helm, but Magnus declined. *Delvion knows who I am, so why bother?*

"Well then… whaddya think?" the smithy slurred through his toothless mouth. He seemed rather pleased with his work. Magnus jumped around in the armour, then ducked and weaved and raised his arms over his head.

"Good, but a little restrictive," Magnus remarked. The smithy scratched his dirty cheekbone nervously.

"Restrictive? What's that then? You can move, can't ya?"

"Take it off my arms." Magnus said. The smithy did as he was told, removing the rerebraces, mumbling to himself as he went. He kept the vambraces in place, but with his upper arms free Magnus could move around a lot more. He stripped the armour from his thighs to good effect as well. "That's better. Thank you."

"Anything else?" the smithy grumbled.

"One more thing." Magnus went over to the weapons arrangement and picked out two small daggers, each about five inches long. "Can you loosen these a little, just enough to conceal them?" Magnus pushed the tips of the daggers into his greaves.

"Ah! Good idea." The smithy did as instructed, helping Magnus place the two hidden weapons up against his calf muscles, such that the handles could be easily accessed when required. Satisfied, Magnus took the two black blades that had served him well the previous day and twirled them about, familiarising himself with their weight and balance and feeling warmth shift through his limbs.

"I am ready."

Carlo shook Magnus's hand with a strong, firm grip. Magnus could feel the man's hopes and anxieties in that shake and, for a moment, felt sorry for him. Just like his own, Carlo's fate was in Delvion's hands. Magnus considered that this was the fate of anyone living within Ba'rrat's walls.

That shall not be me.

Magnus looked out to the arena. The morning sun had risen over the eastern grandstand. Morning dew steamed from the black granite ground, giving a mystical quality to the event. The stadium was filled beyond capacity. Many stood in the aisles and even then were jostling for position.

He could hardly believe all this was from his outspoken behaviour in the arena the previous day. So much had changed for Magnus since then. He was overwhelmed. *Six months of nothing and then everything...* He questioned whether seeing Catanya was a dream, as with Sarah escaping, but the beating he endured because of it was testament to its truth. As for Delvion's confession to holding Bonstaph and Ganister captive—at least now Magnus knew where he stood.

He was entirely unsure how the events in the arena would play out, but there was only one way to find out. Magnus stepped out of the armoury. The crowd spotted him, erupting in cheers. They started chanting his name as he walked to the centre of the arena.

"Balgur, Balgur, Balgur, Balgur..."

Magnus lifted the blades above his head and the crowd raised their chants to a deafening roar. Magnus was alarmed at all this commotion. He was glad for it though, for it was surely making Delvion nervous. When he stood at the centre of the arena, Magnus turned, taking in the mass of people and wondered if they truly supported Delvion and his regime in taking over Allumbreve.

There were over thirty guards around the perimeter of the arena—a change from the usual five or six. Magnus wondered if it was to prevent him from fleeing or to keep the excited crowd in order.

No number of guards could control this crowd.

Trumpets blared from the top of the four towers surrounding the great arena. The crowd fell to respectful silence and focussed their attention on the arena's two gigantic wooden doors to the southeast. Magnus had never seen them used before. Now though, they groaned as they opened. *Clunk, clunk, clunk...* the enormous chains rattled across the gears and held taut as the doors peeled apart. The trumpets fell to silence and an announcer in the northern tower spoke.

"Rise and welcome your King and future ruler of all Allumbreve!"

The crowd applauded as if on cue. It seemed to Magnus that they were doing it out of politeness more than for love of their leader. A procession entered the arena led by two wyverns that sniffed at the ground and snarled at the perimeter guards. They moved aside to make way for two enormous warhorses—the likes Magnus had never seen before. Far larger than a Wardemeer, they were broad chested with large feathered hooves like the draft horses used to pull the quarry carts back in the Uydferlands. They had a foul disposition about them with rolling blood shot eyes and drool excreting from their maws as though suffering from an insatiable appetite. Mounted on each were Quagmen dressed in full black battle armour with their paired swords sheathed by their sides. Their faces were concealed by their usual spiked helms and kerchief-wrapped faces.

Next came an enormous black wyvern whose size rivalled that of a dragon. Magnus had no idea wyverns could be this big. On its back was another warrior. This man wore a flowing cape in a dark shade of purple that covered a more refined set of armour than his subordinates. As he entered, he removed his helm. It was Delvion. His dark eyes immediately locked on Magnus. Magnus sneered at Delvion's excessive showmanship.

The two horsemen dismounted and joined Delvion for a private discussion. Their leader nodded as the Quagmen spoke to him at length, but his eyes never left Magnus. Magnus was convinced Delvion was deliberately trying to intimidate him, but knowing so made it no better.

Magnus stood and waited. The confidence he had felt as he walked in was waning and he started to feel very small standing alone among Delvion's army of men. Finally their conversation concluded and Delvion dismounted from the wyvern and raised his arms in the air.

"My fellow Quagmen!" he bellowed. The crowd were silent. "On the field of the arena today we have a champion among slaves. A slave who calls himself *Balgur,* giving praise to the greatest fire dragon that ever lived."

The crowd were stirred and began to cheer once again. Magnus looked Delvion over. Even in the open arena his height was apparent, yet the truth of his strength was hidden beneath the flamboyance of his cape and armour.

Delvion continued—"But, as the people of the Fire Realm know all too well, *Balgur fell.*" The crowd booed and hissed. "He fell under the hands of Quagmen!" Cheers rose again.

"How do I know of Balgur's fate?" Delvion drew the fire-sword and held it high. "It was *I* who wielded the sword that slayed the mighty dragon. *This* was the sword that smote the oppressor and paved the way to our future."

The crowd were ecstatic. Delvion knew how to put on a show, Magnus conceded.

Delvion waited while the crowd settled, then pointed the fire-bronze sword at Magnus, who still stood at the centre of the arena. "Now it seems Balgur has returned. He has not learned from his defeat and requests that we teach him once again." The crowd booed and hissed at Magnus and many shouted abuse at him. "Let us teach him his proper place in history. Let us see if we can tame the beast," Delvion roared.

These were the words Magnus anticipated—*tame the beast*. Magnus knew it was Delvion's precursor to Magnus swearing fealty with him. It was a spectacular turn of events. Delvion had taken Magnus's show of strength and made it his own. And he held his father and Ganister as guarantee that he would yield.

Delvion ordered his entourage out of the arena. He mounted his large wyvern, took flight, and landed at the southern tower high above the common folk where an entourage of well-dressed dignitaries awaited him. The procession left the arena and the heavy gates closed once again with a heavy crash of chains and a dull thud as the doors slammed home.

Magnus was alone once again, standing at the centre of the arena, only this time, he did not have the crowd's support. He was left to wait alone for a few more agonising minutes before a small door within the larger gates opened and his first opponent appeared.

This is the one I am supposed to kill...

It was most certainly a Quag warrior, though not one Magnus recognised. He was dressed as all Quag warriors were but for one difference—he carried the fire-bronze sword Delvion brandished moments ago. He wore a confident smile across his well-scarred face. The crowd recognised him and began to chant his name.

"*Hermön... Hermön... Hermön...*"

He raised his helm to the sky and roared to the crowd with a scratchy, hoarse voice. *No doubt from the deep laceration to his throat*, Magnus spotted. Hermön replaced his helm and broke into a run toward Magnus.

As a side effect of his recent healing process, Magnus felt as if he were overwhelmed with energy. Hermön approached and Magnus vowed to keep his secret to himself. *You cannot have it Delvion... I am the chosen one.* Besides, he knew an outward display of his powers would elicit a reaction from Delvion that would put his father and Ganister's life in danger.

Hermön charged at Magnus as fast as he could. His sword fell hard but Magnus shifted with unnatural speed, leaving Hermon to overextend. Magnus hesitated and skipped back, away from Hermön.

Damn it… Magnus was anxious.

Hermön took a deep breath and came at Magnus again. Magnus brought both his blades about, ready to counter Hermön's swing. It was what Hermön wanted. His blow was single handed, leaving his other hand free to pull a knife from his breastplate and swipe it quickly at Magnus's face.

Magnus let go of one of his blades and pulled his arm to his head, blocking the knife with his armour. Hermön swung the fire-sword again and Magnus moved swiftly out of the way. Hermön overextended once more. Magnus was not going to give the Quagman a third chance to best him. He twisted his body about, using his elbow to push Hermön further into his overextension. Then, while Hermön was busy shuffling his feet to regain his balance, Magnus buried his blade in his back beneath his tunic and out through his stomach, never relenting until the blade pierced through his armour. Hermön's body slumped to the ground.

Magnus took a step back. The crowd was quiet except for a few isolated claps and cheers that soon died down. Magnus looked to Delvion who sat in his tower silently.

Magnus went to retrieve his black blades when he eyed the fire-bronze sword resting beside Hermön's body. Bending to one knee, Magnus wrapped his left hand around its grip and stood again, holding it aloft. He felt its weight and examined it. It was a truly impressive sword—beautifully constructed and well balanced. Up close, Magnus admired the exquisite detail in its engravings that started at the hilt and continued down either side of the curved blade.

He recalled his dreams back in Froughton Forest. Balgur had told him, *"I will show you the way to the salvation of our people."* It seemed fitting that he now stood in Ba'rrat's arena holding the very sword that killed the great dragon, wielding it against Delvion's men. He hoped it would some day slay Delvion himself.

Magnus stood his ground, waiting for his second opponent to appear. Sure enough, the small door opened again and two men entered. Magnus recognised them both. One was Briet, the other Crugion. They both stared at Magnus with expressions of absolute hatred.

Magnus had no doubt—*they know who I am*... He considered what a thorn he had been in their sides back in Froughton Forest and how Crugion must have gloated to his father about killing Bonstaph's son, only to have his father find out he was lying—or a fool. Either way, they would want vengeance.

Crugion and Briet exchanged words, looking from one another to Magnus. In the end though, it was Briet who placed his helm upon his head and took up his two black blades. *The predictable choice,* thought Magnus. Delvion would not risk sending his own son, regardless of what agreement Delvion supposed he and Magnus had made.

That must surely pain Crugion.

Crugion stayed with the guards at the entrance, pacing the ground in an obvious display of frustration. Briet walked to meet Magnus at the centre of the arena. He stopped just out of reach, removed his helm and discarded it, then stood and stared at Magnus.

"I should have ignored Crugion and finished you off myself in the forest. I'd have spared you a prolonged death." Magnus looked at the big warrior in silence. "You've got nothing to say? You just wanna get this over with?" Briet grunted in his usual uncouth manner. "Let me tell you this—you *are* going to die today. You are going to die a slow and painful death."

Briet took a step closer and Magnus felt his palms turn to sweat. There was no running from Briet this time. Not the way he had at the Hugmdael Inn. Not the way he had in Froughton Forest when he hid behind the oak tree. This time, he was facing the man in a fight to the death.

Magnus let his fear turn to anger. He wanted to kill the tyrant for his part in killing Breona. He pictured his body flying in a ball of fire like he did the guard the night before in the dungeons. Magnus could feel the turmoil in his mind and body, the inner dragon who wished to unleash all its power on Briet. It seemed like the perfect chance to test his strength, but he forced himself to conceal his powers.

No, Magnus asserted. *I'll kill him the same way I've killed every other man in the arena. If I can defeat Briet then the people of Ba'rrat will know a warrior of the Fire Realm can defeat the best of Delvion's men.*

Magnus attacked first. The fire-sword sliced through the air silently. Briet did not bother to move. He used his brute strength to absorb each of Magnus's blows with a single sword in a single hand and countered with his other, slamming his sword down with more ferocity than any of the one hundred opponents Magnus had faced before.

Magnus was quick and danced about Briet, but he was shocked at his opponent's speed. Magnus tried to distract Briet with Sarah's enchantments but he was too clever to fall for cheap deceptions.

Each of Briet's attacks was meant to kill. As the fight progressed, Briet grew increasingly frustrated, putting more strength behind each blow and recovering slower after each move. Finally, his speed waned and Magnus made a strike to Briet's right thigh, cutting deep into the muscles and throwing him off balance. Magnus stood back for a moment, disbelieving he had injured him.

The crowd oohed and aahed, but gave no favour to either contestant. Rather, they were savouring the duel between two contestants they had never seen beaten.

The wound angered Briet and he came at Magnus harder than ever. He seemed to unleash every trick and combination he knew. Magnus fended off blow after blow until Briet was able to land a heavy strike across Magnus's chest armour. It knocked the wind out of him, stalling him long enough for Briet to slash his sword through Magnus's right shoulder. Magnus fell to his knees, still holding his sword as Briet held his own above his head, readying himself to strike.

With heat searing through his body, Magnus pushed forward, driving his body into Briet, sending him tumbling back. They fell over one another, Magnus recovering first. Standing over Briet, he drove the fire-sword down. Briet shifted quickly to avoid it. Magnus went to repeat the strike when the horn sounded. The low sound resonated through the arena. Delvion's words came to Magnus— *"You will yield at the sound of the Quag horn…"*

Magnus swore loudly in frustration, his sword ready to strike again.

"Or witness Bonstaph and Ganister die alongside you…"

Magnus shook his head, dropping the fire-sword to the ground. He could not risk it. He could not kill Briet.

"I'll not make that mistake again!" Briet gloated. Magnus looked down at the repulsive man as Briet thrust his own sword at Magnus's midriff, burying it perfectly beneath his rib cage, piercing his armour and thrusting it out through his back.

The crowd fell silent as Magnus fell to his knees.

The Quag-horn continued to blow, signalling Briet to stop.

"Enough!" called Delvion.

Briet got to his feet and stood back, surveying his handy work. A familiar grin returned to the Quagman's face.

It was too painful for Magnus to breathe so he stopped and waited as the healing heat took over his body, searing through him and attacking his wounds. Magnus grasped the hilt of Briet's sword. It was hot and getting hotter. He peered down as the sword began to glow red. Briet stepped away, watching in awe as the blade glowed brighter and brighter, turning brilliant amber before igniting and crumbling to molten ash that fell to the ground.

Magnus gasped as his breath returned and his heart pumped hard and fast. He stood and looked at Briet, knowing his long-kept secret was no longer.

"What are you?" Briet asked, recoiling, a look of incredulity across his face. Magnus reclaimed the fire-sword, pointing it at Briet. He let all his fear and rage turn to heat that coursed through his body and funnelled into his left arm. Magnus glanced at his clenched fist. As the heat peaked, small flames oozed from the pores in his skin. They quickly grew, merged, and formed an eddy of flames that swirled around his fist and up his forearm. The flames picked up speed, spiralling down the length of the sword and burst out toward Briet, engulfing him in flames. The large Quagman screamed and ran to and fro in abject madness. The flames seemed to have a mind of their own, dancing around Briet's body until eventually, the screams ceased and he fell to the ground—charred and smouldering.

Briet was dead.

SORCERER

The first reaction to Magnus's fire display came from the crowd. A woman let out a blood-curdling scream that tore through the silence, giving rise to a chorus of similar responses. Some of the crowd tried to flee but most remained frozen and wide-eyed.

The flames around Magnus's arm dispersed. He backed away from Briet's corpse and turned to the main entrance, where Crugion stood, staring in shock. Magnus lifted his gaze to the southern tower. Delvion was on his feet, staring down at Magnus, shaking in anger. Magnus knew retribution would come swiftly.

A dreadful screech from behind made Magnus twist his body about. He caught a glimpse of a wyvern just as it landed, knocking him flat on his back. The fire-sword slipped from his grasp and clattered away out of reach. The wyvern came over to him as if walking on all fours with its spiked wing tips clattering across the hard ground.

Magnus reached for one of the blades hidden in his grieves and pulled at it. It was stuck. He reached out an arm, trying to muster a ball of fire, but quickly retreated when the wyvern snapped at it. It screamed directly at Magnus. Heat and saliva whipped at his face and the smell of its breath almost made him pass out. Then the mental attack came, just as it did when he fended off the wyvern that attacked Lucas.

Thump, thump, thump.

The wyvern was trying to tear his mind to pieces with its barbarous thoughts. Magnus looked into the wyvern's sickly yellow eyes. Its pupils shifted furiously. Then the heat came, just as it did to heal his wounds, only it bathed his mind, holding the wyvern's pounding thoughts at bay. The black beast's eyes dilated furiously and Magnus got the upper hand, forcing his way into the knotted, twisted depths of the wyvern's mind. It was pure hatred. There was not a hint of rationality to reason with. But then, as quick as a flash, a change seemed to come out of nowhere and the wyvern projected

287

absolute terror. Magnus pulled his mind free, not wanting to be a part of it. A moment later the wyvern slumped to the ground—dead.

Magnus shoved the beast's leathery head off his leg and saw in the sun the silhouette of someone standing on the wyvern's back. Twisting his head to the side he saw who it was...

"Catanya?"

Catanya pulled her lance from the base of the dead wyvern's skull.

"Aye." She jumped to the ground and took Magnus's hand, pulling him to his feet. Without thinking he gave her a firm kiss. Catanya seemed to choke on it, a surprised expression on her face.

Magnus drank in the vision of her. Unlike the robed priest she was last night, Catanya was dressed in a Ferustir suit that revealed her lithe, muscular body. He was speechless.

Catanya looked herself over, frowning, then smirked at Magnus. "You scared me half to death before," she said. "I thought that Quagman had killed you."

"Briet—because of him I may not get the chance to swear fealty to Delvion."

"You wouldn't dare!"

"It crossed my mind." Magnus thought of his father and Ganister.

More screams from the stadium made them both look about. Several more wyverns had landed among the crowd, flinging bodies out of their way as they crawled down through the rows of abandoned seats toward the arena. Their eyes were locked on Magnus.

"How did you get in here?" Magnus asked Catanya, still looking at the wyverns, wondering which would approach first, yet still astounded Catanya was in the arena.

"People were coming into the city in droves." She spoke frantically. "All talking about the *'Mighty Balgur'* and the battle you were to fight." Magnus looked at her. "And so I just walked back in—blending with the crowd. Not a question was asked."

"You're amazing," Magnus said.

"Where's Delvion?" Catanya asked, stepping back toward the centre of the arena.

They both looked up to the heights of the arena. Delvion was gone. Magnus turned to Crugion who was shouting at one of the guards near the entrance of the armoury. The guard opened the door and two men were shoved out into the arena. They both stumbled and caught their footing. They were not Quagmen, wore no armour and their beards and hair were as dishevelled as Magnus's only greyer. They each carried a sword and shield from the dismal armoury selection. The two men walked tentatively, shielding their faces from the morning sun, seemingly at a loss as to why they were there. Magnus would never have recognised them were it not for the remnants of familiar clothing they were wearing when last he saw them.

Father! Ganister! Forgetting the wyverns, Magnus ran to them. Both men turned toward him and readied their swords for an impending attack. Magnus stopped short. "Father!"

Bonstaph froze and stared at his son. Ganister moved around Magnus, still ready to fight.

"Magnus?" Bonstaph said. "Magnus, is that you?"

Ganister lowered his sword and shield, shaking his head. "No, it cannot be."

"Father—it's me!"

Bonstaph stared in disbelief and Ganister wore a broad smile. Bonstaph reached Magnus and they embraced. Magnus held his father tight through the convulsions of his father's tears, as though all problems of the moment could vanish with that one embrace.

"My son… my son…" Bonstaph sobbed as he held Magnus.

Ganister came behind Magnus and grabbed him by the shoulders, shaking him excitedly,

"Magnus!" Catanya shouted, appearing at his side.

The three wyverns leapt into the arena, pushing two guards at the perimeter aside. The rest of the guards shifted about aimlessly, unsure what to do in the confusion. The wyverns however, were still focussed on Magnus and his accomplices. The smallest of the three made a lunge for them. Catanya skipped toward it, twisting alongside the black creature and avoiding a strike of its barbed tail. Ganister followed her, shouting at the wyvern to distract it, giving Catanya the chance to sink her lance deep into its neck. The creature wailed in pain.

Two Quagmen appeared from behind the wounded wyvern and intercepted Ganister before he reached Catanya.

"No!" Magnus shouted. He knew Ganister was a powerful man but his enslavement had worn him—or so Magnus thought.

Ganister charged hard and fast as the Quagmen raised their swords. Magnus and Bonstaph both ran to join him but they were still a distance away when the Quag swords fell upon him. One splintered Ganister's sword to pieces, the other shattered his shield in two. Ganister fell to his knees as the Quagman came at him again.

Magnus was twenty paces out. In his left hand he gripped the fire-sword, his right hand cast out before him. Instinctively, a jolt of fire leapt from the palm of his hand, striking the nearest Quagman in the chest. His burnt carcass launched backward across the stone floor of the arena, where it landed beside Briet's.

Magnus continued forward, flames still dancing around his hand. The second Quagman turned from Ganister to Magnus. Bonstaph was upon him before Magnus and attacked him with all his resolve.

Magnus had never seen his father fight before, but even with his dull sword he pummelled the bewildered Quagman until he fell. His attack was relentless, his swordsmanship unforgotten. Ganister retrieved the burnt Quagman's swords and threw one to Bonstaph, who caught it and finished off the second Quagman.

Magnus ran to Catanya, who withdrew her lance from the now-dead wyvern. Together they regrouped with Bonstaph and Ganister, standing with their backs to one another. The two remaining wyverns paced about with their backs arched, cautious after seeing their brethren slain by a Ferustir. Some of the perimeter guards were fleeing and those remaining were as apprehensive as the wyverns.

With a moment's reprieve, Bonstaph took the opportunity to talk. "Magnus. How in all of Allumbreve did this happen?"

"It's the longest of stories, Father!"

"It is beyond your call to Knighthood—that much I know!" Ganister laughed.

"I'm no Knight of Allumbreve, father," Magnus said.

"No," Bonstaph replied. "You are far more than that!"

"So you know then why we are here?" Catanya said. "You know why Magnus must survive this?"

"Aye, young priest. But I see no need for *any* of us to die this day," Ganister said.

"If we are to die it will not be to this wretched lot, in this wretched place," Bonstaph added.

"There is more to fear than Quagmen and their beasts," Catanya countered.

Magnus did not know what she was talking about, but before he had a chance to ask, the main gates groaned and the chains started to move, opening them once more. Magnus swallowed hard. There was something scratching and pounding at the door from the far side—some impatient beast trying to get in. A dreadful screeching sound, all too familiar to Magnus, came from beyond it.

"What darkness lurks behind those doors?" Bonstaph asked.

The gates had just opened enough for Delvion's immense wyvern to push its head through. It shouldered the door, tearing it from its iron hinges. Behind Delvion sat a hooded companion.

"Kill them!" Delvion commanded the perimeter guards with ferocity in his voice. "Bring this heinous man before me," Delvion screamed, pointing at Magnus. "I want him dead! I want his blood!"

The guards regrouped and moved toward Magnus and his companions.

Magnus turned a hand upright and allowed a ball of flame to form in his palm. He threw it at Delvion, who watched him, unperturbed by the threat. Moments before it hit him, the cloaked man behind him raised an arm, sending forth a syrupy cloud of black matter that absorbed the flames, protecting Delvion.

A sorcerer? Magnus wondered.

Delvion held firmly to the wyvern's leash and commanded it to move forward. His face held a look of absolute fury. The guards surrounded Magnus, Catanya, Bonstaph and Ganister, none of whom took their eyes off Delvion, the most deadly of his company.

I must kill Delvion… no matter what happens, Magnus promised himself.

He pointed his sword toward several guards closest to him. Flames started to spin about his hand. Noticing this, the guards stopped in their tracks. Further back, a pair of dark robed figures dropped into the arena from the crowd above. They advanced toward them, removed their robes and drew lances, igniting them as Catanya had. *More priests!* Magnus felt relieved at their presence.

The two Ferustirs reached the nearest guards and attacked with more skill than Magnus ever knew possible. Their feet hardly touched the ground as they spun and twirled their lances, forcing the ring of guards to break. Magnus stood beside his father and put the fire-sword to good use again, slaying a guard who came too close.

The priests continued to slay man after man and soon stood beside Magnus and his father.

"Austagia!" Bonstaph shouted to one of the priests. Recognising the name, Magnus turned to look at the priest whom he had hated so much in the days after losing Catanya to the priesthood. The tall priest greeted Bonstaph with a nod and looked at Magnus, nodding to him also. Magnus looked to the other priest and saw it was a woman with hair and outfit similar to Catanya's.

Magnus caught sight of Catanya who, with Ganister's help, was dealing with two more guards with as much efficiency as the other priests. Her attention however, seemed focussed on the other two priests. Once finished with the guards, Catanya stopped to confront Austagia.

"Austagia… Jael… What are your intentions?" she demanded.

"We come before the storm, Semsame. We must get him out of Ba'rrat immediately." Austagia pointed at Magnus.

"You are here to support us?" Catanya demanded.

Magnus wondered why Catanya questioned her uncle's objectives. Austagia saw Magnus watching and spoke gently to his mind.

"You carry the blood of fire. We are with you, not against you." Magnus could feel the priest's conflicting thoughts and worry over their predicament. Magnus looked to the priestess beside him, whom Catanya had called *Jael.* She eyed him with equal curiosity.

Suddenly, an ear splitting roar echoed around the arena and shook the ground beneath their feet. *That was no wyvern,* Magnus thought. A large fire dragon, its wings extended to their full span, landed on the highest precipice of the arena's northern grandstand. A second dragon landed upon the western tower and a third to the east. Each in turn announced their arrival with equally terrifying roars. Each carried a priest upon its back. Magnus caught his breath. The crowd was hysterical, fleeing in every direction. Some simply fell to their knees in fear.

The first dragon to arrive leapt from its tower into the arena and landed heavily, sending splinters of granite spinning across the floor. It released a torrent of flames that incinerated half the remaining guards on the arena's floor. Those left stopped their attack and fled for the main gates.

The two smaller wyverns sprang at the dragon. A brawl ensued and all who remained in the arena stopped to watch as the three beasts tumbled over the ground violently. Magnus cringed at the sound of bones breaking under the clench of powerful dragon jaws and the screech of wyvern claws against the dragon's armour-plated scales.

The wyverns were cunning and worked together to try to best the dragon. As one of them pulled free of the scramble, it paced around directly in front of Magnus—its attention solely on the dragon. Magnus loosened one of the blades from his grieves and threw it at the wyvern's head, where it sank into its jaw. The black beast reeled away and screamed, alerting the dragon to its whereabouts. Turning from the other wyvern it blew a jet of flames over the injured beast, scalding its leathery skin.

Seizing the opportunity, one of the priests ran at the injured wyvern. Magnus saw it was Jael. She jumped upon the wyvern's back and plunged her lance into the base of its thick neck. Magnus was awestruck by her tenacity. She did not stop until the wyvern sank to the ground, dead. Meanwhile, the dragon continued its battle with the other wyvern as the priest who rode it alighted, walking toward Jael with his lance drawn. To Magnus's surprise, Jael reignited her lance and stood her ground, apparently waiting for her kin to attack.

Magnus suddenly felt a firm grip upon his right upper arm. He turned—it was his father.

"Let's take advantage of this chaos, Magnus. We can escape this place." Ganister was with him, keen to make a move. Catanya however, was not. She ran to support the other priestess.

"Catanya!" Magnus shouted. She could not hear him over the screaming chaos that had consumed the arena. The crowd were reduced to half their numbers, wailing and shouting as they toppled over one another in their attempts to escape.

The arena's floor held the remains of dead guards, Quagmen and burning piles of rubble. It was all but consumed with smoke. As the dragon in the arena finished off the second wyvern, tearing it limb from limb, Catanya and Jael were arguing with the newly arrived priest. Looking like they were about to fight, the hulking black beast carrying Delvion and the sorcerer lunged through the smoke screen, grabbing the rogue priest and running him through with its enormous fangs, killing him. Delvion then instructed the wyvern to attack the priest's dragon while he and the sorcerer leapt from its back and made their way toward Magnus.

"Come, Magnus," Bonstaph insisted.

"We have to kill Delvion," Magnus insisted. "We have to end this."

Delvion's wyvern threw itself at the fire dragon. They collided with a thud that sent shock waves across the arena, twisting and cracking the stone ground. A ghastly gnashing of teeth and scales commenced. The two other fire dragons glided into the arena to join in the conflict, their priest-riders leaping free to join the fight.

Is this the storm Austagia spoke of? Catanya said there was more to fear than Quagmen...

Three more wyverns entered the arena and joined the fight of beasts. Magnus however, was more concerned with Delvion and his accomplice.

Turning his head quickly to take stock of those who were still present, Magnus saw Austagia moving in to confront the other two priests. Jael turned and stared briefly at Magnus with intense eyes before continuing on to support Austagia. Catanya was coming around to support Magnus and they stood once again with Bonstaph and Ganister. From the main gates, Crugion came running to support his father. To Delvion's other side was the cloaked sorcerer.

"Who is that?" Bonstaph asked.

"You did not see? It is a *sorcerer*," Ganister warned.

The sight of Delvion with his two companions was all-too-familiar to Magnus. "It cannot be," Magnus spoke aloud. *It cannot be Lucas.*

"What is it Magnus?" Catanya asked.

"The sorcerer, it cannot be him."

Catanya threw a throwing knife at the mysterious man. He lifted a hand and whispered something, creating more of the black mist, dissolving the knife before it struck him. Magnus drew the remaining knife from his gauntlet and threw it at Delvion, but the sorcerer was quick to protect his master— disintegrating the knife with another stream of black matter.

"Curse this dark magic!" Ganister swore, and led the charge.

Out of the corner of his eye Magnus could see a blur of priests locked in battle. It was obvious now that there was division within the priesthood. *Who then, are the outcasts?* The fact that those against him rode dragons did little for Magnus's confidence.

Delvion drew his sword and Crugion followed suit. Magnus and Ganister came at Delvion who dealt blows as ferocious as Briet but with more precision.

Catanya took her lance to the sorcerer and Bonstaph took his sword to Crugion. Magnus had nothing to hide now and he allowed his sword to ignite into flames as he attacked Delvion with everything he could muster. But he was concerned for Catanya's safety. Lucas or not, he had no idea what the sorcerer was capable of. Ganister was with him and dealt blow after blow at the Quag King, shouting profanities as he did. Delvion was clearly skilled in the art of combat, fending off the two-man attack and still managing to strike back.

To Magnus's left, Catanya took a heavy fall at the hand of the sorcerer. Magnus broke away from Delvion to support her. The hooded man drew a sword and parried Magnus's first strike. Their swords locked together, pushing against one another. Magnus glanced at the sorcerer's sword—it was Lucas's.

Magnus had no doubt—*It is Lucas.* "Lucas!" Magnus could just make out his eyes beneath his hood. "Lucas… it's me!" Lucas paused for a moment then pushed hard against Magnus sending him stumbling back. He pulled his hood back from his head, raising his sword to attack again, his dead eyes looking from Magnus to Catanya. Magnus lowered his own sword and stepped toward his friend with a hand raised in friendship.

"Lucas…"

"Magnus…" a weak thought came to him. Other thoughts followed, but were silenced immediately when Catanya threw a piece of burning rubble in Lucas's face, making him reel away. Then Magnus heard a terrible scream.

He turned to see Delvion's attention was on his son, who had fallen to his knees. Crugion's right arm hung limp and bloodied and all but severed at the shoulder. Bonstaph was inches away from taking Crugion's life. Delvion roared with anger and came at Bonstaph—but he was too late. Bonstaph swung his blade and severed Crugion's head.

Delvion paused in shock, watching as his son's head rolled from his shoulders and onto the ground. Taking advantage of the moment, Ganister moved to strike Delvion when a dark shadow suddenly shifted behind him then across to his front. Ganister arched back and fell to his knees. Magnus could see a sword had slashed him deep across his back. Lucas pulled his fleu-steel sword from Ganister's chest. Blood dripped from the blade. Ganister fell forward, landing hard on the stone ground.

Magnus looked about as if trying to find reason amid the insanity of what he had just seen. Delvion was running toward the brawling dragons and wyverns and disappeared into the throng of dust and mayhem. Lucas had dropped his sword and was right behind him.

With no immediate threat of foe, Magnus and Bonstaph fell to Ganister's side and turned him about, onto his back.

"I wasn't expecting that," Ganister mumbled.

"We must help him to his feet!" Magnus looked to his father.

Bonstaph shook his head, looking Magnus in the eyes. He pointed to the ground beneath Ganister where a pool of his blood was draining quickly.

"Is it as bad as all that?" Ganister laughed, choking on blood.

"It was your job to kill Delvion, you old fool," Bonstaph feigned a smile.

"Apologies… next time," Ganister whispered.

"Never mind. I'm an older fool than you," Bonstaph held his old friend's hand.

Magnus put Lucas out if his mind for a moment and thought of Sarah. "Ganister, Sarah is well and safe. She has been with me these past six months and now has her freedom."

Ganister sighed a deep, comforting sigh. "Thank you Magnus, you bring me peace. Give her my love." he coughed and searched for breath. "Find Lucas if you can. Tell him I love him too."

"I will," Magnus said, his heart breaking.

Bonstaph took Magnus's hand and placed it over Ganister's, then embraced them both with a firm grip. Magnus felt Catanya's hand rest on his shoulder. Together, they whispered their final farewells to Ganister.

Through the dust and smoke, Delvion emerged on the back of his large wyvern and took flight, spiralling upwards over the northern wall and beyond the Black Cliffs of Ba'rrat.

His sorcerer sat behind him.

FÄRGD

At the foot of the Romgnian Mountains, five miles south of the Dormiul Path, Färgd extended his forelegs out in front of him, lowering his belly to the ground. He stretched and stretched, splaying his claws and stretched some more until he felt his shoulder joints pop. Satisfied, he looked out at the rising sun beyond the Neverseas.

He was not, however, satisfied about the sleepless nights of late. At first Färgd attributed it to the tough, sinewy sheep he had eaten a while back that had not agreed with him. But no, it was not that. There was something else.

It was around the time I met the young priest... Catanya...

He recalled how he had met Catanya at the base of the Dormiul Path and carried her along the coast to the shores before Brindle. He remembered how she had spotted the approaching pair of wyverns before he had. *Impressive...* Färgd had thought of her much since that rainy night. Her mind was troubled and Färgd hoped she had been able to find the resolution she was seeking. But as much as she appeared in his thoughts, his concerns were not just about her. It really started two weeks later when he spotted a second priest-girl taking the same path on foot toward Brindle.

Demi... the sour-dour looking one. Never have I seen her smile. And never has a priest made this journey on foot... without my assistance... Why is that so?

Färgd had offered Demi a ride to Brindle and inquired as to the purpose of her journey, for he was not informed of it. She was quick to dismiss him.

There was malice in Demi's heart. Her journey was born of ill will and would lead to suffering. I could feel it in my bones.

Yes—it was this that had caused Färgd his sleepless nights. But this morning there was something more. He woke to a red sunrise to the east. *Such crimson hue warns of a disturbance to the west. A warning that comes in two forms. The second upon an unseasonal wind this morning—a wind that carries the smell of blood.* And it was not the blood he liked to smell on an empty stomach—it was the blood of man, the blood of wyvern and...

Dragon blood...

To the west there is malice at play...

He sat up on his hind legs and growled from deep within his chest.

Färgd peered over the sparkly blue sea and watched as a school of dolphins danced through a peeling wave before it broke upon the shore. The dragon cursed them, for he knew dolphins were too salty for his palate and besides, he would now have to forego his breakfast and travel to Ba'rrat.

Perhaps there I will find means to resolve the issues that plague my sleep.

SEPARATE WAYS

The clash of beasts in Ba'rrat's arena had spread to the skies, where wyverns and dragons attacked one another with tooth, talon, and brute force.

"Curse Delvion and his sorcerer. I will kill them if it be the last thing I ever do." Bonstaph paced about, waving his Quag blade to and fro.

"Father," Magnus had found Lucas's sword resting on the ground, its scabbard beside it. He handed it to Bonstaph, who fell silent, as he looked the blade over.

"There were two of such blades."

"I know where the other is," Magnus said. He did not know how to tell his father.

"This blade was forged of love. Now it slayed its forger?" Bonstaph looked hesitantly at Magnus. "Tell me the wielder were not its intended owner." Magnus's silence spoke truth.

"That sorcerer—was Lucas?"

"Aye."

"These past months, locked in Delvion's dungeon… what atrocities did I miss that led to this?"

Austagia interrupted them. "This is far from over," he explained in haste. "The elders of our order have sanctioned Magnus's death."

Austagia's words were like a fog. Nothing surprised Magnus at this point, but then nothing seemed real, either. Forgetting Ganister for a moment, Magnus let Austagia's words sink in. *The priests want me dead…* In the back of his mind Magnus feared as much, but he would never have believed it without hearing it. Bonstaph stepped over to Austagia and stood such that their noses almost touched.

"They would approve the murder of *my* son?" he shouted. His knuckles were white from gripping his sword. "One of their own blood? *My* son?"

Austagia spoke calmly to Bonstaph. "Your son is the chosen one. He is the *Electus*. The Order wishes to see one of our own assume such power."

"And what would you wish for, Austagia?" Bonstaph continue to shout, oblivious to the mounting threat around them. Although the guards had fled the arena, war cries could be heard from beyond the gates, suggesting a fortification of the Quag army. Magnus knew it was only a matter of time before they plucked up the courage to make a unified attack.

"Father..." Magnus appealed for his attention. But Bonstaph was having none of it.

"What about *you* priestess? What would you have happen to Magnus?" He looked to Jael, as did Magnus. Jael said nothing. Austagia spoke for her.

"Jael, as with Catanya and myself, believe Magnus is the rightful *Electus.*"

After a moment's consideration, Bonstaph gave a nod and took a breath. He walked to Magnus, looking briefly at Catanya—an expression of recognition on his face for the first time. He gazed into his son's eyes. "*Electus...*" Bonstaph looked to Catanya again. "Look at you two. What a pair you've turned out to be." Magnus looked at Catanya who raised an eyebrow.

"It's time we leave," Austagia said.

Bonstaph cleared his throat. "Aside from the main gates, does anyone know of a way out of here?"

"Follow me," Magnus said. There was no way to fix the wrongs in the arena now. He made a dash toward the slave's entrance to the armoury with his father, Catanya, Austagia and Jael behind him. From here, he led the way back through the underground tunnels he had grown to know so well. "No one will think we are going this way," he insisted. Together, they made their way through the dark corridors and down the steep stairways.

They reached the dungeons where Carlo and two of his guards had stowed themselves away, no doubt to avoid the chaos above ground. Carlo looked terrified when he saw Magnus and the company he kept.

"You..." Carlo squinted. "You are the *Electus.* All this time you've hidden away here... and with such power at your fingertips. Why?"

Magnus thought of Sarah. "You know why, Carlo." He seethed with anger but wanted no more blood spilled than necessary. "Get into the cage—*now,*" he demanded.

Carlo nodded. He and his two guards moved into cage six and Catanya locked it with the guard's key, stashing the key into her suit, while Magnus and the others worked to free the rest of Carlo's slaves from cages one through five. There were ten freed slaves in total. Magnus cursed that he was only a day away from being able to free Brutus.

"This way." Catanya took the lead.

The freed slaves joined them and, in single file, they wound their way through the endless corridors. They encountered not a single guard. Even this deep beneath the surface, the repeated boom of a city falling under siege resonated through the walls of Ba'rrat's underworld. Magnus figured any remaining guards had long fled.

Magnus was right behind Catanya. Close behind him was Jael. Magnus could feel her brushing close to him. They reached a choke point along a corridor where some of the wall had partially collapsed inward. Catanya climbed up and squeezed her way through the rubble. Magnus was about to follow when he felt a hand rest gently on his shoulder. He turned—it was Jael. He stopped and looked at her.

"You have much to learn about your new powers, Magnus." Jael shared her thoughts. *"Your abilities go far beyond what you already know. Do not be hasty about going into battle. Give yourself time to heed counsel and learn more about whom you have become."*

Jael's touch seemed to fill him with a form of lightness that permeated through his body. Magnus felt elated by her touch. He could feel the heat of his own energy course through his body, toward Jael's arm. Her eyes widened and she took a deep breath. Her shared thoughts suggested she too felt the same elation.

"Are you coming?" Catanya's voice called from the other side of the rubble. Jael removed her hand from Magnus, but not before looking him over with sultry eyes. She moved ahead of Magnus and moved through the narrow gap in the fallen wall.

"Ba'rrat will be brought to ruin this day," Austagia's voice droned off the close walls. Magnus snapped back to reality and looked at the priest. He wondered why the battle was ensuing if the priests were there to kill him, rather than wage war with the Quag.

They continued on, the staircases now taking them gradually back to the surface. "We're nearly there," Catanya said, turning a final corner.

Magnus could see sunshine paving the way up a final stairwell leading to the outside world. At the top, Catanya pushed open a gate. The ten freed slaves gave thanks and bid farewell to Magnus before fleeing across the courtyard beyond.

Catanya closed the gate again with Magnus and the others still on the stairway. She stood her ground and confronted Austagia.

"What are we to do now? Who are we to trust?"

"You are to trust no-one," Austagia said.

"What of the dragons? Are they trying to kill me also?" Magnus wanted to know where he stood before stepping out into the battle zone.

"They know there is a chosen one and believe they are here to find you, but not of the agenda to kill you. If they learn of that, they will no longer have trust in the priesthood."

"They will no longer have trust in mankind," Jael added. Magnus looked to his father to gauge his reaction to all of this.

"She is right," Bonstaph said. "The Irucantî was formed to maintain an alliance between The Fire Realm and the Couldradt dragons. This deception could lead to a war far greater than anything the Quag have sanctioned."

"Your presence here gave cause for a war to reignite," Austagia explained. "The dragon's fury has been woken. They will not stop so long as the Quagmen and their beasts fight back. They *will* destroy Ba'rrat." Austagia addressed Magnus directly. "This is not the time nor place to reveal yourself."

"Very well," Magnus said. "The battle will run its course and we must leave."

Catanya had more questions for Austagia. "Why did you not come to meet me in Brindle?"

"The Romghold went into lockdown after you disappeared. Being your uncle, they suspected me and I was being watched at all times."

"How did Demi track me down?"

Jael spoke up, "Demi suspected you had fled and took it upon herself to find you. By the time I'd learned she had tracked you down the Dormiul Path, I could do nothing to stop her."

"It was three weeks before she arrived," Catanya said.

"It was only a week ago she left," Jael added. "Do you know what happened to her?"

"I killed her." Catanya raised her eyebrows, returning her gaze to Austagia.

With a hint of a smile, Austagia looked out to the open sky. "What we need now are three or four dragons."

Everyone was looking at Austagia for an explanation.

"To fly us out of here," he added.

"I'm happy to walk," Magnus said. He moved to Catanya's side and looked out across the courtyard before him. It was bedlam. The city's residents fled in all directions, while guards struggled to restore order. Quag warriors regrouped, ready for an offensive. Delvion, however, was nowhere to be seen.

Magnus looked at his father. There was a burning question he had to ask him and he sensed his father knew what it was. "Magnus, about your mother," Bonstaph spoke gently with a look of concern on his face.

"Is she alive?" Magnus desperately wanted to know.

"Aye, I believe she is. For what it's worth—it is what my heart tells me."

"What happened that night?"

"There was nothing we could do. We were captured on the ride out to Overpell." Bonstaph shook his head sadly. "They brought us back to the homestead and burned it before our eyes. At first we feared they would catch you and then feared you would die in the fire."

"You know then it was Ganister who saved me."

"Aye. He was captured soon after," Bonstaph chuckled. "But not before he killed half a dozen Quagmen. He told us you were safe, thank the Gods."

"And Mother?"

"For years I had begged your mother to take you back to the Rhyderlands—to her people's lands—where you'd be safe. She was stubborn. She would not leave my side."

"I wouldn't have left either," Magnus added.

"I know. But on the second night in that prison carriage, I begged of her again. We had stood together but did not need to die together. Not so long as our son were still alive." Tears in his eyes, he placed a hand on Magnus's shoulder.

"And so in the night, we said our farewells and she slipped away," Bonstaph sighed. "No prison could hold a woman of the Ice Realm... not my Alavia... not your mother. Ganister and I made enough of a scene to distract the guards."

Bonstaph smiled for a moment, then turned serious once again. "She went looking for you, Magnus. Having not found you, I do not know.... Perhaps she went back to her people for help."

Bonstaph looked out at the chaos in the streets. "She is alive, my son," Bonstaph repeated. "It is what my heart tells me."

Magnus told his father of Sarah. He explained how Catanya rescued her. Catanya then explained to Bonstaph that she was safe and headed eastward to Brindle.

"Then I must meet her and break the news of her husband," Bonstaph decided.

Magnus held Lucas's sword and looked it over. He handed it to his father. "Perhaps you should give this to Sarah."

"No, Magnus. You keep it. The swords were forged as a sign of brotherhood between you and Lucas. Besides, I don't think Sarah could bear the full truth—not just now." Bonstaph handed the sword back to Magnus. "Perhaps... perhaps you may have the chance to return it to him and find common ground."

Magnus took the sword, feeling the weight of his father's hope. For Sarah's sake, he hoped he could make peace with Lucas. Another part of him would never forgive him.

"What about you, Magnus? I take it you won't be joining me?" Bonstaph asked.

"Your son is now the most important man in all of Allumbreve," Austagia interrupted. "When the Couldradt dragons acknowledge their own *Electus*, we will be able to put an end to this feuding. Perhaps even restore virtue among the priests," Austagia said.

"Magnus chooses his own path," Catanya said, peering into the court. "There is no virtue worth saving in the priesthood."

Austagia hung his head resignedly.

Magnus knew his path was of his own choosing. He longed to go with his father but so much had changed since he left home many months ago. The future of Allumbreve seemed to be weighing on his shoulders. He looked to his father again, wishing he would tell him what he should do.

"You've changed Magnus. You've become more of a man than ever a father could wish for. I am proud of you, whatever path you choose to take. Just be sure to take the path that is right for you." Bonstaph smiled at his son.

"Thank you, Father," Magnus said. He knew he was parting ways with his father once again, but glad it was on good terms. More than anything he wanted to find his mother. He also wanted to help reclaim his homelands and help put an end to the battle in the Uydferlands. Then there was the issue of the Authoritarium. For that he would need the support of dragons and it could be some time before that would happen.

Magnus considered his options, taking on board the words Jael had imparted to him. "I know I have much to learn about my powers," Magnus began. "But I am yet to be convinced about whom I can trust. I have a responsibility to the Couldradt dragons and to my people first and foremost. But before I can do so I need to get out of this place. Too long have my father and I been trapped here. But I do not wish to bring trouble to any of you."

"You should not go on alone, *Electus*," Austagia said.

Magnus agreed with Austagia that they would stay together, at least until they were clear of the city.

Before leaving, Bonstaph confided in Magnus that once he had found Sarah, he would reunite the freed people of their realm and return north through the Red Pass. From here, he would traverse the Outer Rim of Froughton Forest back to the Uydferlands to help reclaim the Fire Realm. Somewhere along this path Magnus hoped to meet up with him again.

Magnus bid his farewells and watched as his father left for the southern gate. He vowed to be with him again soon.

STEYNE

The streets of Ba'rrat were a battleground. The city walls and buildings were buckling and many had fallen to ruin from the brutal attacks of the fire dragons. As the number of dragons grew, even more so did the number of wyverns. From beyond the Black Cliffs, the black Corville wyverns came in storms—strong in number and ferocious in their appetite for blood. It was an old battle reignited and there was no controlling it.

Outside the walls of the arena, the city guards had fled whilst the Quag warriors regrouped and formed counter attacks against the dragons and the Ferustirs. The priests were few compared to the Quagmen, but were the superior warriors.

Magnus kept the company of Catanya, Austagia and Jael. Together they ran through the labyrinth of narrow streets and blocked-off alleyways, working their way toward the northern gate of the city. It was the very gate through which Magnus had entered Ba'rrat over six months ago. With the ongoing battle gravitating away from the north, it seemed the best direction to go. They were, however, being hunted.

A wyvern picked up their scent. It soon had them cornered in a street that was blocked by a fallen house. Magnus and his companions finally overpowered the wyvern at the expense of time and anonymity. Now, they had two more wyverns closing in on them. The wyverns let out an eerie howl when they caught their scent. The howling came from two directions and was closing in fast.

"We should split up," Jael suggested. Magnus was not so sure. He did not want to risk losing them and not being able to find them again.

"I agree," said Austagia. "There will be a hundred Quagmen upon us soon enough. It is imperative Magnus gets out of here alive. If Jael and I can create a diversion it may increase your chances of escape."

Before they had a chance to go their separate ways, a host of six Quagmen seemed to appear out of nowhere. Magnus generated a ball of fire between the palms of his hands and focussed on making the ball larger and larger until it was three feet across in size. He cast it at the men and as it neared them, Jael yelled a spell.

"Exploda fara gin mara!"

The fireball exploded violently, killing all six Quagmen and destroying the walls of the buildings either side of them. Magnus was impressed.

"I'll have to remember that one," he smiled at Jael.

"There's so much you will learn from us, Magnus," Jael responded demurely.

Magnus glanced at Catanya whose eyes locked on Jael for a moment.

The dragons kept the brunt of the battle to the city's south, yet the howling wyverns were getting closer.

"Get clear of the city walls," Austagia instructed. "We will deal with these wyverns."

"We will find you on the other side," Catanya said.

Austagia and Jael darted off down a side alley. Magnus and Catanya continued north along a narrow street. The tall, ancient buildings abutted one another, leaving them nowhere to go except forward.

As Magnus rounded a corner a city guard appeared on the road ahead with his back to them. Magnus stopped, grabbing Catanya's arm and pulling her to a halt. But they were too late. The guard turned and saw them and began to blow into a small horn that rang loudly in the narrow streets, raising the howls of the wyverns even more. Magnus sprinted toward him, determined to silence the horn but the guard fled back around the corner. As Magnus rounded it, he came upon eight waiting Quagmen. Magnus turned, sprinting back the way he'd come with Catanya right beside him and the eight Quagmen on their tail, shouting promises of a painful death.

Catanya threw a series of throwing knives back up the road. Each one scored a hit taking a Quag life with it, but now there were at least six more guards heading their way from the opposite direction.

There was one small passageway to their left, partially blocked by a collapsed wall. They turned down it, traversing its sharp turns with the tenacity of a pair of scalded cats. They sprung off walls to change direction and hurled themselves over fallen objects and bewildered townsfolk who scrabbled for their belongings amidst the rubble. They were easily outpacing the Quagmen until they ran headlong into an impassable obstacle—an Irucantî.

"Joffren!" Catanya exclaimed.

The priest ignited his lance and so Magnus drew the fire-sword, ready to fight. Catanya pulled him back away from Joffren.

"No, we must go back," she insisted.

Magnus would have rather faced a single priest than a dozen Quagmen, but there was no time to argue. He started back down the passage, right behind Catanya. She was moving even faster than before and Magnus had to muster all his strength to keep up with her. The tall priest was not far behind. The passage turned to the left, then the right.

Another hundred feet and we'll be among the Quagmen, Magnus calculated.

From out of nowhere, a figure in an old weathered cloak stood out in front of them, hand extended.

"Stop!" the stranger insisted with authority.

Catanya pulled up—startled—causing Magnus to nearly topple over her. Both had weapons ready to attack the stranger.

"There is no need for that, I am a friend... hide here now!" the stranger hissed.

Catanya needed no encouragement, throwing herself into the narrow crevice in the stone wall to their right, dragging Magnus in behind her. Magnus thought it strange she should be so trusting of a stranger, yet this priest she called *Joffren* had her running scared. The cloaked man hushed them to silence. He threw a blanket over their heads and all three of them crouched beneath it. "If you wish to live," he whispered, "remain silent and keep your minds guarded."

Magnus and Catanya did as they were told, frozen on the spot. To Magnus however, there was something familiar about the hooded stranger. *I know that voice.* Nevertheless, Magnus did as he was told, guarding his thoughts as he peered through the thin blanket covering them.

The priest ran past them. Catanya hugged Magnus tightly and he could hear her trembling breath. *Why is she so afraid of this priest?* He cleared his mind once again as the priest doubled back, searching along the walls and checking a locked doorway opposite where they lay hidden in the dark crevice. Catanya's breath stopped altogether, but her grip became vice-like. The stranger behind them began to whisper rapidly, forming a spell. Magnus looked at the blanket as several waves of golden lines shimmered down the fabric. *He's placing enchantments on the blanket.*

Joffren turned from the door, walking across the passage to the crevice. He peered at the blanket—his steel blue eyes hunting for them. Magnus could sense the priest's probing mind. He was searching for any signs of thought.

But the spell wielded by the stranger was cunning and guarded not only Magnus's and Catanya's presence but also any trace of the spell itself. Magnus was impressed. *This stranger must be an accomplished magician to be able to hide from an Irucanti.*

The Ferustir gripped his lance and peered at them, as though staring straight through the fabric. The moments to follow seemed an eternity to Magnus, but eventually the priest looked to his left as the Quagmen set upon him. He ignited his lance and moved out of sight leaving them with just the sound of the altercation occurring further down the alleyway.

"Move now!" hissed the stranger, pulling the enchanted blanket away and dragging Magnus and Catanya to their feet. He stepped out of the crevice, into the passageway. Magnus looked him over. The old brown cloak he wore covering him from head to toe told nothing of his identity. He whispered another spell that opened the wooden door opposite them. He turned back to Magnus and Catanya. "Come!" Once they were through the door, the hooded stranger shut it and ushered them further inside.

"Who are you?" Catanya demanded.

The man pulled back his hood, revealing his old, bearded face and long, motley grey hair. Magnus immediately recognised the man and grabbed him, pinning him against a wall.

"Eamon!"

"Indeed I am, and I am pleased to see you, Magnus." The old man responded in his usual genial manner.

"What?" Magnus grunted, forgetting his need for silence and pushing Eamon even harder against the wall.

"Best you be quiet. There's a priest out there who'll stop at nothing to have you dead."

Catanya walked to the door and went to peek out when Eamon suggested otherwise. "I wouldn't, young priestess. I have placed wards on the door protecting us from prying minds. They will be broke should you open it."

Catanya stepped back from the door and looked Eamon over. "Who is this man, Magnus?"

"This man *betrayed* me. He turned me over to Crugion and his men and profited from it. He sold Breona to Crugion."

Eamon shook his head vehemently. "That is far from the whole truth, young fire-blood, and most certainly scarce of motive. Allow me voice so that I may explain myself."

Magnus let Eamon go and turned away from him. He held no desire to look at the man any longer. He walked to the back of the small, single-room dwelling they were in. His eyes were still adjusting to the darkness of the room—darkness he found unsettling after having finally escaped the dungeons beneath the arena. It made him distrust Eamon even more.

Eamon followed him and Catanya joined them, resting a hand upon Magnus's shoulder. Eamon looked at them both, apparently intrigued by their intimacy. He began to explain himself.

"Back in Guame, Crugion and his men arrived soon after us. By the time word had reached me, they were in the Great Hall, beyond my influence. There was no way I could warn you. What I could do and did was move Breona to safer ground."

Magnus looked at Eamon but said nothing.

"It was hours later they emerged and placed you in the prison carriage. But you weren't alone. They had three other prisoners. One was a dear friend of mine. A man who knew your father well."

"Barron," Magnus said, remembering the man.

"Aye. I gather he did not fare well?"

"He died during our escape."

"Oh," Eamon leaned closer toward Magnus, "I feared the worst for you but then, I had an idea," Eamon smiled. "I'd convince Crugion to take Breona by stating her importance to your family. 'Twas no easy feat considering he wanted me dead also. However—within Guame I have friends and enemies... but *more* friends, who by virtue of their number convinced Crugion to leave me well enough alone. Unfortunately, I could not convince him to do the same for you."

"You were saying you tried to get Crugion to take Breona," Magnus sighed, trying to hurry the conversation.

"Yes! This appealed to him. He gloated of his triumph in enslaving your mother and father and now you. Having your mother's Astermeer completed his undertaking nicely. I thought if Breona were in your company you would have a chance of escaping. After all, only a fool would try to enslave an Astermeer."

"Did you give any thought to how Crugion's men would treat Breona? They *beat* her into submission!" Magnus shook his head in disgust.

"'Tis much to regret that which cannot be undone, Magnus. It was a risky proposition." Eamon looked contrite. Magnus considered Eamon's story. It seemed plausible and he knew for certain he would never have escaped without Breona's help. "Very well then. But how did you end up here in Ba'rrat?"

"It took some doing, but once Mr Overstreet and I were reacquainted, we tracked you through Froughton Forest as far as the clearing. It was there we came across the dragon youngling and Breona."

"Thioci," Magnus said. "The youngling's name was *Thioci*."

"Indeed. But something was not right about him. His body was protected by a powerful spell—one unfamiliar to me. But there was something more. Something was missing. It was then that I knew. The youngling had given itself over to another. I knew it was you, Magnus. I knew you had received the bond of fire." Eamon frowned. "Finding where you went from there was a task."

Magnus and Catanya exchanged glances.

Magnus did not know what to say. He let Eamon's words sink in as he relived past events for the thousandth time. Catanya, however, had questions for Eamon.

"If you knew, why did you not tell the order of the Irucantî about Magnus?"

"I have no business with the Irucantî, nor owe them such accord. Besides, with what you know of the virtue of priests, would you give them such knowledge? I can see where your loyalties lie. Apparently, they are not dissimilar to mine."

"You speak of the virtues of priests. What do you know of priests?" Catanya asked. She stepped closer to him. Magnus looked at them both but became distracted as the sickness of *Anunya* took hold of him once again. It was the second time that day.

"Not now..." Magnus mumbled. Waves of nausea started to course through his guts. "Oh, not now."

"*Anunya,*" Eamon said.

"What did you say?" Catanya asked Eamon. She placed a comforting arm around Magnus as he began shaking.

"You know of what I speak," Eamon said. "You've experienced it yourself."

"What do *you* know of *Anunya?*" Catanya insisted.

Magnus fell to his knee and retched. Sweat formed across his forehead. Catanya knelt beside him and held him in one arm but kept the other on her lance and never took her eyes off Eamon.

Eamon rummaged through a small satchel that hung from his shoulder. "You've been using your new powers a lot of late. I imagine it has triggered the sickness. With time you will adapt and it will no longer occur."

"How do you know such things?" Catanya asked.

Eamon removed a small emerald vial and prised its sealing cork free with a thumb. "Here, have him drink this."

"What is it?" Catanya asked. She took the vial from Eamon and sniffed it. "It smells just like the healing nectar we have back at the Romghold." She sniffed it again. "Honey, camomile, ginger... but there is something more."

"Yes—rhuderburry."

"Rhuderburry? Where does that grow?"

"Where does it grow indeed!" Eamon tapped the side of his nose.

Catanya frowned at him. She put the vial to Magnus's lips and he sipped eagerly of the nectar. Within a minute, his fever subsided. He sat up coughing and licked his lips.

"What was that?" Magnus took the vial from Catanya and drank the rest. "That's the best thing I've tasted since I arrived here in Ba'rrat—that's for certain. I could have done with that many a time."

His vision clearing, Magnus could see Catanya frowning at Eamon. Eamon, however, was preoccupied with the bronze fire-sword Magnus had acquired, lifting it from the ground and examining it. "What do you think?" Magnus asked him, deciding to cast his doubts about the man aside for a moment, yet he could see Catanya shifting her body, ready to strike with her lance should the need arise.

"I think it should have been destroyed with the rest of the fire-swords long ago."

Magnus shrugged. "I think it's a good sword."

"*Good* you say?" Eamon shook his head and his face became sombre. "This blade killed the greatest fire dragon that ever lived."

"Balgur," Magnus and Catanya said together.

Eamon snapped out of his daze and looked at each of his companions in turn. "Never again. It is in better hands now."

Eamon extended his arm to hand the sword back to Magnus. Catanya seized the opportunity and placed a hand upon the side of Eamon's face, sweeping his long grey hair free of his temple revealing the markings he bore upon the side of his head.

"You are a priest!" Catanya said.

Magnus examined Eamon who, for the first time since he had met him, was speechless. Eamon dropped the sword to the ground where it struck the stone, ricocheting a metallic echo through the room.

"*Steyne!*" Catanya said. "You are *Steyne*—the priest who fought Delvion. This was your sword." Eamon said nothing in his defence. "That's why you know so much about priests."

"That's why you know this sword." Magnus got to his feet. He looked Eamon over and considered him in a way he never had before. After all his riddles and intimations. *This makes sense.* "Is this true, Eamon?" Magnus spoke assertively.

The old man did not respond, but picked up the fallen fire-sword and handed it to Magnus. "Take it." Magnus did not take the sword. "Take it!" Eamon insisted. "Return it to the Romghold... to the Temple of Fire where stands the statue of Balgur. Place it at his feet."

"How do you know of the statue of Balgur?" Catanya asked. "It was built *after* you fled from the priesthood—years after Balgur died."

Eamon pointed an accusing finger. "You'd best get your story straight, young priestess. I did not *flee*—I withdrew from the priesthood in the aftermath of Balgur's death at the Battle of Fire for reasons that are becoming apparent to you."

Catanya fell to silence and so Magnus interceded. "Whatever your reasons, we are here together now, Eamon, or *Steyne*..."

"Stick with Eamon."

"Very well, *Eamon*. I am guessing you know how we can escape the city?"

"Your biggest problem is Joffren." Eamon pointed at the door. "It seems his allegiance is with the priesthood and he will stop at nothing to kill you, Magnus."

Magnus could see the pain in Catanya's face. "This priest—Joffren. He means something to you, Catanya?"

Catanya shook her head. "He was my Semsdi—my teacher. All my time in the Romghold I was under his tutelage. How can he support a decision to kill the *Electus*? To kill *you!*"

Magnus was astounded the priesthood had fragmented over the pursuit of power. *This makes them no better than the Authoritarium.*

"I have known Joffren a long time, priestess," Eamon said. "He was my Semsarian before I left the priesthood. I did not take the time to explain fully my reasons for departure. Perhaps a sense of abandonment makes him loyal beyond reason." Eamon gave a soft chuckle as if to lighten the mood. "Righteousness is not a call for self-righteousness."

Catanya chewed the side of her bottom lip, her eyes lowered to the ground. "Righteousness," she said. "He has laid judgement upon me then. Thank you, Semsame," she said out of habit.

"No need to call me *Semsame*, priestess, I hold no honour in that name."

"Then there is no need to call me *priestess*. I am Catanya."

Eamon bowed in agreement.

Magnus appreciated that Eamon could help Catanya resolve her issues with the priests, but Ba'rrat was crumbling around them and they needed to get beyond the Capitol's boundaries.

"As I asked before, Eamon…"

"Yes," Eamon said, rubbing his bearded chin vigorously. "Continue up the alleyway eastward. It takes you to the city wall. I will make sure none follow, including Joffren."

"And once at the wall? It is forty foot high at its lowest," Magnus asked.

Eamon looked through his satchel again, this time removing a stone that he handed to Magnus. "Take this."

Magnus looked the stone over. It had a familiar warmth and purple hue to it. "A Juniper stone," he said.

"Aye. I assume you have lost your other one?"

"I have. But not before it saved my life."

"Then let us hope this one serves you as well. You remember what to do with it?" Eamon asked.

"Yes, but through a stone wall?" Magnus was not convinced it would work.

"Not so long ago you doubted you could walk through a tree."

Catanya gently took the stone from Magnus's hand and examined it. "It's warm. I have learned of the powers of Juniper stones. But walking through walls? That's impossible."

"Only if you believe it is." Eamon grinned the way Magnus remembered, and it was usually in the face of adversity. His fondness for the old man was returning, but with greater respect.

"You really were a priest?" he asked.

"Aye!" Eamon grinned again.

THE EASTERN WALL

The alleyway was clear. Magnus and Catanya made fast progress with Eamon close behind. But as they ran, Eamon fell further back.

"Keep moving. I'll be there soon enough."

They weaved their way onward. The city's eastern wall loomed large overhead. Magnus was in front of Catanya when they came to the end of the alleyway and ran out into an open quadrangle that ended at the city wall. It appeared a lot taller than Magnus had first thought. Worse still, perched atop the wall's crenelations was a huge fire dragon with its tail hanging down the inside of the wall, almost reaching the ground below. It sat still with only its head turning as it scanned the horizon from north to south. Magnus and Catanya backed up and hid around the corner of a building to the north of the quadrangle.

"That's Färgd," Catanya said. "He is the dragon who brought me to Brindle when I fled from the Romghold."

"We'll wait here for Eamon to catch up," Magnus said, giving Catanya a kiss on her cheek.

"Careful... you'll make Jael jealous," Catanya said, and then cursed to herself. Magnus looked at her and thought of his interaction with Jael earlier. "Sorry, I shouldn't have said that," Catanya added, but still looked at Magnus as though gauging his reaction.

Magnus paused, unsure of what to say, but knew there was a right answer Catanya was waiting for. Just then Eamon came barrelling around the corner into the middle of the quadrangle, drawing to a halt at the sight of Färgd. He joined Magnus and Catanya behind the building.

"Sorry, I can't run like I used to." He looked at Magnus and Catanya. "Did I interrupt something?"

"Not at all," Catanya and Magnus said in unison. Magnus cleared his throat, feeling even more awkward.

"That's Färgd ... on the wall over there," Catanya spoke quickly.

"Ah... I should have recognised him." Eamon peeped a look at the dragon. "He's got a long tail, though not as long as Brue's. No chance he'll fly us out of here?"

Catanya rolled her eyes. "He probably carried another priest to the city. Maybe it was Joffren. I can't imagine he'd be keen to leave without him. Did you see Joffren back that way?"

Eamon shook his head.

"We can't get out this way as long as Färgd stands guard up there," Magnus said. He turned to Catanya who was counting her throwing knives. "Do you think you could convince him to carry us out?" he asked.

"I don't know," Catanya twisted her lips to one side as she thought. "He will surely have many questions—particularly about you two."

"I agree with Catanya, it's too risky," said Eamon.

The crack of an igniting lance echoed through the quadrangle. All three of them turned and looked back—it was Joffren. He advanced toward them.

Eamon, Magnus and Catanya spread out, readying themselves for a fight.

"Joffren, no!" Eamon called, pulling back his hood to reveal who he was. Joffren squinted, studying the bearded old man closely. His eyes widened.

"Steyne!" Joffren exclaimed. He looked then to Catanya. "Why do you choose to support these two over your brethren?"

"They *are* my brethren," Catanya retorted, igniting her own lance. "And they are my kin... and so are you."

"I am your Semsdi. I order you to lower your weapon."

"And I am *your* Semsdi, Joffren," Eamon said. "I ask the same of you."

Magnus watched Joffren carefully.

"You relinquished that role when you broke your priest's vows, Steyne," Joffren continued.

"As you broke yours when you chose to kill the *Electus*."

The large fire dragon turned to face the commotion before him.

"Catanya... the dragon," Magnus said, but she was too angry with Joffren to listen.

"I believed you, of all people, would do what was right. But I see that's not the case, so now I make a stand." Catanya stepped toward Joffren. "Now I do what is right, Joffren. *Now* I am at my most righteous as you foresaw."

"Catanya!" Magnus shouted, looking at the dragon.

Färgd jumped off the city wall into the Quadrangle, landing with a trembling thud. He tucked his wings back and crouched forward, looking at the four people before him. He quickly spotted Catanya.

"Young Catanya—I thought I smelt you. What are you doing here?" His words pierced through Magnus's mind with more power and presence than any creature he'd encountered.

"I am trying to leave the city with my friends," Catanya answered. *"This is Eamon and this is Magnus."*

Färgd sniffed at Eamon and considered him for a moment. *"I know you,"* he said, then turned to Magnus and sniffed him too. Färgd reeled back and his eyes widened. *"What is this?"* Färgd asked Catanya, demanding an explanation. *"Who is this one of ashen scent? He carries not the blood of man!"*

Färgd's thoughts ripped through Magnus's mind as though he'd been struck by lightning. Magnus winced as he tried to gain control of his own thoughts and not let those of the strong creature run rampant through his head. As with the wyvern in the arena, he allowed heat to bathe within his skull, and he soon regained full control over his thoughts.

"You have much strength, yet you're no sorcerer. WHAT MAY YOU BE?" A deep, thumping growl rose from within the dragon's belly.

Magnus held his ground and turned to Joffren, whose lance still held its blaze.

"Tell Färgd the *truth*, Joffren," Magnus demanded.

Joffren ran at Magnus, twisting his lance about. Magnus swung the fire-sword around, ready to parry off Joffren's first blow.

"No, Magnus!" Eamon called to him.

Färgd let out a mighty roar directed at Magnus.

"The sword, Magnus. The *sword!*" Magnus blocked Joffren's first blow. He was hardly ready for the aggressiveness of the priest's attack and all the while, he came to realise how he had so angered the dragon.

"DRAGON SLAYER!" Färgd's words made a brutal attack on Magnus's mind. He tried to fend him off while Joffren continued his attack.

"Stop, Färgd!" Catanya shouted at the great dragon.

The commotion was drawing attention. Numerous Quagmen began to gather around them, but none dared get involved in the confusing and violent play of politics occurring in front of their eyes. Joffren twirled his lance with the skills of a true master, finding weaknesses in Magnus's defensive moves before he had even made them. Occasionally, Magnus saw opportunities to counter Joffren's manoeuvres but did not take advantage of them for fear Färgd would attack.

Then Magnus felt another presence within his mind—it was Eamon. Glancing over to him, he could see Eamon standing with his eyes closed, trying to communicate with the great dragon.

"Färgd... Magnus is a friend. He carries the blood of dragons. He is the Electus!"

Färgd's mental assault on Magnus's mind weakened and Magnus could sense his confusion. Färgd turned to Joffren, who offered no counter argument, and so he turned to Catanya.

"Catanya! You call this man your friend yet Joffren attacks him as foe. Explain!"

Magnus understood why Färgd was looking to Catanya to explain the situation. *Obviously Joffren is blocking his mind to hide the truth*, Magnus calculated.

Joffren's lance scored a blow to Magnus's chin, splitting it open with a deep gash. Still, Magnus heeded Eamon's warning and avoided retaliating with the fire-sword. Magnus thought to reach for Lucas's sword that was strapped over his back but Joffren never afforded him the chance.

Two of the Quagmen wandered closer to the action. Färgd swung his tail, crushing their bones and sending their shattered remains flying back down the alleyway, where they slammed into the side of a building. The rest of the Quagmen backed away.

"We are all together, Färgd—Joffren does not see it." Catanya desperately tried to negotiate with Färgd. Magnus could sense the dragon was at an impasse and once its mind was made up there would be violent repercussions. Magnus realised then that it was he and only he who could reason with Färgd.

Joffren's attack was interrupted as he suddenly lost his balance, falling to the ground. Magnus saw it was Catanya—she had pulled his feet out from under him with her lance. She did not allow Joffren respite, coming hard and fast at him, as he had done to Magnus. Magnus was astounded by her ability. Taking advantage of the moments respite, he joined Eamon and opened his mind fully to Färgd.

"Färgd... what Catanya and Eamon... Steyne... say is true. I am friend and come in support of you all. The youngling—Thioci—has gifted me his blood. He has chosen me as Electus. He has presented me before your ancestors. Balgur spoke, telling me I carry the legacy of the Fire Realm."

Magnus looked deep into Färgd eyes, keeping every facet of his mind open for scrutiny. He could feel the dragon probing deep, uncovering every memory and every emotion he had. At one point Färgd stopped to look at Catanya, apparently considering the love between them. Finally, Färgd found what he was looking for.

"Thioci... Young one..."

Magnus fell to his knees as he realised—Färgd had found Thioci *within* him. Magnus felt the presence within himself of the two dragons conversing. He felt the youngling's affection for Färgd who, it seemed, was a relative. Thioci then spoke of his love for the people of the Fire Realm for whom he was born to protect and guide, and Färgd finally understood.

"Färgd, I have chosen Magnus as Electus. He is most worthy and gave his life in defence of mine."

Magnus realised his role was far greater than he had ever comprehended. He was a channel, through which all of his realm could communicate, to find common ground and establish peace.

Eamon—who had witnessed the exchange—withdrew from Magnus's mind. Magnus looked to him. His face was overcome with emotion. Magnus turned to Catanya and Joffren who were still locked in battle. Magnus knew Joffren had to be stopped lest he hurt Catanya.

"Lose the sword, Magnus," Eamon warned again. This time, Magnus did as Eamon told him, dropping the fire-bronze sword to the ground. He started toward Joffren, drawing Lucas's sword.

"Use the Juniper stone," Eamon said.

Magnus dropped the fleu-steel sword and took the stone from within his forearm's vambrace. Holding it in his left fist he felt its warmth. He had no time to question what Eamon was suggesting, but gave over to faith in his old friend. *If it can work through trees and it can work through walls...* He knew now what he had to do.

He broke into a run, keeping light on his toes. Catanya saw him coming and drew Joffren's attack to give Magnus the greatest advantage possible. By the time Joffren turned, Magnus was upon him. He held the Juniper stone palm forward so that it hit Joffren's chest before he barrelled into the priest himself.

Magnus collided with Joffren. But he did not pass through as he had done with the trees in Froughton Forest. Their bodies melded together as one. Magnus could feel Joffren thrashing about, trying to break free but Magnus held him in a firm embrace. His arms were clasped around his waist while the rest of his body, including his mind, merged with Joffren's as if they were one.

Magnus could see Joffren's immediate thoughts, but he kept his barriers up, hiding anything that would compromise his self-control. Magnus, however, opened his mind up to Joffren, who was forced to witness everything—everything that Magnus had experienced with Färgd, with

Thioci, the entire process of receiving the bond of fire and everything he had been through since leaving his home all those months ago. Joffren witnessed it all in the space of a few moments. As the experiences came to him, Joffren began to release the hold over his own mind, revealing a terrible sense of regret and remorse. He revealed to Magnus how the priests had become obsessed with the desire to achieve the power afforded the Electi of the other realms. He revealed how their culture changed over time from wanting to serve the dragons and the people of the Fire Realm, to wanting power for themselves.

Magnus recalled Delvion's words about the desire for power and shared them with Joffren—*"All virtuous beings eventually come to desire power."* These words deepened Joffren's sense of shame.

Magnus experienced many of Joffren's emotions and memories, yet gave him pardon, letting him keep those of his intimate past to himself. He gleaned from him the hurt he felt over Steyne abandoning him and the genuine care he had for Catanya. These last feelings Magnus took for Eamon and Catanya's sake, for he wanted to help them find closure.

Finally, Magnus learned of the Romghold. The two High Priests remained there in the temple under protection of many wards and spells and the guard of two dragons—Rubea and Liné.

Once Magnus had imparted all that he could unto Joffren and learned all there was to know from him, he pushed himself free of the priest's body. Joffren collapsed to the ground while Magnus allowed a jolt of heat to sear through his body, cleansing him and healing the gash in his chin in the process.

He took a deep breath, opened his eyes and observed the sight before him. A crowd had formed, including many Quagmen, who were dumfounded at having witnessed the spectacle. Also present were Austagia, Jael, and two other priests who sat upon dragons. All were silent, staring at Magnus. His body pulsated with shimmers of amber and orange light that spiralled about his body. Threads of heat coursed through him like acid through his veins, working to heal him of the damage caused by his unusual altercation with Joffren. Even Catanya stood wide-eyed at the marvel before her.

Magnus felt Färgd's presence at the perimeter of his mind and realised the dragon had witnessed the experience for himself. *"Now you know the truth, Färgd of the Fire Realm."*

Several long minutes passed and Magnus felt the heat subside—its job done. He turned to Färgd and knelt, bowing his head before the great fire dragon.

"You are indeed the chosen one, Magnus of J'esmagd," Färgd declared.

A GATHERING

With a loud beating of wings, the Couldradt fire dragons converged at the eastern wall to see what all the commotion was about. Each dragon was paired with a priest and they all bore the scars of battle. All of the dragons had blood stained teeth and talons, chipped scales and gnawed underbellies courtesy of the brawling fights with wyverns. Some of the priests bore wounds, yet none were fatal and certainly not as serious as Joffren's injuries.

There were twelve dragons in total, including Färgd. Some perched upon the city wall, others on rooftops, sending tiles skittering to the ground below. A smaller, sprightly dragon landed in the Quadrangle. It sniffed at Magnus just as Färgd had. Alarm came to its fiery eyes and it recoiled, turning to Färgd for explanation.

With such a large number of dragons in attendance, the Quagmen fled toward the southern city gates. Only one dragon pursued them, making sure of their departure. The rest were far more interested in Magnus.

Magnus stood his ground. Catanya was quick to come to his side followed closely by Austagia and Jael. Eamon gave his attention to Joffren. He cast spells upon him to hold what health remained in good stead until he was better able to devote himself to healing his former Semsarian. He then joined Magnus and the others.

Magnus looked at his companions. The day had been long and arduous. Throughout it, the four of them had stood staunch with him and survived. The next few moments however, were vital. Magnus guessed they knew this, too.

Eamon made polite suggestions to Färgd about how to explain matters to the other dragons. Magnus was careful not to intervene. He thought it best to let those more familiar to Färgd do the talking. Färgd however, was not at all indecisive and was quick to share what he had learned about Magnus.

"The Electus has been chosen." The dragon's thoughts rolled forth like a clap of thunder. His words brought absolute silence among those in attendance.

He directed his next words to the priests. *"Who among you disputes this? Who claims a right to this power over that chosen by my kin?"*

There was no objection voiced among the priests or the dragons. One by one, the dragons made their way into the open space of the quadrangle and examined Magnus. They looked him over and sniffed him. Magnus felt each of their minds cautiously touching his own.

"Remain open," Eamon advised Magnus. "Let them see who you are. Reserve nothing of yourself. They seek the truth."

Magnus swallowed hard with a parched tongue. His breath trembled and he searched for the comfort of Catanya's hand. Knowingly she took it, clasping it firmly with her own. The dragons became aware of their shared intimacy and examined her as well. Magnus could feel Catanya's mind open to the dragons, which gave him confidence to do the same. The powerful minds of the dragons explored his thoughts and learned his story just as Färgd had done before them. It was unnerving to have such powerful creatures delve into his mind. He felt like a baby being passed between the hands of great warriors, each careful in their caress yet capable of destroying him at any moment.

Magnus could also sense the minds of the priests, dancing apprehensively at the periphery of his consciousness. Aside from Austagia and Jael, each of them seemed to be in conflict, struggling to accept Magnus as the chosen one. Austagia intervened, giving gospel to assure them that the right choice had been made in Magnus. Some of the priests seemed to listen whilst others withdrew. Magnus knew it would be some time before he could trust them all.

Färgd had more to say but directed it to the other dragons. They each withdrew from Magnus's mind as smoothly as they entered it and turned their attention to Färgd. All but one, that is. For Brue stayed within Magnus's mind, lingering on his memories and thoughts of Thioci. After a while, he too withdrew, but kept his gaze on Magnus for some time before turning his attention to Färgd.

Eamon seemed most pleased with the proceedings. "A dragon protects its kin above all others, Magnus. You are now their kin. And in time, the Irucantî will come to respect you as they have sworn to."

Magnus remained sceptical. He recalled the priest named Demi who tried to kill Catanya, and Joffren's determination to kill him. Even with the full support of the dragons he would not rest easily in the company of priests.

In the absence of the High Priests and lack of knowledge as to how their allegiance would sway, Austagia took command of the order. He sent four of the priests and their dragons to the southern gate to support the one dragon already there. They would assess the situation and, if possible, bring the battle to a close. Five dragons kept counsel with Färgd while Brue set off with three priests to ensure no Quagmen or city residents remained in hiding in the northern part of the city. Catanya asked Austagia if it was wise to send Brue alone with that many priests, what with their questionable loyalty. Austagia however, believed Brue to be the most adept of all dragons present to deal with any resistance that may arise.

Joffren was in a poor state of health. Eamon and Jael administered several healing potions and cast many more spells to keep him from declining further.

Magnus's journey had come to an impasse in many ways. There were a lot of issues that remained unsettled. He knew some things would take time to resolve such as facing the Quag army in the Fire Realm and finding his mother. He had mixed feelings toward Lucas and a huge sense of guilt about him. *What if I were attacked by the wyvern and treated by the Uydfer healers whilst Lucas went on to Guame?* He knew their places had been decided by nothing more than chance, yet he recalled Xavier's words about Lucas—*"He strives for the approval of others. A corruptible quality where loyalties can shift."*

Magnus wondered—*would I have been immune to Delvion's manipulations?* But then he thought of Ganister dying in the arena and all compassion vanished.

Magnus decided he needed space and time to clear his mind and think about what he should do next. He excused himself from the company he was in. Catanya offered to come with him. He thanked her and explained he just needed to take time for himself.

Magnus walked back down the alleyway he and Catanya had sprinted along only a short while ago. Halfway along it, he happened upon the bodies of three Quag warriors. *This is why Eamon took longer to get to the Quadrangle. So much for being slow...*

Magnus stared at the men's bodies that lay awkwardly across the alleyway. A vision of Ganister came to him again. He drew Lucas's sword, examining Ganister's fine craftsmanship. Magnus recalled his father's words when he handed the sword back to him *"Perhaps you may have the chance to return it to him and find common ground."* He sheathed the sword again, aware of the burden of its weight.

Magnus continued down the alleyway until he came to the door on his left—the door to the dwelling Eamon had taken him and Catanya into, where they hid from Joffren.

Joffren...

Magnus opened the door and entered the room, closing the door behind him.

I nearly killed him...

A chill ran from the nape of his neck down his spine and the hairs on his arms stood on end. He stood in the centre of the room, waiting for the sensation to pass, expecting a charge of heat to follow as it usually did. But none came for he was not injured. He appreciated having some sense of feeling that was not manipulated by his dragon blood.

In the darkness of the room, he allowed the silence to wash over him. Magnus sat on the ground, his back to the wall—a habit that had grown on him after the countless hours locked in cage number six. He placed Lucas's sword beside him and removed the armour he had worn since his battle in the arena, laying it beside him also. Magnus felt the cool stone soothe his back as he used to in the dungeon. He allowed the thoughts and confusions of the day to fade away into the darkness.

Magnus slept.

BRUE

Dreams washed through Magnus's mind, giving voice to calamities he was entirely responsible for, or so they told him. He dreamed of Lucas. Magnus tried to explain that he did not abandon him in the Uydferlands and that he longed to return to him. Lucas stared back in silence. The more Magnus tried to reason with him, the more his face receded back into the darkness of his hooded robe until his eyes were cloaked in shadow. Eventually, Magnus could not see him at all. He shouted after him, *"Lucas! Lucas!"* But there was no reply. Nothing. In a moment he was gone. Jael appeared in his place.

Magnus looked around again for Lucas.

"Lucas?"

Nothing. There was Jael again. He turned again but Jael was right there, in his face.

"Do you know where Lucas is?"

He repeated the question several times but Jael did not respond. Her face was closer to his now. He tried to look past her, but she always moved into his line of sight. Eventually he looked at her. Then he forgot about Lucas as he was drawn to her dark, mysterious eyes. As before, they were sultry and alluring.

"Come." Jael knew what he wanted. Magnus knew she did. *"Let's go Magnus. You do not need this. I can show you everything you need to know."*

Magnus looked away for a moment. There was something… something he was meant to do, or know. She was even closer to him now.

"Come." She placed her hands on his chest. He felt that feeling again— lightness and tingling through his chest. It was invigorating. But she was standing too close to him. He looked around, trying to remember what it was he needed to do. Jael grew impatient and her eyes sharpened. Magnus was drawn to them again, scared he had offended her in some way.

He was about to speak when Jael's body jerked violently and a look of dismay came to her face. She opened her mouth as if to speak. A thin trail of blood ran from her mouth down her chin and she paused for a moment before falling to the ground, dead. Behind her stood her assailant upon a field of pure white snow, holding a white sword smeared with red blood. The blood then turned to vapour, rising from the blade and dissipating into the air. Magnus looked at Jael's assailant, dressed in a noble azure robe that fell elegantly to the ground over grey, pointed boots. Her blonde hair flowed to her waist and she stood motionless, flanked with a legion of warriors. They were the Rhydermere of the Ice Realm and she was their leader.

She was his mother.

Magnus sat up, startled by the dream and a repetitive pounding. He turned to the door of the dark room and saw daylight streaking through splinters in the wood.

Thump.

The door gave a little and more light pierced through. Magnus leapt to his feet in an instant, sword drawn and ready just as the door exploded inward, sending daggers of wood hurtling across the room. He shielded himself from the debris.

Through the open doorway came the massive maw of a dragon. A deep burbling sound rose from its belly, then it roared, shaking the room violently. It drew a second breath and Magnus guessed what would follow. He turned his back to the dragon and a jet of flames exploded through him. The flames lashed over him and his body seemed to burn from the inside out. It was a burn like he had never before experienced—like he had been dropped into a vat of molten iron.

When the flames subsided, Magnus fell to his knees, his pants all but disintegrated but his flesh and the fleu-steel sword unharmed. He caught his breath and spun about, looking at the dragon. He did not want to give it the chance of a second coming and so he came at it, thrusting his sword hilt-deep into its pointed nose. The beast screamed. Magnus recognised the dragon.

"Brue!"

Magnus held fast to his sword as Brue pulled away, backing out of the doorway. In his place, three Irucantî ran into the room—the same three who had left with Brue earlier. Magnus opened his mind, trying to get a read on their thoughts but they were quick to block him from any mental intrusion.

The room hung thick with the sulphurous fumes and smoke from Brue's attack and the wooden beams overhead were on fire. The priests ignited their lances—the glowing engravings within them throwing shards of light through the smokey room. It made anticipating the priests' attack easier in the gloom and afforded Magnus a slight advantage.

Magnus cut deep across the ankle of one priest, severing the bone, and did the same to the fingers of another, making him drop his weapon.

Magnus knew that no injury short of death would stop any of them and one against three would soon wear him down—perhaps only for a short time, but long enough for one of them to kill him. And kill him they certainly would. Magnus doubted his capacity to heal would help him here, for surely a severed head or limb, or impaled heart, would not heal. Magnus needed to finish this quickly.

He lunged backward as the third priest sprung off a wall, placing himself behind Magnus. As he did, the wall creaked and the hardwood beams overhead shifted, sending dust and charred wood to the floor. Magnus glanced upward at a thick beam that had turned to charcoal from dragon fire—it had cracked through at its centre. *It won't take much for the roof to come down.* He recalled his escape from his burning home back in the J'esmagdlands and the ceiling that nearly caved in on him. *The same could happen here...*

Magnus saw an opportunity. He waited until he was positioned in the middle of the three priests—a vulnerable position, but necessary. As two of them came at him with their lances, Magnus back-flipped and severed the brittle beam with his sword. He landed beyond the third priest at the door and dove for the exit as the roof crashed down behind him.

Once clear of the door he turned to see that the roof had collapsed entirely. The doorway was still intact and one of the priests lunged free of the room, covered in debris. He coughed and stumbled and took a moment to recover but it was too late. Magnus came at him hard and fast, slashing at the Ferustir's neck, chest and abdomen—skilfully finding the weak points in his armour. The priest was soon dead. He waited a moment for the other priests to come through the doorway. None did.

Magnus headed back up the alleyway.

"Finally," he said to himself in a resolute manner. *"I know what I need to do to end this."*

JOFFREN

Joffren was a broken man. Catanya knew his chances of recovering were slim at best. His body and mind had suffered inexplicable damage with the assault Magnus had made upon him.

"You know, Catanya, things could have turned out a lot worse than this," Eamon said as he knelt beside Joffren.

"I know," Catanya said. Still, it did little to appease her seeing her teacher and companion of the last six months close to death. Eamon had been diligent with his attention to Joffren. Catanya could see he left no stone unturned in doing what he could to heal the priest. Jael stayed with Eamon, following his instruction to the letter.

"Eamon is good," Jael said to Catanya. "His skills as a healer are very good." Coming from Jael, who was a good healer herself, these words gave Catanya confidence.

After Joffren's battle with Magnus, Catanya listened to Magnus explain how Joffren's mind revealed his loyalty to her as his Semsarian. She tried to find comfort in this knowledge but still, she needed to know—*Did Joffren know about Demi's attempt on my life?*

"We've done all we can for now," Eamon explained. He stood and placed a hand on Catanya's shoulder. "Time will tell," he smiled. "What I should do now is find Brue." He peered out of the open door of the small house they had appropriated near the eastern wall. "He was to return here before now, so that we could leave and seek Marsala. She is a healer, among other things. Joffren will have a greater chance of survival with her." Eamon excused himself and walked outside leaving Jael and Catanya to tend to Joffren.

Jael looked Catanya over inquisitively. Catanya sensed that she had questions for her—questions about Magnus. She pretended not to notice Jael's enquiring eyes. *What was it she said to Magnus? 'There's so much you will learn from us.'* But it was not so much the words as the way she looked at him that caught Catanya's attention.

"Where do you intend to go from here, Semsame?" Jael asked.

Catanya stared at Jael without saying anything for a moment before answering. "I want my old life back. The further away from the Romghold I am, the better."

Jael fell silent. She tried to get Joffren to sip some tea from a small pot she was holding. "That would be a shame—after all you've been through. After all your training."

"If you had been through what I had, would you go back?" Catanya tried to keep the bitterness from her tongue, but it tainted her words nonetheless.

"I've been through plenty, Semsame." Jael smiled weakly and Catanya felt shamed. She still knew nothing of the ordeal Jael had been through in the six months she was missing in Froughton Forest. Catanya looked at Jael. Her scars were healing well, but she dared not assume her mind had recovered. "But things have changed now," Jael continued. "The priesthood will no longer be what it was. We have the High Priests of our order to deal with, then…" Jael's voice trailed off with her thoughts.

"Then, what?" Catanya asked.

"Then a new beginning… a new era."

Catanya looked at Joffren. It was more so to break eye contact with Jael than anything. Beads of sweat ran down his forehead and over the markings across the side of his head. She raised a hand and ran her fingers over her own markings, somewhat hidden now by the growth of hair over the last month. She had deliberately avoided the ritual of clean-shaving the area. She thought it helped maintain her anonymity during her weeks in Brindle, but now it served to distance her from the order that betrayed her.

Jael reached out to her and felt the side of her head also. Her touch was gentle. "Don't hide who you are, Semsame. Be proud."

Catanya looked at Jael again. She had admired how refined and pretty she was when they first met. Now she resented her for it. There was a seductive quality to her and Catanya wondered if Magnus found her attractive. Catanya held Jael's wrist and gently removed it from her face.

"Do not call me Semsame again, Jael. I am no longer a part of the priesthood, regardless of what comes to pass."

Jael smiled. "We need you. Magnus needs you."

"Magnus is with me, regardless," Catanya said snidely.

"Hmm," Jael looked to Joffren as Catanya had done before. "There is a big future for Magnus. Are you sure you are up to being a part of that?" She slowly looked back to Catanya—a challenging expression on her face.

Catanya could feel heat rising to her face. "The last priest who tested me was Demi. Things did not end so well for her. Are you sure *you* are up to that?"

Jael sneered. She stood and drew her lance from over her shoulder. Catanya jumped to her feet and freed her own lance. The two Ferustirs stared at one another, neither saying a word.

Eventually, Jael looked down to her weapon, stroking its casing with her thumb. "I think I'll see what Eamon is doing," she said and left.

Alone with Joffren, Catanya tried to calm herself. She sheathed her lance, concentrated on her breathing and removed further thoughts of Jael from her mind. Kneeling again, she held a damp cloth to Joffren's forehead. It seemed to settle the tossing and turning and anxious mumbling he was working through in his semiconscious state.

"Shh..." Catanya whispered. Joffren's eyes suddenly shot open. Fear seemed to grip him and he shouted a nonsensical jumble of words. It was strange for Catanya seeing Joffren like this—he was always a man of absolute control and confidence.

"Why didn't you do what was right? Why did you listen to the poisonous words of the High Priests?" She spoke directly to him. She hoped some part of him, beyond the damage and delirium, would hear her.

There was no response. Eamon had explained that his wounds ran deep. Every organ and bone had been twisted or cracked. *"Only the Gods know the damage done to his mind, Catanya,"* Eamon had said. *"That seems to be causing him the most grief."*

Catanya sighed and stood to leave the tent when Joffren took a firm grip of her lower leg. He looked at her with eyes wide, as if in shock. He gasped in short breaths, blowing frantic whispers from his trembling lips. Catanya knelt beside him, her head bowed so as to hear him.

"Semsa... Semsa..." His voice was frantic.

"Semsarian? Is that what you are saying? I am here, Joffren." As much as she pitied him she couldn't bring herself to call him *Semsdi.*

"Semsa..." he repeated. "Sorry... I'm sorry."

Catanya nodded, holding Joffren's hand. "Joffren," she said. He blinked as if acknowledging her. Catanya drew breath and forced the question from her mouth. "Did you send Demi to kill me?"

Joffren's head shook and his eyes widened even more.

"Did you, Joffren?" Catanya spoke louder and shook Joffren's shoulders. "Did you sanction my death?"

"I… I'm sorry… I'm so sorry," Joffren stammered repeatedly.

Catanya stared at him. Tears welled in her eyes and her face twisted into anger. She cast his hand aside and walked out of the tent. Eamon was talking with Jael. He turned to her to speak but Catanya spoke first.

"Let him die in there. Let him rot alone." She stormed off, hoping to find Magnus.

FAREWELL

Magnus stormed toward the priest's encampment at the eastern wall. He cursed under his breath. "Wretched priests and their fickle dragons." The first person he happened upon was Catanya, who came down the alleyway toward him. She appeared as vexed as Magnus but stopped dead in her tracks at the sight of him.

"What happened to you?" she asked, looking Magnus over. She covered her open mouth.

Magnus looked at himself for the first time since the incident. His body was blotched in black from head to toe with soot and ash. His pants had not survived Brue's flame attack and the strips of melted leather that did remain clung to his flesh. "I apologise for my appearance. But we've three less priests and one less dragon to worry about."

"What? Which dragon?" Catanya asked.

"Brue. It appears his loyalties remain with the priests who would rather I were dead."

"*Brue*... Are you sure?" Catanya looked him over again.

"I'm sure. I got a pretty close look before he tried to burn me to a cinder."

Speechless, Catanya scanned the ground with wide-eyes.

"Catanya. We're not safe here. I don't know whom we can trust. I think we should leave now." Magnus's words were harsh. Catanya said nothing. "Catanya? We should leave *now*."

Her head went from shaking in disbelief to a fast nod. "Yes, we should leave. It's true then—we cannot trust anyone."

Magnus could see more than his incident troubled her. "What is it, Catanya?"

"Joffren all but admitted to me he sanctioned my death." Catanya's face turned cold.

Magnus held her close. "I hope he lives to regret it."

Together they turned and headed back down the alley to find another way out of the city. He hoped any remaining Quagmen were otherwise occupied as he was in no mood for any more fighting. As they walked, Eamon's familiar voice called after them.

"Magnus! What… What happened to you?"

Eamon was jogging at a slow pace, his wild hair flowing behind him. He looked as surprised at Magnus's appearance as Catanya had been. Magnus explained in detail what had occurred in the small room, leaving out the particulars of his dreams.

"This is most grave news, Magnus. We should get back to the Quadrangle and inform the others." Eamon shook his head in disappointment. He removed the cloak he was wearing and threw it around Magnus's shoulders.

"I don't think so, Eamon. There is none we can trust short of you."

Eamon looked at Magnus then Catanya as if for further clarification.

"In the company of priests and dragons, whom can we trust?" Magnus said. "Where can we sleep without fear of our lives? What if Catanya had been in the room with me just now? It seems I cannot be destroyed by fire. But can you?" He could see Eamon understood by the despondence in his face.

"Yes. Yes I see that now." Eamon looked drawn. "Just now—you were about to leave?" Magnus and Catanya looked at one another but neither admitted he was right. Eamon nodded. "Well then. I'm glad to have found you before you do. Pray tell—where will you go?"

The moment his altercation with Brue and the priests ended, Magnus had hatched a plan. "Joffren revealed to me the minds of the High Priests behind this madness. It is they who've poisoned the minds of the Irucantî and it is they who need to be brought to justice. They have hidden away in the Romghold with wards and dragons as their guards. I am going there to see them repent or fall."

"*We* are going there," Catanya said.

"Yes—*we*. We go without warning and without anyone knowing. It gives us the element of surprise. Then we finish this."

Eamon twisted two locks of his beard between his thumbs and forefingers. "Yes, it is what needs to be done. I can see, too, that even if Austagia and Färgd alone were confided in, the process of deliberation would certainly raise suspicion among their brethren. News of your intentions could lead to a revolt by those sympathetic to the High Priests."

"We would ask you to come but I believe you are needed here," Catanya said.

Magnus appreciated that Catanya could see what he had not—Eamon's desire to join them. Yet he needed to look after Joffren and support Austagia.

"You can see my predicament, Catanya," Eamon said. "I would see you safe to the Romghold on the back of a dragon. And my advice would have been as much just hours ago. Advice that may have cost you your lives."

"It seems fate has a cruel way of showing us what we need to know," Magnus said.

"Indeed," Eamon agreed. "You know of course, without a dragon your journey will be long and arduous?"

"Aye," Magnus agreed.

"We'll have each other." Catanya added.

"Indeed you will. And what a formidable pair you are!" Eamon chuckled. He reached to Catanya and held her hand then did the same to Magnus. He looked at each of them in turn. "I am proud of you both."

Eamon turned his full attention to Magnus. "You have done well, Magnus. I, more than most, have seen you go through fire and brimstone to protect those you love and defend what is just in this world. I can think of no finer man to bear the title of *Electus*." Magnus thanked him. Eamon then handed Magnus the fire-sword he had carefully wrapped in a suede cloth for safekeeping. "Keep this, Magnus. Return it to the Romghold and place it before Balgur in the temple. There it will rest as it belongs."

Catanya stepped closer to Eamon. "No, Eamon. It is you who needs closure on the matter. I think you need to make the journey to the temple. Here, you can leave with it, the priest who once was *Steyne*. Perhaps if Joffren is well enough he can accompany you and together you can reach a mutual understanding," Catanya took the sword from Magnus—who nodded his assent—and she handed it to Eamon.

Eamon smiled to her. "For the second time today you have left me speechless. Something none have done for many a year. You are wise beyond your years, Catanya." He looked at Magnus again. "Take care of this one, Magnus—she's a keeper." He winked at him before slapping him across the shoulder. Eamon looked over the wrapped sword and allowed his thoughts to trail off for a moment. "Memories... good and bad. Nostalgia and regret paint with different palettes."

Magnus considered the old man. He had saved his life and taught him much. Eamon—the man who at first frustrated him, whom he then grew fond of, before hating him so much for so long, only to admire and respect him all over again. Now they shared a common goal, yet Magnus knew they needed to part ways.

"Eamon, thank you—for everything. I would not be here now if it weren't for you. From the moment we met in Froughton Forest you have put my needs before your own." Magnus stopped talking, for his heart had risen and choked his words. He was tired and worn from saying farewell to those he loved.

Magnus stepped up to Eamon and embraced him with a long, firm hug. He stepped back again and Eamon smiled at him the way his father did—with pride and love. "Thank you, Magnus."

Catanya did the same, hugging Eamon affectionately. "I've only known you a day but I see you as an old friend." She wiped away a tear.

"Old... yes! A friend... most certainly," Eamon said. "Now, be off you two. When I can I will get word to you of my whereabouts and of Joffren's progress. And anything else of importance. Look to the skies for the Ahrona swallow."

With a final wave, Magnus and Catanya headed back down the alleyway and south toward the city gates.

BEYOND BA'RRAT

Outside the eastern walls the land was a scattering of ancient ruins that predated Ba'rrat itself. The pale stonework was crudely made of brittle sandstone from the coast built long before the people of the known ages started mining the more resilient black granite from the cliffs. The ruins sat upon parched, lifeless soil long sucked of its fertility, making the bleached landscape a striking contrast to the foreboding black city. Blood was splattered all over the ruins—evidence of the airborne battles of dragons and wyverns. Magnus and Catanya walked around the body of a dead wyvern that was draped over an old stone wall where flies busily made a feast of the bloody mess. The smell from its carcass made Magnus gag and he could see Catanya fared no better.

A Quag horn blew, bringing Magnus and Catanya back to reality. Somewhere beyond the Capitol the Quag were reuniting. Magnus and Catanya started to run, weaving their way around the ruins, occasionally hidden by smoke from smouldering fires lit by the flames of dragons. A dragon's roar followed by a screeching cry came from Ba'rrat. Magnus looked to the sky and saw a dragon tearing at a wyvern before releasing it from its bloodstained claws, letting its dead body fall to the ground behind the city wall.

They kept running—Magnus fuelled by the blood of dragons and Catanya by her flawless training. Neither needed to temper their pace for the other. Progress was fast and, within an hour, the violence and deceptions of the city were out of sight.

"Over there." Catanya pointed to where the land sloped away to form a gully lined with a neat row of tall poplar trees. They broke into a sprint, desperate to close the gap between them and the shelter of the gully. Magnus's hairs stood tall on the back of his neck at the sound of a galloping horse approaching from behind. He looked at Catanya just as her body jolted forward and she lost her footing. Magnus caught her and came to a standstill. Catanya had an arrow protruding from her back. Magnus saw the approaching Quagman on horseback with a second arrow loaded in his bow. He released it.

Magnus felt Catanya's heart beating against his chest. He held her tight, taking the weight of Catanya's body in one arm. The arrow spiralled toward him. He raised his free arm, allowing the arrow to pierce through and embed itself into the palm of his hand. Still the Quagman came, drawing his two black swords, spurring his angry warhorse forward.

Holding his hand aloft, Magnus allowed the arrow to burn to ash. His hand healed with an ascending ring of flame. The Quagman saw this and pulled back hard on his reins, drawing his great horse back—its hind legs sliding to a halt.

"*Electus!*" The Quagman yelled, before turning and charging back toward the city.

Magnus carried Catanya the short distance over the steep embankment to the gully below where a creek flowed weakly back toward Ba'rrat. He sat on the ground and laid Catanya in his lap.

He took a hold of the arrow in her back and tried to gently pull it free but it was stuck fast. Catanya recoiled from the pain and wrapped her arms around Magnus, squeezing him tight.

"Try again!" she cried. Magnus was hesitant, knowing the gnarled arrowhead may cause more damage than when it went in. "Please Magnus, just take it out."

Magnus place a hand on Catanya's chest to see if the arrow had pierced her through but it had not. It had found its way through a small gap in her Ferustir armour to the right of her spine. He was sure it had missed her heart and hoped it had missed her lungs. The only choice he had was to pull it back the way it went in.

He took a grip of the arrow once again, then thought for a moment. *Can I turn it to ash as I do to myself, or will this burn her inside?* He thought carefully about trying this approach, for he could not bring himself to pull the arrow free with force. *If I heat the arrow it may sear the flesh and stop the bleeding...*

"Catanya," Magnus began to explain.

"Hmm." Catanya shook from the pain. "Whatever you're thinking, just do it. I trust you." She forced a smile. "Can you heal me the way you heal yourself?"

"I don't know," Magnus confessed. Nevertheless, he held the arrow and felt the heat from his hand flow through its shaft. Catanya gripped even tighter and grunted through gritted teeth. Smoke began to rise from the shaft of the protruding arrow. Magnus pulled gently but it was still firmly lodged in Catanya's back. He did not want the arrow to ignite into flame.

Magnus looked at the arrow and thought of the crude metal head, for it would surely hold more heat than the shaft. He closed his eyes and pictured the arrowhead turning to molten metal and reshaping itself into a smooth extension to the arrow, allowing him to pull it free. Catanya pushed her face into Magnus's chest and mumbled what sounded like a spell.

"Namon hama fara meo…" She said it twice over then gave in to screams of pain. Magnus pulled on the arrow again, drawing it easily free of her body and examined the glowing metal head—it bore the smooth shape he had envisioned.

Catanya's body slumped and she took deep breaths, recovering from the ordeal. Magnus put a finger to her wound and saw it was cauterised by the arrowhead, stopping any further bleeding. *Hopefully it will stop any infection.* He held Catanya tight.

"It's over, Catanya. It's over."

"Thank you," she mumbled.

"What was that spell you cast?"

Catanya breathed deeply, "Something Färgd taught me… to protect against damage from fire."

"Thank you Färgd…" Magnus whispered.

He stood, lifting Catanya to his chest. She wrapped her arms around Magnus's shoulders, resting her head on his chest and her thighs around his hips. He carried her further up creek like this, walking on the soft sand of the lower embankment.

The sun began to set over the poplar trees that followed the top of the embankment, taking with it the warmth of the summer day and replacing it with a damp chill. Catanya shivered from the cold. As night wore on the creek widened and the lush vegetation flourished with more trees, grasses and summer flowers. The sound of water cascading down a small waterfall lifted Magnus's spirits.

"Are we home?" Catanya mumbled half asleep, her head under Magnus's chin. Magnus smiled and stroked her forehead. She looked so beautiful and he felt blessed that they should be together again.

"No, we're not home yet, but we will be soon."

The waterfall reminded him of the Nuyan River, as it no doubt had Catanya. Thoughts of home came to mind—more so than in times past. He had been so focussed on protecting Sarah and finding his parents that he had given little thought of returning home. He thought of his mother and of how his father said she had gone looking for him. *To what end?* Magnus wondered. Returning home was of no interest to him unless he found his mother. His father would soon look for her himself. He yearned to be by his side searching for her.

Most of all, Magnus's heart was with Catanya. He wanted more than anything to remain by her side. Now that they were together again Magnus knew her desire more than any other would be to return home—to reunite with her mother and Hannah. With her skills and Magnus's own they would be of great help in the fight to reclaim their lands. But first he needed to gain the support of the dragons and the Irucantî whose very existence was for the protection of his people. For this reason he could never give up. For this reason he had to reach the Romghold and deal with the High Priests—either through negotiations or otherwise.

Several hours passed as Magnus carried Catanya upstream. The creek was now a broad river bringing with it good coverage along the banks, and so Magnus waded across to the northern side in search of an area to spend the night. He was aware Catanya had not slept for several days and, with her injury, needed it even more so.

He eventually happened across a good area to stop. The land rose to a slight hill affording him uninterrupted views from the east to the southern coast and to the west. Behind them loomed the Black Cliffs and further on he could see the faint glow of lights several miles away. He assumed that was the town of Brindle. Magnus calculated Ba'rrat to be nearly twenty miles back. On this side of the riverbed, Magnus settled on an area with low hanging beech trees that would hide them through the night.

He lowered Catanya onto the soft grass beneath a tree. She lay down and asked Magnus to lie beside her, but he preferred to sit up and keep watch through the night. Catanya rested her head on Magnus's lap and he shared with her the large cloak Eamon had given him, wrapping it around her. He watched as she fell into a deep sleep. At one point Catanya turned over to her right, revealing the markings over her left temple. Magnus felt the silkiness of the dark hair she allowed to grow over the markings that were still visible.

Magnus looked at her resting eyes, her beautiful face and how content she was. Catanya had confronted the greatest of warriors to find him and save him. And all she wished for in return was to be with him. "Just as you promised me long ago," Magnus said. Catanya opened one eye and looked to him.

"Hmmm?"

"It's nothing. Rest Catanya. I love you."

"I love you too."

EPILOGUE

The old man woke with a start.

It was how Trager always woke, thanks to the nightmares that plagued his sleep. He sat up in a sweat, grunting through gnashed teeth and cursed the Gods as usual. But this night was different. There was commotion beyond his bedroom quarters and that woke him instead.

"Dermot!" Trager shouted with a shrill tone. "Dermot—what in damnation is going on out there?"

The young servant opened the huge doors that led to the Elder's sleeping quarters.

"Your Greatness... The city has been breached!"

Trager scrambled out of bed, stumbled across his room and out the door. "Rubbish! Guame's city walls cannot be breached. And there certainly is no breaching this cathedral. If you're wrong boy, you'll hang for waking me."

"It is true, your Greatness," Dermot quivered.

Pounding started on a second set of doors across the large gallery. In moments, the doors splintered and flew inward off their hinges.

"What in all the realms is going on?" Trager shouted.

Through the open doorway, six Astermeer horses and their riders charged into the hall and formed rank with three to a side, allowing a seventh to ride between them and approach the Leader of the Authoritarium. Trager looked at the men with their long, blonde hair and dark blue robes that fell by the sides of their white steeds—each of whom stomped angrily.

"*Rhydermere!*" Trager whispered, his sunken grey eyes widening.

The seventh rider raised an arm and the six Rhyders drew their white Icerealmish swords. A flash of white light danced along the blades of each.

"What is this outrage?" Trager trembled as the Rhydermere elder dismounted and walked toward him. It was a woman. Her blonde hair flowed to her waist and she wore an azure robe that fell to the ground over her pointed grey boots. Her blue eyes—as brilliant as sapphires—stared at Trager.

"What is it you want of me?" Trager demanded.

EPILOGUE

"Your life." The woman drew her sword and thrust it into Trager's heart. His eyes popped from their sockets and his mouth opened wide. The Rhyder twisted her Icerealmish blade making Trager scream in pain. "All members of the Authoritarium are now dead. This day marks the beginning of the Fourth Age of Allumbreve."

Trager stared at her in disbelief. "I know you..." he stammered through bloody lips. "You are Bonstaph's wife!"

"I am Alavia. And I take your place as ruler of the four realms..."

THE END

www.ingramcontent.com/pod-product-compliance
Lightning Source LLC
Chambersburg PA
CBHW032234010726
47494CB00002B/487